GNOSIS

A NOVEL

AMY RUSSELL

DEDICATION

When I was 12 years old, my grandfather, Gigum, asked me what I wanted to be when I grew up. I told him I wanted to be a writer. He smiled proudly and shook his head saying, "No, don't do that! You'll never make any money. I should know."
I guess I didn't listen to his advice, although he was right! This book is dedicated to him and my parents who always encouraged me to go after my dreams.

CONTENTS

CHAPTER ONE

SARAH

AUGUST, 2016, PHILADELPHIA

Finally, the stalwart organ music of the closing hymn swelled up, as the scraping sound of the congregation's soles against the bare wooden floors moving from kneeling to standing, muffled the first bar. I picked up my red hymnal and straightened my clergy stole as I prepared to join the tail end of the choir, recessing down the short steps of the chancel. I felt myself slowly releasing my held-in breath, a check against the anxiety that had awakened this morning along with the first rays of dawn. As I raised my head, singing "Joyful, joyful, we adore thee," my voice streamed up to join the congregation and choir. Carefully negotiating the shiny marble steps, holding up my white surplice slightly with one hand, I stepped down, then looked up to the over two hundred expectant souls filling the dark wooden pews, eyes seemingly fastened on me.

My first service with this Philadelphia congregation, St. Philips Episcopal Church, as their first woman priest was coming to an end. But as I looked out over the congregants facing me, some with dubious expressions, some with faint encouraging smiles, and others with curious but blank looks, I felt that strong inner desire to be accepted as who I was. Just a young woman, carrying some hopeful optimism that I could build something here, something of value. And maybe, make a difference in people's lives.

As I moved down the center aisle of this historic church, with its stone walls and heavy oak beams, I noticed that most of the congregant's ages were at least 20-30 years older than me. White hair and weathered faces all appraising me, the new young priest. One elderly man grasping a cane held my gaze as I stepped down and passed his pew. He seemed to challenge me with his haughty stare. What can I possibly offer those with the life experiences of marriage, children, career, and all the obstacles that come with those events?

I smiled warmly at a young family, the woman holding the baby against her shoulder and the father tending the standing toddler perched precariously on the pew, her small hand grabbing his shoulder. They smiled back with hopeful encouragement. Maybe I had something fresh and new to offer them.

Nodding at Jeffrey Trainor, the Senior Warden, sitting next to his wife in the middle of the sanctuary, I noticed his thin smile, not happy exactly, but satisfied. I hoped the sermon was good enough. He's a tough one. I could see that the first time we met when his business-like manner never faltered despite my desperate attempts at humor. But Elaine, his wife, acknowledged me with a nod. She's one of those always happy to help parishioners. She had greeted me this morning at the door, telling me how pleased the congregation was to welcome their first woman priest.

As I passed the back rows, I picked out an older woman from the vestry, Irene, I think? A sixtyish, retired woman, who dressed conservatively in a slim navy pantsuit with a light blue flowered scarf tied skillfully around her neck. She had been the vestry liaison to the Search Committee and had seemed very eager to have St. Philips'

Vestry approve my call. Looking up from her hymnal as she sang, she dipped her head in a slight nod of approval.

As I continued to recess toward the back of the sanctuary, I tried to put aside my concerns as I prepared to greet this congregation informally for the first time. At 30, I am young; the youngest priest they've seen since the fifties. Jeffrey called me a "breath of fresh air," intimating my youth and inexperience. Irene had told me over the phone that she felt a new day had come to St. Philips after years of what she called, "a male dominated leadership," implying her own impatience of a patriarchy long overdue for change.

Arriving at the rear sanctuary doors, the choir turned to finish the hymn, the cross being held up over the congregation's heads. The hymn ended with the long held "Aaaa-----men!" The organ flourishes struck the air, then left a resounding silence. All the waiting faces turned toward me. I raised my arms to hold the shape of priestly authority and projected my voice up and out, pronouncing the benediction: "And may the Lord bless you and keep you. May the Lord make his face shine upon you and be gracious unto you. May the Lord lift up his countenance upon you and give you peace." The organ pounded out the postlude and I turned toward the doors, handing my hymnal to the nearest choir member, thanking them for taking it.

As I stood by the chancel doors, greeting parishioners and trying to learn their names, I could feel something inside being aware of this moment. I was becoming their priest, somehow, as unlikely as that had seemed for so long during my years-long journey to this moment. And as unlikely as my call to this congregation seemed to some of my professors in seminary who viewed my unorthodox approach to theology as bordering on heretical. My theology professor would sometime call me "Doubting Sarah" since my questions were complex and full of skepticism about doctrine. But that doubt would sometimes give way to an explanation deeper than the one given in the textbooks. I thought it was something that would feel relevant to what I imagined everyday parishioners might need. That's why I stuck it out. Here I was, wanting desperately to make a difference in these people's lives, and I just hoped they would let me.

***

Earlier that week, driving into the parking lot for the first time in my fluorescent green VW bug, I noticed the elegantly painted sign attached to two stone pillars, "St. Philips, Episcopal Church, Established 1890." The new addition that hung below read, "The Rev. Sarah Piper, Rector." A little squeeze in my heart region was a silent reaction to the clear evidence that I was really here, my first day of ministry, even if I wasn't quite sure if I was ready for it.

I checked myself in the rearview mirror, pushing back my long, blond curly hair held off my face with a clasp, took a deep breath, collected my canvas bag, and launched myself out of my car. Seeing my reflection in the car window, I felt a bit dubious about what I chose to wear today. I tended toward vintage denim, boyfriend jeans with a frilly blouse, but I knew I'd need to dress more professionally with my new role. That first day, I compromised with a pair of smart black slacks with a tailored striped cotton blouse. I hoped it looked professional but not stuffy. I really didn't know what young clergy wore since all my mentors were older men, who almost always wore the 'backwards collar' over suits. None of my classmates opted for that kind of dress, and many considered wearing a clergy collar outdated. I guess I'd have to find my own style.

Both of the church buildings, sanctuary and office, were grey stone with Gothic arches over stained glass windows and dark stained oak doors, ivy curling around the foundations. I headed toward the side office building. Pulling open the heavy door, I slipped through, remembering that the office area was down the hall to the right.

Peeking into the glassed-in office area as I approached, I saw Jeffrey Trainor with his tailored dark grey suit, talking to the middle-aged office administrator, Mary, who sat primly behind her desk. Mary looked up when I entered, offering me one of those genuinely welcome smiles. She stood and came around her desk reaching out her hand to greet me.

"Good morning, Rev. Piper! And welcome!" Mary carried herself in a shy manner as she kept her head slightly down but met my eyes.

Jeffrey came forward, "Good morning, Rev. Piper. I know you met Mary, our office administrator, when you came to interview. I'm sure you heard all about how key she is to this place."

We chatted informally for a few minutes, Jeffrey playing the role of host and a bit of the manager welcoming a new staff member. Jeffrey and I had met by video conference when the Vestry had followed the Search Committee's recommendation and arranged a meeting with me to confirm their choice. After taking my coat, they showed me the "Priest's Study", off of Mary's office, Jeffrey leading the way.

"You probably saw the office when you were here for your interview, but I know Mary has done some cleaning and re-arranging to make it more comfortable."

The rather outdated pine office desk and bookshelves had been polished with a sheen. The sofa against the wall and the two easy chairs covered in a green and blue flowered cotton looked comfortable and inviting, despite their worn appearance. Some white roses had been arranged in a small blue vase on the desk.

Mary pointed to the empty shelves. "I just moved some of the stuff that had accumulated on the shelves over the years when Rev. Hogan was here. But there's some basic supplies here in the desk."

Jeffrey seemed a bit anxious as Mary began to describe all the kinds of supplies she could order for me. He put up a hand to stop her.

"I'm sorry, Mary. I'm sure Rev. Piper will be happy to tell you exactly what she needs. I hate to interrupt, but I just want to check if you want a short tour of the building before I have to shove off. I'm afraid I've got an 11:00 meeting downtown." He looked at me inquisitively.

Just then I saw someone else entering the outer office. I recognized Irene from my interview with the Vestry, with her neat, greying bun, nicely dressed in slacks and a tailored blouse. Jeffrey saw her as she came to the office door and with a raised eyebrow, pulled his face into a polite smile.

"Irene, I see you're here to welcome Rev. Piper as well."

I held out my hand to Irene, and greeted her, as she stepped forward nodding to Mary. All this 'Rev. Piper' stuff was beginning to get on my nerves. I had grown up in a fairly low-church environment where we had called our priests by their first names. So, I decided then and there to try to change this practice before it was too late.

"Jeffrey, I'd really like it if you would all call me Sarah. I mean, I really don't need all the formality of a title." I watched Jeffrey's face look surprised, while Irene nodded approvingly.

Jeffrey held up his hands in response. "Well, okay, if that's what you want. But I must say that really isn't the custom here. Is it, Mary?"

Mary shifted uneasily, being put on the spot. She didn't want to correct the new priest. Irene saw her discomfort and spoke up.

"We've usually used the Reverend title, except for some of the priests who wanted to be called 'Father'. But Sarah, you should be able to be addressed as you see fit. Some people will always be more comfortable with the formal titles, and some won't."

I was grateful to have Irene's opinion. While she had been fairly quiet during my interview, I had noticed that her questions seemed astute and thoughtful, designed to ferret out a candidate who wasn't ready for what might have been seen as a challenging congregation.

Jeffrey cleared his throat. "Well, how about 'Rev. Sarah' instead of 'Rev. Piper'? That would give people the proper understanding of your role without being too formal. What do you think?"

While this wasn't what I had asked for, I could see that Jeffrey was making an effort to let me understand what might be most acceptable in this congregation. I agreed with a small nod. "Yes, I think that works."

Jeffrey then mentioned again his need to get going and Irene offered to help get me settled in my office. I was quick to accept her offer of help since I wanted some time to get to know her. I sensed she might be a good person to have as an ally, if I needed an ally. She pulled out some blueberry muffins from her tote and offered them as a welcome gift. I already liked her. Smiling, I turned to Jeffrey.

"Jeffrey, thanks for being here this morning to welcome me. I really do appreciate it."

Jeffrey held up a finger, and riffled through his briefcase, searching for something. "Wait," he said, pulling out a folded paper with some kind of coloring on it. He handed it to me while smoothing out the folds.

"This is from my daughter, Emily." I looked down at the cray-oned drawing. There was a vague oblong looking body, a squished head with scribbled yellow fuzz adorning it. It was obviously some-one's hair.

"Oh, I see. I guess that's me?"

"Well, she's only four. But when she saw your picture, she said she thought your hair was like an angel's." Jeff looked somewhat embarrassed, but pleased.

"Wow, angel hair! I've never been characterized that way before! Such a compliment! Thank Emily for me."

Jeff nodded, smiling proudly, and putting his briefcase back un-der his arm, went hurriedly out the office door, offering to get back to me later in the week.

Once Jeffrey was gone, Mary emitted a sigh, maybe of relief, I wasn't sure. Irene offered to help carry in some boxes that she had noticed I had stacked in the back of my car. Glad to get more time with her, I agreed, and we went out to the parking lot. As I handed her a box of books, she looked in and saw one of my poetry books. Her face lit up as she pulled it out and showed me. It was one of Mary Oliver's books of poems.

"Oh, this is one of my favorites. I love the one about 'my wild and precious life'," she said with delight.

"Me, too. And I'd love to hear more about your wild and precious life, Irene."

"Well," she said smiling, "I'm sure you will hear more than you want to hear about it eventually."

I smiled at that prediction. "I look forward to it."

When we started to unpack the boxes of books in my office, Irene pulled a blue baseball hat out of the top of the first box, and held it up, the red B emblazoned clearly.

"Clearly a Red Sox fan! I should have known since you're from Boston. So, who's your favorite player?"

I took the hat and put it on playfully. "Oh, Mookie Betts, of course! Are you a baseball fan?"

Irene shook her head. "Sadly, no. I'm kind of a washout when it comes to sports. But you'll find some real Red Sox fans here in Philly. There's a whole bar dedicated to Boston fans down on Broad. So, will you be looking for tickets to the games when the Red Sox come here to play the Phillies?"

"Oh, yeah! Maybe I'll invite my Dad to come visit then." I placed the blue hat on a bookshelf thinking about how important baseball was to my dad. It was one of the only things we still shared.

Over tea and muffins, we talked about St. Philips and its traditional character. The way the Vestry had refused to include women until the 1960's, and had always called male priests. Irene was carefully filling me in on its history, which she knew well having been a member for 30 years. She seemed to want me to know a fuller picture than I had perhaps gathered with my time with the Search Committee. After asking me what I thought about the Supreme Court's decision a year ago which legalized same sex marriage, she watched my face carefully as I answered.

"Well, I'm very pleased with that outcome which has been much too long in coming. And I was happy to hear that St. Philips is welcoming to LGBT people. So, why do you ask, Irene?"

Irene sighed, considering her answer. "So, did the Search Committee tell you that St. Philips' Vestry voted last year to not move forward with same sex marriage, but to pause that decision?"

"What? They did not tell me that! They implied that it was very welcoming and I assumed that meant open to marriage equality! Oh my God, why didn't they tell me that?"

"I think they were afraid they'd lose you. "

I was upset when I heard that, but tried to keep my cool. "Irene, you were a part of the Vestry interview process. Why didn't you tell me?"

Irene shook her head and sighed. "I had assumed the Search Committee had told you since they assured me they had 'put you in the picture'. But later, when I asked Jeffrey, he tried to gloss over it, saying you had been given all the information you needed. I'm sorry that you were misled."

Irene didn't seem shocked, just disappointed. I got the sense that this was why Irene had come in to see me this morning. "So, this seems very important to you as well. Is it?"

Irene nodded. "Yes, I'm lesbian."

Now I began to see why Irene had perhaps allowed me to come here not knowing St. Philips' stance against marriage equality.

"Irene, did you suspect that I was pro-marriage equality, and might not have come knowing the Vestry's decision?"

She looked down and then up, her reluctant nod confirming what I suspected. "Yes, I also wanted you to become our next priest, both because you were young, a woman, and because you probably would want to change the Vestry's minds. Was I wrong?"

I chewed on my bottom lip as I did when considering something. "I just wonder if my being here isn't the best thing for this church. I mean, I will try to change that and if they had hired a more conservative priest, things might never change. But, wait, do you think St. Philips can accept gay marriage?"

Irene nodded, answering me reassuringly. "This church may be ambivalent about marriage equality, but personally, they have been more than supportive to me. Yes, I do think they can change given the right leadership. But it may take time. I think slow and steady wins the race in this case."

I felt slightly encouraged. "Good, that's what I hoped. Well, maybe with your help, we'll be the leadership they need!"

Wrapping my mind around the situation that now confronted me was daunting. A vestry against gay marriage, in Philadephia, in 2016? I knew the bishop had encouraged the parishes to make their own decisions. But I'd been led to believe that almost all churches had embraced the new law. I felt betrayed by the Search Committee. But Irene was offering me another viewpoint. That I was here for a reason. To make something new happen here. And wasn't that what I was looking for in my ministry?

I felt comfortable with Irene. Her manner was respectful and open, signaling that despite my age, she really trusted that I had something to offer. I had noticed this during our first interactions during the interview. She seemed to get me, even when I had been rather reserved with the Vestry, she had drawn me out with thoughtful questions.

Today, after agreeing that we'd need to discuss the situation further, Irene left promising to check back with me later in the week. I hoped I hadn't come across as too upset by the news she shared. I was naturally on the serious side and always had been. My mother used to say I'd try to outthink everyone around me.

Growing up with very intellectual parents, I had been pushed into achieving academically from an early age. AP classes, debate team, applying to the top colleges, getting the top SAT scores, all of this was the drumbeat of my parent's expectations. Somehow, they identified me as the one who was going to achieve, while my sister, Pam, was excused due to her poor health.

In college, I began to realize that my achievement orientation sometimes found me judging others who didn't push themselves. When I'd meet someone, I'd want to know what courses they were taking, what books were they reading, and what they wanted to get out of college. Once on a date when I was asking these kinds of an-noying questions, the guy looked amused and asked if I wanted him to take an intelligence test to prove he was worthy of me. Mortified, I apologized and retreated into an embarrassed silence. Needless to say, there wasn't a second date.

Then in seminary, my expectations for others seemed to be more oriented toward judging the sincerity or commitment of the people I met.   But I had begun to realize lately that my approach to other people was prematurely judgmental. As soon as I met someone, I often immediately tried to ascertain whether they were smart, sincere, or compassionate. If not, I tended to turn off my interest. And here, with the members of the church, my judgment of others was still in play. Already, I could feel myself judging Jeffrey, trying to stick him into a preconceived stereotype of a stuffy businessman. And that wasn't fair to him, nor was it "Christian."

I decided to spend some of my prayer/meditation time focusing on accepting others as they were. The God I believed in wasn't a judgmental being who made rules for others to follow. The God I imagined was unconditional loving energy who loved us no matter what we did. It wasn't a question of being forgiven; I wanted to believe we were already forgiven before we acted wrongly. That kind of non-judgment for humans was impossible. But it was what I wanted to consider as an ideal. I realized that many Christians were all about judgment and little about forgiveness. But that wasn't the Christianity I would ever ascribe to.

CHAPTER TWO

IRENE

Last Sunday's sermon from Father Tyler, the white- haired retired priest who had been filling in during the summer, was still lingering in my mind. He had ended with: "While we sometimes wonder at the inherent inequality of the sexes in the time of Christ, Peter, while a product of his times, wasn't really the arrogant, misogynist we assume he was, because he was letting us know that everyone has a role to play, and everyone is valued by the Lord." He finished with a smug, paternalistic smile, obviously pleased with how 'modern' he was.

Yeah, right, I thought to myself, *with women's roles assigned to the kitchen and the bedroom*! I was literally sick to my stomach. Whenever a priest asked to be called "Father" it scared me away. I didn't need another father; the first one having been one too many.

But I had spent the time half-listening, imagining Rev. Sarah Piper instead, whose bio sent to the Vestry sounded like someone with some life in her. Her experience with teaching inner city kids was probably good training for the care and feeding of working-class older folks who were also rather ornery. But I worried about her ability to handle the over-privileged yuppies who had begun attending a few years ago. Their sense of entitlement even surprised me, and I had taught in a private school for a while. Until someone outed me. But I was eager to know Rev. Piper and what kind of changes she would bring to St. Philips. I decided to arrive on her first morning to give her some support and maybe a view into what kind of church she would be leading.

Wednesday morning, I arrived at 9:30, trying to give Rev. Sarah a little time to settle in, but I was too late. Jeffrey Trainor was already there, throwing his weight around along with his perceptions. We had crossed horns on several occasions over the past two years since he had joined the Vestry. It was clear to me what was not so obvious to others; Jeffrey's agenda was to keep St. Philips the conservative middle-class church it had always been. While he was always pleasant to me, I knew that he was the one who had shanghaied the Vestry to vote to keep the pastor from performing same-sex marriage, despite the bishop's invitation for churches to accept the new Supreme Court ruling that marriage equality was now here to stay. Over Jeffrey's dead body, I guess.

Meeting Rev. Sarah for the first time, I was struck at how confident she was for such a young woman. She seemed to see through Jeffrey's bluster right away, and dispatched him in record time, seeming eager to talk to me, for some reason. We talked for nearly an hour over tea and the muffins I had brought with me. My mother taught me that everything goes better with something sweet. She also taught me how to bake, a skill that seems to have been lost in an age where the local grocery chain carries bakery items that masquerade as homemade but taste like the chemicals additives they're filled with.

Our first conversation was enlightening, for both of us. As I suspected, the Search Committee had not clued her in on the church's stance on gay marriage. But when I assured her that I thought the congregation was ready for new leadership on this issue, she seemed heartened and ready to take it on.

I felt an immediate relief and sense of rightness enter me. I had been right about this young woman. Heaven had sent us help!

Later when we were shelving some of Sarah's books, I noticed out of the corner of my eye her carefully unwrap some framed pictures that she dusted and placed gently on the bookshelf behind her desk. I asked her if they were pictures of family. She smiled but seemed to hesitate before answering.

"Yes, those are my parents," she said holding up the picture of a well-dressed couple standing close together in front of a building, the woman standing stiffly next to her husband who was smiling warmly.

"Do they live close by?"

"No, they're in Boston. Close enough," she said, as though glad for the distance. She positioned the picture on the shelf. Then she picked up a picture of two girls, young teens it looked like. She smiled down at this one and held it for a moment before handing it to me.

"This is my sister, Pam, and me when we were teenagers." Then as I opened my mouth to ask how old Pam was now, Sarah cut me off saying quickly, "But ... she died." She realized, I guess, how abrupt this sounded, so she added, "She was twelve. Of course, that was many years ago."

I didn't know what to say now, since she had seemed to want to head off any elicited sympathy by the disclaimer. Not knowing Sarah well but sensing this was a conversation for another time, I just responded, "The two of you looked close." I gazed quickly at the picture, but handed it back when Sarah reached for it, seeming eager to move off the subject.

As we chatted, I began to realize that while Sarah was young, she seemed ready for this fairly daunting task of serving a growing congregation. She didn't seem fazed by my description of the real differences between the older, working-class folks and the younger, more upwardly mobile families with their BMW's and country club memberships. She asked me whether the values between the two groups were noticeably different. It was a good question and took me a moment to consider.

"Well, I guess you could say that our life experiences are very different and that leads to somewhat different values. Folks my age, and I'm over 60, have worked hard to have a stable lifestyle and aren't afraid to pitch in to make the church work. We've all taught Sunday School or washed the dishes, mowed the lawn, and cleaned the bathrooms. Some of the older ones are resentful of these younger families who seem to want to pay to hire people to do things. Like we have a lawn service now and a sexton. Now we're talking about hiring a Christian Education Director. Don't get me wrong, I think this is the best direction to go in, especially now that we have more kids in the Sunday School. But some of the older members and people who've been attending the longest feel we're moving too fast toward what they might say is a 'professional' church. It doesn't feel like the homey place they're used to. I guess they kind of feel that the new younger folks should be putting in the elbow grease like we all did for so long."

Sarah nodded slowly, listening. "But do the newer members pledge more and so does the church benefit from having them here?"

"Yes, that's the rub. The younger members are pledging higher, but the older, longer-term members feel like they're buying their way in. Like they haven't done their time, so why should they have the upper hand in decision making?"

"So, what about the make-up of the Vestry? Is it heavily weighted one way or another?"

"Pretty evenly divided. Jeffrey Trainor, as you know, as Senior Warden, is one of the newer members who gives a large pledge. Sorry, you can't help but know these things when you work with the pledge drive like I do. But Jeffrey and his wife also give a lot of time to the church, so people were glad to ask him to become Senior Warden. I sit on the Vestry, and as you know there are two men, one of them Frank Trumbore, the Junior Warden and another older, more conservative man. They want the church to slow down and not change so fast. So, about gay marriage? Those two men and Jeffrey are the ones who voted to prevent the priest from performing them. The Vestry is seven people, and out of the four women, three of us voted to approve it. Jeffrey is very influential with the men. But the fourth woman is a retired lawyer, pretty wealthy. Her family is one of the founding members of the church. She tends to vote with Jeffrey as well."

"So, the vote was 4-3 against marriage equality?"

"Yep. And not likely to change right away."

"Well, as you pointed out earlier, you help me get settled here and we'll tackle one issue at a time. No need to hurry on this, right?"

"Well, it may not be a hurry for us. But we don't know when we're going to have a couple who will want to challenge that rule."

Sarah smiled and finished putting the last books away in the upper shelves over her desk. "Well, when that adorable gay couple comes in, falls in love with us and us with them, then we'll have our perfect test case. Right?"

I felt my heart lighten at knowing who this pastor was and what she offered us. Yes, Sarah was the right choice. Young, full of hope, and ready to make change.

Chapter Three

JEFFREY

It's not that I didn't like her, I just thought she was too young to be St. Philips' next priest. When the Search Committee sent her credentials packet to the Vestry, I thought, "Oh, geez, another young woman who thinks she can jump to the head of the line and start imparting her feminine wisdom like Mother Theresa to guys like me." I mean, I've got enough of that at work, right? Rev. Piper, oh, sorry, I mean, the *Rev. Sarah* is now our priest. Somehow, I'm having trouble considering some young woman as my spiritual advisor. Someone I'm supposed to look to for advice? Not some 30-year-old whose only work experience is at an inner- city high school in D.C. She may know how to grade English papers for high schoolers who need to get their asses wiped, but how is she going to help those of us with mortgages, kids with ADD, and marriages with a sell-by date?

But I looked over her sermons and they weren't bad. I mean, I really liked *What Would Jesus Tweet?* and *Does Forgiveness Mean You Get a Do-Over?* Her writing is not bad and her ideas about getting churches into partnership with the community has some relevance, but what does she know about a church budget? Or about supervising staff? Or for God's sake, about giving advice to people who are married?

Anyway, the Search Committee makes the recommendation and the Vestry basically just gets to rubber stamp it, or it seems that way. After we interviewed her, a couple of the Vestry said that having someone young would be like a new start. Being only five years in the church and brand new to being Senior Warden, I sure wasn't going to rock the boat by rejecting her because of her age. Wow, that could have resulted in a lawsuit! So, I went along.

The Vestry had done her interview by video call, so I had met her virtually, but was surprised meeting her in person at how good-looking she was. I mean, for a priest. Blond wavy hair, nice-looking high cheekbones, and a fairly trim figure. She's 30, so she hasn't had time for childbirth to wreck her waistline and 2:00 am feedings to add wrinkles to the corners of her eyes.

She was very pleasant when I welcomed her as she entered the office. Mary, our administrator, bounced up, eager to please, holding out her hand like a dog waiting for a bone. Everything was all nicey, nicey, until Irene showed up, home baked goodies in hand, plots of congregational uprisings hatching in her mind. Irene is our resident lesbian hippie. I mean, she was a hippie back in the 70's before they allowed lesbians in churches. And now that the Supreme Court has blessed those blasphemous unions, she's all ready to get St. Philips to join the fray. I could see in her eyes the plot of getting Rev. Sarah on her side had already begun. When some women meet, it's just like you can see the viscous vapor of estrogen move between them. I saw it happening right then with these two women. Eye to eye, they just tuned into each other like they were on the same radio wave.

I guess it is good to have someone younger who can perhaps learn from a congregation that's been around the block. There are some good stable families here who founded this church and are not interested in change for change's sake. I think once Sarah sits down with someone like Phyllis Trimble, she'll begin to get the lay of the land. Phyllis' family were the wealthy industrialists in this older neighborhood when steel was still king. I can see Phyllis inviting Sarah over for afternoon tea and setting her straight about St. Philips and the founding families' intent to create a more 'moral presence' in the minds of the young. Ha, I'd love to be there to see that! Sarah will have to figure out on which side her bread is buttered. There's much to learn in a church about how communities work and how churches are supported. Rev. Sarah's salary is dependent on the older founding families as well as some of us newer families who moved into Oak Park when the new townhouses were built.

My wife, Elaine, is not very happy with the decision that the Vestry made about holding off on gay marriage at St. Philips. She thinks I'm too old-fashioned and that we should move ahead with the times. That's just because she has a cousin who's gay. But while some will see it as behind the times, the ones who agreed with me on the Vestry are the ones who are the financial pillars of the community. They think this liberal nonsense may all pass. We'll see.

Chapter Four

SARAH

After Irene left, I sat in one of the side chairs and relaxed, glancing out the double windows in my new office. I could see the full view of the front walkway that led into the office area, as well as the tall oaks bordering the courtyard and the tidily planted end-of-summer hostas, their dark green fronds browning. Tangerine colored day lilies poking out from a central bed with some red begonias surrounding them still held on in the end of August heat.

Mary came to the door and looked in. She looked over the rows of books now filling the shelves with two or three boxes still to unpack. I could see her scanning the poetry books set next to the biblical criticisms and theology texts.

"Settling in? It's starting to look like you belong here."

"Mary, I hope so. I'm looking forward to meeting the whole congregation this Sunday."

"I know the congregation is excited to have you as our first woman priest! I can't think of anything better than working for a woman. I've worked for men all my life. And have always had male priests as well."

"Well, I guess a lot of women have had that experience. Perhaps having a woman priest will help some people relate to the church more. At least the women, maybe?"

Mary nodded. "Yes, I think so. We've been lucky here to have had pretty good priests. But the Catholic Church with all those pedophiles? Oh, my, that is just too hard to believe! How can religious men act like that?"

"Oh, jeez, it's so hard to believe that they got away with it for so long. But, you know, it wasn't just the Catholic Church. I guess most churches have had their bad apples. It almost turned me away from ministry completely."

"So, why didn't it?"

"I think it had to do with my experience with a good priest. A damn good one who was there for me when I needed it."

Mary looked interested in hearing more, but I changed the subject. Not quite ready to lay the whole sad tale of my life on her. Not on the first day anyway. We talked some more about our experiences in our respective churches. Mary had grown up Lutheran. She had some pretty old school priests who taught a lot of fire and brimstone and that's when she decided to try the Episcopal Church. As a young woman, she had started bringing her kids here to St. Philips and later, after they left for college, and her husband died, she had accepted the office manager's job. She had found her place as the administrator, finding that she had an important role in building community.

Mary went back to her desk, and I finally had time to just breathe. Moving around the desk, I sank into the chair with a sigh of finality. Here I was. Finally, here. I realized when I felt my feet slightly lifted off the floor that the chair was set too high for my stature. Obviously, Rev. Tim, the interim, had much longer legs. Oh, well. I'd check about getting the chair adjusted later. For now, it seemed obvious

I would need to grow into the daunting stature of the people who had sat in this chair before me.

Pulling open the desk drawers, I emptied the few items from a tote bag I'd brought into one. Then I glanced at the photos on the bookshelf behind the desk, my eye catching one showing my sister Pam and I when we were teen-agers. Each of us held a wedge of bright red watermelon, Pam in the midst of a bite and my mouth dripping red juice. Our dad, taking the picture, had captured the hilarity of our taking turns spitting the seeds in front of us, seeing who could spit the furthest.

"You cheated," I remember her sputtering through the giggles, "you have a bigger mouth than me!"

"Oh, yeah, well, better to spit at you, my dear!" I had gasped, turning my focus of spit to aim at her. I launched one that landed splat on the front of her shirt. She gasped and looked down at it, her eyes meeting mine as she gathered saliva in her mouth to lubricate the next missile. I started backing away as she followed with a gob of drool and black seeds falling harmlessly into the grass. Our laughter died down as we collapsed like spent balloons onto the ground, the watermelon rinds carelessly thrown to the side.

The photo was taken about a year before she died, before her leukemia diagnosis permanently changed our lives. Back when we were still in the joyous, carefree existence before chemo drips, hospital beds, and nausea. Before the idea that she could die was even a possibility. Before.

The picture next to it was of my parents. It was an after picture. Taken on my college graduation day, when they dutifully came to the ceremony, hugged me, told me how proud they were, and then trudged back to their car, driving home that same afternoon. You could see the tiredness etched on their faces, the resignation of how life would never be the same again. Even when your other daughter made you proud, it just wasn't enough.

And here I was. Starting my career as a newly ordained priest in my first parish, about eight years after that college graduation. Staring out the window again, I realized that despite the uncomfortable height of the chair I felt something right settle inside me. I might have found that place where I could make a difference. Where the scars I bore from losing Pam could finally become places of healing where I could help others who were hurting. Even if it felt like it was a stretch right now.

Telling Mary I wanted to tour the building by myself just to get the feel of the place, I sauntered through the hallways toward the sanctuary. It felt so different to move through this church now than it did when I had come for my interview, when I was so distracted by the impression I might make. I remembered my initial feeling when walking into the worship area with the high vaulted ceiling, dark polished beams, and hanging round chandeliers. The light filtering in through the blue and rose-tinted stained glass gave the space a quiet, sacred feel that I had so loved growing up in a similar church. But I felt a different kind of energy take hold as I realized that I now carried a huge responsibility for creating a place where people came to be fed and nurtured, as I had been growing up in a church. Could I be that kind of pastor that my priest had been for me when I really needed it?

As I walked out of the sanctuary to the parish hall, I saw the row of priest's portraits in gold filigreed frames. Some were oil portraits of heavily-jowled, older men with thick brows of concentration. Then there were a couple of photographs of priests in their robes, holding up the silver chalices, offering communion. The long history of men who had shaped this church by seeing it through difficult times and maybe in also limiting ways weighed on me. I was going to be part of the history here. My picture would be hanging on this wall one day, I assumed. Maybe the first woman with that honor, but hopefully, not the last.

After I finished my tour, I asked Mary if we could take some time just to talk. Mary suggested going into the kitchen where she put on the kettle for tea. I mentioned as I sat down how helpful Irene had been in telling me about the church. As Mary got out the teacups and a cannister of tea bags, she paused for a moment.

"Irene is like the wise grandmother of the church," she began. "She's not the mother, trying to fix everything. She's not the gossipy cousin who complains about everybody else but does nothing to help. She's like the grandmother who listens to everything then adds just the right comment at the right time. She seems to keep herself above the fray."

"Above the 'fray'? And what is this 'fray' usually about?" I asked, raising an eyebrow.

Mary sighed, "Well, whenever the conversation turns to the budget. And right now, whether or not we're going to hire a Christian Education Director."

I remembered a long conversation about this during the interview. It seemed that the young families with kids and more income were anxious to hire a part time religious educator to manage the Sunday school. Some of older members who had been managing the Sunday school with volunteers for decades now were adamant that the church couldn't afford it. Mary told me that this issue was going to be on the Vestry agenda next week.

"Mary, is Irene a good person for me to trust on this issue?"

Mary nodded. "Yes, she has a long view having been here the last time the church could afford a Sunday School director. Which was about 20 years ago, I think. She was very involved with the Christian

Education program here at that point. And she's always volunteered with the Sunday School."

"Is it okay if I ask you your opinion of some of the other members?"

Mary pursed her lips considering, then responded haltingly, "Well, I hope...you'll feel like you can do that... and maybe take it with a grain of salt or two. I mean, I've been here a long time, so I've seen a lot. But I might also have a slanted point of view." She seemed apologetic.

"You mean, you aren't absolutely objective, all the time?" I asked, raising my eyebrows sarcastically.

"Well, I'm afraid being in a church this long doesn't necessarily make someone accepting. I'm afraid it can make you a little, not jaded, but I certainly don't take people at face value anymore."

"What do you mean?"

"Well, there are people you meet and you know right away they're the real deal. You can just sense that they are who they say they are. Like you, for instance."

"Oh, thanks." I dipped my head in acknowledgment.

"But then, there are people you meet, and unfortunately, there's just as many of them in a church as there are other places, who are...well, shall we say, not necessarily showing you their full story. You know what I mean?" Mary asked hesitantly.

I sensed this was leading somewhere. "Yeah, I do know what you mean. But is there someone in particular you've been feeling this about?"

Mary frowned, then continued cautiously. "I don't want to give you a bad sense of someone before you've really had a chance to get to know them. You know?"

"Okay. What if when I get a feeling about someone who might be hiding something, I'll come to you and check it out? Would that work?" I asked.

Mary thought a minute. "Yeah, I think that would make sense. Thanks. I appreciate you not pressing me on it."

We continued our conversation about church leaders, committees, and meetings that I might be expected to attend. I felt a sense of relief that at least in Mary, there was someone who could help steer me the right direction. She wasn't eager to gossip or share her opinions right away and I appreciated that. I needed a chance to get my feet wet, meet everyone, and form my own perspective before I grappled with other's opinions. I have always counted on my intuition about people, but I realized that also came with a heavy dose of judgment.

At the end of the afternoon, after Mary had gone home, I slipped back into the sanctuary, finding a seat in one of the back pews. Breathing the musty air, I let the silence envelope me. The long, tall stained-glass windows all the way down the sanctuary filled the room with glowing vibrant colors and the images of heroic figures of the Bible. I could name each of these figures, St. Philip being the most prominent in the front window with his gathered robes and the two loaves of bread at his feet in a basket. I thought about the passage in John in which Philip, the Apostle, is mentioned in the story of the loaves and the fishes, one of my favorites. I made a mental note to include it in one of my first sermons.

That first week, my apprehension built thinking of my first Sunday service with my new congregation. What they expected of me seemed incomprehensible. I didn't have any great wisdom to impart. Just some simple understanding that might be helpful to people in understanding what God might be like. Something that would have relevance in their lives.

As I met and talked with more congregants that week, I began to realize that they were excited to have me there and eager to be present for the first Sunday. That day, despite my anxiety, all seemed to go well. At coffee hour after the service, Jeffrey Trainor introduced me to those gathered as "our delightful new priest who has graced us by accepting our call". My face beaming, I shared a little about myself and promised they would hear more. It was what you might call an "auspicious" beginning.

Chapter Five

SARAH

After a restless night, my eyes opened early that second Sunday morning around 6:00 a.m. with the sky still smoky dark. I lay in bed watching the horizon beginning to suffuse with faint streaks of light. It was in this kind of rosy lighting in the rising dawn that I often found myself most connected to that sense of something sacred. In that hour, my mind opened to what was unseen but felt before the daily anxieties took hold. The waking dawn with its unwritten promise.

Working on the sermon all week, I pronounced it done the night before around 11:00 pm. Anyone who writes for a living is familiar with that unease of wondering when to pronounce something done. You can always overlook something you might want to say, but you can also commit death-by-editing.

My second week at St. Philips had seemed like a merry-go-round with various committees and members shifting up and down, in and out, all wanting my attention. I'd wake in the night, thinking about how to do something differently, better than I had. I felt that rising tide of hopeful anticipation that maybe I'd found my place here. A few nervous twinges in my belly questioned that optimism.

Each morning, after I did my morning meditation and prayers, I found myself checking my phone to ensure there weren't any pastoral emergencies. That Sunday morning, I saw a message from Marilyn, my close friend from seminary and the reason I had chosen a church in Philadelphia. She had helped me move in when I had arrived two weeks before. She came bearing a welcome gift of a bag of bagels from down the street and cleaning supplies both of which were very appreciated.

[Hope your first week went well. I was so overwhelmed here at St. John's that I could barely look up to see what day it was. Let's get together this week. Dinner, Monday night?]

I replied with a thumbs up.

Marilyn had swept into the classroom in those first few weeks of seminary plunking down next to me in Hebrew Testament class. I noticed her right away as she was carrying not just the Hebrew Testament required for the class, but also a novel by Octavia Butler, a black feminist author who made wondrous sci-fi worlds into spiritual adventures. Anyone who could study the Bible and carry it next to spiritual fantasy was someone I had to know. When she leaned over and whispered, "And another day of the Holy Patriarchal Trio," I covered my mouth to keep from losing it, then smiled to her, nodding.

Later in the semester, we both received terse notes added to our papers about our "irreverent and arrogant" attitude toward scripture. Having someone who could love God and still joke about "what would Jesus do" when the toilet in the ladies' room overflowed was really the only way I got through those days. Marilyn would stay up past midnight with me as we struggled to answer those nagging questions about sin and atonement. We both felt it was more important that we figure out the relevance of Jesus' teachings to the problem of homelessness rather than whether Jesus believed he was the Messiah or if he just wanted to do good work.

Squeezing into the narrow kitchen of my small apartment between the boxes that were still unpacked, Filling the tea kettle with water, I took out the granola from a glass cannister, poured it into my favorite blue-green ceramic bowl, adding plain yogurt and grabbing a spoon from the dish drainer. I sat at the small kitchen table I'd put together from IKEA, with the two painted chairs from my parent's house, a soft flat embroidered pillow under me.

I opened my laptop to the last iteration of the sermon for today. As I reviewed it for the umpteenth time, I read aloud some of the sentences I just hadn't been sure about, changing a few word selections as I went. It sounded okay. Just okay. Did it tell them that I was pretty open religiously? Did it tell them that I wanted to make scripture relevant to daily life? And did it tell them that I wanted to relate to their needs as a congregation? No sermon could do all that. But maybe it was a start.

Earlier in the week, when I had started this sermon, I had not yet met with many of the members. As several people came in to see me over the week, though, I had begun to see the congregation more clearly. The shape of my sermon had begun to form around what I was seeing. There were some dramatic differences between some of the people in the congregation. I mean, I had been warned that there were a couple of octogenarians from the wealthier founding families, then "the long-term members" who had been described as "working-class", and the younger, more "up and coming" people, but now I began to put a face to what that meant.

One long term member was Peg, the forty something divorced mother with her squinting anxious eyes and glasses pushed up on her forehead as she told me about her two young girls. Working in a retail store, often having to work weekends and leave her kids with her mother, she told me she didn't have much time but would love to talk briefly. Peg had made an appointment for 5:15 so she could swing by and see me before she had to pick up her girls from daycare. She came in clutching a large tote bag and seemed to slump into her chair when I invited her to sit down. She jumped right in without my even having to prompt her.

"You know, Rev. Piper, I really love this church because I know that people have got my back. When I was going through my divorce, I would sometimes just break down and cry during Sunday service. No one made me feel ashamed. Someone would just come and sit with me. I knew that I wasn't alone. I can't really give much money to the church and that makes me feel sad but I didn't feel that anyone expected more from me. When I first came, I felt like I could just give what I could and it would be okay."

Then Peg had shared that some of the newer people who could give a lot more seemed to expect everyone to give a certain amount. They didn't understand how hard it was to make ends meet. Peg was glad these new families had found the church and supported the church financially, but sometimes it made her feel like there were the "haves" and the "have-nots" dividing up the church.

When I began writing the sermon I thought about Peg's words. Being inspired by the image of St. Philip in the front stained-glass window, the story of the loaves and the fishes had become the centerpiece of the sermon. Philip had said to Jesus that it would take at least "two hundred days wages worth of food to feed the huge crowd that had gathered and that they had only five loaves and two fish." Phillip was practical and was showing Jesus how insurmountable was the task before them. But Jesus directed the disciples to bring him the baskets with the food they had. He took the food, and he gave thanks to God. Then he gave it back to the disciples and told them to give it to the people.

Can you imagine St. Philip when Jesus handed him this paltry amount of food and told him to feed the thousands of people in front of them? Can you see Philip's eye roll? Can't you just hear him sighing and his whiny voice, "But Jesus, we can't possibly feed thousands of people with that!" But the disciples reluctantly did as Jesus asked, doubting this could ever work. I would imagine they were fearful, too, that the crowd could get angry and out of hand and demand more food. When the disciples looked out at the crowd, they probably saw lots of different kinds of people gathered there.

There were people who stood proudly with brightly colored robes and shiny jewelry showing off their wealth. Some of these people had been rather skeptical about Jesus' preaching fearing that he wanted them to share their wealth. Then there were the merchants who were well fed and plainly dressed but seemed eager to hear more from this so-called prophet who spoke aloud of the kingdom of God and His great mercy. Then there were so many of the people who wore simple clothes and who were thin and looked worn out with work. The poor among them were probably the most faithful to this teaching which spoke about everyone being seen as equal in the eyes of the Lord. But these were the hungry people. The disciples probably worried that these truly hungry ones might cause trouble when it became evident how little food was available.

But when the baskets with the food had been distributed, everyone had enough to eat! They were no longer hungry! And there were 12 baskets of leftovers! Imagine Philip's face. Jesus had told them to trust the Lord and be okay with what was asked of them. That the Lord would provide. The disciples were amazed and thought it was a miracle!

Okay, there are different ways to interpret this story. Some of us might think that Matthew and John are telling us in this story that Jesus performed a miracle and waved his hands over the baskets, and food just multiplied before their eyes. Right? That's one way to interpret this story. Jesus performed a miracle. But another way that many interpret this story is that when the baskets were passed around the crowd those who had plenty of food would put something in the basket as it went around instead of taking something out. Those who needed food, took food out; those who had plenty, shared what they had into the baskets so others could eat. So, at the end, there was plenty to go around and plenty left over.

You've all seen this happen, haven't you? We hold a potluck at church and at first, we look around and there's only the mac and cheese that someone brought and put on the table and then a tossed salad appears. If we're there early, we might start to worry, "Will there be enough?" Then several come in with hummus, right? Always plenty of hummus! And then someone comes in with a sliced ham. Someone else arrives with soup and some brownies. Then as more people come, the food on the table multiples right before our eyes. We all go around the table spooning up the delicious smelling treats brought by everyone, and we sit down and break bread together and we're stuffed! And there's plenty left over. We end up taking some home because we couldn't eat it all.

Is this a miracle? Something being created out of thin air? Or is this the miracle of community? Of what happens in community when we share a common purpose- a spiritual purpose. The purpose has something to do with feeding each other, right? We nourish each other spiritually. And the purpose has something to do with the miracle that God always provides for us, somehow, someway. Even sometimes when we can't quite see how it's going to happen.

I had also remembered what Irene had shared about some of the more secure families who had begun joining the church a few years ago. The ones who lived in the new development built where the old steel mill was razed. With its three and four- bedroom new construction townhomes, built from four different models but looking very similar in design, the neighborhood attracted families who worked in the city but wanted the amenities of suburban life. Surrounded with treed lots and a few fenced in "pocket parks" with small playgrounds for families, it was the ideal suburban enclave built in the middle of the city. The families who had joined the church from this newer neighborhood were considerably more financially secure than the working- class families that made up the majority of the congregation. That had given St. Philips more financial stability recently. I had thought about how I would speak to them in this sermon as well.

Many of us are practical people like Philip. We don't see how our church budget is going to cover all the needs of the congregation. We work hard on the pledge drive bringing people together to help them understand the importance of the vision of the church. But we can't see how it's going to happen. But everyone steps up and gives what they can. Somehow, by some miracle, it happens. We make the pledge goal. We squeak by again. We do it with everyone helping. This spiritual community of God comes together, and we feed each other. We nourish each other with love and care.

You may be wondering how we're going to make this miracle happen this year. Here you are, you've called a new priest and that had some expense to it. You've committed to making some repairs to this building. Now we're going to be deciding if the church can hire a Christian educator. So, it's a lot. But it all comes down to this. I won't say faith- because I don't want to imply that you don't have enough faith if you think we should pare back the budget. No, it comes down to the strength of community. Whatever we decide should be our vision for this church year and the budget that supports that vision, together we'll make it happen. With everyone's help. With some help from God. But God doesn't usually perform miracles without our help. The miracle is the strength we find from the experience of working together to make this happen. The miracle is in the hands of the people. All of you.

St. Philip (point to the blue robed figure in the front window holding a basket) was also a practical man and might have questioned a visionary budget at first. But after seeing what that crowd could do starting with five loaves and two fish, he became a believer. He became a believer not just in the Lord, but in the power of community as well. That's the kind of faith we can learn from this story. We learn the faith of what we can do together, each one doing their part with love for this community. Each one of us different in our own unique ways. Different in the way we work, different in the way we interact, different in the way we love. But all doing their part to make this Beloved Community.

This second time I preached for them, I was more aware of who they thought I was, this new priest, thirty years young, hopeful, and expectant with possibility. But I hoped that they would see me putting the pieces together from all the introductions this week forming a picture of who they were.

Under my black robe and white surplice, I was sweating. I could feel the drips running down my neck. My stole was slowly growing damp. I grabbed my handkerchief out of my robe's hidden pocket and furtively dabbed at the back of my neck, while glancing around at the sea of faces, hoping they didn't notice. Mostly the faces looked encouraging, egging me on, giving me their whole attention. Some I already knew from meetings during the first week, but many were new to me. While I felt good about the sermon, noticing the number of smiles and nods in response, I also noticed many of the older members sitting in the back with staring, blank faces. I had no idea what they might be thinking.

In the reception line, I stood at the front door to the sanctuary, shaking hands and meeting more of the members I hadn't yet met. I tried to remember names by using a trick one of my colleagues had shared. Looking at something about their appearance, I'd try to relate it to the name. "James" had a dark beard, just like St. James might have had. William had two children pulling him away from the line insistently- he looked like a friend of mine, Bill, who also had two children. I also was very grateful for the ones who wore name tags and thanked them for doing so.

One balding, middle-aged man with a baggy tweed jacket shook my hand and introduced himself. Then pausing and looking a bit sheepish, asked if I was single. I had to stop myself from asking why he wanted to know, thinking it was such a rude question. But clearly, he just thought it was important to my role somehow. I replied that no, I was not married, with a puzzled expression. He laughed and said, "Oh, don't you worry. I wasn't trying to hit on you!" We both laughed and it became a light moment. Other people in the line asked me where I lived and if I needed recommendations for doctors. I began to understand that these people wanted to know me, everything about me. I would need to learn how much of my private life I was willing to share.

But overall, I felt the sense of welcome coming from this community. For it was a community, not just a bunch of individuals. They had called me as their priest, and I was slowly being welcomed into their already formed religious community. But I did worry that my unorthodox approach to Christianity might come right up and hit me in the eyes when it became more apparent to this community.

My seminary papers had questions scrawled all over them from the more conservative professors. "What is your salvation theology?" they asked over and over. But I had passed with fairly good grades, my approach to stories from the Bible laid against modern life giving them relevance.   The Search Committee emphasized to me how they were looking for someone "younger" who could speak to the younger parishioners that they were starting to attract. But would the older members be able to relate to my theology?

In the first day of my second year of seminary, I was sitting in my New Testament class waiting for it to begin having my typical thoughts of "what am I doing here?" Thoughts that fluttered here and there throughout my seminary education. But particularly as I had begun the more "Christian" parts of what going to seminary was all about, my doubts were sticking their necks out like an un- wanted busybody. The doctrine of Christ's sacrifice as a substitute for punishment for humanity's sins which was the central Christian concept continued to nag at me. I continued to question what it meant.

While I was having one of these annoying conversations with myself waiting for the New Testament class to start, I noticed an older woman with graying, wavy hair with a single gray braid resting on her shoulder sitting in the back of the room. I hadn't noticed her before and wondered if she had just begun her seminary education. We were a small seminary, with only about 30 people in each class. But sometimes there were students who were from the community attending to just learn more about the Bible. I wondered if she was one of those.

At the start of class, Professor George, whom I knew from my Hebrew Testament class the previous year, asked us to introduce ourselves and to say where we were in our seminary education. As we started around the room, I was half-listening knowing most of the students who had begun last year with me. But when it came to this woman, we all seemed to lean in wanting to hear more about her.

She looked around the room at the mixture of younger students and many second career students who were in their fifties. She smiled a kind of knowing smile. "I am Gloria. I guess you are wondering when I turned up? Kinda old to be heading toward seminary, right? Well," she said speaking slowly with a soft Southern accent, "I guess you could say I'm a Bible tourist. Just here to learn more about the Bible. More for my own education, than anything else."

The professor nodded and motioned for the next student to speak, continuing until everyone had spoken. He explained the syllabus with the Gospels, the Epistles, and Acts as the main content. He went on to explain our assignments and the grading system. Finishing up, he paused and asked for questions. Gloria raised her hand.

"Yes, Gloria?"

She looked a bit frustrated. "So, is that it? Are we just studying the approved cannon?"

Professor George narrowed his eyes in confusion. "What do you mean?"

Gloria looked down at the floor and shifted in her seat. "Well, I mean, are we going to study some of the Gostic Gospels?"

"The Gnostic Gospels? You mean, like the ones found in Nag Hammadi?"

"Yes, the Gospel of Thomas or others?"

Professor George shook his head, looking a bit thrown off. "Well, Gloria, this is a course in the New Testament, the Christian scripture, so, no, we're not going to study ancient documents that were not accepted canon by the established Church. I mean, it might be interesting to examine them to compare them to the approved cannon and understand why they were not included. But that could be done just by an individual who wanted to do further study."

Gloria nodded her head, "Uh, huh. Okay. That's what I figured."

The professor pursed his lips at her obvious disappointment. "Hmm. Why don't you speak with me after class? I would be happy to have some discussions with you on this topic offline."

She looked unmoved. "Okay. I see." She said, sighing deeply.

The professor decided to move on. I was intrigued and wanted to know more. I had heard about the ancient Gnostic Gospels and had even read a bit about the Gospel of Thomas as an unapproved gospel found in Nag Hammadi, Egypt along with several others. Stashed in a sealed earthenware jar, and hidden away in a desert in Egypt, they hadn't been found until 1945 by accident by a wandering peasant. The Church fathers had obviously not been keen on having people find these. And once you read some of them, you could begin to see why. The theology that was hidden beneath the simple words from these first or second century writers was much different than the thrust of the New Testament. Even I could see that these words might have made the founders of the church take note of the difference and hatch a plan to make sure they didn't see light of day.

After that class, I decided to start reading the Gospel of Thomas more carefully and what I found called to me.

Jesus said, "If they say to you, 'Where did you come from?', say to them, 'We came from the light, the place where the light came into being on its own accord and established itself and became manifest through their image."

    • *Gospel of Thomas*

I began a spiritual practice of reading a verse from these Gnostic Gospels before bed. The image of humans "coming from the light" as our source spoke to me in a way that a Father God and male son did not. The verses were filled with a calmness and simplicity that spoke to me. I could imagine God as light more than as a powerful Being with an agenda. When I read these simple verses, I felt like that light was within me, and shining from within all people.

Gloria became a friend when I had stopped and asked her one day in the cafeteria if she could tell me more about the Gospel of Thomas. She half-smiled, shook her braid, and said, "You know, they aren't going to like it if I'm proselytizing about these heretical texts. But..." She looked at my intrigued and open face and invited me to sit down. Over our lunch, she began to open new doors for me about what Jesus was all about. The ideas coming out of these heretical gospels were more about finding God everywhere, in everything thing we did or said. As she talked, I felt that kind of shaky feeling you get when you know something meaningful is happening to you even when you're not sure what it is. Gloria's eyes got brighter and her face opened up with what you might call "religious fervor" or what felt to me like inner joy.

We had begun a regular email interchange that kept our discussions lively when we couldn't meet for coffee. I remember a conversation we had one afternoon, sitting in the quad on one of the benches, on a bright sunny afternoon. I was bemoaning a New Testament paper we had due in a week. She raised her eyes at my discomfort.

"You're struggling with something. I can see that," she said gently.

I groaned and opened the textbook to find the troublesome quote from Peter I'd been reviewing for the past hour. When I found it and read it aloud, I sighed deeply and put down the book looking over at her.

"So, why does the church draw this conclusion that God sacrificed his son, Jesus Christ, on the cross, so that we can be forgiven? I mean, yes, in Peter, it says that Christ died for our sins to bring us to God. But maybe he meant that Christ was willing to sacrifice himself to prove to us that God is with us, even in our worst moments. That he could die, and God would still be with him and we could, therefore, count on God, despite our sinning." I blew out some air, looking over at Gloria, raking a hand through my hair.

She smiled, laughing at my frustration. "Honey, you just summed up my whole difficulty with Christian theology. I get it! It doesn't make sense to me, either. That's why I keep coming here, taking courses. I'm still trying to figure it out. You know, I'm not trying to convince you to question your faith, Sarah. I really hate to bring this up with other students. But with you...."

I nodded, "Yes, I've certainly always questioned everything. It's kind of how I was raised. My parents weren't very religious."

"So, you'll draw your own conclusions. I don't worry that you will be unduly influenced by me. In fact, your questions have been helpful to me since I've had so many of my own. I just hope you'll be able to find your place in all this...your own faith. I sense that in you. A deep faith which comes from within you. I really see that."

"Really?" I said surprised. "Even with all my questions?"

"Oh, behind those questions is a deep need to draw close to what is true for you. You know that questioning is the best way to deepen your faith, right?"

"Well, I guess that depends on how you define 'faith,'" I said, with a bit of a flippant tone.

Gloria just nodded her head, her grey curls bobbing. "Yes, but I define faith as what is at your root, your essence. And that can't be something that someone else handed to you all wrapped up in a bow."

After that conversation, I wanted more. I wanted to continue our discussion because I felt I was getting something from Gloria that I didn't get from my seminary studies. But a week after that talk, after I finally finished and turned in my final paper for the semester, I tried calling Gloria but she didn't answer. I left several messages and was surprised when I heard nothing. Checking with the dean's office, I was told that she had dropped her status as a part-time student, leaving with no explanation. They didn't have any more information. It felt like the blank stares I received when I started to bring up these non-canonical texts in my classes. Gloria wasn't answering and neither were my professors.

My printed-out copy of the Gospel of Thomas sat on my desk throughout seminary next to my white leather New Testament. Both were equally dog-eared and underlined.

As I began this ministry, I still had lots of middle of the night musings about how I defined "salvation" and my relationship to the Trinity. When I was questioned by the committee in my diocese about my salvation theology, I explained that I saw God, Christ, and the Holy Spirit as three aspects of divinity that were used by God in different ways. My relationship to God was deep and all encompassing. In some ways, it was beyond words, I'd explained. I felt held and strengthened every time I prayed. But, I went on a little nervously, I didn't necessarily see God and Christ having traditional Father-Son anthropomorphic characteristics. The whole picturing God as a father sounded limiting by giving God human characteristics. The God I knew was pure Love. Unconditional Love.

Then why send Jesus into the world if God could do the job, they asked. Jesus, another form of this pure love, but incarnated, was made into human flesh, so had some of the characteristics of humans. In fact, I saw Jesus as human but with the gift of "gnosis", the inner knowledge of how to be human with God's perfect love. That "gnosis" to me was available to us all, even though we were unaware of how to use it.

Anyway, these answers were good enough for most of the committee with the exception of one male priest who asked me twice to explain "gnosis" and how it differed from "Holy Spirit". I said that if I knew that, I'd be ready to lead the whole church, in fact, the whole world. But, I said, I would be aware of my desire to learn more about what "gnosis" was and how the average person could access it. The bishop closed the meeting by blessing my strong passion to learn how to access faith by praying with the Holy Spirit. He said I had the spirit of a disciple who didn't always get it right (like many of the disciples), but who kept trying. He encouraged me to center my prayer life on becoming a true disciple who didn't have to question everything but could take some things on faith.

So, my prayer life was a little different than most Christians, I guess. I truly felt the presence of divine Spirit, within me and surrounding me. But I didn't feel it as a "Being". When I prayed, I wasn't asking for God to do things as most people did. I didn't believe in a transactional God. My prayer was more like presence with God, in that I wanted to connect with the Holy Spirit. If I could be immersed in unconditional Love that God represented for me, then my actions would be filled with love. Or at least that was my intention. As I looked forward to this new life, this new identity as a priest, my intentions would be put to the test. Could I embody even a little bit of that love?

Sitting in the pew after that Sunday service, I decided I would focus my prayer on the image of Mary that was depicted on one of those glossy stained-glass windows. In the window, Mary was shown as usual with her sky-blue veil and golden halo, but as she held the baby Jesus, she looked down on him with tenderness and I thought a bit of apprehension. Like Mary, I felt I was holding this whole congregation in my heart but also with hopeful and wistful expectation. The hope that I could be the best shepherd for them, guiding them toward that "gnosis" of understanding the mystery of

God. But also fearing that I wasn't at all sure that I wouldn't lead them astray somehow.

Chapter Six

IRENE

After speaking with Sarah briefly after her second Sunday, I swung by her office later that week just to check on how she was doing. I could see that Sarah had great confidence and enthusiasm but maybe a bit of näiveté. I could almost remember having that kind of upbeat optimism and it was uplifting to see it in Sarah. But I also remembered the letdown that followed when people disappointed you. I didn't want her to start in this ministry with unrealistic expectations. On the other hand, her hopefulness was encouraging.

I knocked on her door, and since it was open, I stuck my head in. She seemed focused on her computer screen.

"Hey, don't want to interrupt you, but I just thought I'd stop by and see how your week is going."

Sarah looked up and smiled, motioning me to sit down.

"Hey, thanks for coming by! I need a break, so come sit for a minute."

"So, this is week three. Have you learned where the bodies are buried yet?"

Sarah laughed and waved at the window showing a glimpse of the cemetary in the back. "I sure hope they're buried out there."

"Well, yeah, most of them,." I said teasing.

"Oh, now you tell me. Okay, where else should I look?"

"Oh, you might check the basement near the boiler. I hear that some Vestry members might have been moved along by putting them down there." I smiled and winked at her. "So, you've been at the welcome lunch with the "Oldies but Goodies" bunch. Oh, and then there's the Friday brunch with the Ladies Guild tomorrow."

"I know. It's all wonderful. I missed you at the Oldies but Goodies. But I guess you're not old enough for that group. And will you be at the lunch tomorrow?"

I laughed. "Well, I'm certainly old enough. And I'm certainly of the female gender. But no, those two groups are not my thing."

She looked surprised, "And why are those not your thing?"

"Oh, there's nothing wrong with either of those groups. I just don't quite fit in with the "grey hairs" even though I have plenty of grey hair. I guess you might say, I've shocked them enough over the years to make myself rather unwelcome."

"I see. What have you done to become an outcast?"

I smiled and paused. "Well, just being lesbian is enough.. But if that's not enough to scare away those nice church ladies, then there are the times I've been arrested down at city hall. All in the name of some relevant political issue."

Sarah chuckled. "Wow. I wasn't warned that we have a real rebel in our midst."

"Oh, you never know," I added, smiling.

"Seriously, I know you play an important leadership role in this congregation. What kind of a role do you play?"

I had to think about that for a minute. "Well...you're right. I do play some kind of leadership role. I guess you could say I am often the devil's advocate. But mostly, I just ask a lot of questions."

"In my experience, asking questions is a very good tactic to get people thinking. About whatever they're about to do."

"Yes, that's often my intent. There are many times when a process I call "group think" has taken over and the group has wandered onto thin ice but hasn't noticed because they thought they were on solid ground."

"Hmm. What makes you stick with this church despite some of this thin ice?"

"You know, despite the people who are stuck in their ways, when it comes down to it, this church is my home. They show me they care when it really matters. Like when my mother was ill and they were there every day with casseroles and visits. And then, after she died, they just handled the whole memorial service when I just couldn't manage it somehow. They were there for me."

"Earlier, did you come out when you were in a congregation? An Episcopal one?"

"Yes," I sighed. "That was hard. It was one of the hardest things I've ever done. But it was amazing, really. I couldn't come out when my dad was still alive because he would have stopped talking to me, so I kept it to myself all through high school and most of college. My dad died when I was in college, and I finally got the courage to tell my mom. She said that she already knew. Figured it out when I was in high school and I didn't want to go to the school dances. But when I told her I wanted to let the priest know, she was hesitant."

"She didn't think you should come out?"

"Well, Father John, the priest at that church, seemed a bit conservative. He talked about not going against God's plan, which seemed like code words for, you know, not being gay. But in high school, I had worked in the nursery with the little kids. And there was one little boy there who liked to dress up in some of the dress up clothes that parents had brought in. He loved the pink frilly dress and the tiara. He kept putting it on and asking me to dance with him. I loved his little proud face when he danced and swirled around in his finery."

"But did the priest object to this?"

"Well, that's the thing. One day, he came in before church looking for someone and saw Joey twirling around in this dress, and he stopped, he smiled at Joey, and came over and danced with him. Really took his time to give Joey that extra special attention. I was, well, surprised, to say the least."

"And did that give you more hope for this priest being open?"

"Well, maybe. Father John also had reached out to me encouraging me to apply for a scholarship for college from the diocese. Anyway, I stopped by his office after church one day and asked to speak to him. I told him that I was having these 'thoughts' about not really...well, not wanting to go on dates and all. And he stopped me. He said, 'Irene, it's okay.'"

"What? He really said that?"

"Yeah. He said, he thought that having these thoughts was okay. That God loved me no matter what I decided. And he didn't think I should make up my mind about it yet. Just to give it some time."

"Wow."

"And so, later when I came back from college. I told him that I had decided that I was a lesbian, and he got up from his chair and gave me a big hug." In remembering that I felt some tears threatening. I took a breath. "I mean, he just accepted it. I was amazed."

Sarah looked touched and waited a beat. Then she asked, "So, did you come out to others then?"

"Slowly and not publicly. Father John just asked me not to 'advertise' but to feel comfortable just being who I was. So, I would tell friends and of course, word got around."

"This was in the 70's?"

"Yeah, things were just starting to open up for gay people, but certainly not in the church."

"Did you get any pushback when you joined here?"

"Just once. When I asked the priest during the 90s if we could gather a group to rally at the statehouse for a marriage equality demonstration, he said that wasn't the purpose of the church. But I gathered a group privately and we went anyway. Later, as I told you I had difficulty with a job where I was a teacher and I was fired for telling my students that I was a lesbian, my church friends gathered a petition with 300 signatures and got me reinstated."

"This church did that?"

"Yep. And even the priest who had told me we couldn't gather for the rally signed it and preached something about how every person has the right to be who they were in their hearts."

Sarah looked surprised. "Irene, it feels like this church has your back."

I smiled, "Yeah, it feels that way to me."

"So, even now when it's taking them longer to get to condoning marriage equality, you think they'll get there."

"Yeah, they'll get there." Then I paused with a slight frown. "But I'm not sure about the Senior Warden. He seems to think he holds all the cards."

"Jeffrey?"

"Yeah.

"And what makes you think he thinks he holds all the cards? And what is he planning on doing with those cards?"

"Hmm. Well, I don't know really. But he's the voice of the older members of the congregation who apparently think we're not ready for marriage equality. Oh, but interestingly, he doesn't agree with them about our hiring a Christian Ed Director."

"Huh. What does he think about that?"

"Well, he thinks we need one and soon. Maybe that's because his wife Elaine has taught a lot in the Sunday School and she has clued him in. But he's a tricky one, I'm afraid. He's very political. Seemed to grab hold of the reins of power by getting chummy with the older families who founded this church. They may not be vocal themselves, but they still have a lot of influence."

"Influence over the Vestry?"

"Oh, yeah. Enough to sway several policies. That's the way church politics go. You mean they didn't teach you this in seminary? Vestry politics 101?"

Sarah shook her head. "Nope. Family systems theory. But nothing spelled out as bluntly as Vestry politics."

"Well, I'm sorry to be the one to break the news to you. But politics exist wherever there's people."

Sarah shook her head sadly. "Yeah, I guess I knew that."

Chapter Seven

JEFFREY

Seeing Sarah standing in front of the bank, I waved to her from across the street where I had found parking. I had arranged with her to meet at the bank and get some documents signed so that she could have signing authority over checks that fell within her budget responsibility. The treasurer and I had signing authority for most of the financial responsibilities of the church, but the priests had to be able to sign checks under their discretion.

She waved back and waited until I arrived at the steps to the bank. She was dressed nicely in black slacks and a sweater. I was glad to see that she didn't wear her "backwards collar" everywhere. I always thought it a bit daunting when priests would show up at a cocktail party with that obvious sign of their religious calling. But Sarah seemed comfortable to be who she was, just a regular person, and I was starting to think she would be a good priest despite her youth.

We chatted as we made our way into the bank and after I signed the register to see the next bank clerk, we settled into their waiting area. She turned to me, easily slipping into a relaxed conversation.

"So, Jeffrey, I was so glad to meet the rest of your family on Sunday. Emily is so adorable, she must keep you in stitches!"

I smirked thinking of what Emily had said about Sarah after church. "Yeah, she is pretty funny. And she loved meeting you, too! In fact, she asked me if you always wore that long dress even when you went to the store!"

Sarah laughed. "I can just see myself trying to push the grocery cart and running over my surplice!" We both laughed at that image. Then the bank clerk interrupted us, and we went into her office to get the business done. When we came out, on the spur of the moment, I asked Sarah if she wanted to go to lunch down the street at a local diner. She agreed, looking surprised and pleased, and we decided to walk there. We entered the small diner and settled in a booth by the window, looking over our menus after the hostess ushered us in. We both ordered sandwiches and iced tea and then I started feeling a little uncomfortable trying to come up with a topic we could discuss. I hadn't really known a priest well before this. Sarah looked a bit anxious as well but cleared her throat.

"Jeffrey, I wanted to ask you about something, but I was hesitant to bring it up."

"What's that?"

"Well, it's about the sanction against gay marriage that the Vestry passed. I had not been aware of it until after I came here. The Search Committee had not brought it up."

She looked unhappy and seemed to be challenging me. I had been cautiously waiting for her to bring this up, knowing that Irene had met with Sarah a few times already.

"Yes, Rev. Sarah. That is true. Did Irene voice her concerns to you about this?"

"Yes, she did. I have to tell you, I was not happy that I hadn't been informed about it during my interviewing process."

"Oh, and you didn't ask about it?"

She looked taken aback. "Well, I had asked if the church was open and affirming. I had been told that indeed, it was very welcoming to people of any sexual orientation. But I just assumed that meant that the church was affirming of marriage equality since the bishop had approved it a year ago. But I understand that St. Philips wasn't ready to sanction it."

I could hear the challenge in her voice. She was not going to let this go, I could see.

"Rev. Sarah, I'm sorry you made that assumption. The bishop has also made it clear that each church in the diocese should take their time in moving toward this decision. And we on the Vestry didn't feel our congregation was ready to make that decision." I felt myself getting a bit red in the face, feeling defensive.

"I see." Sarah didn't seem to see at all. In fact, her sour face expressed her disappointment in St. Philips.

But I didn't want her to get all worked up about this. I tried another tack.

"I can see that you're not happy about this. I certainly don't want you to think that we're, well, entrenched on the issue. I mean, the Vestry was divided in the vote. I think it might be that in time, we might see some change. Certainly, we've all seen churches divided over this issue. I don't want to see that happen. That's why we decided to just put this issue on the back burner, especially since we were getting ready to call a new priest. We didn't want to push it on people who weren't ready to deal with it."

"So, who are the people who aren't ready to deal with it?"

I didn't want to share my own discomfort. "Well, there are some older members. Some of the biggest givers, in fact, who just aren't comfortable with the idea of sanctifying something that we'd been taught by the church was wrong. So, I think you may need to meet with some of these people. Talk to them. Get to know them. And then, if they trust you, they might change their minds, you know?"

Sarah considered this. "Well, I can see that might be a good tactic. So, will you speak to some of them and tell them I might want to meet with them?"

I agreed and we moved on to other church issues like the hole in the ceiling in the sanctuary. I could see that Sarah wasn't someone to shy away from crucial issues. She was smart and forthright. I admired that. But I also didn't want her to think that she had to worry about some of these financial issues like the hiring of the Christian Education Director which the Vestry was ready to approve. She seemed satisfied to hear that. All in all, it seemed like we could work together. But I could see that she saw herself as the decision maker in some of these issues. I just wasn't sure that she had the experience for that. So, I tried to throw out the idea that maybe in these first few months, that she could concentrate on getting to know the members and planning worship. She looked confused.

"I'm not sure what you mean. Of course, I'm doing all that. But as the Rector, I need to be involved in all areas of staff management, including the hiring of a new Christian Ed Director. That's part of my responsibility,"

"Well, of course, we want your opinion on the matter."

Sara kind of narrowed her eyes and looked at me suspiciously. "Jeffrey, hiring is part of a Rector's responsibility."

Realizing that I was getting into a touchy area, I demurred. "Well, of course. But you are so busy right now, let the Vestry help with this."

Sarah pursed her lips and raised an eyebrow. "I'm not too busy, Jeffrey."

I realized I'd gone too far. "Yes, we'll be sure to work together on this."

When she looked puzzled, I changed the subject quickly toward a more general topic of religious education and the new curricula that were available. She seemed much more aware of this kind of detail than I expected. She had helped with the Christian Education program during her internship.

By the end of our lunch, I felt we had moved past the stickiness of the hiring issue. I hoped so anyway. I wanted her to work with me. But I didn't want her to know everything.

She told me about some of the people who had come in to meet with her. I was really glad that Sarah was meeting with lots of different people. She would hear how some of these older wealthier families were against gay marriage. She would begin to see a bigger picture.

I grew up Catholic and I have to admit my experience with Catholic priests probably tilted my judgment a bit about the whole religion thing. I had worn my best Sunday suit to church clutching my mother's sweaty hand and when we were supposed to pray, I quickly squatted on that uncomfortable kneeler with my little grubby knees. I'd look at the bottoms of the feet of the people in front of me and notice when they had holes in their soles. Or when someone had slipped their shoes off to be more comfortable. Then I'd hear the priest's voice announce the next part of the service and all the people would groan quietly as they stood up. My mother would be reciting something that I didn't understand. It all made no sense to me, either as a child or later as a teen. I mean, how was the "Lamb of God" supposed to take away the sins of the world? Christ dying a bloody death on a cross was supposed to somehow make up for all of us crummy people and the things we got up to? What kind of sense does that make?

Then there were the priests. I mean, at the time none of us were aware of all the pedophiles. But just the power those guys held? It was unbelievable. My father wasn't one to buy into all that stuff, anyway. He'd come to church on Christmas and maybe Easter, but most Sundays, he'd sleep in. When we got back from church at noon, he'd just be getting up and sitting at the kitchen table with his coffee and paper. When my mother would mention something the priest had said, Dad would grunt something like, "Does that priest have to get up at 7 a.m. in the morning and go to work at an office trying to make a buck? Trying to put food on the table? No! All he has to do is put on some dress-like thing and chant some magical words and you all buy it! I don't need that stuff!"

Once when we were supposed to meet with the priest for our confirmation class, I asked my dad why I had to go when he didn't have to. He looked disgusted and shook his head. "You do it to make your mother happy. That's all. If you don't believe it, you can do what you want once you're sixteen."

My mother, hearing this, would pick up her coffee cup and leave the table, muttering something about how you could lead a horse to water. Then later when I was sixteen, my parents divorced. Surprisingly, it was the church people who supported us then. One woman helped my mom get a job. I mean, I couldn't leave the church because they were like our lifeline. Hell, I even volunteered with their food pantry while I was in college. I didn't stop attending on Sundays until I left to take a job in New York. Then I just never found another church where I felt comfortable.

So, when my wife suggested we try this Episcopal church right in our neighborhood, I said, why not? Couldn't hurt. It surprised me that I've found a place here. I'm known and respected. It was pretty great when people asked me to join the Vestry and then later insisted that I'd make a great Senior Warden. I was flattered. I thought it wouldn't hurt my business either, to tell people that I played a leadership role at church. So, all in all, being a part of a church has worked well for me and my family.

I just hope that Rev. Sarah is not some rabble rouser activist priest. That would make my job much harder. St. Philips just isn't that kind of church. It's older and traditional. That's what I like about it. We'll see, though. I know there are a lot of younger members who are pushing for change. I don't mind change as long as it makes sense. Like I know we need to hire a Sunday School director. That makes sense. And she agrees, obviously. We just don't agree on the process yet. We'll see about that.

CHAPTER EIGHT

SARAH

Why is it that you just feel uncomfortable with some people right away? After our lunch, I realized that Jeffrey was one of those people. I'd ignored the feeling when I'd first met him during my virtual interview, but during this lunch I could almost feel this queasy uneasiness sneaking up on me, like indigestion after eating really greasy food. Why didn't a belief in the divine spirit being present in all people help me see that in Jeffrey? I wanted to see his innate goodness. He volunteered all this time for the church. Volunteering for the Christian Education committee and sitting on the Vestry. I could see he sincerely cared about the church. And he seemed to be a good dad. I mean, he was doing all those things you'd think would create the picture of a devoted servant to God. But somehow, I thought up all these ulterior motives for him. So, when Peg called and asked to come back to see me, I guess I wasn't that shocked about the topic.

She came on her lunch hour, hurrying in and hanging her raincoat on the coatrack, looking a bit nervous, her hair frizzy from the rain. I welcomed her and asked what was on her mind. She hesitated, and rubbed her hands together, glancing at me nervously.

"So, Peg, you can feel free to tell me anything you want me to know. You don't need to worry about it. But if you're not ready to share, that's okay, too."

"Well, you know, I don't want you to think that I'm a gossip," she said biting a corner of her lip. "That's why I didn't want to tell you. I don't usually share things like this. But I think you need to know."

I nodded, and looked at her attentively.

"Well, I've told you that I really do agree with the idea that we need a part-time Sunday School Director. I'm one of the main proponents of hiring someone. I've taught Sunday school practically every year since we joined. And now that I'm divorced and working full-time, I just can't do it anymore. I need some time to myself. Now that we have grown the church and have so many more kids, we really need someone to manage that whole program." Peg said emphatically. But then she paused and gave me a serious look.

"But you should also know that the candidate, Terry LeBlanc, who is being considered. Well..." Peg suddenly fell silent.

"Yes?"

"It's hard to say this, but, it's pretty clear from what I've observed that the main reason that Jeffrey is promoting her candidacy is because, well, because he is sort of interested in furthering his relationship with her." Peg pushed out the last sentence in a whoosh, then looked deflated.

I nodded, swallowing a nervous reaction, and attempting to keep my tone neutral. "Uh-huh. I see. And furthering it in some unhealthy way?"

"Well, yes. I think so."

"I see." But I didn't want to see.

Peg looked worried. "Well, I have seen the two of them whispering in one of the Sunday school classrooms. And then, I was having dinner at a diner that's in another part of town, and I saw the two of them together. Having dinner. I was so shocked and embarrassed I didn't speak to them. I don't think they saw me."

I sighed and looked down. There I was in a place we call "church" and here was evidence of life and all the real stuff that made it hard. There was no escaping it.

"So, Peg. I appreciate you wanting me to know about this. But, would you feel comfortable with someone making an assumption about you based on who you ate dinner with? I mean, maybe they were just meeting to discuss the RE curriculum, right?"

Peg looked chastened. But then she raised a finger. "Of course, that's possible. But you have to notice how they've been talking to each other. All flirty! It's pretty obvious. But--"

I cut her off there. "You might be completely right about your assumptions about Jeffrey and Terry. But you realize that I can't judge someone based on that kind of observation. Right? Nor would I want to. It's not my job to judge people."

Peg's cheeks were red. She stammered in reply, "No, well, sure. I get it. But what do we do about Jeffrey promoting the idea of Terry being hired?" She sounded indignant.

I answered calmly. "Peg, we will handle this hiring like any other. We'll examine the candidate's qualifications, interview her about the job, and make a decision with what we know about her. Not what we don't know or suspect about her."

Peg nodded, not convinced, her hands fidgeting. "Yeah, okay. That makes sense." Peg shifted uncomfortably in her seat. "But, Rev. Sarah, um, do you think, well, do you think badly of me because I shared that with you?"

I smiled. "No, Peg, I do not think you're a gossip. I think you're a person who cares about their church and wants to do best for everyone here. Does that make you feel better?"

Peg frowned. "Well, I don't know. I feel bad for Terry. I think she's being taken advantage of. And for Jeff's wife, Elaine, of course. But I trust that you will do what's best."

I pushed my hair back, thinking about how to remain positive. "You know, Peg, I'm pretty new at this job. But I feel like this congregation cares about each other and together we'll figure out what's best for everyone. Do you think I'm naïve in thinking that?"

I cocked my head, looking for her judgment. Peg shook her head.

"No. I do hope we can do that. Anyway, I appreciate you listening and not jumping to conclusions. I think you're right. We can all make wrong assumptions. Thanks, Rev. Sarah."

Grabbing her coat and purse and thanking me for listening, Peg left hurriedly.

At the end of the day, when I was finishing up my sermon and getting ready to leave, I got a call on the office phone. I considered not answering because it was really after five and I was thinking about stopping for a pizza on the way home. Mary had left a couple of hours ago, but I didn't want to miss something important. So, I answered with what I had been hearing Mary say all week, "St. Philips, how can I help you?"

A faint woman's voice asked, "Is this Mary?"

I replied that no, that I was Rev. Sarah, the pastor.

"Oh, goodness. I'm sorry to bother you. Well, I should just call back when Mary's there. When will she be there, tomorrow?"

"Yes, tomorrow at 9:00, Mary should be here."

"Oh, good. Well, then." The soft voice hesitated.

"Yes, is there something I can help you with?"

"Well, I don't know. Um..."

"You can tell me, if you want."

"Mary told me about a fund that was available to help people pay their rent or gas bill. But this, was, uh, maybe a year ago. I really needed help then. And Mary told me this fund was available. It was called the Vestry Fund."

"Oh, I see." I hadn't yet heard the particulars about this fund. "So, do you need help now?"

"My daughter needs help now. She's pregnant, and well, she's in her seventh month. She had to stop working because the doctor told her to. So, well, she can't pay all of her rent this month. I don't know if you all would help us again, though. You were so nice to help me last time."

I thought about whether I could trust what she was telling me. I didn't know if there was such a fund. I had to find out more. "So, can you tell me your name?"

"Uh, Ginny. My name is Ginny Sherman and my daughter's name is Jill Sherman."

"Okay, Ginny. I'll need to find out more about this. Can I get your number and call you back tomorrow?"

Ginny gave me her phone number and I promised either I or Mary would call her back the next day. Then I remembered that Mary was off the next day. I'd need to get this taken care of. I decided to call her and find out about it.

When I called and apologized for bothering her at home and explained about Ginny's call, Mary was quick to tell me that I could call her anytime at home. Then she explained that the Vestry Fund was something that had just been put into place two years ago by the Vestry.

"In fact, you know, it wasn't really the Vestry's idea. Do you know who brought it up and began the fund by depositing the first $500 into it?"

"No, who?"

"Jeffrey Trainor. Yeah, it was Jeffrey who insisted to the Vestry that the church needed to have funds available when people who were having emergencies called and we verified their need. After he wrote a check and handed it to the Vestry secretary, all the members of the Vestry wrote checks. So, we always have funds available."

I was floored. Jeffrey. This was the Jeffrey that I didn't yet know. I asked Mary if Ginny's need had been verified last time and she said that yes, the priest had met with her and had given her the money for her gas bill. Mary told me where the check book was and luckily, this was one of the budget lines that I had been authorized to approve at the bank. I could write a check for Ginny's daughter. I thanked Mary and hung up, calling Ginny back and making arrangements for her daughter to come in the next day.

I sat for a while in my office, looking out at the wet grass in the courtyard, the light rain falling on the end of the summer day lilies. The pavement edging the garden darkened with its slick surface as the rain fell. Wet, yellow leaves were already starting to pile up on the ends of the lawn, evidence of fall beginning its earthy advent. Already, I was seeing a new season in this new city of mine. And a new look at someone I thought I knew.

Pulling out my well-used copy of the Gospel of Thomas, I looked for the phrase that would offer wisdom.

His disciples said to him, "When will the kingdom come?" Jesus said, "It will not come by waiting for it. It will not be a matter of saying 'here it is' or 'there it is.' Rather, the kingdom of the father is spread out upon the earth, and men do not see it."

The kingdom or the queendom of God was right here under our noses, and we didn't see it. I had to keep reminding myself that each one of us was a part of that holy kingdom, each playing out our own divinity. But that was so hard to see sometimes, wasn't it?

Chapter Nine

SARAH

September, 2016

Marilyn was one of those angels in disguise that had made my faith clearer when we became fast friends while attending seminary. She was always pointing out in a class when a biblical passage would be helpful to nudge a congregation to act boldly when they might be hesitant. She had been raised a Baptist but had become an Episcopalian when her beliefs were just a little too north of the Baptist doctrine to be acceptable. I remember the week the gay seminarians had gathered in the front of the Baptist seminary down the street to protest when their convention had voted to exclude LGBT ordination. Marilyn had led the vigil with a prayer remembering Jesus' words from John. "Beloved, let us love one another, for love comes from God. Everyone who loves has been born of God and knows God." The students had kept chanting "Love comes from God. All love is holy!"

So, not only was she someone I really admired but she was also the kind of friend who is intuitive and notices when something's going on with you. Once when I was picking at my food, my demeanor not my usual, cheerful, "get along with everyone" mood, Marilyn picked up on it right away.

"Got your period?" she pried nudging me playfully with an elbow.

"No," I responded, annoyed.

She looked at me, eyebrows raised. "Oh, so everything's fine, I guess."

I tried to ignore her, but she kept staring. "It's nothing. I mean, it's just my parents again."

"Oh," she said with a knowing look. "Making you feel bad about going to seminary?"

I moved the food around on my plate, pushing the beans under the mashed potatoes. I could see she wasn't going to let this pass. "Well, they want to give me some money."

Marilyn rolled her eyes, "How terrible of them. How dare they imply that a seminary student might need money." She was so annoying sometimes, seeing right through me.

"It's more the way they do it. When I told them I was going to teach in the inner city, they tried to give me money to rent an apartment in a 'better' part of town. Then when I turned it down and rented an apartment near the school, I ended up with my computer being stolen and my apartment being ransacked. So, that sucked since they had been right about that neighborhood. But I was happy that I stayed in that job for four years, until I was called down by the administration for 'favoring one student' and I quit."

"Sounds like a grave error on your part," she commented wryly.

"Yeah." I shook my head in exasperation. "So, now they want to give me money so I'll leave seminary and go to law school."

Marilyn looked stunned. "Law school?"

"Yep."

"And why would you want to go to law school all of a sudden?"

"Because they thought as a lawyer, I could really make a difference in people's lives instead of thinking I can just get them to pray more." I replied acidly.

Marilyn winced. "And because you have such a deep interest in the law and all."

"Yeah."

Marilyn was always the one to listen to these ridiculous arguments with my parents and remind me that I had a "calling" even if they didn't believe it. I sometimes wondered myself what that "calling" was about and if my parents would get proven right again.

Marilyn had graduated the year ahead of me and had left to lead an inner-city church here in Philadelphia, moving with her husband, Bob. When I was in search for the right city and the right congregation where I might be happy, she had nudged me toward Philadelphia. She wanted me close by, and she thought I'd like the city.

Ever since our first dinner together when I arrived in town, I had been looking forward to attending the meeting of the interfaith clergy group she had described. I drove downtown, planning to meet her there and have lunch afterwards.

Being anxious to find a parking place and get to the meeting on time, I arrived a few minutes early for the meeting at Christ Church, a downtown Episcopal church. I hoped to catch Marilyn and have a few minutes to chat. She had told me that there had already been a few meetings about the plan for a foodbank to be housed in a deserted church building near the city center, where the homeless ended up. Getting St. Philips involved in a project like this was the kind of hopeful direction I wanted to take the church, but I realized that it was early days in my ministry. Building the congregation's trust and respect would be necessary before I launched them into this kind of project.

As I entered the stately brick church, a middle-aged man wearing a clergy collar greeted me and introduced himself as Dave Potter, the rector. After welcoming me to the area, we chatted briefly about the difficulties of older church buildings with their costly maintenance. Looking up into the lofty arches in the narthex of this huge structure, he sighed, telling me that this building would probably outlast him, but not without considerable expense. We commiserated at the lack of congregational energy for meeting those challenges. He excused himself to greet other ministers who were entering behind me.

As I moved and sat down toward the middle of the church, I saw Marilyn arriving in the back vestibule with another woman. Recognizable in her purple clergy shirt with a lavender paisley scarf adorning it, Marilyn always looked stylish despite her large frame. She turned and waved to me while talking softly to the other woman for a few minutes, before moving toward me, a wide, welcoming smile filling her broad face. Marilyn had one of those infectious personalities that drew people in just by her smile and her ironic sense of humor. Some people might be put off if they thought a religious professional shouldn't be quite so ready to poke fun at herself and the church, but most people were instantly charmed.

Marilyn's brilliant blue eyes flashed as she greeted me. "So, here you are. God, I'm glad to see you! Oh, thank you, Jesus, for sending me Sarah!" She dumped her heavy cloth bag onto the chair next to me, and grabbed me around the neck, hugging, while swaying back and forth. I had stood to receive this hug but was nearly knocked off my feet by her joyful exuberance.

"Sit down and tell me all about how it's going!" Marilyn gushed, pulling on my sleeve to sit next to her. I readjusted my sweater, feeling a bit disheveled after the overwhelming hug.

"Well, like I told you at dinner, there were some real surprises waiting for me at St. Philips, and this week has been even more interesting to say the least," I said in a low voice.

Marilyn leaned forward closely and whispered loudly, "Really? Now what?"

I shook my head, looking around at the steady stream of clergy starting to fill in the pews. "Not here. I can't talk about it here."

Marilyn glanced around at her colleagues. "These folks? They all have similar landmines in their congregations. They will not be the least bit shocked. In fact, most of them could tell you things about their congregants that would knock your socks off."

I laughed and turned to face the front where Dave had moved with a stack of papers and was conferring with a colleague. "Let's talk afterwards at lunch," I whispered. Marilyn nodded and we turned to listen as Dave introduced himself and began to summarize the project. We learned that the proposed food bank was to be housed in the large stone meeting house, which had held a Quaker congregation until ten years ago when they moved out and donated the building to the city. The Quakers had specified that while the building needed repairs, that the city could use the building for any purpose that "directly impacted the homeless in the city for their betterment."

Dave then introduced a youngish man standing next to him as Edwardo Sanchez and asked him to speak. I noticed right away as Edwardo began to speak with a slight Latino accent and a strong confident tone, that he was attractive. Dark curly hair, nice build, and probably around my age. You could tell that he believed this project would make a real difference in this city, providing much needed food and community support. Introducing himself as a social worker with the city who had been tasked to promote a project that would support the homeless, he had this air of invitation about him, beckoning people to care about this project as much as he did. Many there nodded as he spoke. After Edwardo finished, Dave got up and thanked him for summarizing the needs of the population well. Then he invited the clergy who wished to speak about their congregation's involvement to raise their hands. Several raised hands, including Marilyn. I wished I could raise my hand but knew that my church was not ready to commit until I had done the hard work of convincing them of the importance of this work. I wasn't even sure that it was the right year to bring this up until they trusted me more.

Dave pointed to Marilyn, inviting her to speak. She stood and looked around the room.

"Friends, I am Marilyn Jennings. Many of you know me and know I have a loud voice." Several people around the room chuckled and nodded agreement. "Well, I have a loud voice when it comes to justice, and this project has been motivating me to raise it. You also know that my congregation is small and is mostly low income. We would not have anything significant in our budget to give to this project, and many in my congregation will need the food bank themselves. But we do have members that can volunteer. I think we need to plan levels of involvement so that congregations that can't afford to give a large donation can still hold up their heads and say they are partners in this venture. As Jesus would have said, the widow's mite is just as important as the rich man's dollar, so let's make sure that we have an equal opportunity for all to be able to contribute!"

Marilyn ended with her typical flourish and several clapped in support. I nodded to her with a smile. I thought of all the times in seminary when Marilyn had spoken up about justice issues and how the other students looked up to her. Now, again, she was truly showing her leadership.

At the end of the meeting, Dave wrapped up the discussion thanking everyone for their ideas of how to move forward and promising to get back to the clergy once the founding board had drawn up a policy for the way congregations would be asked to support, both financially and with volunteers. I noticed that Dave turned to Edwardo, as people began to get up, preparing to leave. Marilyn introduced me to a few of her friends as they came by. I was a little overwhelmed by all the names and faces and whispered to Marilyn that she would have to help me remember them all.

As Edwardo, walked by, and Marilyn called to him. He smiled, then came over, giving Marilyn a half hug as she congratulated him on the great meeting. She turned to me and introduced him with a hint of an impish grin on her face. I noticed him kind of taking me in, maybe? Had Marilyn mentioned me to him? I remembered Marilyn being anxious to get me to this meeting, said she had someone she wanted me to meet. As she introduced him, I noticed his face, his strong jaw and dark eyes.

"You know, Edwardo was the person who dreamed up this whole idea," Marilyn said to me, placing a hand on his back affectionately.

Edwardo's face broke into a bashful smile, shaking his head and waving a hand toward her.

"No, no, that's not true, Marilyn. You know as much as anyone, that it was that small group of us, yourself included who met down there one day to try to imagine what we could do with that space. I was just the first one who put the idea into words, but we all were thinking something similar." To me, he said, "Your friend here, who has only been here about a year, has already had an impact on those of us who've been hoping for this kind of project for a long time."

Marilyn shook her head but beamed. "Edwardo, I simply arrived at the right time. You and Dave are the movers and shakers." She took my elbow, moving both of us along to the door. She had a knowing smile directed at us both which started to make me nervous. "I want you two to know each other. So, I'll invite you to dinner with Sarah sometime soon." Edwardo nodded and agreed that would be good. I was annoyed with her then, being so obvious. But judging by Edwardo's smile, he didn't seem to mind. He seemed agreeable, saying he looked forward to it, before saying good-bye and moving off to speak to another group near the door. But I was frustrated. I pulled her aside after we left the church.

"Why do you feel like you have to 'fix me up'? Really, Marilyn! It was so obvious!"

Marilyn patted my hand, and pulled me along the block, pointing out the restaurant where we were heading. "Now, Sarah. I'm just introducing two people who deserve to know each other. It doesn't have to be romantic! It could just be that you have so much in common, you're friends." I looked exasperated, but she assured me. "You have to agree he's really good-looking, right?"

I sighed, "You are too much!"

Marilyn chuckled and hooked her arm through mind. "Yes, but you love me." I couldn't argue with that.

We took our time walking along the tree-lined downtown street with tall elms rising from well- manicured flower beds. Entering a small casual restaurant with colorful red gingham tablecloths, a young woman with long brown hair escorted us to a table near a window and we settled in.

Looking around at the other diners discussing business and their lives, it seemed everyone was buzzing with new ventures and ideas. It felt good being in a city where there were endless possibilities popping up. I leaned over the table to Marilyn, beaming at being here with her. "So, here we are again. Having lunch and hatching plans to change the world."

Marilyn looked doubtful. "Huh, I don't know about changing the world, but I do know about changing your life a bit." She immediately took out her phone and scrolled through her calendar. "Okay, let's set a date right now for you to come for dinner with Edwardo. How about two weeks from Friday?"

I eyed Marilyn suspiciously. "Why such a hurry?"

Marilyn opened her eyes wide. "Oh, no reason! Just that he's the most attractive thirty something guy I know who also happens to be single and I, in my great wisdom, know that the two of you would get along famously!"

I groaned. "Marilyn, I'm not in the market right now."

"Who says that anymore? 'In the market?'" she teased.

I bristled as I stared at my friend. "There's so much on my plate right now. I don't need to get involved with someone."

"I'm not asking you to get involved with him. Just meet him. That's all."

"Yeah, I just met him. And I know you. You have the rest of our lives plotted out."

"Hon? I saw your face when he came over. I don't believe for a second that you don't want to...*meet* him. You turned the slightest shade of pink." Marilyn let out a laugh then cut me off before I could protest. "Just come to dinner and get to know him and then tell me you're not interested."

I groaned. "You are too much. *Okay*, I'll come. But only if you promise to stop playing matchmaker. And that you won't embarrass me by making this more than it is."

As we ate, I filled Marilyn in on the disturbing suggestion that Peg had made to me about the very married Jeffrey Trainor, Senior Warden, possibly being involved with the woman who was being considered for a religious education role. I told her that I hadn't approached anyone else to check it out yet, since I knew it was a bomb waiting to go off but wanted to get some confirmation before I brought it up. Then I described the conversation I had with Jeffrey earlier that week when he told me not to worry about the hiring process since I was "too busy." Then learning that he was recommending the woman he had been seen having dinner with. Marilyn listened carefully, asked questions, then sat back with a sigh.

"Nothing is easy, is it? Here you are, all ready to get started on whipping up this congregation into a frenzy of social justice and spreading goodwill and this ugly stuff lands on you. It's not fair! And in your first couple of weeks!"

I nodded, putting down my fork. "You know, I think I need to slow down and not react to this. I'm getting the feeling that everyone wants to come shock me with all the church secrets to somehow get close to me. Did you experience that when you started?"

Marilyn thought for a moment. "Hmmm. That's interesting. I can't say I remember that. I mean, they did want to come share their own shocking stories to pull me into their drama, but I didn't get much sharing of congregational secrets. Maybe that's because my members hardly have time to get involved in the church because they're mostly all involved in their own survival." Marilyn paused, then sat up straighter. "Oh, but yes, there was one shocker shared that I learned early on. It was about one of the former priests and his indiscretion with the former secretary. That was a juicy one! Someone walked in on them getting it on in the choir room. Oh, boy! The things people think they can get away with!"

"Marilyn, these are the things they just don't ever talk about in seminary. The real mud you get stuck in. My parents stayed away from getting involved deeply in our church because of it. But what do you do when you just don't trust someone?"

Marilyn sighed and wrinkled her nose in exasperation. "I know. It's so hard sometimes when we are expected to be these superhuman people and love everyone. I mean Jesus didn't really expect us to love slug-balls, did he? I mean there's got to be a limit to this 'love everyone crap', doesn't there?"

"I don't know. Maybe we love some people because they're flawed, not despite their flaws, right? I mean, some of them have kind of adorably glaring flaws."

Marilyn made a face. "Why do you say that? I can think of plenty of people I have to hold my nose in order to even like let alone love."

"No, I know you," I replied, shaking my head. "I know that you have more love for those drug dealers and alcoholics in your congregation than anyone I know. And I know that you practice the ministry of compassion every day. So, don't tell me you don't love them."

Marilyn emitted a "hmph" kind of noise, "Oh, I wasn't referring to the drug dealers and alcoholics. They are my people."

I added, "Yeah, I get it. It's not the flawed, down in the mouth people I have a hard time with. It's the prep school, custom-made suit, businessman that I have a hard time loving. I happen to have a few of those in my congregation. So, I've got a lot of atonement to make before I take communion on Sunday. Consider this a confession."

Marilyn put her hand on my arm. "Forgiven. And then some. Just try not to murder anyone before Sunday."

After our lunch, Marilyn reminded me that she would be getting back to me with a date for a dinner with Edwardo. I told her just to slow down a bit.

That evening after I had fixed myself a salad, I sat down to review my emails. There were a few from congregants that I looked over but left for dealing with tomorrow at work. But then I saw an email from my mother. She usually called, so this email so probably her passive-aggressive way of nudging me to call. But I just didn't have the emotional energy to soothe her anxieties about me. I sent a brief email saying I'd call. I thought it was going well, I said. I didn't share that I was still finding my feet. That every time I got in that pulpit, I wondered what I was doing here. That I was trying to be a "pastor" to people who didn't want to accept gay marriage. How the hell did I think I could change that environment? Once again, was I bringing my arrogance by thinking I could help people?

And then, as usual, in the midst of my doubting, Pam, my little sister was there, crowding out my thoughts. She might as well have been sitting in the corner of the room in the chair by the TV, staring at me. My failure at helping Pam always loomed largest when I started doubting myself. I couldn't help her when she really needed me. I had done so little when she was going through hell. As many people did when faced with uncertain circumstances and uncomfortable pain, I had turned away from it, turned away from her, despite her need. Nothing I did these days seemed to make a difference in my grief and guilt.

I thought of a day at the hospital when she had been recovering from pneumonia that she'd gotten as a result of her poor chemo-riddled immune system. One of her few good days. I had arrived after school and was telling her about this new guy at school, Gary. He had asked me to help him at the school library when we were both there doing research for our history papers. He had asked me a little about myself and I had told him about Pam.

She winced and asked, "So, what did you tell him?" She looked interested in what I'd said about her.

"Well, I told him you were getting treatment for cancer and had to spend some time in the hospital and that's why you weren't at school."

"Huh. So, is he cute?"

"Kinda'," I said considering. "He's kind of different. Like he doesn't seem to care about what other people think. Like he wears old ratty t-shirts with flannel shirts over them. And he doesn't seem to fit into any particular group at school. He's not a jock, or a nerd, or a goth. I don't know what he is. But I like him," I said thoughtfully. "I think you'd like him, too,"

Pam looked amused. "So, do you think he was flirting with you?"

"I don't think so. He's just friendly to a lot of people. "

"Do you think he likes you?"

"Hmm. Maybe. I don't know yet."

"I think you like him."

I blushed, but realized that I wanted to share this with her. I wanted her to know more about my life since she'd been having such a limited one for the past year. While I wouldn't usually talk to her about boys and such, I wanted her to have a view into my life.

"Maybe I do. He asked me about the museums in Boston."

"Why don't you invite him to go to the art museum with you? You love it there. Maybe he'd like it."

"Hmm. I don't know. I couldn't ask him to go with me. That's like asking him on a date. No way I could do that."

Pam looked wistful. "Why not?"

"Are you nuts?"

"Well, you know. You are always talking about women's rights. Why shouldn't the girl ask the guy out?"

"Yeah, well, I'm not that brave. Or stupid. He might think I'm trying to date him or something."

She shrugged. "Well, aren't you?"

I shook my head. "No, I'm not. Just telling you about a guy I know."

She looked disappointed and sighed. "Sarah. I'm probably not going to get to date anyone. Maybe not ever. So, I just think you shouldn't waste your time. Why not do whatever you want?" She picked up the book she had been reading. The conversation was over, I guess. And I didn't know what to say. I didn't respond.

Thinking about that conversation now, I remembered it as another way I had failed her. She had probably wanted to talk about her possible death. But I couldn't do it.

My fingers hovered over the keyboard as I tried to end the email to Mom. There was so much I just couldn't share with her. Especially since my parents weren't that thrilled with my career in ministry. I remembered the night I had shocked my parents at dinner with the announcement that I had left my teaching job and was planning on attending seminary in the fall.

My parents had looked dismayed. Dad had pointed out that maybe I could figure this out while working and supporting myself instead of going back to school. That's when I had decided I would move out of my parent's house and go to seminary while working part-time. I found some cheap student housing in Brookline and enrolled in the Boston University School of Theology where I was awarded a full scholarship. I stayed in touch with my parents but no longer counted on their financial support. Marilyn talked about this as my "emancipation" from my parent's expectations. I just wished that I was not so caught up in what they thought. While I felt deeply that I had finally turned my life in the direction I needed to go, I still sought their approval.

Thinking about my parents now and their disappointment, I felt again the heavy mantle of doing something significant with my life that would fulfill this nagging need to help people. I kept hoping they would see it as a meaningful direction for my life. But here I was, pursuing my ministry with people like Jeffrey who didn't want me applying my so-called higher standards when they thought things could be simpler. Yeah, that seemed to be the way the world wanted things done, quick and easy, and not in a way that might change things or make a mark on the world.

Chapter Ten

SARAH

Monday morning as I was making my tea, I still felt a little bleary from a night of more worry than sleep. From the two conversations I'd had, one with Irene and one with Peg, I knew that I was already in over my head. For God's sake, how did I wind up walking right into a scene from a Sinclair Lewis novel in my very first weeks of ministry? A Senior Warden with possibly wandering eyes and a prejudice against gay people? A Vestry still mired in fears about gay marriage? I tried to remember the class I had taken in seminary on "Healthy Congregations" which described all the ways a congregation might be unhealthy. I remembered one thing very explicitly: get close to the situation, ask questions, don't make assumptions. Okay. I could do that. Getting closer to the situations felt like the right move. I finished up my tea and granola and dressed hurriedly to get to church early. I had calls to make.

I texted Jeffrey first at 8:30 hoping he would still be at home. I texted him asking if we could meet after work. He responded that he'd swing by my office at 5:30.

I spent the morning reviewing the notes from the last priest about Christian Education during his ministry and notes from the

Christian Education Committee meeting that Irene had sent me the previous Friday. She noted that the Christian Ed committee had seemed frustrated by Jeffrey's instructions sent to the Committee Chair several weeks ago. He had apparently asked the committee to interview Terry Lablanc as soon as possible as a potential candidate.

I decided I'd better call the chair to understand the situation better. I talked to her and learned the committee was not in any hurry to hire someone and would be happy to slow the process down, write a job description, and interview candidates from outside. I was glad I had a better handle on all this before I met with Jeffrey.

I spent the day writing the sermon for the next week all about process theology and how God was suffering with us, not thinking up ways to punish us. It was modern theology, and I thought the younger people in the church should be open to it. I used it to describe how I had come to feel the presence of God after losing my sister. I wanted them to know my experience and what kinds of events in my life had given me a deeper understanding of what God could be.

At just thirteen, I hadn't been all that clear about God being with me, but certainly my priest, Rev. Doug, had been with me and that started to feel like God being with me. Anyway, it was enough to encourage me to explore what God meant to me. I found it very comforting.

I remember one day sitting in class about a year after Pam, looking out the window, thinking about her and how she used to love to snuggle with our cat. She would scoop her up, bundle her under her sweater and then collapse with her into the velveteen easy chair in the living room. You could see the cat's little face peeking out of her sweater as Pam spoke little soft whisperings into her face. All of a sudden, sitting there, tears started leaking down my cheeks. I knew I had to get out of there before I completely lost it, so I just hurried out the door with my head down, hoping the teacher would assume I was going to the restroom. I went to the nurse's office, and broke down there. The nurse called my mom who came to pick me up after about a good twenty minutes of me trying unsuccessfully to stop the sobbing. My mom, perplexed, since it had been six months since Pam's death, put her arm around me, apologizing to the nurse as we made a quick exit. On the way home, I asked Mom if we could stop at the church to see if Rev. Doug was there. She agreed and called the church to check. The administrator told her that the priest would be happy to see me, just to drop me off and he would bring me home. Mom looked a bit worried since she wasn't someone who shared her problems with anyone, but I had been seeing the priest off and on over the past months. She dropped me at the door after I had successfully stopped the tears that had been falling relentlessly for the past hour.

When I went into Rev. Doug's office, he held out his arms and gave me a comforting hug and the tears started all over again. It felt like all the grief that I had been able to contain pretty well since I started back to school had been pent up inside me and was now pouring out. I let it come, and he welcomed it. He didn't stop me or pat my hand telling me it would be better someday like my mother sometimes did. He just waited until it stopped. When I finally looked up, Rev. Doug asked if it was okay if he said a prayer. I nodded again. The prayer was thanking God for being with me during this time. I knew it was his way of letting me know that God had been with me that whole day. I started to look at my grief not as though I was alone in it, but that God was sitting beside me—also grieving.

The idea of God sitting beside you when you're in your dark night of the soul, reaching out to tell you that you're not alone, and that God was suffering too, was life-changing for me. I learned in seminary this was called 'process theology' and I tried to convey this amazing possibility in my sermon, making it simply comforting, not theological. I had just about wrapped it up when I realized that I had only about an hour before Jeffrey would be dropping by.

My anxiety started ringing a very loud bell about what the hell I was going to say to Jeffrey. Deciding to take a brief walk just to clear my head, I wrote a note to Jeffrey and stuck it on my office door saying I'd meet him behind the church in the garden. I threw my sweater over my shoulders and headed out the door.

Just making the effort of walking briskly down the shaded block, my arms swinging, looking around at the beautiful fall day, I began to feel my anxiety level slowly begin to soothe out. The maple trees were just starting to yellow, but the oaks already showed flashes of bright orange here and there. Fall was the most beautiful time of year in Philadelphia, and I realized that I had not taken the time to notice. Hiding myself inside my office and apartment, I had been so caught up in the human challenges whirling around my brain that I had not even considered that the cycles of nature were moving on without me. My tendencies toward seeing the worst possible outcome ahead of me were grabbing control of my mind, despite some real attempts at focusing on centering prayer. The anxiety was winning the battle.

I focused on the sunlight filtering through the branches, with dappled shadows dancing everywhere. Opening myself to what else was possible instead of the dreary situation I'd been rehearsing over and over, I felt a heavy load lift.

After 20 minutes of walking, I swung back around to the church and headed to the courtyard, taking one of the benches that faced the church. I sat with my eyes closed for the next few minutes, deepening the peacefulness I'd begun to feel. Soon, I heard some rustling of leaves behind me, and I turned finding Jeffrey, looking puzzled at seeing me here instead of in the office.

"Hey there!" I greeted him warmly, and stood, offering him a seat beside me. "Would you mind if we met out here? It's just so beautiful, I couldn't stay in the office."

He looked amused. "Well, sure, a little fresh air never hurt anyone." He seemed a bit uncomfortable but took off his suit jacket and sat on the bench, looking around the courtyard like he'd never imagined sitting here.

"Rev. Sarah, how's your week going? Settling in, okay?" Jeffrey's tone seemed sincere, like he regretted not checking in with me.

"It's been an exhausting but productive week. I've met several church leaders. And I realized that at our lunch together, I didn't really ask about you, and your history with St. Philips." I looked expectantly at Jeffrey.

"Oh, well. Yes, that's a great idea. I mean, I got to know a lot about you during the Vestry meeting with you, but you haven't really had a chance to learn much about me." He looked pleased that I had asked.

"Tell me about why you and your family joined this church. It was just a few years ago, right?"

Jeffrey nodded and seemed to relax. "That's right, about five years, I guess. I've been Senior Warden for a year, and before that I had been on the Vestry for another year as Junior Warden. But why we joined? Hmm, that's a good question. I guess, we joined like many families whose kids are reaching that age of reason, you know, around ages 10-12. They had started asking questions about church and why we didn't attend when many of their friends did. Elaine and I, we just weren't that religious, but we realized that a church community and the people you meet in it are an important part of feeling like you belong somewhere. We had both grown up in church communities. Elaine was a Presbyterian and my family had been Catholic. Not strict Catholic, just the basic Ten Commandments and such. So, when we found St. Philips right here in our neighborhood and we gave it a try. We liked it." He smiled and shrugged.

"What did you like when you came here?"

"Well, I guess we liked the people. They were friendly and seemed to welcome us. And the Sunday school was good. The kids told us they liked it. I don't know. We got involved in some things like the Bible Study and I tried the Men's Group. It just started becoming more and more like something we needed in our lives. Community. Some basic teachings from the Bible."

I nodded my head. A typical story from a young family joining a church. But I was still curious.

"And how did you get so involved that you got roped into serving on the Vestry?"

"I was surprised when they asked me. But I thought if this church is important to my family and my kids are getting their religious education here, I should do my part. Step up. So, I did." He swung his arm at that statement like he was stepping up and proud to do it.

"Taking on the Senior Warden position is quite a 'step up'. That's unusual for someone who's rather new to a church. But good for you. I've been hearing a lot about this Christian Educator position. The Vestry has approved hiring someone. What do you think is the next step?"

"Oh, hiring someone soon is really important. I know that some of the older members are reluctant to spend so much on someone to manage this program. But I also see that not all the volunteers really know how to do their job. And sometimes, they don't even show up! I mean, a couple of times, Elaine has been called downstairs to take over one of the classrooms since the volunteer teacher didn't show up. I think it's time this church upped its game and hired someone to do this important job. Oh, and by the way, we have a perfect candidate right in the church. Someone who has been a volunteer in the program for a while. She's perfect!"

"Oh, is that Terry LeBlanc?"

Jeffrey looked surprised. "Yes, that's right. Have you met her yet?"

"No, but someone mentioned that she's being considered. What are her qualifications?"

Jeffrey looked momentarily stumped. "Oh...well...I'm not sure. She has a two-year degree, but I don't know what it's in. But she loves teaching Sunday School. I'm sure she would be good. And this job is just 3/4 time."

"And has the Christian Education Committee written a job description with some basic job qualifications?"

"A job description? Well, I don't know. But do we really need all that formal stuff in a church this size? I mean, we need someone to start doing the job. So, why not just move ahead?"

"Well, when you hired me, the church followed all the formal protocols, right? Sometimes, when you're beginning a new position, you might want to ensure that it's clear what the job entails and if you've got someone with the right skills. Don't you think that might be important to get the right person?"

"Rev. Sarah, I know you've just come from seminary and they probably taught you all the 'right ways' to do church. Having job descriptions and search committees and all that stuff that businesses do. But we're just a small family church. Only about 300 members. We don't need to be formal about these things, right? We had to follow protocol to hire you because we were competing with lots of other churches. But for a Sunday School director, at three quarters time? It's best to get someone who's one of us. Someone who knows us. So, listen. I'll bet you have so much on your plate right now. Right? You don't need to worry about this. The Vestry can just move ahead and you can interview Terry to make sure you get along. But why make this such a lengthy, difficult process?"

My inclination to call "bullshit" was strong. But this man was essentially my boss. *I didn't want to get fired in my second week,* I thought. *So, I'd better find a compromise.*

"What if I ask the Christian Education Committee to write a job description quickly? Like, right away," I offered. "There's probably one they could find on the diocesan website. And the Vestry can review it at their next meeting or even by email. Then the committee could advertise it on the website and in our own newsletter. And in a couple weeks after we get some applications, we can start interviewing. It wouldn't take more than six or eight weeks. That's fast enough, isn't it?"

Jeffrey looked non-plussed. He stared at the ground, not responding. Then he looked up. "Well, I guess you've made up your mind about this, huh? Who talked to you? Irene? I bet it was Irene. She is always making things more difficult. Sarah, I think the Vestry should handle this. It's a hiring decision and therefore it can be done just by the Vestry. I think you should concentrate on writing sermons, visiting the sick and thinking about our next pledge drive which is in two months. We really don't need you to worry about this."

I looked at him pointedly. I wasn't going to back down—and I think he was starting to see that.

"Jeffrey, I'm sorry. But I was hired as Rector and part of my responsibilities is to be head of staff. Making hiring and firing decisions as all head of staff positions require. I'm not too busy to do this. In fact, I have to insist that I'm key to this hiring decision and how it's done. If you don't agree, I'm afraid you'll need to re-negotiate my contract with the Vestry."

"I see," he said quietly, but his brow was furrowed, and I saw the muscle in his jaw clench. "I guess we don't agree on this. I think the hiring process should be discussed by the Vestry. So, I'll make that happen. And then I'll get back to you." He stood abruptly. Picking up his jacket, he threw it over his shoulder, and turned to leave.

I spoke up before he could leave. "Jeffrey, I'm sorry we don't agree. But this issue needs to be handled properly. So, I would be happy to discuss it with the Vestry—together."

"Hmm. We'll see about that. I think that churches tend to discuss things to death. Sometimes, we just need to act. Since you aren't ready to act, I can ask someone on the Vestry to expedite this process. Really, Sarah, it's not that big a deal," he said shaking his head. Then he sighed and looked back at me. "I do think you could help make this transition easier. A lot easier." With that, he stalked off to his car.

I took some deep breaths to stave off the anger rising in me. I did not know how I could deal with a man like this. But then a passage from Matthew came to me:

Jesus said, *"You see the sliver in your friend's eye, but you don't see the timber in your own eye. When you take the timber out of your own eye, then you will see well enough to remove the sliver from your friend's eye."*

Certainly, I had enough of a timber in my own eye that I should start there. Perhaps. The timber in my eye was my suspicion of Jeffrey and what he was up to in this congregation, using his male authority to move things his direction. I decided to pray then and there to try to understand why this man moved me into a place of anger so quickly. That tendency certainly wasn't serving me. But, damn it, he wasn't making it easy!

Chapter Eleven

JEFFREY

I was pissed; I admit it. Getting into my car, I could feel the anger getting the best of me. How dare she pull administrative bullshit on me! She was barely out of seminary with no experience hiring people let alone understanding the needs of this church. It just burned me that this young chick thought she could hold a contract over my head. In her third week! Jesus! I knew this church and what we needed much better than she did. And I was essentially her boss! At least that's the way it worked in business. And anyway, the Vestry was pretty much mine. I had the two other men on the Vestry. And then there was Phyllis, the old timer. She really thought she owned the place since her family had been one of the founding families way back in the dark ages. She didn't like change much. But maybe she would come around to hiring someone for the Sunday School. She wouldn't want to fool around out looking for some higher-priced, college-degreed person just to run the Sunday School for God's sake. This wasn't some private school we were talking about. Just an hour-long program once a week and some family activities.

Elaine was in the kitchen chopping vegetables for a salad, when I came in. She asked about my meeting with Rev. Sarah since I had texted that I would be late stopping at church after work. I described the meeting as she listened. I told her how pissed I was at Sarah's reaction to my proposal of moving ahead with the hiring process.

She put down her knife and looked down at the cutting board for a minute, silent. Then she looked up at me, seemingly frustrated. "Jeffrey, calm down. She's just getting used to this new job. Don't start a fight with her when she's barely arrived. Please don't make a big deal out of this!"

Elaine's face tightened like I had caused this problem. She basically went silent the rest of the evening while she fixed dinner. She does that sometimes. Just stops talking, and I have no idea what I've done. The dinner conversation that night was a bit stilted. Emily noticed it and asked if Mom was mad at her. Elaine assured her that she wasn't mad at anyone. I knew better.

That night I was supposed to meet Terry at church to discuss the job and how we were going to move forward with it. But I realized that I just didn't have all my ducks in a row and didn't want Terry finding out. So, I texted her that we'd have to postpone. She sent back a "Got it!" and then our code, "MYRB" which she had come up with. It means "miss you real bad" but no one reading it would get that. I thought it was kind of dumb, but okay.

I thought about her mostly at night, when I couldn't sleep. I'd be lying there, my mind going around and around thinking of her, while sleeping next to Elaine. How could I do this?

I love Elaine. I mean, we were really in love when we met in college. Got married just a couple of years after we graduated. I guess it was a miracle that we didn't get pregnant before we got married. But then when we started trying it didn't take for a couple of years. However, when I think about it, that was a good time in our marriage. We wanted each other so badly that we could barely wait to get home from our jobs to be together. I mean, it got comical when Elaine would get home first, put some dinner in the oven and be waiting at the door with just her underwear on. She'd say "Didn't want to bother to change into clothes when I knew you'd just take them off when you got home." And I'd back her up to the wall and kiss her and pretty soon we might even be doing it there in the hall. Oh, my God. What happened to that feeling? I guess kids is what happened. Elaine finally got pregnant and then we were so ga-ga over the idea of a baby that we continued with our hot and heavy times. But then near the end, she didn't want sex any more. She said she just didn't have any energy, but I think she was worried I'd squish the baby or something. I was also a little worried about that, so I didn't mind.

After Alan was born, and two years later, Paul, it seemed like one long night of babies crying and both of us looking at the other like who was going to cave and get up first. Elaine had quit her job at that point and she was so bored and tired by the time I'd get home, she would just go back to bed. I would take over with the kids, feed them and put them to bed. She would finally come down and make us some dinner. Sometimes, we just had peanut butter and jelly for supper because neither one of us had any energy for real cooking. That was a hard time, but we felt like we were a team somehow.

But once they were out of diapers and Alan went to preschool, I thought, we're going to be okay. Elaine even took a little part-time job helping out at a fabric shop. She really loved going there and doing something other than babies for a change. She started wanted sex more, too. Thank God, because I was wondering if I'd ever get any again. She had fixed herself up a bit, too. She was happy again, and we'd have date nights on Saturdays. We'd leave the kids with the baby-sitter and go out to dinner. Just some Italian place, soft lighting, hushed music, and wonderful pasta. It felt like maybe we were human again.

Then her mother died. Just like that, gone from a stroke. Only 65. And Elaine fell apart. Even though her mother didn't live close by, they talked probably once a day, at least. Elaine was always calling up to ask advice about the kids. When should they get solid food or how to get them to use the potty. And of course, her mother loved giving advice! But losing her mother was life-changing for Elaine. Other than me, her mother was the person she counted on. We went to DC for the funeral. I figured once we came home, she would slowly come out of it.

But I have to say, that's when everything changed in our marriage. I mean, she wasn't *in* our marriage anymore. She wasn't even all that present for the kids at first. I tried to gently ask her if maybe she'd like to talk to someone. She hesitated before answering that no, she'd be all right, then she'd try to smile to make it seem like that was true. I think she really did need to talk to someone since she wasn't talking to me about it. She didn't have her mother anymore. Tammy and Jennifer, a couple of good friends who had been around more after the funeral, reached out. As far as I know, Elaine may have gotten together with them, but it didn't seem to help. Her friends probably expected that she'd moved on.

But I could see that Elaine hadn't moved on. She stopped fixing her hair. Just pulled it straight back into a ponytail and dragged around in jeans and a sweatshirt from college, even when she was working. When I nuzzled her cheek and moved over in bed, she'd go along, but it was like having sex with a mannequin. I stopped bothering. It was quite a surprise when she got pregnant with Emily. We'd hardly slept together at all. Having Emily seemed like just one more thing on the pile of things she couldn't handle. She quit her part-time job, but she seemed even more miserable.

That was probably when I started noticing other women more. I guess it's some kind of built-in male reaction when you're not getting what you need. I noticed a woman at work who wore these revealing tops. She would sometimes sit near me in the cafeteria. She'd smile and we'd chat a bit. Nice face and great bod. But I wasn't looking for anything.

When I started volunteering at the church and was invited to join the Vestry, that's when it happened. I was assigned to be liaison to the Christian Education Committee. I guess they asked me because I have kids. Terry was on that committee since she taught in the Sunday School. I had noticed her because she seemed shy, but lonely. I mean, she wouldn't initiate a conversation but once you asked her something, she'd just really light up. She had a really nice smile. She kind of half-smiled but her eyes did most of the smiling, if you know what I mean.

At one point, the committee needed someone to develop a plan for the curriculum for the middle school and Terry volunteered. I found myself saying that sure, I could help, too. Why not? My kids were that age and I thought I might be able to help figure out what they'd like.

So, we'd meet in the church basement and start planning. She was great to work with. She'd have new ideas for fun activities for kids, crafts and games. I'd have my laptop and would record what we planned, emailing it out when we were done. Proud of what we'd put together, I started looking forward to those times. I'd notice that she seemed to brighten when she'd see me. I mean, she was *really* glad to see me. We'd stay afterwards just shooting the breeze. She was so easy to talk to.

One evening, it had gotten late, and we hadn't stopped for dinner. So, I just suggested we grab a bite to eat, and she thought it was a great idea. I took her to a pizza joint. We had a couple of beers. Then

I started realizing what was happening. We were not just talking about church anymore. We were developing a relationship. Yeah, attraction, sure. I mean, she's a good-looking woman and I'm not blind. I noticed that she liked it when I'd accidently brush by her side, sitting together. But I started caring about her, like having real feelings for her.

One night when we had finished a curriculum plan and were cleaning up, she laughed at something I said. I leaned over to get some paper towels, and I realized that I was really close to her. I leaned over further, and just kissed her. I mean, *we* kissed. She leaned in just as I did. It just happened. I hadn't been planning it. But I had been thinking about it, I guess. That's how it started.

I felt terrible at first and told Terry right away it was a mistake. I called her the next day to tell her that I was sorry, but I couldn't do that again. She sounded disappointed, but I told her that I was happily married and couldn't have an affair. I didn't believe in it.

Or so I told myself. I just couldn't stop thinking about what I could have with her. So, after a committee meeting when everyone else had left, I kind of fumbled an awkward invitation. Something like, well, since we seemed to like each other so much and that I was certainly attracted to her, that well...and she responded with a slow smile. Yes, she said, let's. So, we drove to a cheap motel. One of those places where you wouldn't run into anyone you knew because no one you knew would ever go there.

It seemed tawdry at first. Looking at each other when we were done in that cheap motel with the nylon bedspreads and the cheap molded plastic chairs, it felt kind of desperate. I was embarrassed, but also amazed at how good it had been. Terry looked at me like I was really hot. I mean, those feelings you have when you first kiss and first touch each other. Jesus! Her body. Her mouth. Oh, my God.

I felt like a teenager discovering sex for the first time. I just couldn't give that up.

But of course, I also felt huge amounts of guilt. When I got home that night, I had a hard time looking Elaine in the eye. So, I just gave her a buzz on the cheek and avoided eye contact. I thought she could feel the heat coming off of me from carrying this secret. I was sure she would smell it on me. Or notice a button undone or a smudge of lipstick. All those clichés, that turned out to be true. I never was so meticulous in my dressing as I was when we left our little sessions.

But Elaine didn't seem to notice a thing. She had gotten a little better in the past couple of years, since we joined the church. She was teaching Sunday School and had made some friends. She was more cheerful and was very involved with the boys' basketball parents' group. She was the mom who brought brownies and remembered to have their Gatorade cold. Elaine never let her depression affect her parenting, at least that's what it seemed.

But the Elaine that I had married was no longer present in our marriage. So, it kind of felt like I had good reasons to be involved elsewhere.

CHAPTER TWELVE

SARAH

When Irene mentioned the Friday night potluck earlier in the week, I had kind of inwardly groaned as the gas in my internal tank was beginning to read empty. I think of myself as a shy extrovert, someone who gets energy from being with people until I've used up my reserves. Then I need time alone. I had attended just about every committee meeting and met with many of the leaders of the church one on one and boy, I needed a break. I was hoping to have a weekend to myself to explore my new neighborhood and the city. But, of course, this was important. It was the first church potluck this year where all the leaders were expected to show up and bring a dish to share. Apparently, these were held every other month on a Friday night. Luckily, the priest was not expected to bring a dish since so many of their priests had been male and not all of them married.

I decided not to get there early and help out as I usually did with church events, realizing that helping in the kitchen was generally a female thing in this church like many I had been in. I didn't want to end up being seen as another woman in the kitchen. I had certainly been doing my share of cleaning up, but I didn't want anyone to expect that as a part of my duties. I guess I was overthinking things as usual, but I made myself wait until it seemed like the right time.

I finally wandered into the parish hall when I could see that the potluck table was almost full and several people were clumped in groups, talking and holding back the claws of hungry kids who wanted to dig in. Glancing over the spread, the typical potluck fare reigned supreme: lots of potato salad, hummus, green salads, meatballs, sliced ham, and several kinds of casseroles with hamburger and pasta. Someone had brought a cheese pizza which didn't look very appetizing as the cheese had already congealed in a sticky mess. But goodness, when I thought about these families trying to arrive here after work and bring a dish to share, it couldn't be easy. So, bringing a pizza or any pre-made dish was just fine by today's potluck standards.

I saw Peg and Irene and two other women carrying in plates, napkins and all the utensils needed. When Irene saw me, she waved and came over.

"Hey, there! Did I ask you if you could do the blessing tonight?"

I smiled ruefully. "Yes, Irene. You've only mentioned it about six times since Sunday."

Irene chuckled. "Well, we wouldn't want you to feel overlooked, would we? Oh, and if you wanted to use this opportunity to talk about anything on your mind during dinner, this is also often used as a kind of update time for the priest to speak."

I must have looked horrified since Irene had not mentioned that small item of importance ahead of time, so she started to backtrack. "Oh, I'm sorry, I guess I forgot to tell you. Well, you certainly don't need to speak tonight. Could you just do the hostess thing after the blessing? Just thank people etc.?"

"Of course, I can do that. Just give me a minute and I'll think of something to say. No problem, really. After all the meetings I've been in this month, I should be able to come up with something."

Irene thanked me and disappeared back into the kitchen. Noticing Jeffrey standing with his wife, I went over and greeted them. I felt Jeffrey stiffen a bit as I approached, obviously uneasy with our last interaction. But Elaine smiled widely and took my hand when I got closer.

"Rev. Sarah, we are just so glad to have you here. You know, the Sunday school teachers have been talking about how they are really sad they can't hear your sermons since they're in class during service. They've been hearing about what they're missing! I've only heard one of your sermons, but I really enjoyed it."

Jeffrey looked directly at me and smiled stiffly before saying, "All the more reason to get a Christian Ed Director on board who could manage the rotation of teachers, so they don't all have to miss out."

Elaine blanched. I guess she now knew this was a point of contention between us. But she gently smoothed out the moment suggesting we move to one of the tables since Irene was holding up her hands to get people's attention. I allowed myself to get herded to the seat at the head of the nearest table and looked to Irene. She held up a chime and rang it loudly three times. The people quieted and moved quickly to find their seats. Irene glanced over at me to check if I was ready. I nodded.

"Let us pray together to bless this wonderful meal we're about to share. We are so blessed to have our new priest Rev. Sarah here with us tonight. Would you please gather and join hands as we ask Rev. Sarah to bless this meal?"

I reached over and took Jeffrey's hand although he gave me a reluctant glance and then took Elaine's in my other hand.

"Gracious God, you who has brought us together here in community. We thank you for the good food that has been so generously offered by the loving hands of our dear friends. We thank you for the hands that prepared the food, the hands that have laid the tables, the hands that care for our children, the hands that offer comfort to one another, and the hands that are clasped together in holy community here, now. We offer this in your holy name. Amen."

Jeffrey dropped my hand quickly, looking decidedly uncomfortable about having had to stay in such close contact. Elaine, on the other hand, squeezed my hand softly as she let go. I mentioned to her that I hoped we could get together soon to chat. She nodded and smiled agreement.

Irene announced the order of the tables for getting in line. She wisely asked the tables at the front with the most kids at their tables to go first, and a couple of kids yelled, "Yes!" their hands shooting up with glee. The rest of us sat down to wait our turn.

Elaine turned to me and asked about how my week was going. Jeffrey seemed to redden at this question, thinking of our last conversation.

"You know I have been delighted to spend so much of my time recently getting to know so many of our members. And Jeffrey, when we met, told me how important the church has become to your family over the past years."

Elaine looked pleased that I had brought up their family. Their daughter, Emily, the four- year-old, was giggling softly to a friend, as she pressed a paper napkin to her head making some kind of hat out of it. I loved the way kids could turn anything into a game. Elaine looked over at them with a fond glance.

"Yes, Emily loves going to Sunday School here. We have such creative teachers."

"Jeffrey has told me how important that program is. And you have enjoyed being a teacher as well?"

Elaine nodded, "I really have."

Just then Irene called our table and the kids jumped up to rush over to the serving table. Elaine excused herself to quickly follow behind them, trying to prevent them from jumping ahead of others. Jeff got up and motioned for me to go ahead of him, magnanimously offering me a plate from the table. I took it and started adding items to my plate while he followed.

We didn't talk as we chose our food. I was suddenly not very hungry and just took a chicken thigh and some of the salad. I added some potato salad but at the end of the table decided that I would branch off and visit some other tables before returning to ours. I moved over to the first table where two families with several children of various ages were already halfway through their meal and there was much merriment shared as they argued who could finish their meal the fastest so they could return to the dessert table. I greeted some of the parents and laughed as a red-headed freckled eight-year-old shoved the last piece of pizza into his mouth and threw his hands up. "Done!" he shouted, then raced off to grab some sweets. Peg, who was there with her girls, motioned me over.

She leaned closer, whispering softly, "Have you met with Jeffrey yet?"

I nodded and assured her that I was working on getting the hiring process slowed down. "Don't worry. We'll get this done right."

Peg looked doubtful but held up her hand like she had said her piece. I went back to my table and sat down with my food. Elaine was there with her daughter and her friend, supervising them as they ate, giggling more than chewing. She nodded at me as I settled down and began to eat. She looked a little uncomfortable. Jeff had disappeared somewhere.

Elaine said quietly. "I would like to come talk to you. Can we make an appointment in a couple of weeks?"

I took out my phone to check my calendar and agreed on a time that would work. Elaine looked serious as she noticed Jeffrey coming back into the room from the hallway. He hurried over to another table and bent over the table to talk to Frank, the Junior Warden. They talked seriously, looking over their shoulders at me a couple of times. I imagined they were hatching a plot about the hiring.

Then I noticed Terry, the person that Jeffrey had been promoting for the position coming into the parish hall from the same hallway where Jeffrey had appeared. I noticed Elaine's eyes watching her enter the room as well. Then Elaine looked down and became absorbed in Emily's dinner directing her to finish her food before she went for dessert. She looked like she didn't want to notice Terry but couldn't help it.

Irene came over and asked me if I wanted to speak as people were finishing up their dinners. I suddenly had an idea. I agreed that if she could get people's attention, I would speak for a few minutes.

Irene went to the front of the room, chimed the bell a couple of times with no result. People were too busy chatting and eating. She raised her voice over the crowd. "People, may I have your attention, please. Hello!" Congregants noticed her and started shushing the ones around them. The kids were still talking but one dad raised his voice, "Quiet, please, the lady is talking." Everyone became quiet then and looked expectantly at Irene.

"Our Rev. Piper has been with us now for about five weeks! Can we give a round of applause for how excited we are to have her here at our first potluck of the year?" Some clapped and the ones who were still eating raised a cheer. I stood and went to the front of the room, where Irene had grabbed the microphone and turned it on, handing it to me.

I thanked everyone for the delicious food while thinking fast about what I'd say next. I told them that we were so lucky to be privileged to have enough food but that as we knew, not everyone was so lucky. I looked around at their puzzled faces, no doubt wondering where I was going with all this.

"I'm new to this city and new to this church, but I've observed how generous the people of this church are. So many of you do volunteer work in the city. Some are tutoring in the schools; some are working at homeless shelters providing meals. I'm beginning to see that the members of St. Philips care deeply about what's going on in this city. I'm hoping that means that you want St. Philips to make a difference as a church community. Am I right?"

Many nodded their heads, but others looked confused. Jeffrey had a skeptical scowl on his face like whatever I was about to say would cause him to have an ulcer or a heart attack.

"So, if I'm right, I hope you'll be interested in what we can do as a church community to help the people of Philadelphia who don't have enough food. Remember what I preached a couple of weeks ago about Saint Philip? About how he was skeptical that the five loaves and two fishes could possibly feed the thousands who showed up to hear Jesus preach? I see some of you might be skeptical about how we could possibly make a difference to the people who are hungry. Well, I've learned about a new food bank that's going to be forming with an interfaith coalition in the downtown area. Some of our friends at St. Martin's and St. Paul's are going to be partners. So, let me ask you. Do you want to make a difference in the city of Philadelphia for people who are hungry?"

The faces staring back at me were a mixed bag. Some still looked confused, some interested, and some nodded enthusiastically. I looked over at Irene to see if I was making a faux pas and she looked a bit startled. I guess I should have run this by her first. But here I was. I might as well go the rest of the way.

"So, I'm just wondering, who might be interested in learning more about this possible downtown food bank in which we could participate?"

Irene raised her hand immediately. A few joined her. But then some of the teen-agers started that finger snapping thing to show their support. I smiled gratefully. Jeffrey kept his head down, his face blank. Obviously, I should have run it by the Vestry first. New priest mistake, I realized. Everything is political. I backtracked a bit.

"We'd have to learn a whole lot more about it before we could commit. But I hope you'll be open to considering much more involvement in the city. We are somewhat isolated here in our neigh-borhood but there's a whole lot of need."

Irene started clapping, and I sat down quickly, realizing I didn't need to put my foot in it any more than I had. I remembered my conversation with Irene. We need to take it slowly. And yes, I needed to slow down.

Chapter Thirteen

SARAH

October, 2016

One afternoon, I was in my office when Marilyn called reminding me of the dinner on Saturday with Edwardo, her friend whom I had met at the food co-op meeting. I could hardly forget him, given that he was probably the best-looking thing I had seen in a long time, and I was very much looking forward to the dinner. Still, I didn't appreciate Marilyn's pushiness on the subject.

"Just want to make sure you're not going to back out on me."

"No, of course not. I'll be there. And I'm bringing dessert."

"Good. Edwardo is definitely coming, too. I can't wait for you to two to get to know each other," she chirped knowingly.

"Well, don't get your hopes up. That's the worst way to jinx it. Please don't expect us to like each other and then act like we've disappointed you."

"Oh, relax. It's just that I like you both so much that I think you'll click."

"Yeah, well, no pushing!"

"Okay, okay. I'll see you Saturday." When Marilyn hung up, I went onto Facebook, looking up Edwardo's page. While downplaying my attraction with Marilyn, I guess I was kind of cyber-stalking him, spending ten minutes perusing his picture. He had that kind of dark almost beard that was so sexy. Gray, almost black eyes that seemed to be hiding something deeper. A confident but not arrogant smile, if that's possible. But I hated it when my friends did these set-ups. It just put the whole thing into a light of expectation that made it awkward. Oh, well, it was just one dinner. I could always go back to my "I'm just not in the market" line. I couldn't shake off the anticipation I was feeling about the dinner, but I didn't want Marilyn to be disappointed.

When I arrived Saturday a few minutes early, Bob answered the door, taking my lemon meringue pie from me, and welcoming me warmly with a huge hug. I had gotten to know Bob during those days in seminary when many of our friends would gather at Marilyn and Bob's apartment for celebrations. Bob was the host in the background, doing most of the cooking, pouring drinks and generally making it all work behind the scenes. Bob had that quiet, welcoming nature which set against Marilyn's exuberance was a perfect contrast. Together, they became the campus parents, the glue that held people together and the ones people sought out for comfort. After I got to know Marilyn early on, I felt extremely lucky when we hit it off and became close. Knowing Bob and seeing their complementary pairing, I also yearned for such a good partner in life. But I hadn't ever had a relationship where I felt the kind of demonstrable support I saw between these two.

Bob delivered my pie into the kitchen and came back with a glass of wine. "If I remember, you like white wine?" I nodded, grateful for someone in this city who knew me. "So, Sarah, how is the church treating you so far?" Bob asked as he offered me a seat in the living room.

"Well, they've been pretty welcoming. Lots of lunches and teas. And people coming in and pouring out their souls. You know, the sharing of secrets so they think they'll get closer to you?"

Bob chuckled. "Yeah, and then you find out which of those secrets are really true and which are self-serving gossip. Right?"

I shrugged. "I haven't gotten that far yet. Only have the early responders. We'll see. But it's going well. I think the biggest hurdle I have is getting them to consider taking part in the food bank."

"Oh, you're going to try that? In your first year? That's brave." Bob raised an eyebrow.

The bell rang. Bob went to the front door as I perused the charming living room. I heard Bob welcoming Edwardo, taking his coat. The sound of that deep, slightly accented voice gave me a bit of a fluttery feeling in my belly. As Edwardo entered the room, turning to me with this broad smile, I felt my cheeks grow warm. He was much handsomer than I had remembered. Really a kind of attractiveness that was way over what I judged as my own physical desirability. I mean, why would this guy be interested in me? I was just okay attractive, but jeez, this was level 10! I pushed down my anxiety and tried to hide it with a smile.

"Hi there, Sarah, is it?" Edwardo said, extending his hand. "Edwardo Sanchez. I'm glad to see you again. We didn't get a chance to talk much at the meeting." Bob came in after hanging up Edwardo's coat. After exchanging niceties, we all sat down, Edwardo noting the brightly colored wall hangings from Haiti, where Bob had done a short stint in the Peace Corps.

Bob and Edwardo talked briefly in Spanish as Edwardo remarked on the origin of one of the wooden statues gracing a bookshelf, also from Haiti. He delighted Bob with something humorous in Spanish, but quickly turned to me to translate so I wouldn't feel left out.

Marilyn came hurrying down the stairs, dressed as usual in something lavender and gray, looking casual but well-dressed as usual. When Edwardo saw Marilyn entering the room, he stood up like gentlemen of the previous generation had always done.

"Oh, no, now don't start that formal bowing and scraping that you do. You don't need to impress me. I know you're a gentleman. And a 'gentle man' as well." Marilyn said kissing Edwardo's cheek. She winked at me and leaned down to give me a side hug. "So, let me get the cheese plate and some wine. Edwardo, white or red? White, right? Sarah, would you come help?" Marilyn disappeared into the kitchen, motioning me to follow.

Marilyn pulled out cheese from the refrigerator shelf and was opening a top cabinet door when she whispered, "Isn't he delicious? Couldn't you just eat him with a spoon?" She smiled raising her eyebrows.

"Well, sure," I whispered back. "But, okay, that's enough matchmaking. It's just embarrassing. And will probably backfire." Marilyn handed me a packet of crackers and a white platter, while she unwrapped the cheese.

"Okay, okay. I'll stop. But don't say I didn't fix you up good," she said, her head doing a little happy shake. "Anyway, what's going on at St. Philips? What's the newest in the Senior Warden sleezeball saga?"

"Oh, the secrets continue to spill."

"Do tell."

"I can't tell you everything but there's more evidence of the reported affair."

"Really? Oh, goodness, this really is turning into the plot of a bodice ripper. And what are you going to do about it?" Marilyn looked intrigued.

I finished arranging crackers and looked at her. "Nothing. I don't plan on doing anything."

"What? You can't let the guy get away with this!" Marilyn looked indignant.

"But Marilyn, it's not my job to become the sex police, is it? I mean, I think this is a private matter that needs to play itself out. I can't tell them to stop having the affair, right? I mean, that's not my job! What would you do?" I asked, exasperated.

She looked momentarily stumped. "Hmmm. I see what you mean. You can't just march in there and tell your Senior Warden what to do, I guess, but doesn't a Vestry member have to follow a certain code of ethics? I mean, we no longer put people on trial. But doesn't the Episcopal diocese have some document that dictates the kind of ethics we expect?"

"I don't think we follow that kind of thing anymore. And I wouldn't feel comfortable with it, anyway. But if either of them comes to me, I can counsel them about what this means to their lives and to the church. But I don't think I can just act like judge and jury with them. I don't believe in that kind of ministry." I felt at a loss especially since Marilyn didn't seem to have any answers either. She was usually full of advice and resources. But then I added sadly, "But I certainly do feel judgy about it."

Marilyn hesitated. "I see. I guess you're right. I'd feel like beating that man around the head, but I guess that isn't our job, is it?" Marilyn handed the cheese platter to me and picked up wine glasses for herself and Edwardo. "I guess we won't solve this tonight. So, let's go have fun, shall we?" I nodded and followed her back to the living room, placing the platter on the coffee table in front of Edwardo and sitting down next to him.

Marilyn led the conversation as she usually did, drawing out Edwardo to tell something of his childhood in Mexico City and how he came to Philadelphia. I was surprised to learn about his well-to-do parents who owned businesses in Mexico, sending him off to boarding school in Mexico City and then college at Carnegie Mellon. They wanted him to be an engineer but after failing a physics course, he changed directions and started taking courses in psychology and business, finally deciding on a major in social work. His parents apparently threatened to not pay for his final years in college, then gave up and let him go his own way. I could relate considering my own struggle with my parents and their upper middle- class expectations.

Marilyn asked him how he had become interested in doing social work. He thought about it for a moment, before replying playfully, "Can you explain how you became interested in doing ministry?" Then he looked at me. "Or you Sarah, how did you? We know it wasn't for the money!"

We exchanged laughs. Marilyn replied sarcastically, "It wasn't for the power either!" We all smiled at that foolish thought.

Edwardo's expression grew more serious. "But I suspect that you both felt the way I did. That people suffered terribly in this life and if I was going to do anything meaningful in life I needed to deal with people's suffering." My heart did a little two-step hearing this. Here was someone who might get me.

Marilyn looked at me with a knowing glance before responding. "Hear, hear! But I'm lucky in that I married someone who can support me while I save humankind. Unfortunately, you two haven't figured that out."

Edwardo turned red, seemingly embarrassed, but then recovered himself laughing, and added, "Yes, if you know any wealthy single ladies, please let me know."

"Oh," I responded with a sarcastic tone, "you haven't heard about the very large salaries Episcopal priests make?" Turning pink, I looked away, feeling like I had gone a little too far.

***

Holding up the colorful bangle earrings that I had bought in a church craft fair last year, I imagined how they would look to Edwardo. He was coming to pick me up for dinner in 20 minutes. I was nervous, but excited. A little too excited, I thought. I had been telling myself not to get my hopes up just because this guy seemed like the real thing. Someone who might share my values. Not like so many guys I had seen my friends dating who wanted to make a lot of money and impress women with their BMW's or townhouses. But I didn't know who he was, yet. I had no idea, really.

Examining myself in the mirror, I tried to see myself as he would see me. My bright fuchsia blouse with the dark skinny jeans were fine, I thought, for a date at a casual restaurant at the downtown open-air market. While they were one of my favorites, maybe the earrings look a little too bohemian. I took them off and tried a more sedate pair of smaller gold hoops. No, not quite right. I finally just fastened on the plain gold knots I usually wore, shaking my head that I had just spent 20 minutes worrying about earrings, of all things.

At the dinner at Marilyn's, I found myself suddenly worrying that I was trying too hard. Smiling too much. Talking too much. Touching my hair way too much. *Oh, my God,* I thought, *I was so obvious.*

I had been staring at him; I realized to my horror. But I was drawn to his wide, open face framed by dark, curly hair. Edwardo's warmth, the way he said something in a questioning voice, followed by a quick, amused smile was so enticing. I waited for that smile, almost coveting it.

But every time I saw Marilyn watching me, I'd play it down and try to react in a nonchalant way. I guess I wasn't surprised when Edwardo called the next day. He said that he wondered if I'd like to meet and get to know each other better. I guessed with the set-up Marilyn had engineered, it was almost expected of him. I hoped that wasn't the reason he was calling, instead that his response to me that night was genuine.

The doorbell rang as I was applying my lipstick. Opening the door, I felt a small surge of excitement as I saw the warm smile and expectant face with which Edwardo greeted me. Smiling, I grabbed my sweater and suggested that since I was ready, we could leave right away.

Edwardo seemed a bit nervous, smiling and exclaiming about the nice fall weather. He was apologetic about the state of his older dark blue VW station wagon, as he opened the car door. But when I sat down, I saw how he must have carefully tidied the seats and floors. It was a little shabby but immaculate.

"That Marilyn, she's something, isn't she?" I started hesitantly, as we started off.

"She really is, so welcoming and friendly to someone just coming to the city," Edwardo responded warmly.

Uh-oh. Does he mean that he's just taking me out because Marilyn asked him to welcome me? Or is he talking about himself?

"Yes, she is. How did you get to know her?"

"I met her right away at that interfaith group. She invited me to her home like right away!"

"Yep, that's Marilyn. And Bob, of course, who is the host making it all work behind her."

Edwardo nodded while waiting for the turn onto the boulevard that led down to the market. "I am amazed at how well they work together at this hospitality thing. They could easily run an inn! Always welcoming everyone. I mean, they even invited the whole group to their house last Christmas. That was above and beyond."

"Oh, didn't you go home for Christmas?" I then realized how intrusive this might sound. I tried to pull it back. "I mean, do you get a chance to visit your home often?"

Edwardo kind of frowned, then responded evasively. "Um, well, not very often. I've only been a few times since I moved here four years ago."

We chit-chatted about where we grew up and our families. But after we had parked and were walking around the market, looking at some of the shops, I suddenly remembered when Edwardo had asked me at Marilyn's about why I went into ministry. That was the moment I knew that this man wasn't just a surface kind of guy. He had revealed that he cared about who I was and what was important to me. Thinking of that, I jumped right in with a question that may have been a bit much for an opening salvo on a first date. But I couldn't help it. That's who I was.

"So, Edwardo, you asked me the other night why I went into ministry. And I asked you in turn why you were a social worker. But what you didn't tell me was what was that compelling motivation that meant you had to do what you do. Was there some kind of underlying reason?"

"Oh, you mean, why I couldn't do anything else than choose the most poorly paid profession I could possibly find? Boy, you don't fool around, do you? Go for the gold, right away, right?" He looked at me with a knowing look. "I shouldn't be surprised, given that you're a friend of Marilyn's."

I grimaced, sorry that I was so direct sometimes. I had regretted it before when I was just beginning relationships that I would come on too strong.

"I'm sorry, I didn't mean to be so serious. My mom is always warning me about that."

Edwardo smiled again. "No, I like it. I like to know what drives people. And yes, there is a story, as you guessed. Why don't we sit down and have a glass of wine, and I'll tell you, if you really want to hear." I agreed and we moved toward the casual seafood restaurant Edwardo had chosen at the center of the market.

After we were seated and had ordered, Edwardo picked up where we had left off.

"So, you wanted to know how I ended up in social work, right?" I smiled and nodded.

"Well, this is kind of a hard story to tell. And it might sound sort of like a white guilt story. I was in high school when this happened. I went to a private school which meant that most of the other students in my school were also from a background of people with more European descent and fairly well to do. I had little contact with the poverty in Mexico City. Except that, where I grew up, we had servants who were all indigenous Mexicans and poor. Our cook's son, Mario, had grown up pretty much with me. We had always played together and been like close friends, despite the differences in our families. He wasn't allowed to eat with us, but I was frequently down in the kitchen area, helping out and being in the way. His mother, Lupine, was so sweet and always treated me like a part of their family. His dad had never really been a part of the picture. Once when I was in boarding school and I came home for the holidays, I learned that Lupine was in the hospital. She had been suffering from colon cancer and had been receiving treatment for months. But before I arrived home, she had fallen seriously ill.

When I learned this, I immediately left for the hospital. I hoped I could see her and be with Mario as he waited for her. I arrived there and went straight to her room, where I could see a whole team of doctors surrounding the bed. I could just see glimpses of what was going on, but near the door, Mario stood anxiously."

Edwardo stopped speaking to take a sip of wine. I could see him hesitating, taking a deep breath before he continued.

"As I said, this is a hard story, but it describes what affected me in so many ways. The doctor who was holding the defibrillator ordered everyone to stand back. Pressing the paddles to Lupine's chest, he watched the monitor, then tried again. After a minute with no response, one of the nurses noticed Mario there and tried to shepherd us away from the scene. Mario wouldn't leave; his face was terrified. After another couple of minutes, we saw the doctor shake his head. The nurse whispered to Mario that she was sorry, that they had done everything they could."

Edwardo stopped. He looked troubled just relaying the memory.

"I'll never forget that moment. I realized that my friend, Mario, was alone in this world. We were the only family he had. I also realized over the years, that Lupine had not had any insurance and while my parents had gotten her some treatment, that it hadn't been the kind of treatment they would have arranged for someone in my family. I felt that my family bore some responsibility for her death. I began to have this sense of responsibility to care for people who were not given the benefits I had growing up. I guess you could say, I'm kind of... what do you call it 'a bleeding heart', or maybe a sap?" He looked a bit embarrassed to have shared this.

"I understand. It must have been so hard to watch Mario struggle with his loss. And to feel helpless." Edwardo raised his hands in a shrug.

"Well, much harder for Mario. I just felt responsible for my family not doing more."

"So, what happened with Mario?"

Edwardo shook his head a little in frustration. "Well, my parents did look after him. They paid for him to attend college. He did well. Then he started his own business with a little help from my father. But after that, he seemed to resent me. I've tried numerous times to reach out, but there's some sort of block he has. Really, I can hardly blame him."

Edwardo took another sip of wine before shifting gears. "So, after trying in college to connect to the idea of becoming an engineer which was really my father's dream, I eventually realized that I had to do something in my career to address the inequities I've lived with."

"So, social work is your way of addressing those inequities?"

"Yes. Maybe not a very effective one," he said raising his eyebrows, "And some days I feel like it's an extremely ineffective one. But there it is." He looked at me expectantly. "So, I've told you my long and boring story. I'd like to know more about you. You just told me a little bit about losing your sister. Tell me more about that. If you like."

Talking about Pam's death wasn't something I freely talked about, but Edwardo had deeply shared the experience that had changed his trajectory in life. He seemed sincere in asking. I sighed.

"Okay, I guess it's my turn." I twisted my earrings nervously, as I looked up at him wanting to measure his ability to understand.

"My sister, Pam, was two years younger. When she was diagnosed with leukemia, I was 13. It didn't really register with me at the time that it was serious. I mean, I kind of felt like she was getting a lot of my parent's attention which seemed like a relief so I could go off and do what I wanted. But as she got sicker, I started realizing that she could die. I tried to spend time with her, but she rarely felt good enough to do anything other than just watch a movie or listen to me read to her.

But I was getting involved with my church youth group and I was caught up in my own life. What I mean is, I wasn't really there for her. I was off being a teen instead of spending any real time with her. Then when she died, I felt such a huge load of guilt that I hadn't been there. And my parents just...shut down. They tried to get me some counselling, but I had already found the priest at my church who had reached out to me. He was my main support. So, later, when I started teaching but found that it was just a lot of administrative bullshit with so little freedom to do much good for people, that's when I thought about what my home priest had done for me. Changed my life, basically. I mean, if he hadn't reached out to me, I would have been alone. Very alone."

I sat staring at my hands on the table. Then I looked up. Edwardo's eyes shimmered with emotion. He gently covered my hand with his own. "Sarah, I'm so sorry," he said quietly before pulling his hand back.

I tried to recover—both from the memories flooding my brain, and the feel of his hand on mine. "Yeah, it's okay. It was a long time ago. And I'm fine." I cleared my throat, smiled, and pulling back my hand, took a sip of my wine.

"So, did you enter ministry to help people? Was it a debt you felt you were paying back?"

I thought about it. "Well, kind of. But it was more something I had to do. I had to find a way to feel good about myself, which I didn't after she died. And ministry seemed to be a way to do that. I feel good when I help someone wrestle with their questions about life and death. It feels meaningful in a way that teaching wasn't."

"So, is it a debt you're paying to God?"

"Oh, no. Nothing like that. My religion is very practical. God to me is like the ultimate expression of love. God is everything in life that is sacred. The God I know is not a typical father-like figure. Oh, that's probably TMI. I could talk religion all day long, but it would probably be very boring." I smiled apologetically.

Edwardo looked interested. "I find that fascinating. That you're a priest but not very traditional."

"Yeah, well, Episcopalians are often pretty open in their theology. And I am extremely open in mine. Sometimes it gets me in trouble. I'm just hoping it will play okay in this church."

"So, tell me about this church of yours. It's in an interesting neighborhood. Mostly working class?"

"Well, that's been its history over the past 30 or so years. But it was built in the late 1800's when the neighborhood was quite well-to-do with the families who had built the steel industry. St. Philips was founded by some of those families. But then when the steel industry declined, the families that had founded that industry were also affected and many moved away. The area became somewhat rundown until working class families bought some of the older homes and refurbished them into apartments or boarding houses."

"But do you have some families from Oak Grove Park? Some more upwardly mobile families?"

"Yeah, we do. Our Vestry president is from there. And there are probably ten or so families from there now. They have really saved the church from decline. They support us well. But they also have a loud voice about what they want."

We continued talking about the differences in the congregation between the more well-to-do families who wanted more paid staff, and the working-class families who were used to doing things themselves. How the newer Oak Grove families wanted a paid religious educator to be hired sooner rather than later.

"But is your congregation interested in being more involved in the community?" Edwardo asked.

"Well, they say they do. But I have to admit, I haven't seen much evidence of that. I haven't gotten much traction on the idea of the food bank. But I haven't done a real push on it. I don't think I have enough political capital yet."

"Oh, that's okay. It's a struggle even for the big churches. I don't know if this project is going to fly. It's a really good idea. And it never would have gotten off the ground without Marilyn and David's help. But the economy's not that good. So, churches and donors are a little hesitant."

"But you really see the need?"

"Oh, yeah. I have families, many of whom are immigrants, some undocumented, who are going to food banks across town and using food stamps and they still don't have enough to feed their families. And they're working two, sometimes three jobs."

"Wow, I can't imagine trying to make that work with kids."

"Yeah, the kids often bear the brunt. They don't see enough of their parents. They don't have enough to eat. They don't have help with their homework. Just a never- ending cycle of poverty. Not a new story. And now we have this guy who's President who wants us to send all the immigrants home. Just don't get me started..." Edwardo ran his hand through his hair in frustration.

The waitress brought the food, a shrimp salad for me and baked fish for him. The conversation shifted to the kinds of food we liked and the music we both followed. Phish for me, and Coldplay as one of his favorite bands. As we were finishing, Edwardo's phone buzzed. He looked apologetic but picked it up frowning.

"I'm sorry. I'm afraid I should take this. It's a client of mine who is in crisis." I nodded and waved my hand for him to go ahead. Edwardo picked up his phone, got up and moved to the front of the restaurant by the windows. I could see him speaking quietly in Spanish, then listening and responding hurriedly, before hanging up. He came toward me with a troubled look.

"I'm so sorry, Sarah, I have a client who is undocumented. The police are there and are threatening her. I'm afraid I need to go and see if I can help sort it out. I could drop you…"

I spoke quickly, "No, just go. I can get a taxi and talk to you later."

Edwardo looked apologetic and quickly took some cash out of his pocket and put it on the table. "Could you get the bill taken care of? I hope this is enough…man, what a way to end an evening! I am so sorry, and I hope you won't think badly of me."

I waved him away. "Just go. Don't worry. This happens in my line of work, too." I stood and patted his arm to reassure him since he looked uncomfortable. "Really, I understand." Edwardo took my hand and squeezed it, before hurrying out the door. But as I watched him disappear down the street, I felt good. Edwardo had understood me. He was interested in what I had to say and didn't even seem phased when I talked about my beliefs. I felt hopeful about how the evening had gone. Finally, here was someone I found interesting and attractive!

I had dated a little during my teaching days and found the guys struggling to find their careers and make their way in the world. I had been too, but these guys were often focused on getting "ahead" to some vision of success that I didn't care about, and I found the talk about current bands or movies left me empty. I didn't necessarily expect them to be trying to save the world, I just hoped for a guy that had something more interesting in mind than a 401K and a Porsche.

The friends I gravitated toward in college were usually people my dad would describe as "causies." I had found a small group of four friends whom I had met while volunteering at the local foodbank. We usually hung out at the student union together or attended local political rallies after meeting our sophomore year. We hadn't dated each other, preferring to keep things friendly and casual so we could always come back to report to each other on the miserable dates we endured. We had something we called the "Mr. Rogers score" we'd assign to each possible date, citing the Mr. Rogers quote "look for the helpers". If someone was involved politically, volunteered in the community, or was majoring in Women's Studies or African American Studies they would get a 6 or a 7. If they had run for student government on a political issue like getting a more diverse teaching staff, they'd get an 8 or 9. No one got a 10. But most of the poor fools who were 2's or 3's were cut from the same cloth. They grew up in the white suburbs without a clue that they should care about anything except their GPA or how hot the band was that was playing on campus. We were pretty brutal in our judgment. It was only later that I realized how much our judgmental clique kept me from knowing other people.

As I paid the bill and went outside to flag down a taxi, I thought of Edwardo hurrying off to help someone deal with the police. I smiled considering his score.

The next morning, I woke up to a gray, drizzly rain with a feeling of damp cold permeating the apartment. I realized anew that my windows were not well insulated. Living in an older building had its drawbacks, despite its charm. But I loved the high ceilings and wide crown moldings, classic painted patterns etched in the front lobby walls, and dental molding gracing the ceiling. When I had first come to look at the apartment with an agent, right away I noticed the 1940's art deco details of recessed niches in the living room and scratched marble floors in the front hall. The agent kept emphasizing how "classic" it was. Classic, yes, but then there were these annoying features such as no insulation on the windows and the heat coming from old cast-iron radiators which clanged on making the apartment toasty and freezing when they went hissed off. There was no in between. If I could insulate a little, the heat might modulate better. I made a note to stop at the hardware store and pick up some of those plastic sheeting kits for the windows.

Snuggling down in bed, I made a warm nest, pulling the comforter up to cover me better. I loved my brass bedframe with its intricate patterns in iron and the brass finials on each post. It had just reached out and grabbed me one day when I had been meandering through an estate sale my first week in Philly. It magically made the place feel more like home.

Creating my own home had been an elusive goal in my short adult life. This was the first time I had begun to feel something right about what I had chosen. A home, a career, people I cared about.

I picked up my phone from the bedside table and was checking my texts, hoping for a text from Edwardo since he had to leave so abruptly last night. Then I saw it. A text apologizing for having to end our date and asking if he could make it up to me.

A floaty, hopeful kind of feeling came over me. While not allowing myself to think too much about a possible future, my mind held those fleeting possibilities. It felt really strange to actually consider a serious relationship since I had been putting that idea into a box marked "Not Now" for so long. The emotional muscle of pulling myself back was tired.

My therapist in college had pointed out that since Pam's death, I had not allowed myself to feel much of anything, except that slightly hidden wedge of guilt. Becky had continued to remind me to "feel" and to report those feelings. One of the annoying things she pointed out was that when I dated, I held myself back.

She had also remarked that I kept coming back to the need to help others. She wondered where this need came from, implying, I think, that it came from guilt. But when I asked what was wrong with this need, she admitted that there was nothing wrong with needing to help others as long as I understood where it was coming from.

I texted Edwardo back: [Don't worry about it. Got a taxi home.] And then I waited to see if he responded. It didn't happen right away. But after scrolling online for a few minutes, my phone pinged.

[So sorry I had to leave last night. I was having a really good time. Would you be interested in lunch tomorrow? After church? No problem if you're not available or if you just aren't looking to further this relationship right now.] It was followed with a smiley face. I felt my heart give a little elated zing. He was interested. Yes!

I texted back that I'd love to do lunch and asked where to meet. Edwardo texted back immediately with a thumbs up and the suggestion of a picnic in the park. I sent back a smiley face. I watched the dots under his name percolate for what seemed like an eternity—then ping, he sent a thumbs up and the name of a park and where to meet.

I rolled over, a warm, delicious feeling spreading throughout my body. I started to think about what I would wear and thought of running down to the little consignment shop on Elm that always had cute things in their window. But then I thought of a pretty, lacy blouse I hadn't worn in a while. It might do.

I got up, poured hot water over an English Breakfast teabag into my favorite light blue mug, then added a little honey. Sitting at my kitchen table next to the tall window which condensation had totally fogged up, I opened email on my tablet. Scrolling through, one caught my eye. It was from Terry, the much-mentioned, suspected lover of Jeffrey. The email was entitled "Need some assistance."

Opening it and scanning it quickly, I saw that Terry wanted to meet with me as soon as possible, after church tomorrow, in fact. Oh, hell! I so wanted to see Edwardo. Maybe he would agree to a later time to meet.

I quickly texted him and was relieved when he said he could meet later. I emailed Terry and arranged to meet in my office after the service.

My phone rang and it was Marilyn. "Hey, are you thanking me this morning for introducing you to Mr. Right?"

"Well, yes, I guess so. We'll see."

"Okay, give it up. How was it?"

"Um, it was fun. He is really interesting."

"Interesting? Oh, give me a break! We're not talking about a library book! He's a hunk and a sweetheart! So, tell me. What did you talk about?"

"Well, we talked about our families and our lives. I don't know... just things...."

"Things? Oh, I see. That means you're not going to tell me whether he made a move."

"Marilyn! It was just dinner. And he had to leave early."

"What? He left you early? No, can't be. I was sure that you two would hit it off! Don't tell me you put him off with all your theological musings!"

"No, Marilyn, nothing like that. He just got a call from a client and it was an emergency. He had to leave right away from the restaurant."

"Hmph. That sounds fishy. But okay. Are you seeing him again?"

"Yes. Just got a text. After church on Sunday."

"Huh. An afternoon date. Doesn't sound promising. So, no hanky-panky. I can see I'm going to need to be patient with the two of you. You're both so serious. But that's why I think you're good for each other. So, are you still interested after last night?"

I hesitated, feeling annoyed at Marilyn's nosiness. I was never one to share with girlfriends about my love life. "I don't want to encourage this adolescent need of yours to know everything about our personal business. But...yes, I like him. That will have to suffice for now, Mrs. Nosy! Just chill."

Marilyn made a frustrated grunt. "All right. Fine. Be that way. Just don't forget who it was who thought of you and introduced you when you finally realize what a catch this guy is. So, I've got to run, but I'm waiting for any updates. Later."

I hung up, shaking my head and chuckling at Marilyn's impatience. I fixed my usual breakfast of granola and toast and threw on some yoga pants and a t-shirt. I was looking forward to a day of just being in my new apartment and making it homier.

I spent the day arranging the study, emptying a few cartons of books into the bookshelves I had bought at the unfinished wood place. I had planned to stain them before filling them up with my books, but I hadn't found time. As I picked up each book, I enjoyed that feeling of connection I got from these familiar covers of the precious ones like the poetry books of Rumi's with intriguing covers of turbaned seers, or the pictures of banks of cattails framing water on the books by Annie Dillard. Each of these treasured books were like friends, containing pieces of my history. They could be traced back to important times when I had relied on them.

At the top of the next box, I found a thin cardboard box, taped carefully and marked "Pam". I opened it slowly and removed the framed piece from the bubble wrap. Inside the frame was a watercolor sketch that Pam had given me on my thirteenth birthday, when she was eleven, a year before she died. It was a sketch she had made of the two of us, copied from a photo. The photo, taped to the back of the frame, showed us with an arm around each other's shoulders, sitting on the top steps of our house on a sunny, summer day. We had done up our hair identically in twin ponytails caught up in blue ribbons, our faces open, happy, and grinning. Despite the ponytails and the grins, it was clear how different we were from each other. Pam with the straight cornsilk hair, clear blue eyes, and freckles covering her face. At that awkward age before her body had begun developing, her t-shirt hung straight, no evidence of the budding breasts.

In the photo, my curly dark blond hair was such a contrast with my bangs frizzing wildly on my forehead, my ponytail bursting out with stubborn wily strays. On my cheeks were two glaringly obvious pimples, but they weren't pictured in Pam's sketch. Hers showed us looking much more alike: ponytails, clear skin, and flat chests. But Pam had somehow captured both of our unique grins. Mine, sort of awkward and stand-offish, and Pam's wide and sincere.

I stared at the sketch, remembering what Pam had said when I opened it. "This is for you to see how much alike we are, even if you don't want to admit it." I smiled thinking of how much my sister wanted us to be alike when we were so obviously very different. I could see my somewhat stiff serious face; the older sister having moved away from the world of childhood leaving Pam feeling somewhat abandoned.

Seeing that silly, childish grin of Pam's, I thought of how she would relish the girlish imaginings that I was enjoying today after meeting someone new. I could just see the amused look on her face if she was here now and how she would make up some embarrassing way to tease me. I missed that possibility.

CHAPTER FOURTEEN

IRENE

My gaydar wasn't very good when it came to young gay men, but when I noticed a couple of young women who had started to attend a few times, I thought to myself that maybe they were it—the lesbian couple we were looking for.

When I accosted them at coffee hour, the dark haired, slender woman introduced herself as Justine and her friend as Abigail, petite, blond, and very feminine. Justine shared that she had been raised Episcopalian in a suburb in DC, in one of the more conservative parishes. Laughing, she said growing up in a white bread suburb where she was encouraged to "pray away the gay" didn't work with her. Looking uncomfortable with sharing any personal information, Abigail only mentioned that she had been raised in an evangelical church. Justine seemed to speak for both of them (while holding firmly to Abigail's hand) when she told me confidently that they were "together" and were looking for a church that could accept them as a couple. Abigail looked nervously around the room as Justine shared this, then dropped her hand, transferring her coffee cup to the other hand.

Justine seemed to relax a little when I said that I was one of a couple of lesbians in the congregation and I wanted them to find acceptance here at St. Philips as I had. I shared that the congregation had voted to be open and affirming some time ago. Justine replied that when they had learned that on St. Philip's website, they decided to attend. I introduced them to another young couple, Brad and Jennifer, who were refreshingly friendly.

When they returned the following Sunday, we had a longer conversation when Justine told me they were looking for a church where they could be embraced as a married couple and later as a family. They had been looking into international adoptions, but one of the hurdles was being legally married which was now possible with the recent Supreme Court decision. I told them that was something I hoped the St. Philips' congregation would support.

Abigail gave me with a shy glance and asked quietly whether St. Philips was supportive of gay marriage. I sighed and looked straight at her and spoke from my heart. "Abigail, I think this church wants to be supportive of all people's marriages."

"Really?" she asked, looking doubtful.

I wanted to be honest with them, but didn't want to scare them off. "I've told you that the congregation voted to be open and affirming?" They both nodded.

"However, the Vestry has also voted that same-sex marriage would not yet be allowed in our sanctuary." Abigail's face fell.

"But I have always been supported by the majority of this congregation. They've had my back over the years. I think the vote by the Vestry was not representative of the congregation as a whole. So, I'm hoping that once our new priest feels comfortable, we will launch a campaign to get that Vestry policy changed. I can tell you that our new priest is very anxious to make that happen."

Abigail looked unsure, but Justine's expression was hopeful when she asked, "So, when do you think that might happen?"

I thought for a minute, weighing the possibilities. "I think within the next six months. And I say that because Rev. Sarah is not going to wait around very long before she makes it an issue with the Vestry."

Justine smiled. "Good. Because we were thinking of planning a wedding in the spring. In May. And we'll need a priest and a church to hold it in." I smiled back.

"Good. I'm hoping we can be that church."

What I didn't tell them was that Sarah wanted to take it slow on the gay marriage issue, which I get. But now that I knew there are folks like Justine and Abigail who are interested in St. Philip's, the process needed to hurry up.

Very sweet and decidedly middle class, this couple was well-dressed and well-educated, just the kind of people this up-wardly mobile congregation would like. And they needed us. They wouldn't push any buttons with straight folks, like having butch haircuts or dressing non-binary or stuff like that. It's not that I mind that, in fact, I think it's great that young people can be them-selves in today's world, but that's not the kind of gay folks who are going to grab the hearts and minds of the typical church-going St. Philips congregant. These folks are very strait-laced. Literally. With Justine's pencil skirts and Abigail's demure heels, they fall into the category of "lipstick lesbians," and they are the ones we need. Let's just hope they're ready to be the poster children. I'm not sure with Abigail's extreme shyness whether she'll be up for it. But Justine, I can see her standing up and asking this church to support them in their marriage.

Over the next few weeks, as I got to know Justine and Abigail better, I noticed their tender interactions with each other. Justine's hand on Abigail's back as we stood for hymns. Abigail's shy face looking up at Justine for reassurance when they were talking with me. How they would grab each other's hands when they were walking back to the parking lot. It touched me that they were beginning to feel comfortable enough to show these signs of affection more openly. The small curl of hope within me was growing. We were building that community that I had only dreamed about.

But I needed to slow down. They hadn't even become members yet. One thing at a time.

When I mentioned Justine and Abigail to Sarah, she said she had noticed them attending. When she noted my expectant look, she reminded me that we had decided that we should go slow on moving the church along. Wait until the congregation trusted her before we asked for real change. I wonder though, when will that be?

Chapter Fifteen

SARAH

The soft hush of the church building when I arrived early Sunday before anyone else felt sacred, like entering a prayerful space. The only sound was my quiet shuffle echoing in the hallways and the soft snap as I turned on the lights, illuminating the dark gray walls with the heavy gold picture frames with scenes of Jesus walking in gardens and hills. The walls were brightened only by occasional bright spots of children's art hung in the classrooms. Everything about the quiet stillness of the church gave me some comfort, despite the gnawing anxiety I always felt before preaching.

The kitchen jumped to life when I flicked on the overhead fluorescent lights, a slight buzz slicing the stillness. I filled the electric teapot with water and got out a ceramic mug, placing my teabag over the edge.

While I was waiting for the water to boil, I stared out the kitchen window. Irene stuck her head in the door, saying hello. I gave her a questioning look as I greeted her.

"Irene, good morning! Why are you here so early?"

Irene explained that she was there to take another look at the ceiling in the sanctuary before she called someone for an estimate.

She shared that she had offered to take care of this task since she had always helped Rev. Tim figure these things out. I looked dubious as that was often the task of the junior warden.

"So, does that mean, you're consulting with Frank Trumbore about this since he's the one who should be taking this on?"

Irene laughed. "Well, let's just say Frank was happy to give it up."

"I would hope the vestry would appoint a committee to handle these matters and the Junior Warden could supervise it."

Irene chuckled and pointed at herself. "Yeah, the committee they appointed was me. No, no. Don't worry. I'm working on Jerry Wright, who has been a building manager and has just retired. I think he has a few ideas of a couple of other retired people who will help but just don't want to sit on a committee."

"Why do committees get such bad reps? I think sitting on a committee is a good way to serve the church. Don't people here like committees?"

Irene turned up one lip in a half-sneer. "Not so much. I think what happened was at one point, Rev. Tim took a seminar on church management, and they taught him all these formal structures that committees should follow. He was so disgusted with the whole thing that he suggested that we have one or two person teams instead who rallied the volunteers they needed when they needed them. Committees were a waste of time in Tim's estimation. I kind of agree with him. Committees that I've served on have just spent a lot of time arguing about something when one person could have made the decision and moved on."

I realized how much work I had in front of me to introduce the idea that doing church work could create community that was drummed into me in seminary.

"So, could I get you to consider the kinds of relationships that we could build on committees? You know, people getting to know each other in a deeper way than just the chit chat that we engage in at coffee hour?"

Irene sighed. "Hmm, maybe we could postpone this discussion for a time when we have something stronger to drink in front of us."

I acknowledged that with a nod. "Okay. Got it. So, what's up with that email you sent me about the Vestry meeting? You said that I should be careful as we move forward with the hiring process for the Christian Ed Director? What did you mean?"

Irene pursed her lips and lowered her voice.

"I just mean that Jeffrey is telling the Sunday school committee that Terry LeBlanc is eminently qualified and they don't even need to advertise the position to get other candidates."

"Oh, okay. I see what you mean. Don't worry. I will outline to the Vestry that we should try to attract qualified candidates through the diocese. I'll even get the job description posted on the diocese web site."

Irene looked amused. "You're assuming there is a job description."

"No, I already found out that needs to be done, and I've got the committee chair working on it. Okay? Don't worry, I'm on it!" I waved to Irene as she disappeared out the kitchen door.

The service that day seemed particularly moving to me, with Joanne, a woman with cancer whom I had spoken to briefly before the processional smiling to me from the front pew. Irene, near the back, chatting with other women her age. And Elaine, sitting next to Jeffrey, nodding to me as I moved past. As I was getting to know these people more, sitting up front on Sunday morning seemed more like being at a family table with all the relatives sitting around it. The family members weren't all glad to be there. Jeffrey seemed to be glaring up at me today. But the fact that they were there meant that we were a family, stuck together, like it or not, to learn how to be with one another. On a morning like this, I felt like I was finally a part of the family. Not the mother, of course. Not the wise aunt, yet. But the respected older sister, perhaps. The one who was expected to hold things together because the parents were too busy. An older sister who might be able to rally the troops around them.

When I was young, the whole church community had pulled around our family when we lost Pam. I sensed that St. Philips had that caring at its core, that loving community. Even right now, when people seemed a bit divided over the budget issues, they were still held together by caring for each other. Maybe it was not the budget that divided them but what was expected of each person and how those gifts were appreciated. Maybe that was at the root of the divisions. What did each have to bring to add to the soup and how would that soup be used to nourish all?

I had met with so many people who had shared stories of times in their lives when this community had come through for them. There was the widow whose husband had died of MS at age 55, dying a slow death, with his faculties gently slipping away. The widow had told me about people coming over and just sitting with him, reading to him, or helping her to move him. She had finally hired help. But during the transition, someone had created a schedule of helpers who showed up in the morning and evening to help her, bringing meals and washing dishes. She shared with me that after he died, she had felt some relief but had also felt so alone. Two of the other widows in the congregation had taken it upon themselves to show up for her. They knew what it was like to lose a spouse, even if they were older when it happened. They remembered waking up to a cold empty space in the bed next to them and learning to live with the painful silence during lonely meals of frozen Mexican dinners for one. They came and took her out for lunch, shopping, or just sitting with her.

I had learned that the last priest of St. Philips, Rev. Tim, had been that kind of caring presence and had fostered that kind of unusual community. But I also knew that communities take on their own character that seemed to last through the tenure of different kinds of priests. This community had not always had a rector who had that sense of building community. They had had their share of the pulpit pounders who saw their mission as hammering the gospel into people whether they liked it or not. Priests who wouldn't be caught dead sitting beside someone quietly in the hospital, keeping vigil. And yet, the members had cared for each other during these times. The stories still hung around about strong women and a few older men who did the pastoral care during the times when the rector didn't see it as his job.

Irene represented the strength of this church community, I mused, seeing her in the back pew, her head with her short white hair bent over the pew railing. I had known women like her in my own church growing up. I knew that ministry was not done by just priests. It was shared across a congregation. I only hoped that I could find the "ministers" in this one and rally their strength to elicit the mission of this congregation. Well, maybe mission was too fancy a word. Just to help find their direction, what they wanted to be in this world. I hoped I was up to the task. As I looked out over the congregation with this growing sense of belonging, I felt more confident about being the kind of priest that could help lead them.

After the service, I waded through the parish hall, greeting people and having quick conversations, and eventually found Terry waiting in my office. She had not been in church earlier. She seemed like she was a little antsy, looking around to see if I was alone.

"Hey there! Sorry that it took me a while to extricate myself from coffee hour. You know how it is," I said, closing the door. I sat down in the chair next to Terry's, wanting to avoid seeming officious.

Terry seemed to be in her late thirties, with a very short dark hair in a sleek cut, which tapered to a point in the back. She was slender and well dressed, with higher heels than I ever wore. She didn't seem like the "religious educator" type, which in my experience usually meant wearing jeans and cutesy sweaters. Or things that could be worn while wrestling kids and paints.

Terry looked nervous, her face frozen into a polite smile. nodding as I opened the conversation with chatter about the church and about getting used to the ways things were done at St. Philips. I was hoping to ease into Terry's candidacy for the Sunday school position. But when I asked Terry about how long she had been at the church, Terry held up her hand.

"Wait, before you go on, let me tell you why I'm here." She took a breath and frowned. "I'm here to confess, basically."

I felt my heart jump. "Oh. What do you mean?"

"Well, you've probably heard the rumors already."

I played dumb. "What rumors?"

Terry looked dubious. "Well, I've heard that people have already shared with you what I came to tell you. That Jeffrey Trainor and I, well, we... we're having an affair." Terry looked straight at me, raised eyebrows, seeming to want to shock me. I tried to look surprised.

"Oh, I see. Well...I don't know what to say." This was true. Her admission had stunned me, and I had no clue what to say next.

Terry's shoulders relaxed, relief filling her now that she had finally unburdened herself. She seemed like someone who was a bit lost, but who really wanted direction. She looked me in the eyes, not displaying any great burden in what she just shared. Her demeanor shocked me, not really caring that she was confessing adultery to a priest!

I tried to figure out where to go with the conversation. We never did any role playing in seminary about this scenario. I remembered one role play in which someone shared that they were thinking of having an affair, but not with the married Senior Warden.

"Um, so...why did you decide to come tell me?"

"I thought you should know. And honestly, I just want some help here."

"What kind of help?"

Terry sighed and shook her head. "Well, I don't know. I feel bad about this. I know it's wrong. I never wanted to hurt Jeffrey's wife. But we just fell into this somehow. I don't know what to do now." Terry put her hand over her eyes, like she felt guilt, but somehow when she looked up, it felt a little false, like she was acting.

I was silent for a few beats. What did they tell us in seminary about guiding people through moral quandaries? Something about helping them get in right relationship with God. But what about getting what they want? They didn't seem to mention that.

"So, Terry. Have you prayed about this? Do you have a prayer practice?"

Terry looked totally perplexed. She hadn't really thought about that, I guess. She looked down, then up at me, her eyes narrowed, like she was trying to psych out what I wanted.

"I mean, I know it's wrong. And I guess I should ask for forgiveness? But I don't know how to do that when I don't know if I'm ready to end it. Is it wrong to love someone?" she asked a bit defiantly.

"Terry, it's not wrong to love. But it's wrong to act on that love physically when you are hurting another person. Jeffrey is not free to love you."

Terry sighed, sounding disgusted, like I was scolding her like a child. "Yeah, I *know.*"

"So, what are you hoping will happen with you and Jeffrey?" I asked.

Terry thought for a few seconds. "Well...we're in love. I mean, it's complicated, but that's what's happened. We had been working on a plan for the Sunday school together. We didn't mean for this to happen, but it did. We just clicked. I feel terrible about Elaine and her kids, but sometimes these things can't be helped."

I nodded, considering her words. "I see. And what do you think Jeffrey should do about this?"

"I think he should tell Elaine and leave her. He's been saying he will. He just... well, he just..."

"He just what? Hasn't gotten around to it?"

Terry agreed sadly with a nod. I felt a slow anger rising. Not at Terry. But at Jeffrey. How he had manipulated the situation to suit himself. To get what he wanted. To have an affair and to keep his standing in the community. To keep his family, too. How could someone be so selfish and so misguided?

"Terry. Do you think he really intends to leave Elaine?"

Terry looked around in confusion. She finally sunk down with a breath, smoothing her hair down in the back. "I don't know. I mean, he seems sincere. He loves me. But... well, I guess he doesn't really know himself what to do."

"Yeah. I think you're right." I took a moment. "But if he really loves you, and if he sincerely wants to do what's best for everyone, do you think he should figure this out and finally tell Elaine?"

Terry looked at me but didn't respond. I felt so sad for her and for Elaine. And for the kids. And in some small way, sad for Jeffrey to be this stupid and selfish.

I tried again. "I wonder what you could do to make him decide and act?"

Terry thought for a minute, looking down at her lap. "I guess I could force him to act by cutting off the relationship until he made up his mind." She sighed and looked deflated like she was finally coming to terms with what was happening.

"Do you think he would respond to that?" I asked, lifting my eyebrows.

Terry nodded slowly, raising her head. "Yeah, I guess so."

"Do you have the courage to stop the affair? Because it's the right moral thing to do. And right for everyone involved in this."

Terry's face collapsed at the thought. "Yeah. Well, I guess."

"Terry, I think you should pray about this. Start with confessing and asking for forgiveness. Ask God to help you to get back in right relationship with others around you. Maybe you'll see this more clearly if you pray."

Terry looked lost. "I suppose. I don't really pray very much except in church."

"Would you like me to help you with what that might sound like?"

Terry nodded slightly, not really sure about whether she wanted to do this. And I certainly had never offered a prayer like this before. But here I was, trying to figure it out. I bowed my head as Terry bent hers. I fastened my eyes on her shoes as I searched for something that maybe she could accept.

"God of love, who loves us more than we can imagine. Terry is confused and hurting, Lord. She wants to do the right thing but she's not sure what that looks like. Stay with Terry, letting her know of your presence as she considers her choices and how they might hurt other people. Let her find a way to act morally and to ask for your forgiveness. May she begin to know your loving presence and how that love can be used to heal her. In the name of all that is holy, we say Amen." Terry whispered an "Amen," in a faint voice, looking uncomfortable.

We ended our session with Terry promising that she would talk to Jeff and get back to me after she did. I tried to reassure Terry that what she shared with me would be in confidence, and that I would simply wait to hear back from her. I suggested that Terry try prayer as a daily habit during this difficult time. She left composing her face for anyone she might meet going out.

I closed my door after her, checking the hallway for anyone waiting. Sinking into my chair, I sighed, exhausted. I felt a sense of disappointment in the role I was being thrust into. The role of Mother Confessor. It seemed that Terry expected me to be able to sort out all the moral quandaries of life and then just help her get what she wanted despite the obvious immorality. The expectations that people were beginning to place on my shoulders felt enormous, and misplaced. Certainly, they didn't expect someone like me to be able to play judge and jury and peacemaker for all their sins and troubles. Jesus Christ! (*Yes, I still swore to myself.*) What had I taken on? And why?

Feeling discouraged, I picked up my now tattered copy of the Gospel of Thomas, remembering a passage.

Jesus said, "*If you bring forth what is within you, what you bring forth will save you. If you do not bring forth what is within you, what you do not bring forth will destroy you.*"

I guessed that's what Terry was feeling, a sense of something inside her that would destroy her if she didn't share it. Would "bringing forth" this knowledge 'save her'? It might save me since I could now work toward resolving whatever Jeffrey was attempting to do to manipulate the Vestry to hire her. But what would it do to Terry? I had to be careful that I wouldn't use this knowledge just for my own means. I needed to remember that I was here to minister to her, not to be a powerful manipulator. I could leave that up to Jeffrey. Oh, hell! How could I possibly do what was right by either of them? I wondered if it was time I should be calling the bishop.

Chapter Sixteen

IRENE

Sunday, as I watched Rev. Sarah follow Terry into her office and close the door, I wondered what that was all about. I figured it must be confidential. But with Jeffrey insisting on Terry as the best candidate for the Christian Ed position, I'd sensed something fishy going on. I hoped Rev. Sarah was going to get to the bottom of it.

I had seen Justine and Abigail at service and was going to share with Rev. Sarah my hunch that this was the couple we'd been waiting to test the waters. I so hoped to bring the congregation into the more progressive era, wanting them to welcome everyone and approve same-sex marriage. Now that I had started imagining Justine and Abigail being accepted at St. Philips, showing the congregation that other gay couples were so similar to them, I had begun to see a different kind of life here for me as well.

I knew there were people in the congregation who were certainly on my side. Much of the congregation supported me when I needed them. But ever since Jeffrey joined the board, I could see the culture changing slightly. The Vestry being more hesitant to make any change. But especially when marriage equality was made legal by the Supreme Court just a year ago, and the states had to allow it, I had expected St. Philips to follow our liberal bishop and welcome marriage equality. But I think Jeffrey had been working on people behind my back. I felt it in that fateful meeting when they voted to not allow same-sex unions in the sanctuary. Their wording was vague so people might not figure it out right away. Something about "taking a cautious approach to following a popular trend in same-sex marriage" and "waiting until the spirit informs us of the Biblical direction we should invoke." Biblical direction, my foot! They were just stuck back in the last century with Jeffrey!

But lately, with Rev. Sarah in the pulpit, I began to feel hope. Despite her youth, and maybe even because of her youthful optimism, I thought that I now had an ally. I could start to move forward with my strategy with this picture-perfect lesbian couple.

When I went into the parish hall, Justine and Abigail were talking to another younger couple. I waited until that conversation seemed to peter out when I walked up and greeted them, getting a warm response from them both. We exchanged small talk about the weather before Justine glanced at Abigail, who nodded slightly.

"So, we've been wondering. Irene, do you think this thing about the Vestry not being ready for marriage equality will change, and soon?"

This is what I'd hoped they'd ask. "Yes, and if you two decide to stay with us. I hope you'll be our first celebration of that." I raised my eyebrows hoping for agreement.

Justine looked at Abigail. Abigail was not smiling, looking a bit tentative. Justine hurried to say, "We just don't know yet. You know, we have to be sure that we'd be welcome."

Touching Abigail's sleeve, I responded, "I get it. It's not something you can be sure about until you feel it with your own hearts. So, I'm here to help you feel comfortable, but I won't push you."

Abigail gave me a small smile. "Thanks, Irene. That would really be helpful. I'm not a risk taker like Justine. She is very patient with me. I hope you will be as well."

"Of course," I said with a nod. "I have waited thirty years for this. I'm not going anywhere. But when you are ready, will you make an appointment with Rev. Sarah about moving forward?"

Justine took Abigail's hand and told me that they would and probably soon.

Just then a new young couple came over with an infant, maybe six months old, and introduced themselves. Abigail immediately began cooing to the baby in one of those high, sing-songy voices. The baby's face lit up with the attention, her bright blue eyes following Abigail's chatter, her smile enchanted. When Abigail asked if she could hold the baby, the mother passed her over gratefully. As I watched Abigail, her face bright with joy, my heart warmed to her. She was so obviously ready to be a mother.

Lately, I'd begun to feel something growing in me as well. Some kind of feeling of wanting more family. I only have my brother Brad left, and he lives in Portland with his wife, Alice, and his college-aged son, Tim, whom I don't know well. Too far away to be close. Over the years when I've talked to Brad on the phone at Christmas and his birthday, I heard all about Tim, the soccer trophies, and the broken bones that kept them running to the ER. He almost always says offhandedly that he wants me to visit soon. But I've only seen Tim a few times, once when I took my mother out there just after his birth, and a few times since when I've visited. But lately when I've gently suggested a visit, Brad has come up with excuses why they're busy with visiting Tim at college or travelling with business.

"Not fun travel. Detroit and Chicago. Just conference rooms and hotel meals. Ugh. No fun."

When I asked when they might visit me in Philadelphia, Brad was quiet, then said that maybe someday when Tim was out of college and they had more discretionary income.

I'm the age my mother was when she became a grandmother. She certainly wanted me to have children despite the fact that she accepted me as I was. She knew I could only be who I wanted to be, the "straight lesbian" she called me. She called me that because she said I dressed so nicely that no one would ever guess I was a lesbian. I guess she thought all lesbians looked a certain way. She always told me that she was so proud of me just the way I was. She did ask once if I thought I would ever find a partner or have children. I had shared with her my relationship struggles, never finding someone who felt comfortable with being out and being whole with their sexual identity. I dated a couple of women who became significant in my life. And I always longed for these relationships to end up in a long-term partnership, but it never happened for me.

One day while I was visiting Mom in the hospital, she got quiet, reached for my hand and said, her voice strained, "Irene, you have made my life worthwhile. I love Brad and his family, of course. But, in a way, you have been my life partner. We've been through so much together. I don't want you to think that you have disappointed me in any way. You've only deepened my respect for you by living your life without pretense. I mean...you have made my life richer." I held her hand as her eyes closed and she was quiet. A few hours later, she left me.

Being so close to my mom meant that losing her was hard. I found myself shutting down for a time after that. Not wanting to go to church because then I'd have to explain to people that I was feeling lousy and lonely. But then two good friends from church demanded that I go out with them one night, and they goaded me into sharing. I don't share easily, but that night after dinner at our favorite Thai place, they suggested that we take a walk. When we sat down on the bench where I had often gone with my mom on walks, I finally told them what I missed the most. Soon after, I returned to the church community, knowing that I could find the support I needed there.

One evening before a church meeting about hospitality, Sarah and I had dinner at a local Italian place. She wanted to know some good but cheap places near church where we could grab dinner before a Vestry meeting, so I suggested Sal's. The Friday night special was a glass of wine, salad and lasagna for under twenty bucks. Couldn't beat that in Philadelphia. We shared a bottle of their family label Chardonnay and on her second glass, Sarah had asked me whether I had ever been in a committed relationship. Sarah was a good listener and I found myself opening up.

"I was in a fairly committed relationship in my twenties. But my girlfriend ended up getting mixed up in drugs and the peacenik community. It just wasn't me. It was quite a relief to let go of that strange and well...limiting friendship. In my thirties, I was so hopeful when I started dating another woman, Leslie. She was mature and warm and so smart. My mother liked her and would talk about her as my 'friend'. But Leslie had never come out to her parents."

Sarah looked puzzled. "Why in this day and age wouldn't someone come out?"

"Well, that was in the nineties. She worked in a non-profit that was founded by the Lutherans, who even today aren't very accepting. So, she really couldn't come out at work. Which meant that wherever she went, I was not invited along. I got tired of asking her to claim herself and along with it, to claim me."

"That must have been hard."

"Yeah. But she had grown up in a religious home, and she thought she would lose her parents if she came out. She finally chose them over me when I forced the issue. I wasn't willing to be her silent partner."

I picked up my glass and drained it, not really wanting to re-hash the pain that resulted from that break-up. Sarah finished up her last bite of pasta, looking thoughtful. Tilting her head, she asked, "So, Irene, who are your people?"

"My people? You mean, who I hang out with? I have a small circle of women friends, none of them lesbian. One is married and one is single, but we still consider each other family. But on holidays, they are usually with their real families and I'm alone. Oh, they have tried to invite me to join their holiday festivities, but there's nothing fun about tagging along in someone else's family holiday."

"What do you do on holidays then?"

Feeling like she was about to try to rescue me, I tried to reassure her. "I've always figured it out, don't worry."

Sarah nodded, but I could see her making a mental note. She was the type of person who tried to fix things. I knew that tendency, but I also knew how dangerous it could be.

Chapter Seventeen

SARAH

After I watched Terry leave, I remembered that I was supposed to meet Edwardo for lunch. I felt this low-level excitement in the pit of my stomach. My imagination was beginning to play with scenarios about the kind of relationship that might be possible with him. But right now, with the knowledge that Terry had shared, I felt a generalized anxiety, my heart beating fast. Why, I wondered? Why was hearing about this mess from Terry affecting my feeling about my new relationship with Edwardo? They weren't similar at all. But my experience of falling in love was so limited that I was generally nervous about the prospect.

I had been in love once in college. It had been one of those heady romances when you feel like there couldn't be an end to the dizzying, addictive rush of desire and connection. Josh had been a philosophy major and we had walked the campus and sat in pubs over warm beers in endless discussions about parallel universes and the essence of one's being. Everything had seemed possible. But when we came back to campus after a summer apart, I noticed his hesitation right away, in the tentative way he held me our first night back together. My fantasies over the summer had been about this great true love, and then when we were back together, it felt like the emotional intensity had been turned off. Like he didn't remember our connection, or I had imagined it. I remember the shock at my misreading of the relationship when I discovered he was so lukewarm. He mentioned something about his having ideas about transferring to a different campus. Even hearing him voice that seemed to be a distancing signal. I kept thinking that the other shoe would drop and he'd be gone. I began to distance myself and saw him mirroring that. My heart wasn't exactly broken, but it was bruised. When I finally told him that I thought I needed time to sort things out, he had seemed relieved and agreed. We'd see each other on campus and wave from a distance.

I hadn't allowed myself to fall hard like that since then. Dating off and on, I was always wary, keeping myself at a kind of emotional distance. Eventually it occurred to me that I wasn't sure I wanted to give myself up—to trust my strongest feelings to another person.

But with Edwardo, I felt those stirrings of wanting; I couldn't help it. I had found myself looking at Edwardo's lips during dinner and feeling the possibility of a kiss. Wanting to feel the weight of a man's body enveloping me. But it was more than just a physical ache. I wanted to have the kind of intimacy where you can tell that person anything and they'll see it a gift, an opening. I had been imagining that since our first date. My yearning for this kind of intimacy was surprising, since it hadn't happened in, well, ever, really.

I shook off these feelings and gathered my things, texting Edwardo that I was on my way. A smiley face followed with a photo of a grassy site and a basket sitting on a plaid blanket.

Following the trail down to the area he had described near the pond, I saw him lounging near a park bench on the blanket I recognized from his picture. I smiled at the romantic setting he had created. Marilyn would make fun of this; I could just hear her:

"Latin lover lays a romantic trap for unsuspecting woman." I found myself chuckling at that. But I could also feel a bit of nervous tension in my chest.

I waved as Edwardo looked my way, raising his hand in greeting. I hurried over, and with an excited sigh, dropped my purse next to the blanket, slipping off my shoes and sinking down, folding my legs under me. Edwardo moved over to make room next to the picnic he had laid out. He smiled and looked relieved, seeing my delight at the feast.

"Oh, my God. This looks great. What did I do to deserve all this?" I asked, beaming.

"It's the least I can do for the lady whom I abandoned in a restaurant."

"Oh. Well, I hope I'll get left again to get this kind of treatment!" Beside the wine bottle, there was a plate of cheese, a blue cheese and some kind of Brie, a loaf of French bread, and a knife. Grapes spilled out of an open bag. Some kind of cookies. It felt like not just an apology, but something more. A hopeful gesture toward building a relationship, maybe? I cautioned myself not to read too much into it.

"Well, I hope I don't ever have to do that again. But you never know." Edwardo pulled out a plastic cup and poured me a half glass of wine, then poured one for himself. "I hope you're okay with drinking wine in mid-day."

"After I preach on Sunday afternoons, it's almost a prerequisite. Whew! What a day. I'm so glad to be here in this idyllic spot, drinking wine and relaxing. I needed this."

"Good, I'm glad this will help. Relax, and tell me about your day. If you want to, that is." He seemed eager to please, but his tone was a bit tentative.

I frowned. "Well, most of it, I can't share. That's the problem about my job. I have to keep almost everything I know confidential. I'm sorry. Does that sound like I'm being difficult?"

Edwardo shook his head. "No, of course not. I totally understand that people don't want their secrets shared. I'm glad you take that seriously. I respect your needing to be careful about people's situations. I also have to respect my client's privacy. But...maybe, you could just share how you feel about your day, not what was confidential? Would that make sense?"

I felt relieved. I wasn't sure how he was going to respond to my reluctance.

"Oh, that makes perfect sense. Let's see...well, I am frustrated by a person who has made some bad choices. And I think I'm kind of pissed at another person who has taken advantage of a situation to get what he wanted. It's not a pleasant story, and I guess I'm a little confused about how I feel about it."

Edwardo nodded thoughtfully. "And why are you confused?"

I paused. "Um. Huh. I guess I'm feeling judgmental about some of these people's actions. And I hate being judgmental. Because I so often am."

Edwardo smiled. "I think the fact that you recognize that you're judgmental is unusual. And shows that you're not taking it lightly."

"True, but my experience tells me that maybe I'm painting myself the way I want to be seen. I mean, don't we all do that sometimes?"

"Of course, we do. But it takes an awareness to even recognize that when we see someone in a certain light, either bad or good, we are making a subjective judgment. That it's not black and white. I like that you're not a black and white thinker."

I nodded, holding onto this thought. That he seemed to value complex judgment meant a great deal to me, because that was just what I had started to notice in him. A pattern of thoughtfulness that didn't just take things on face value.

We spent the afternoon discussing churches and the kind of crazy things that happen in them. Edwardo had grown up Catholic. His family had been very involved in their local parish in their small town near Mexico City. Their priest, Father Michael, had been pretty autocratic and distant. Edwardo had not had any kind of relationship with him, but his mother had sometimes gone to his office for counseling. Or what he called, "prayers and pastoring". After Edwardo had gone away to school, it had been discovered that the priest had been having an affair with one of the young mothers in the parish. His mother had been horrified. She felt so betrayed. But she had stayed faithful to the church.

We talked about the role of ministry, and I shared that I often felt conflicted about it. The priesthood was supposed to be a position of trust and influence. A person who was elevated to a higher standard and expected to have wisdom. I felt this was unfair and unrealistic for people to expect this of anyone. I was working on how I could keep expectations low by being an ordinary person, not a person who raised themselves above others.

"How do you do that?" Edwardo asked.

"I don't know yet. Check back with me later."

"Maybe by just being yourself?"

I smiled and nodded, "Yes, that's absolutely the best way to do that. And I hope people will see me for who I am."

"And who are you?" Edwardo looked pensive as though he truly wanted to know.

I sighed. "That's a harder question. I hope...I hope that I'm a caring person who does the best she can but still makes lots of mistakes and is open about that. Hopefully someone who's open to change, ready to accept different opinions, and someone who knows when to take a stand and when to compromise."

"Wow! If you are all that, you'd be a very good priest. And a very good person at that."

"Yeah, that's probably just who I'd *like* to be. I'm not sure that anyone can truly be honest about every facet of themselves. Can you?"

Edwardo tilted his head thinking. "Yes, I think you're right, that would be a tall order. Maybe honesty is something that grows in a relationship. Maybe we start by revealing some of ourselves, and then slowly, I don't know, maybe more and more? As we become friends?" Edwardo looked a little embarrassed. "I mean, I'd like to be in close friendship with you." He looked at me with a question in his eyes.

Is he trying to say he only wants to be friends? "Close friendship? I like...close friends. Is that what you would like this...relationship ...to be, a friendship?" I tried to keep the disappointment out of my voice.

"Oh! I see what you mean. Should we be just friends or compadres? Edwardo smiled and leaned forward. Stopping a few inches from my face, he looked into my eyes, hopefully. With my heart beating wildly, I closed the distance. It was a small kiss at first, the barest touching of lips. Then Edwardo came back in for a lingering, searing kiss, his hands touching my hair gently. It was everything I had imagined. It was more than I had imagined.

When we finally took a breath, I pulled back a little to look in his eyes. Then, grinning, I said, "I guess that's a no. Unless you kiss all your compadres like that."

***

Driving into the parking lot of my favorite woodsy park a few miles from my house later that week, I felt my anxiety releasing like blowing out a long- held breath. The Lakeview Park path leading into deeper forest beckoned me in.

I had gone into the office that morning, stared at my computer screen and tried concentrating on the biblical interpretation of the weekly scripture. After scribbling a few half-legible sentences and fielding some calls about the Saturday tea, I decided I needed the afternoon off to untangle some knots forming in my mind. I had been coming to this park often. I loved the dense, tall trees surrounding winding trails and the hidden lake peeking out through the lacy green.

Pushing my hands into the pockets of my jacket, I started down the trail as a small breeze gave a slight chill to the mostly warm day. I nodded to the older man with his basset hound coming out of the park. As I neared the lake, a young man in a concert t-shirt and cut-off jeans lounged in a beach fold up chair while his fishing pole sat propped in the calm water. He looked up and raised a hand when I greeted him with a quiet, "Afternoon."

I loved being here alone, although once I'd invited Marilyn to join me. But while I saw myself as an extrovert, loving to interact with people, I had begun to understand just how much I needed alone time, too. Especially at a time like this when I was doubting myself. I needed space to mull over all the conflicting thoughts crashing around in my head like warring enemies.

First my mind drifted over the sweet thoughts of the last few weeks with Edwardo. Every time he called just hearing his voice gave me an excited jolt in my stomach. Walking in the crisp fall air, I sort of wished I had invited him to join me. But being alone was better, especially after last night's Vestry meeting.

As I walked, the voices in my head started up again, arguing this way and that. I heard Jeff's strident voice calling out that the church needed to address the requirement for a Christian Education Director now rather than later. He said the kids were being neglected and the lack of volunteers was stressing out both the teachers and the students. I heard Irene's calm but strong voice addressing the need for a structured process with a job description, a committee who represented both the parents and the other members, an outreach for candidates, and a formal interviewing process. Then I heard the loud, angry voice of an older member who had attended the vestry meeting as an observer calling out the unnecessary expense of hiring someone when volunteers had always done a "perfectly good job" of teaching Sunday school. Then I heard my own voice, trying to remain a neutral mediator asking the Vestry to appoint a committee to come up with a formal proposal for them to consider. Luckily, this time they listened, and a parent had been named to begin the task.

When I brought up the idea of backing the food co-op, Jeffrey shut me down almost immediately. It was a "budget" question he said, and would need to be brought to the Finance Committee first before the board considered it. I felt completely pushed out of my role as spiritual leader of the church with him using procedure to squash the conversation but realized that I had to get support among the members of the church before I brought something this new to the Vestry. It was political, I realized, just like everything else.

Shaking my head, I reminded myself just to breath. *Breath in, breath out. Just be here*, I reminded myself.

After walking and attempting to focus on my breathing for a while, realizing that with all the chaos churning in my mind, I needed something more restful to focus on. I stopped at the overlook to the lake sinking down gratefully on a wooden park bench. Two turtles poked their knobby heads out of the water and scrambled onto a floating branch. I felt the gentle warmth of the sun sitting in the clearing. I imagined myself as a turtle basking in this peace with no expectations, no responsibility.

The disagreement didn't really bother me. It was the lack of respect that Jeffrey had shown for me and Irene, denigrating our ideas of a formal hiring process in front of the Vestry. His sneering tone about the way "formality" would bite them in the rear by postponing the real needs of the church. He knew he was exploiting the traditional informal ways that the church had done things to get his choice railroaded through the hiring process. He was out to get his way, no matter the cost to the church or to me.

I thought of his comment to me after the meeting when we were leaving. I had looked him in the eye, wanting to challenge him, but also knowing that I had to maintain the relationship. His face was tense as he held up a hand stopping me. "You haven't had that much experience, Sarah. You really need to let the Vestry do this their way."

I had felt my anger rising like a hot fire—and I immediately wanted to throw in his face the question of his ability to be objective and bring up the accusations about his relationship with Terry. But my calmer self prevailed and with a cool tone I responded that I had been hired to lead the church, and I was doing that the best way I knew how. He had responded with bitter condescension, "I'm sure you are."

I breathed in the fresh air, the rays of the sun beating down on my head, the leafy fermented smell of the underbrush of the forest filling me. The heady aroma was like a healing potion of nurturing medicine. Nature's medicine, I thought. My breath filled my chest and my belly. A light filled me. A lightness of body and a shower of well-being. This was truly what God was, I thought. God was with me in every atom of sun and breath and light. Not as a powerful being telling me what to do. But as the very pulse of life within me and in this place. In everything. Everywhere. If I could just bring this peaceful moment with me back into the church, I would be okay.

CHAPTER EIGHTEEN

SARAH

NOVEMBER, 2016

I was immersed in writing a newsletter article the next day, when Mary came in to ask a question. She had a young woman on the line who wanted to meet with me. When she said her was name Justine, I remembered the two young women who had been attending service regularly. Irene had mentioned they might be looking for more.

I picked up the phone, greeting Justine and telling her I remembered her and her partner, Abigail, from having met them in the receiving line. Justine seemed relieved that I remembered who they were.

"Rev. Piper, we have been wanting to come in and speak with you. I wondered when a convenient time would be to do that?"

"Justine, I'd be happy to talk with you and Abigail after church or another time if that's better. Can you tell me what you wanted to discuss?"

There was a slight pause, and Justine cleared her throat. "Well, we've spoken with Irene Hall. And she gave us the impression that it's possible the congregation might be ready to consider sanctioning a same-sex wedding in the sanctuary. But we wanted to talk with you about it first."

So here it was. The time was upon us. I wondered if Irene had been pushing this young couple or if they were truly ready for this.

"I couldn't tell you whether they are ready or not. But I certainly would like to discuss it with you. Let's set up a time when we can do that."

I made an appointment with for them to come in during the week when we'd have a quiet time to get to know one another and discuss their possible marriage. I told her that I couldn't promise anything but that it was my hope that we could move forward with this within a few months.

When we met a week later, I noticed that Justine did most of the talking while Abigail typically hung back, listening quietly. They described their hopes for being a part of a community where they could be embraced as a couple.

Justine asked hesitantly, "Rev. Piper, do you think that this church is ready to let us be a part of this community?"

I responded that most of the people in the congregation were open to having a gay couple among them and would welcome them to be who they were.

"But... I don't really know yet. I'm relatively new here and I don't know the congregation that well yet. We have a couple of lesbians, but older women who are not partnered. They are certainly comfortable being a part of the community and have many friends. They play leadership roles. But they haven't tested the waters like you would. They haven't sat with a partner in a pew holding hands. I'd be honored to marry you. But I know Irene has shared that our Vestry has not yet approved same-sex marriage within our sanctuary. So, I would have to work with them to get approval. I'm ready to do that if you are ready to stand up with me and ask for them to change their policy. Or... I would, of course, marry you somewhere..."

Justine finished my sentence. "Marry us somewhere else, right?'

I frowned in frustration. "Yes, I'm afraid that's right. But I would work with you either way to create a wedding that feels true and honest and not like you're hiding something. But I would really love it, if you were brave enough to help this congregation come into a real place of being affirming."

"Well, we want to find a community who welcomes us. The times we've come here, people were very friendly. We've talked with Irene. She's encouraged us to stay. But...I don't know, maybe she has her own reasons. She wants this church to be more diverse, I guess."

"Yes, she does, I'm sure," I agreed. "And she would do everything to make sure that happened. She will go to bat for you. So will I. It's just a question of whether you want to take that kind of risk. I mean, there are other churches in town who will welcome you with open arms and where the priest would be happy to marry you. I can give you their names. There's one downtown, St. Anne's. I know the priest."

Justine responded quickly, "Well, yes, we know that. But we live near here. And that's what we want. A community near us where we can be fully who we are. Where we can get involved and find community. We hope to have kids some day and want a place to bring them where they will be comfortable."

I felt hopeful. Maybe they were the right couple. We ended the conversation agreeing to discuss it more when they had become members.

***

I was sitting with Mary going over the bulletin announcements some weeks later, when I glanced down and saw a text show up on my phone. Edwardo. He had asked me to come over to his apartment that night, promising to cook. I smiled and texted back that I'd be there with a bottle of his favorite Pinot Grigio. We had seen each other a few times in those early weeks, but now it was becoming more regular. Friday nights. Saturday afternoons. A weeknight here and there. It felt so easy. We always had something to talk about. The conversation went from sharing about our jobs to political analysis to stories about our childhoods. I loved this the most. Sharing my growing up years, and hearing all about Edwardo's big noisy extended family in Mexico. I had not found anything about being with him that annoyed me or sent up any red flags that would usually happen when I started dating someone.

Usually, I would notice right away when someone didn't appreciate the kinds of things that I did. Like they would be bored hearing about my family. Or they talked too much about their career. So many annoying habits that I'd tried to overlook. If I discovered they were a smoker, a second date was out of the question. Drank too much? That was the end of that! Talked endlessly about sports—done! I sometimes thought that I was way too picky. My mother totally agreed with that.

"You can't find someone perfect! No one's perfect! Just find someone that you like to be with, that you share some values with. Relationships are hard because people expect to find someone perfect. That doesn't exist!" My mother would argue on and on with her supposed enlightened view of men. I realized though, that if I brought someone home who wasn't liberal enough or intellectual enough, she would cock her head at me and say, "Sarah. You know this relationship just isn't going to last."

But while Edwardo wasn't perfect, the relationship was easy. I always liked being with him. I loved the way he listened to me talk about the difficulties with the job, sharing similar stories with his job. I loved the relaxed, intimate times we shared in bed.

The first time had been at Edwardo's apartment when he had invited me over to make pizza. He had bought the raw dough and the toppings at a neighborhood market. I laughed hysterically as he tried throwing the pizza dough up in the air, only to have it land on his face. We were just being silly and fun. But before I had come over that evening, I had anticipated that this might be the night. I had taken time as I dressed, selecting my nicest lacy underwear.

As we ate together, I leaned over to wipe some sauce from his cheek, and he grabbed my hand, and kissed it. Later, as Edwardo washed the dishes and I was drying them, he turned off the water, took the towel from me, drying his hands, then pulled me towards him, leaning against the counter for a long deep kiss. The kissing went on for some time, when Edwardo stopped and with his eyes suggested a move toward the bedroom. My heart was beating so fast, but I knew this is what I had wanted for so long. It just felt right. I grabbed his hand and led him into the bedroom.

It seemed so natural to share a passionate evening together, then to fall asleep wrapped in his arms. Waking up, seeing his sleeping face on the pillow next to me was for me almost the most cherished part.

When I finally told my parents about Edwardo, my mother was so excited and wanted me to bring him home the next weekend. But I put it off. I just wanted to make sure of my feelings before I subjected Edwardo to my parents' scrutiny. They wouldn't be happy about his choice of profession because they wanted a partner for me who would "provide" well for me. But I knew they would accept him once they met him. How could they help it?

That night, after picking up the wine from the small wineshop near me, I arrived at Edwardo's, anxious to see him. It had been a few days, and I had found myself storing up all the issues swirling through my head I wanted to talk over with him. When I explained something complex and worrisome to him, pulling apart the issue and examining it from one side and then turning it around and looking at it from the other, he would just listen quietly, then ask an appropriate question or two, and suddenly the problem was clearer. His questions, his simple comments, not telling me what to think but simply reflecting what he heard me say, made things seem obvious. It almost seemed magical. He got me. He respected what I was trying to do but understood the complexity of the issues.

After dinner, we relaxed in his small living room with its bright red and blue accents of Latin American bowls and small papier mâché figurines scattered among the bookshelves, listening to some Cuban jazz. We both loved the resonant sounds of the Buena Vista Social Club. We were sitting on his sofa listening to music, my feet in his lap as he was giving me the most luscious massage, kneading away my tension. I was practically drifting off when I noticed the look on his face. Pensive like he was struggling with something. Looking down at the floor, then up at me, starting to say something, then stopping

"What is it?" I asked, suddenly starting to get a little nervous.

Edwardo sighed. "I haven't told you everything about my past," he started, hesitantly.

I was genuinely puzzled. "You mean your 'checkered past'?"

"What? What does 'checkered past' mean?" he asked, looking confused. I sometimes used euphemisms he didn't know.

"Oh, it's a phrase for someone who had caused some *trouble* in their past life," I replied.

"Oh, you mean like a 'troubled past'?"

"Well, yes, but even darker than that. Like maybe you were a bank robber or something?" I joked.

He grinned. "No, I don't mean something I've done that's bad or wrong. But just more about what brought me where I am and who I am."

"Well, I'd love to know about that."

Edwardo started to explain about how his family and another family had always been close, their fathers in business together. How he had been close friends to the daughter in the family, Luisa, and that transitioned to dating in high school. How their parents had always expected them to marry. Edwardo started to stammer, looking nervous. I sat up straight, tucking my legs under me as I studied him. Something was off.

"So...why didn't you? Are you trying to tell me you're divorced?" I couldn't help the worry leaking into my voice.

"Well, not exactly."

"What then?"

"Well, we still have a friendship. But it's not as it was. I mean, we're no longer together as lovers. We barely speak. But there are still some strong ties there."

I frowned. "What kind of ties, Edwardo?"

"Well, I haven't spoken to her in six months. Haven't seen her in three years. So, it's not close. And it won't get in the way of how I feel about you. But I just thought you should know that it's kind of complicated."

I could see that he was concerned, but he was just talking about a past girlfriend. But nothing to worry about, I thought. I leaned close and looked him in the eye. "You know, Edwardo. Our relationship is still new. So, I'm not overly concerned with your past. At least not yet."

Edwardo still looked tense, but he stopped trying to explain. He leaned in and kissed me.

"Sarah, I just want you to know everything about me. So, I really need to tell you this."

I appreciated his wanting to be honest, but who didn't have a serious relationship in their past that ended badly? I wanted him to tell me more, but I also didn't want him to worry and overthink things. Overthinking things always got me into trouble.

"There's time," I said softly. "Really." I stroked his worried face and began kissing him again. Soon, there wasn't anything more to talk about.

Chapter Nineteen

IRENE

On Mondays, I volunteered with a homeless shelter to organize their clothing room, going through donations that had been dropped off, getting them washed, folded and sorted into categories. Most Mondays, my good friend, Shelley, joined me and we spent the time we weren't doing laundry catching up with each other. We relished this time together since she lived outside the city and couldn't get in very often. She had been a fellow teacher in the high school that I had eventually left when I had been outed. Shelley had been the organizer of the group of teachers and parents who went to the administration to ask for my reinstatement. I owed her so much but she would never let me tell her that. We remained good friends even through my eventual departure to go to the community college to teach.

While I was sorting through various sweatshirts and men's shirts, I saw Shelley examining what looked like a small white evening bag, looking into its pockets. "Find anything good?"

She looked up. "Um, there's a photo in here," she said, holding it up. I moved over to get a look. The photo showed a young woman dressed in a white evening gown with a blue sash, her hair swept up on top, carrying what looked like the clutch Shelley held.

I squinted to see it better, "She looks young. Maybe this is her prom? Oh, is that a flower corsage around her wrist?"

Shelley looked closer. "Ah, yes, I think you're right. Her prom. What a special time that is for a young woman," she said sighing. "I remember my Senior Prom. I had a date with a guy I didn't really like, but I wanted to go to the prom, so I went with him. Had a miserable time. But still remember that dress."

She looked wistful. "What did it look like?" I asked moving back to my folding.

"It was beautiful. Light green with a pink flower on a trailing vine. A green velvet sash. Oh, I felt so grown-up. But all wasted on this nerdy guy who couldn't figure out how to move his two clumsy feet without stepping all over my little black heels. My first heels, I think." She put the photo in a box where we kept personal items in case people came back for them. Then she threw the bag into the box for purses.

Looking thoughtful, she looked over at me. "What about you? Did you have to suffer dances with nerdy guys?"

Thinking about that painful time, I winced. "No. Once a guy asked me to a dance, but I just said no, I was busy. Later, I heard from a friend that he had told his friends that I was queer and that's why I didn't go with him. At the time, that really hurt. But he had just figured it out."

Shelley looked at me more closely. "So, did anyone ever call you something nasty to your face?"

"Not until I came out. In college a couple of guys walked by me when I was with my roommate, who wasn't lesbian. After they walked by, they whispered loudly, 'They're lesbos!' looking back at us. I shouted back, 'I am, but she isn't, so leave us alone!' My poor roommate was humiliated. I noticed she kind of avoided going out with me after that. Which was okay since we weren't really friends."

"So, you were pretty open about it in college?"

"Yeah, pretty much. There were just a few out lesbians and I didn't really fit in with them. But I still had other friends who didn't have a problem with who I was."

I thought of how I have been able to be myself for most of my life. Not having to hide. "I guess it's sad that so many can't live the life they imagine for themselves," I said wistfully. "I'm lucky. As you know, I've been out and proud for most of my life," I said, "I have no regrets."

Shelley narrowed her eyes. "Really? No regrets?"

I realized what she was referring to. My lack of a partner in life. My not having a family to call my own. "Well, I have some regrets. But doesn't everyone?"

Shelley nodded, but then looked at me thoughtfully. "But this lesbian couple at church you've mentioned? They seem to mean a lot to you. Maybe more than just a way to change church policy? Maybe?"

Was I more interested in Justine and Abigail than just as a "test couple" to push the church into accepting marriage equality? I guess that was true, but I hadn't really considered why. "Hmm, I don't know. I guess they do remind me of what I never had. A steady partner, someone with whom I might want to have a family."

"Is that what you hoped for with Leslie?"

Shelley remembered the failed relationship that I had hoped would become more. "Well, yeah. But she wasn't ready to commit or be out. So, I knew it would never work. But yeah, I kind of secretly hoped that we could have a family." I thought of those days, the wistful longings, the furtive sex, and the resentment of someone who wasn't willing to put it on the line for me. Or for herself.

Shelley folded some t-shirts into a stack, putting them on a shelf. "I wish you had had that, too," she said, looking back at me. "You deserved it. I mean, I remember how in love you were, and Leslie was great, except for her need for secrecy, of course." She picked up some more shirts, checking them for cleanliness or rips. "But what is it about *this* particular couple that has become so significant for you?"

"I guess since they're really sweet. Rather conservative in their style. Not like so many gay people these days who seem to need to flaunt it. You know I accept them all, but this couple is quiet and polite. Not going to storm the citadels to get what they want. I think they will fit in with the St. Philips crowd. And...I just like them." I picked up a basket to take it into the laundry room. "I'll be right back."

I carried the basket of the clothes that needed washing through the halls and down into the basement. Thinking again of Leslie, I wondered where she was now. She and her mother had moved away soon after we broke up. I think she was afraid I would somehow out her just by how I acted when we broke up. Calling her late at night. Showing up at the doorway to tell her that she needed to come out. She had shushed me and closed the door firmly in my face. That was the last time I saw her. A month later, I heard from a friend that she had quit her job and moved herself and her mother to St. Louis where her brother lived. Pushing me away was a way to silence her fear of the world seeing who she really was.

I thought of Abigail, who was also fearful. But with Justine's support, she seemed ready to move into the church as full members, asking Rev. Sarah to officiate their marriage. She had been through the painful process of losing her family when she came out, thanks to their evangelical righteousness. But that hadn't deterred her to pursue her dream of marriage and family with Justine. Maybe it was easier because the world had become more accepting, allowing her to see that they were not the problem; the people who didn't accept them were. Leslie had continued to feel that guilt that had been drummed into her by the church and her family. Perhaps I'd pushed her too far before she was ready. Was she ever going to be ready? Probably not.

At this age, I had mostly stopped thinking about a possible partner. I felt the closeness of my friend Shelley and a couple of other women friends who were always there for me. What I missed was the idea of progeny, some person who would carry my memory on. That certainly wasn't going to be my nephew who barely knew me. I had been to many funerals at this point in my life and I had always noticed who got up to share stories about the deceased. If the ones sharing were just as old as the one who was gone, it seemed clear that the memory of this person was perishable like all fragile things were. When children and especially grandchildren were present, then I felt some hope that something would be passed on. Then the stories about the amazing chocolate cake they made or the uniquely warm way they spoke to each person would survive the ravages of time. Why did I care about that? I don't know. I guess it was caught up in my human need to have left my mark.

I carried my mother's memory. I remembered her especially at those anniversaries, her birthday, my birthday, the day of her death. I would go to the cemetery at least once a year bringing yellow roses, her favorite. Sitting on a bench near her grave, I would remember things. Her soft hands with elegant long fingers and how it felt when she would touch my face. How she liked to have tea every afternoon with little shortbread cookies. In later years, I would join her and we'd discuss the particulars of our day, or the current news. Who would tell stories about me? Who would remember me? And maybe, even more importantly, who would I share those stories with now?

CHAPTER TWENTY

SARAH

When Elaine Trainor arrived a little late for our meeting, her cheeks reddened from the cold, she didn't seem her usual cheerful self. I invited her to sit down. Her eyes darted to the office door and back, seeming to check if someone nearby was listening. I closed the door and then settled myself across from her.

"I'm really glad to have some time with you, Elaine." I noticed her breath was a bit ragged, showing anxiety perhaps. But I realized suddenly that I shouldn't assume anything about why she was here. She didn't know that I knew the truth about Jeffrey. I needed to treat this like any other meeting with a new congregant. I relaxed my face into my social getting-to-know-you face. "So, tell me about your boys. They're both in high school?"

Elaine looked relieved. "Um, yes, Alan and Paul are in high school. Paul's a junior and Alan's a senior."

I saw her visibly relax a little as she thought of her kids. I decided to stay on that track. "And then you have your daughter, Emily?"

Elaine gave a half-smile. "Yes, she's just turned five."

I pointed to the crayoned portrait that Jeff had given me the first day that I had taped behind my desk. "I've been meaning to thank her for my picture."

Elaine smiled more broadly. "Yes, she wanted you to have it. She said she loved your hair and wished she had curly hair."

"Well, if she had it, she might change her mind on that." I laughed, touching my mop briefly. "It's no fun when you can't get anything but frizz on humid days. But I hope she's not worrying about things like that, yet."

Elaine laughed. "Oh, yeah, they start worrying about their hair early on these days. She's already asked to pierce her ears."

I grinned. "I hope you distracted her from that idea. That might be painful."

Elaine smiled and nodded.

"Tell me a little about yourself. What brought you all to the church? Had you grown up in a church?"

Elaine leaned in a little, then began telling me about growing up in a Presbyterian church in North Carolina, getting confirmed as a teen but not being very involved. Elaine said that when they heard about St. Philips and the close community that it fostered, they decided to try it out. They started attending about four years ago and found it provided them with what they needed for their family.

I listened, watching Elaine as she described her kids' involvement in the youth group and Sunday school. Elaine face lit up when she described helping in the nursery which she had been doing since they started attending. She loved helping with the little ones and how they seemed to trust so easily. Elaine loved the way some of them just came over and gave her hugs so naturally.

"You know, when I was growing up, we didn't get much hugging and that kind of stuff. My parents were, well, a bit stiff when it came to affection. I guess I decided that my kids would get as much loving attention as they could stand. And now, of course, my sons won't let me even put a hand on their shoulders. So, I am glad to have Emily and those little ones to love on." Elaine was sitting back in her chair, relaxed and at ease at this point.

As I listened, I wondered how the picture she painted of their happy family could possibly be over-shadowed with something darker. But as Elaine started to talk about how Jeff had accepted the position as Senior Warden a year ago, her face began to shut down a bit. She talked more slowly, and seemed to search around for her words.

"Jeff has been so involved with the church this year that he's busy a lot. I mean, it's great that he wants to give back to his church and all. But, well, I have been feeling a little like he's...disappeared from our family." Elaine stopped and looked down at the floor. Her face was pensive. She looked up at me, looking for my reaction. I just listened and said nothing.

"You know, I asked him about it, and he got all defensive. Like angry at me just for asking. I was surprised because usually he would tell me that it was just a busy time, and it would slow down. But this doesn't seem to ever get better. So, finally, I called him on his cell a few weeks ago after work when he said he was going to a church committee meeting later that evening. He was supposed to be home for dinner first, but he didn't show up. When I called him, he answered and when I asked where he was, he got all flustered like he didn't remember that he was supposed to be home for dinner. He said he had stopped at a fast food place to grab something to eat. But what I heard in the background was some water running and a radio. It didn't sound like a fast food place." Elaine stopped and sighed, looking hard at the floor.

"Anyway, a friend of mine from church called me later that week. She said that she had seen Jeffrey at a restaurant with Terry. She said she assumed it was a church meeting about the Sunday school position. She tried to act all cool about it, but I could tell that she just wanted to make sure I knew. I pretended like I knew about it, and it was just church stuff." Elaine's hands were clasped tightly. She finally looked up at me, eyes tearing. "Rev. Piper, I think... maybe Jeff is having an affair with Terry." She unclasped her hands and covered her eyes with them. I pulled a tissue from the table and handed it to her. She took it and wiped her eyes while more tears leaked out. When Elaine finally got control, she looked up at me, eyes shining with pain.

I took Elaine's hand and held it. Then, after a moment of silence, I released her hand. "Elaine, I am so sorry you are having this painful time." Another tear dripped down Elaine's cheek. She nodded. "I want you to know that you can come tell me whatever you need to. Whatever you tell me is completely confidential. What you share will not be shared with others."

Elaine nodded again. She pushed a huge sigh out. "But... but..." She couldn't find what she wanted to say.

"But what?"

Elaine picked up a hand waving it in front of her face. "But doesn't this affect what Jeffrey is doing here at church?"

I nodded. "Well, it may affect it. But I can't act on private actions. I don't act like the church police, Elaine."

Elaine looked puzzled. "You don't think the Vestry should know this?"

I frowned. "Do you want the Vestry to know about this?"

Elaine shook her head. "No. I don't want anyone to know about this. But if my friend knows, I'm sure others know."

"Even if they suspect something, this is up to Jeffrey and Terry to share with me. And if they do, it will still be confidential unless they decide to share it with others."

Elaine looked relieved. Her hands lay quiet in her lap. "Oh. Wow. That's really good to hear. So, if they don't say anything, there won't be a witch-hunt to find out what's going on?"

"No, no witch-hunt. This isn't the Middle Ages. People's private lives are their own business. But if someone brings it up, I will tell them that it's Jeffrey's and your personal business."

Elaine sat spent. Her emotions now laid bare, she had no more energy for this. I looked closely at her. "But Elaine?"

Elaine looked up.

"What I really care about is you. How are you going to deal with this in your marriage? How are you going to protect yourself?"

Elaine looked down again, pushing a string of hair behind an ear and then squeezing her hands together in her lap. "I don't know."

We sat quietly for a moment. I thought about what my pastoral care professor would tell me to do in this moment. I thought about all the things I should not do. Give advice. Reassure. None of those, but there was one thing left. Oh, God, help me.

"Elaine, would you like to pray on this for a moment with me?"

Elaine looked blank.

"What I mean is, if you don't know what to do, and I certainly can't give you any answers, maybe we can together just open ourselves to whatever the Spirit sends us. I mean, it can't hurt, right?"

Elaine nodded with a shrug. It obviously felt weird to her. And it also felt a little forced to me. I wasn't one to "let go and let God". But my instinct reminded me of what my hometown priest had done during my crisis when Pam had died. He had sat with me quietly. And then at the end, he would ask if we could just invite Spirit in. At that time, while I hadn't understood it as God coming into the room, there was some kind of feeling like something powerful and peaceful was there. I still didn't understand it. But I remembered how comforting it was.

I wanted desperately to give some comfort to this hurting woman. Maybe this would help. I took Elaine's hand and bowed my head as Elaine did. Holding her hand instantly brought the overwhelming feeling of pain closer to the bone. I felt the hurt of betrayal exuding from Elaine like a wave. We sat quietly. Then I said softly, "Dear Lord, who comforts us when we are in pain, we come to you with our lostness, with our sorrow. Please be with Elaine so that she will know that she is not alone in this. Let her know that your love, which we can't begin to understand, is with her now. Let us continue to seek understanding and the path to love."

We sat in silence, holding hands for a long moment. Elaine's tears began slowly wending their way down one cheek again. She didn't stop to wipe them and I felt one fall on my hand like rain. Rain that wasn't just sorrow but also had the soothing possibility of healing. After a few minutes, I ended the prayer with a quiet "Amen," and released Elaine's hand.

She seemed calmer. When I gave Elaine some referrals for a therapist who could also do marriage counselling, Elaine said that she didn't think Jeff "would go into that kind of thing".

After Elaine left, I sat at my desk, looking out the window onto the courtyard of the church. I watched a squirrel disappear quickly up the maple tree shaking its branches. I could feel the sun start to wane sending deeper shadows across the yard with the scant grass and scrubby weed. Then a memory came to me unbidden: Home. My teenage years.

My father leaning down to pick up the mail which had been dropped through the mailbox slot in the front door. I had been coming down the stairs for dinner but I stopped as I watched him shuffle through the mail quickly. I saw him glance at the kitchen, then quickly pull a letter from the pile and slip it into his trouser pocket. Then, as he turned, he saw me and his mouth pulled down a bit, before he fashioned a smile to speak. His voice sounded false and forced.

"Another bill. They never end."

But it didn't look like a bill.

Later in the week, I overheard my mother in the kitchen on the phone to my Aunt Ellen. She spoke quietly but seemed upset. She ended the conversation as I entered. When I asked her about it, she said she was just talking about Ellen's son, Jack, and some troubles he was having.

I hadn't figured out what was going on during that time. But many years later when I was living at home during my time before seminary, my mother had confessed to me that my parents had gone through a "rocky" time soon after my sister, Pam, had died. My father had been travelling a lot and had started seeing a woman whom he had met in his business dealings. She lived in New York where he had been visiting frequently. My mother discovered it when some letters started arriving addressed to him written by hand. She hadn't recognized the address. When she finally confronted him one night, he had admitted that the affair had gone on for a year but that it was finally over. He shared that the woman had started writing letters to him since he wasn't answering her emails. She was desperate to continue seeing him, but he had chosen his family.

My mother didn't usually share any feelings of her own easily, but when she had described this time to me, she said, "You know, we both had shut down. We were trying so hard to appear like we were functioning normally that we didn't do the kind of grieving we needed. Instead of reaching out to each other, we just pretended we were doing okay. Your father turned to someone else to share his emotions. I was hurt and angry, but I finally decided that I was just at much at fault. I hadn't given him any support. I was just so lost."

I pulled myself back from mentioning that I hadn't gotten much support either. I realized that my mom had done the best she could just to survive. We all had. I had been lucky to have found Rev. Doug who had been there when I needed him. I just wished my parents could have reached out to him as well. But my parents had never trusted clergy. Ironic, wasn't it?

CHAPTER TWENTY-ONE

JEFFREY

A couple of weeks after the potluck at church, when I was on my way home from work, I got a text from Terry. We'd only seen each other once since the potluck. Just a hurried dinner.

[Must talk. Call soon.]

I pulled my car over on a side street and found Terry's number in my Recents. She answered right away.

"Hey, sweetie. What's up? Why so urgent?"

I heard her taking a deep breath and then whoosh of words came blasting out at me.

"I've told the priest. At church. She knows!"

"What? You told Rev. Sarah about us?"

Terry blew into the phone. "Well...basically, yes."

"What? Why? What were you thinking?" I felt the pit of anger rising in my stomach like a heaving mess. Nausea climbed up my esophagus.

"Because. I'm tired of you...promising me that you'll leave Elaine. You keep putting it off. I'm just sick of it! And I won't wait for you anymore! That's it! Either you tell Elaine and leave her, or I'm done!" Terry spit out the words like she was afraid she couldn't be rid of them fast enough. My heart pounded like crazy. This couldn't be.

"Goddamn it! Why did you have to do that? I mean, Terry, really. You know I care about you! But why did you have to go and tell that woman!" I tried to calm myself, to no avail.

"Jeffrey, you say that, but you do nothing about it. I can't take it anymore. It's not right, what we're doing! It's just not right! That's why I told her."

My mind raced as I tried to find a way to get out of this. This would be all over the church in no time. What if she told the Vestry? My God. I had to find out what Sarah planned to do.

"What did she say, Terry? What did she tell you to do?"

Terry was quiet for a minute as she thought. "Well, she didn't act that surprised. I think she already knew."

"What?!"

"I don't know. I think someone saw us. Someone mentioned to me that they saw us at the diner one night. So, I think they told her."

"Who?"

"It doesn't matter who. It only matters that you do the right thing here."

"Which is what?"

"Tell Elaine the truth and tell her you are leaving her. Today! Now!"

"Wait a second Terry," I tried to use a soothing voice like I would with my kids. "Just try to stay calm."

"I am tired of being calm. I'm tired of being used. And of your telling me that this will all work out for us. I don't see that. This is not working for me anymore!"

"But I just don't want to hurt Elaine. You can't imagine how hard this is going to be for her."

"We have both already hurt her by our actions. And I regret that. But you just need to come clean with her. She deserves to know!"

"But...I'm working my hardest at getting you this job. You know that's going to help you be more independent from your ex. Right? Isn't that what you wanted?"

"That's not what I need right now. You promised that you would leave Elaine sometime this year, and you haven't. So, my having a job isn't going to help anything if I can't be with you. I don't want to be used like a mistress anymore! I'm done!"

"Okay. Calm down." I needed to get off the phone and get home to see if anyone had called Elaine yet. That bitch might have blown the whole thing all over town! "Terry, I've got to go. I've got to get home."

"Stop telling me to calm down!! You should tell Elaine!!!" Terry burst out. Then she hung up.

I couldn't believe Terry had done this. We had been so discreet. We never showed anything at church. We texted under false names. We met out of town. How could Terry have ruined this?

But while my churning stomach seemed to be calming as I became used to this new reality, I tried to figure out what to do next. What to say to Elaine so I could figure out what she knew. And what she didn't know.

When I pulled up in front of our house, it looked different somehow. The beautiful three-story pilloried front still looked like one of the nicest, most stately of the rowhouses. But somehow the comfortable security that I had always felt looking at this house was muffled by a sense of impending disaster. Like I knew before I went in that this would no longer be where I lived. That all the hard work I'd poured into my career to get where I could finally attain this level of economic stability and no longer be afraid was disappearing before my eyes. My view of my life as I had known it was slowly slipping down one side of my brain into a pit of doom. I could barely get out of the car, grabbing my briefcase like a heavy log. I felt weighed down.

Elaine's car was in the driveway. She and the kids were home. What would I say? What if the boys heard something we said? What would I do if the boys found out?

As I entered the house, I heard Elaine moving around in the kitchen. I smelled dinner cooking, warm and fragrant. Chicken, maybe. The music from Alan's stereo was pumping away upstairs. Maybe that would mean the kids weren't going to hear anything we said in the kitchen.

I still wasn't sure what to say as I put down my briefcase on the front hall table and hung up my jacket. Usually, I'd call out when I was home and she would answer. But I didn't know what her mood was. What did she know? Had Sarah called her?

I moved into the kitchen doorway and saw Elaine chopping some carrots. She looked up right away. She looked down again, and turned to get more carrots, turning her face away from me. No greeting.

"Hi, hon. Something smells good. How are you?" I asked tentatively.

She stopped chopping and looked at me, like she was deciding how to respond. Was she waiting to pounce, or just tired from a long day?

"How am I? I am exhausted. I've had quite a day." Her voice was flat, maybe angry. She went back to chopping. Like she couldn't bear to look at me.

"Oh? What about it? What did you do?" I asked, alarms going off in my head.

"What did I do?" She replied, laying down the knife. "Well, I went into church to talk to Rev. Sarah."

Christ, I thought, here it comes.

"Why did you do that?"

"Jeffrey, I went in to talk to her because I've heard rumors that you and Terry are having an affair." She gave me a disgusted look. A look that told me that this wasn't new information to her.

"Now, wait a minute, Elaine. We need to talk about that. I don't know who you heard that from." I grasped at straws trying to figure out where to go from here. Do I confess or deny? She had just heard rumors. Maybe she didn't believe them.

Elaine sighed deeply and turned to walk away from me picking up the cutting board and swiping all the onions and carrots into a sizzling pan on the stove. Then she threw the board into the sink. This wasn't good. Leaning against the sink, she turned to me, her arms crossed, her expression like stone, but waiting for my response.

"That's a weird thing to say, Jeff, isn't it? It doesn't matter *who* I heard it from. Who I heard it from is totally irrelevant. Can you tell me honestly that it's not true?" She asked, her lips pursed and her face cold as she unflinchingly held my gaze.

"Elaine. I've been meaning to talk to you about this." I put my hands on the counter. "I'm sorry you heard this from someone else. I should explain."

"Yes, you should."

"So, Terry and I got to be friends when we were working on the curriculum plan. And yes, well, it has grown into a relationship of sorts," I said. Elaine's face began to sag as she heard this. I could see her struggling to keep her composure, but her lips were trembling. "You know as well as I do, we've been having difficulties for some time. I mean, maybe we haven't tried very hard."

That was it—her features crumpled. Covering her face, she began to emit loud muffled sobs and turned around to hide her dismay. Her shoulders were hunched, and her back was like a fence, keeping me out. This obviously wasn't the time to try to go and hug her, although that was my first instinct.

"Honey, I'm so sorry." I waited a few beats until her loud cries died down. She sniffled, pulling a Kleenex from a pocket. "Elaine, I do care about you. I never wanted to hurt you. And that's why I haven't told you. I mean, I've been trying to figure this out."

Her sobbing started again. I waited. She wasn't hearing me, wasn't listening. When she was finally quiet again, I tried to go around the island to her, but she backed away, pushing me with one hand.

"No, don't you touch me. Don't you dare!"

I worried that the kids would hear. "Elaine, I know we need to talk about this," I said quietly. "But maybe we should wait until after dinner and then we could go out, take a walk or something."

Elaine hit me in the face, just slapped me, wham! It hurt. But I deserved it, didn't I? Through clenched teeth she spat out, "You should go pack a bag because you are not staying here tonight."

Then she ran from the room, running up the stairs to the bedroom. I could hear Alan come out of his bedroom. Then I heard him coming downstairs slowly. Oh, God. What would I say to him?

CHAPTER TWENTY-TWO

SARAH

The sun was streaming through my office window in the early November afternoon. Outside my window, I could see the browning leaves hiding the dead grass, bleached out like it had given up its former brightness with the advent of the colder weather. The air had been brisk when I went downstairs that morning to pick up the morning paper, sending me into the sunroom to unearth the boxes marked "Winter clothes." I finally found my quilted navy jacket which I'd really needed in the last few days. The unpacked boxes pushed up against the corner, reminded me that I wasn't quite moved in despite the months I had been here.

Sitting in my church office, my laptop was opened to my half-finished sermon, but my mind kept re-playing my time with Edwardo last night. I felt the deep stir of longing which seemed biologically addictive. Yearning like this might lead to jumping to conclusions about the true nature of this relationship, I thought. Maybe I needed to slow it down. Maybe the endorphins filling my mind were literally brainwashing me into this feeling of being "in love." But oh, what the hell, how could I not see this as a gift from God?

Intentionally pulling my attention away from those seductive thoughts, I looked down at the outline of the sermon I was pondering. I thought of Peggy and her daughters, Rachel and Leah. She had popped in to see me last week, wanting to talk over Rachel's questions about God. Peggy wanted to know how to answer when Rachel asked, "Why does God let some people get sick and die? Why doesn't God make them better?" The questions had been prompted by Peggy's mother's death a few weeks ago. I had felt utterly lost in how to answer that question for a 10-year-old. I gave Peggy a weak, half-hearted explanation about how the God I believed in wasn't the omnipotent controlling force in the universe making things happen a certain way. I described God as the loving force in the universe who was with us in every decision we made and every difficulty we faced. This kind of God was a part of us, suffering with us, not looking down at us from above. More like the soft comfort of a mother's lap than the unmoved King on a throne making everything happen. I immediately saw the confusion on Peggy's face. It wasn't the kind of answer she was looking for.

Imagine if I had suggested that much of what we blamed on God was really just life, in all its confusing and thrilling mysteries. And that maybe what we call God was not controlling any of it but was a universal part of all the pain and all the joy. Maybe God was that energy that made everything move forward. The love, but also the pain. We couldn't really love without pain, right? The joyous heady experience of falling in love, and the tumbling dismay of love gone wrong were two sides of the same coin. Oh my God, I was starting to sound like a country western song. Yeah, imagine if I sang my sermon like one of those sappy country songs.

These were the kind of days when I felt a little tug of being tied down in this profession I had chosen. There was gratitude for finding a more meaningful place in the world, in ministry. A place where I felt I could make a difference and maybe where I could begin to ease some of the sense of uselessness I had always carried from Pam's death. But there was also an almost unconscious desire for breaking free of the heady expectations already placed on me from the anxious eyes staring up from me in the pews. I had not expected the authority that came with the role. The unearned place of trust that came with donning the white collar and the surplice and robe that carried centuries of patriarchal authority.

A healthy amount of feeling like an imposter came with the garments, like tags attached to shiny new clothing demarking "not yet worn in." A costume worn by others who wished for dominance, when I wished for relationship. When I considered taking on this mantle, I had imagined that the trust I engendered would come by the placing of my hand on someone's shoulder as they watched their life partner struggle to take their last breath. I had plenty of experience already in my internship with walking beside people. But now as the "Rector," the burden of responsibility was altogether different. It seemed like a badge given blindly by some whose heavy expectations felt more like a weight, holding me down.

I thought about the glances, handshakes, and half-hugs doled out while I stood robed in my white surplice by the sanctuary door, greeting people on Sunday morning, like someone dressed in costume. The costume said, "Trust me, I'm on your side." Or "I've got all the answers!" But many parishioners had stored up associations with the black and white robes from past relationships that carried all kinds of other baggage. The association of power, of assigning guilt, of hypocrisy. People wearing these robes were not always trustworthy. Unfortunately, in modern times, we had all become much too aware of that. So, as I stood, my smile and my heart seemingly in the right place, I was also aware that some greeting me were not at all ready to give me the title of "Rector" or of seeking any kind of relationship. They expected me to earn this title, and it may never be granted. The polite surface smile pasted on some faces warned me "don't come in, not welcome." It was for those people that wearing the robe felt somehow false or at least not yet earned.

One of those people, I realized was Jeffrey. Despite his stiff guarded friendliness at vestry meetings, I felt an underlying lack of respect. I had thought it was just because of my gender and youth, but now it seemed more personal. In each meeting, I noticed his negligence in asking my opinion on most financial decisions. I was consulted on matters on worship and pastoral care, but with anything that related to church finances, or even stewardship, he skirted his glance around the room, seeking opinions from everyone but me. It seemed deliberate and unfair.

Now that I was carrying the burden of knowledge of his affair, I noticed that I was avoiding him. Last Sunday at coffee hour, I realized that I had slightly adjusted my stance when talking to a new couple so that my back was facing him—just so I wouldn't catch his glance. What a coward I was.

I went back to struggling with the text of my sermon and saw that it was preaching to me as well.

"But I say unto you, love your enemies, bless them who curse you, do good to them who hate you, and pray for them which despitefully use you and prosecute you." Matthew 5:44

Matthew was reminding me that I needed to find a way to love Jeffrey despite his transgressions and his way of treating me unfairly. *Fat chance of that,* I thought.

One afternoon later that week, just as I was leaving my office, Terry called me. She let me know that she had given Jeffrey an ultimatum. Leave Elaine or they were done. I wondered what Jeffrey's next move would be.

"Rev. Sarah, I told him off, finally. I told him that he had better tell Elaine about us soon, or else. I told him we were done until he did that!"

"Terry, I'm proud of you. Now you have to stick to it. That's harder, perhaps."

"Yeah, I know. I really do love him. But I just can't keep doing this! I'm glad you helped me figure this out. Thanks, Rev. Sarah."

"Well, this isn't over, and it's definitely not going to be easy," I said gently. I could tell she wanted this all to end, but this situation was just starting.

"Oh, I know. But one way or another, I'm ready to move forward."

"Good, I'm glad. Let me know if you need to talk."

Boy, I thought, I was in this now. Unfortunately, I was right in the middle of it, and it felt like stepping into a muddy mess of shit that was all over my shoes. I had thought about calling the bishop to get advice but I didn't want to bother him with a tawdry affair. Why would he want to know about that? I was definitely having regrets about getting involved and wished I didn't know.

St. Philips had an old pipe organ that bellowed out its strident tones of the "good news" with so much vigor that often I felt my ears ringing after the recession down the aisle on Sunday. Our organist was a dear older parishioner, Tilda, who banged out the traditional hymns like "Abide with Me" and "Joyful, Joyful" with enthusiastic abandon. I loved to sing out even though I was glad that the vibrant echoes of the organ drowned out my pitiful contribution. While singing these familiar hymns, I often imagined changing the words to something not quite so archaic, something people could relate to. These wild thoughts came to me at the most inopportune times like when I was striding down the aisle nodding to parishioners as I walked. So, when I walked by Jeffrey on the Sunday after my phone call with Terry, I couldn't help but imagine some real humdingers. But I smiled at him and held up my hymnbook as a shield. Jeffrey's pasted-on grimace, paired with a glare, seemed threatening, or so I imagined. I realized Elaine was sitting further back with a friend—that was unusual.

Later, as Jeffrey came down the reception line at the sanctuary door, he turned to me with an unhappy look on his face. He whispered near my ear, "I need to talk to you." I nodded and suggested I meet him in my office after coffee hour. He gave a terse nod before stalking off. I wondered for a minute if I shouldn't be alone with him. But I realized that he wouldn't talk to me with anyone else there. After chatting briefly with some newer folks at coffee hour, I took my mug and made my way back to the office. I saw Jeffrey sitting silently, alone, in the outer office, but his demeanor wasn't what I expected. He seemed almost deflated. Sad. Maybe worried. When I motioned to my office door, he got up, and followed me in, while I closed the door. We sat in the two chairs facing each other.

"So, why did you need to meet with me, Jeffrey?" I tried to keep my tone open and questioning. Jeff narrowed his eyes and paused before speaking. Then he looked up, shrugging. "I'm at a loss here," he said.

I was puzzled. "What do you mean?"

"I know that Terry has shared with you that we are in a... close relationship. But I don't know what to do. I mean, I know what we've wandered into is wrong. But, Rev. Piper, I truly didn't intend for this to happen. We've just found ourselves in a deeply meaningful relationship." He truly looked frustrated and anxious as he spoke.

For a second, I actually felt sorry for him. He seemed absolutely lost. I wondered suddenly what my role should be? Should I be helping him through his crisis as a pastor? What about the consequences for his wife and family? And how he was hurting the church? This was the first time I'd ever counseled someone in this way. I felt uncertain, and sent up a prayer that I'd find the words.

"What are you hoping will happen?" I asked, trying to keep my tone neutral.

"I don't know. There's no good answer here. I know what I've done is absolutely wrong. But, really. Loving more than one person? Is that truly a sin? I mean, I love Elaine. She is such a good wife and mother to my kids. But we don't have that much in common. We can barely find stuff to talk about. Then Terry and I? We start talking and can't stop. I mean, we're friends more than anything. But then it went further, into a real relationship. I just don't want to hurt Elaine. I do have a deep affection for her." He wiped his forehead and rubbed his eyes. The pain on his face almost looked like a small boy who has stolen a cookie and truly wants to be forgiven. But as he looked up at me, his expression turned to one of fear.

"And now Elaine knows."

"Well, I'm glad you've finally been honest," I said. "That had to happen, eventually."

We sat quietly for a minute.

"Well, Jeffrey, I don't know what to tell you. Except that you are hurting Elaine. And your kids. And the church. That's happened because of your inability to make a choice. Of course, you are hurting yourself most of all. All of this is truly unethical behavior. And I'm sorry that you're struggling. Truly, I am. But that choice I talked about? You need to make it and move forward so the people that you are hurting can also move forward."

Jeffrey sighed. "But...I don't really think this is the church's business. I mean, I understand it seems very wrong to you as a priest. But you're still young. You haven't had a situation in your life like this one. I mean, you haven't even been married. And I can tell you, it just isn't as easy as just making a choice. It just isn't."

I felt my hackles raise. My youth and inexperience, again! Where did he get off? He was using it as a cover for his inexcusable behavior. I wasn't going to let him get away with it, but I tried to keep my tone sincere but firm.

"Jeffrey, it is. It *is* just making a choice. A choice for helping the people around you to move forward. And asking for forgiveness. I know it's not easy. No, I haven't experienced this first hand. But I am a human being. I know how hurtful your behavior is to other human beings. That's what I think the unethical part is. That you're hurting people. You can't keep up this cycle of hurting people, including yourself. That's all."

Jeffrey took a deep breath, his face hardening with determination. "Well, Rev. Piper. I *do* think you see this choice as something easily made. You forget that these matters are absolutely confidential. I think you've used your position here to uncover these private matters and thrust my family into the church's business. It's *none* of your business!" With that, he stood, and I tried to gather my thoughts at his abrupt turnabout. He glanced at me, like he wanted to see my reaction.

I stood while considering what to do about his accusation that I had pushed into this. I knew that wasn't true, but certainly it could look that way. I took a step toward him but stopped, wondering wildly what to do. I was out of ideas. The one thing I did know, was that Jeffrey was hurting. It was all over his face. And people who were hurting needed to be reminded that they weren't alone.

"Jeffrey, I know this is so difficult. You've got to be scared. I get that. But please, if you don't want to talk to me about this and find a way forward, would you go talk to someone else about all this?"

"Someone? Who do you mean?"

"A friend? A confidante? Maybe even a therapist?"

Jeff looked disgusted as though I had suggested that he parade his secret out in front of the whole congregation.

"Again, Rev. Piper, this is no one's business but my own. And I warn you, don't share this with anyone else! I mean that!" he barked at me, his face coloring.

I sighed, trying to remain calm and but to address his concerns. "I haven't shared this with anyone. And I didn't seek out this information. It was shared with me by all the parties. I have simply been here to offer my counsel."

I took a breath and held up a hand. "But let's talk about this again when you've calmed down. Let's make a time when we both have taken a breath to discuss this further."

"I think the time for that is over. You know what I think about your ministry here? I think you're wasting your time gossiping behind closed doors about people's personal business. I have heard from so many people how disappointed they are in you!" He hit the back of the chair with that statement, turned and walked out briskly.

My heart was beating like a drum. Now what? How could I help Jeffrey when he wouldn't even consider what his actions were doing to others? I groaned, suddenly realizing that I had wandered into that jungle of lions and tigers that we were warned about in seminary: the triangulation forest. When one person tells you one thing about another, then the other person tells you something else about the other, and you discuss the whole situation without getting the others in the room to talk directly to one another.

I sat in my office, feeling like an imposter. I reached for my well-worn copy of the Gospel of Thomas. Flipping through the pages, I came to a verse that I had re-visited many times, a verse that often puzzled me.

Jesus said, "If you bring forth what is within you, what you bring forth will save you. If you do not bring forth what is within you, what you do not bring forth will destroy you."

-Gospel of Thomas

What was within me was a lot of anger, a lot of sadness, and a lot of empathy for the people who found themselves in this tired knot of misplaced love and blame. But also, within me was my own human failings. How could I blame these people for their failings? How would I bring forth what was within me? How could I help others to bring forth the true feelings within them? Had Jeffrey finally owning up to the truth helped him? Or had it only made the situation worse? He was still mired in a mess of denial and guilt. I thought about the Gospel of Thomas telling us that we had what we needed within us and bringing it out in the world could save us. Was Jeffrey going to be able to find the light from God all around him when he couldn't even admit his bad choices? Or did he need to bring his own transgressions out into the open and ask for forgiveness from those he had hurt? The idea of him coming to God sincerely through prayer just didn't seem remotely possible.

Once again, I felt my own failings acutely. I wasn't doing anything that resembled good ministry with Jeffrey. And once again my own doubts assailed me.

Chapter Twenty-Three

JEFFREY

Driving back to the Embassy Suites where I was holed up temporarily since Elaine had banished me, I felt anger building in my chest after my disastrous talk with Rev. Sarah. Like a heat or a pressure.

How dare she make this about the church? It was none of her damn churchy business. The righteous way she stuck her nose in this thing. Like it was the Middle Ages and the church could legislate morality. How dare she?

She was so damned inexperienced at life! How could she possibly know how complicated marriage was? How at first you were in love, and then you got married, had kids; and then it somehow all turned into a huge fucking responsibility, like an iron weight. Raising these kids when half the time you have no idea what they need or how you will give them what they need. When your wife is always so involved with getting the kids taken care of, washing their clothes, cooking the meals, and constantly worrying about them. There's always some issue that had to be dealt with. Whether they should sign up for soccer, whether they need to go to the doctor, if they are eating right, if one of them isn't doing well in school. It's always something about the kids. And never, at least, almost never, about me or even about her. Or about our marriage. When was the last time we had sex? You could hardly call it "making love" anymore. More like a hurried exercise in getting something done before the kids might need her again. Hurry up! Get this done! I can't even remember a night we had to ourselves.

When this thing started with Terry, it was like the best vacation. It was about her finding me attractive, and me noticing that she was wearing that purple sweater with the lower cleavage that got me excited. But it wasn't just about the sex. She cared about me. Asked about how I was doing, like I mattered to her. Not like at home where I was always runner-up in some contest I didn't even know I had entered.

But still, I needed to make a decision. I couldn't risk losing the kids. I knew plenty of middle-aged men who were living in sterile, beige divorce apartments eating frozen pizza and trying to make a relationship with their kids over weekend bowling, and stupid Disney movies. Trying to have a relationship with your kids through stiff formal chats in the car driving from the ex's place to your stupid one bedroom. I've watched that lonely existence. I didn't want that.

But the times with Terry are so good. The aching, long desire of wanting her and then the physicality of the act with her, both of us gasping with incredible release. I mean, I can't remember it ever being this good with Elaine. Married sex pales in comparison. Maybe it's that forbidden thing. Regardless, it was different.

I don't know. Maybe Sarah was right. Perhaps I did need to talk to someone about this. But who? I didn't have anyone I thought would understand. If we had hired a male priest he might understand. A therapist? How would I even find such a person?

But if I told anyone; it might come back to haunt me. Rev. Sarah knew what was going on. What if she tells the Vestry? I have to get this thing turned around. I need to get the Vestry to hire Terry so she'll be happier and will shut up. I mean, I could tell Elaine that the affair was over, and we could just lay low for a while. I could tell Sarah that we had ended it. Then work fast to get Terry hired by the Vestry. No one outside of Sarah would ever know this happened. She's a priest; she's supposed to forgive.

CHAPTER TWENTY-FOUR

SARAH

After Jeffrey left my office, I sat for some time thinking about how to turn this situation around. I had begun to feel sympathy for Jeffrey. He was swimming in a sea of self-delusion with conflicting feelings and a painful lack of clarity about what his actions were doing to others. I imagined his family at the dinner table where Elaine was sitting quietly hiding all her hurt and anger from the kids. It was a big gray hairy elephant that I'm sure the kids were beginning to smell. Kids always sensed when something was wrong with their parents.

But Jeffrey also probably counted on Elaine's fear of the congregation finding out about his affair to prevent her from sharing it. I was actually surprised she came to me. I guess she saw someone who could be an ally. But now what? My instincts told me to let it alone, but my anger and frustration toward Jeffrey was beginning to outweigh my sympathy.

I spent the rest of the week leaving a portion of my prayer time devoted to sending Jeffrey, Elaine, and Terry God's healing love. It wasn't enough, I knew. But it helped keep me balanced for the remainder of the week. I had been moving forward on many other fronts at church, so I managed to put it in the background.

On Saturday, when I awoke, I immediately had a sense that the day held promise. Looking outside my bedroom window, I noticed the bare branches, dark against the clouded sky. The starkness of winter, like the simplicity of Japanese paintings, was calming. It left an impression of the beauty of stillness.

I had invited Edwardo over for lunch and he said he'd come by after doing a home visit to an undocumented family who needed help with their immigration status. Planning a leisurely lunch and perhaps a walk in the park nearby, I took my time that morning. After washing my hair, I sat in my bed, under my blanket with the hair dryer on while I read over my sermon for the next day.

After my hair was dry enough and I had dressed in a nice sweater and jeans, I straightened the apartment, thinking about Edwardo the entire time. Examining my bookshelf, pictures, and the flowered curtains I had put up recently, I saw everything with new eyes. What would Edwardo think about it? Would he fit into my life? I mean, the thought of possibly living together had begun to slowly creep into my mind in a lazy swirl. What would it be like? Would he even consider such a thing?

My phone rang just I was grating gruyere cheese for the French onion soup I was making for lunch. Rinsing my hands, the phone rang again. Edwardo. I immediately picked it up.

"Hey, are you on your way?"

"Um, almost. But I need to swing by the office and pick up something. How about 30 minutes?"

"Perfect. I'll see you then! Bye!"

I stirred the beef stock with onions and started sprinkling the grated cheese on the slices of French bread I had sliced and laid out on a flat pan to broil. Turning the oven to broil, I checked the time. I still had 15 minutes, so I laid out napkins and cutlery on the brightly colored woven placemats. I loved to make the table look nice. Bright pink chrysanthemums filled a small blue vase. With the sun streaming through the side window, the room looked enticing.

Edwardo had mentioned that he had something he wanted to talk about. He sounded maybe a tad nervous. I couldn't imagine what it was but I didn't want to jump to conclusions. Maybe he just wanted to suggest that he would like to meet my parents. It certainly was time, and I had been thinking of asking him to come with me when I went to Boston for Christmas when I had some time off. My mom had weaseled news of this new relationship out of me when she noticed I was too busy on the weekends to answer her calls. So, they were anxious to meet him, but I'd been delaying it.

I heard the doorbell as I was scrolling through Facebook. Putting down the phone, I stopped at the hall mirror to softly re-arrange my hair and opened the door. Edwardo held up a white bakery bag with a smile and a raised eyebrow.

"Hey, brought you some of those cookies that you like from that shop next to my office. Hope I'm not too late." He leaned down and kissed my cheek, handing me the bag. I remembered the cookies that we had tried one day walking by his office. They were brown sugar with marshmallow topping and reminded me of some amazing cookies that my grandmother had made.

"Hey, great! I love those. Come on in. Soup is almost ready."

Edwardo followed me into the kitchen as I swept the bread and cheese into the oven to broil.

"Do you want a soda or wine with your onion soup?"

"Oh, how about some wine?"

I smiled. "Okay, sure. It's from yesterday. Hope that's okay." I grabbed the half-filled bottle of white wine and handed it to him asking him to pour me a half glass.

Edwardo poured the wine and handed it to me, taking a sip from his glass. He looked a bit unsure of himself, like he didn't know how to start. He cleared his throat, and I could see he was gearing up to say something.

"So," I said trying to make it easy for him. "What did you want to talk about?" I went to the stove and busied myself with filling the bowls, my back to him.

"Let's just eat our lunch and then we can talk," he said, sitting at the table.

A wave of unease washed over me. Maybe this was more serious than I thought. "Well, now I can't focus on anything else. Can you just tell me now?" I pulled the cheesy bread from the oven with a mitt, waving away the steam, and placed the bread on top of the soup and served the plates. I sat down, looking at him curiously.

Edwardo, still standing, ran a hand through his hair and cleared his throat nervously.

"Sarah. You know that the past few weeks have been just wonderful. I have found myself getting more and more deeply involved with you. I'm in love with you. I hope you feel as I do." He looked at me, eyebrows raised.

Now I felt more nervous. "Yes, of course, I do. You know that, Edwardo, I hope."

This wasn't the first time Edwardo had said that he loved me. There were several times during love making that one or the other of us had thrown out those words even if it was during the heat of the moment. Afterwards, Edwardo had often kissed me and murmured how he loved me. I had been so amazed at these feelings over the past few weeks that I was a little scared of them. I had never had this much emotion in a relationship. It seemed very real and solid. So why did he suddenly look so pained?

"I haven't told you this yet because I wanted to make sure that this was something serious before I shared it. But you need to know. I have tried to tell you a hundred times. Sarah, this doesn't change how I feel about you."

"What? What doesn't change how you feel?"

"I, I'm... I'm still technically married to someone in Mexico." Edwardo looked at me with agonizing regret. "But—"

A feeling like a ten-ton truck struck me. "What? You're married? Oh, my, God!" My stomach did a flip, and I felt sick. I pushed back from the table wanting to distance myself from him and this news.

Edwardo reached out a hand to touch me, but I shrank back. "I've told you about her, Luisa?"

"You never told me you *married* her!"

"This marriage isn't real," he said quickly. "We haven't been together for four years. The marriage was a mistake. I married her because it had been something our parents had planned for years. I only went along with it because I didn't want to hurt them. But once we were married, we both could see it was a mistake. I wanted a different life than the life she was planning. She wanted the wealth my family represented. She did not want to come to this country. So, we basically decided we'd separate and tell our parents that we were trying to work it out. But we've just been putting off the actual divorce. I will divorce her as soon as I can. But, Sarah, I know I should have told you this..."

I was barely processing what he was saying. An arranged marriage? How could that be possible in modern times? It didn't sound right.

"Why didn't you tell me this when we started dating?" My voice was cold and hard, and he flinched.

"Because I didn't think this," he said, motioning between us, "would be something serious. I just wanted to see if there was something real here before I told you. I'm telling you now that this marriage was never anything to me. I mean, we were just friends. I agreed to it for my parent's sake. I thought it might grow into something deeper, but it never did. Luisa admitted long ago that she also thought it was a mistake. So…"

I held up my hand. "So, you thought you'd wait until I was in love with you to break the news. How convenient for you! That I would just understand and let you off the hook. But, Edwardo, you lied to me. You misrepresented yourself. How could you do that?"

Edwardo stood and came over to me, his face in such pain. "Sarah, I love you. And yes, I never should have kept this from you. But now, I'm sharing it. I'll take care of it, and we can move on. Please don't let this come between us. I made a mistake, but I will correct it. And you must not think that this represents who I am. I just didn't want to hurt my parents. In fact, I stopped by my office to print out this email that I sent them last week. It's telling them that Luisa and I are getting a divorce. That is what I was waiting for, just to tell them."

Edwardo took out a folded paper out of his pocket and spread it out on the table facing me.

I looked down at the paper. But I couldn't see it. I could only see the troubled expression on Edwardo's face. It now seemed like a false face. How could I have let myself be fooled? I got up and moved to look out the window so I didn't have to look at him.

"I can't do this," I said quietly on the verge of tears. "I can't be with a married man. Edwardo, could you please just leave *now*?

Edwardo stood and tried to move over beside me.

"Please just leave. Now!"

Edwardo shook his head, breathing a heavy sigh.   "I will leave. But Sarah, I hope you will think about this, and we can talk about it further. I never intended to hurt you. I love you too much for that. I hope you'll forgive me for just not thinking this through." He spoke softly with a pained tone, then turned and left the kitchen, picking up his sweater in the hallway and leaving, closing the door behind him.

I waited a few seconds after I heard the door close. Then I turned and picked up my bowl of soup and hurled it into the sink. Then threw his. They clattered against the metal, spilling hot liquid everywhere. Some splashed on my arms, burning them a little. I pulled down a dish towel, dabbing my arms. I felt as if I was on fire. Sinking down into a chair, I put my head in my hands.

"God, damn it!" I screamed, and then the tears came, coursing down my face. More angry than sad. More humiliated than angry. Feeling like such an idiot. I let it all out, screaming into the dish towel. Then I lowered my head and sobbed. My joy at this relationship, how much I loved him, all of it—gone! I couldn't believe it. It burned inside like a knife cutting me. My body shook with anger.

After a while, the tears finally spent, I was exhausted. Lifting my head, I noticed the paper Edwardo had left, now darkened with spilled soup. I picked it up, dabbing it with a napkin.

In the email, I read Edwardo's explanation to his parents of why his marriage hadn't worked out and that he was finally getting a divorce. He described the marriage as he had to me, a marriage only consented to because of the intense pressure that they had exerted on him all his life. That Luisa was always a part of his family and that he had loved her as a sister, but that they didn't have the foundation of a good marriage. They had opposite values and differing interests. He shared that Luisa was also unhappy in the marriage from the start and was ready to make the divorce final.

But then in the last paragraph, Edwardo had added this:

I know you will want to know what has finally prompted me to take this final step. Up until now, I have not had any interest in finalizing

*the divorce since there wasn't any reason to move on. That has changed.
I am in love with a beautiful, smart, and spiritual woman, Sarah,
who I am hoping will eventually agree to marry me. I can't wait for
you to meet her since I know you'll also love her. Please forgive me for
not telling you my true feelings earlier, but I have always tried to be a
dutiful son, and I knew this would be hard for you to hear.*

Con Amor, Edwardo

I felt the intense pain of losing something so precious. Of a
possible life. He had wanted to marry me! He was serious. Maybe
he hadn't just taken advantage of me. Maybe this pressure from his
parents was real. Perhaps I really hadn't understood how difficult it
was for him to stand up to his parents.

I put my head down back on my arms, leaning on the table, unable
to bear the weight. Exhaustion overwhelmed me. Too tired to figure
this out. Maybe I just needed time like Edwardo had suggested. Or
maybe this was a sign that he was not to be trusted, and it was good
that I found out now. But the pain in my heart felt like it was ripping
itself in two. One half yearning toward what this could be, and one
half pulling away with fear.

I spent the rest of the afternoon laying on the couch, alternating
between crying and cursing. Throwing pillows across the room, and
then stomping around to collect them, pushing them down under
my head only to have another angry outburst which caused me to
pick them up and throw them again. After an hour or so of that,
I thought about calling Marilyn. I wanted to call her, desperately.
But the thought of making her feel guilty for having introduced me
to Edwardo and for having not seen this coming put the kybosh on
that. I didn't want her to see me this distraught. After all, it was my
fault I'd gotten this involved with him.

But when you see someone's heart, or you think you see someone's heart, you can't help but move toward that glimpse of some-

thing real. Something in me had seen something familiar in Edwardo's heart. His kindness, his concern for vulnerable people.

I kept turning over and over our conversations to see where I went wrong in not getting the truth from him. It wasn't anywhere apparent to me where he had been hiding something. Other than when we started talking about other people we had dated, and he had mentioned that he had had a long- term relationship that had turned out to be just a friendship. Had he said something like he still had "ties" to her? I couldn't remember. He had said this woman was a friend of the family and was very close to his parents. But nothing about a marriage!

When my head finally ached from all the endless speculation, I realized that I hadn't eaten any lunch and that it was almost dark. Cleaning up the kitchen, I managed to rescue some of the soup that was still in the pot and ate it with toast.

I was too restless to watch TV. I knew my mind was too worked up to just meditate, but I needed to find a place of peace. All of a sudden, I remembered a Saturday evening church service called "Compline" that was held in an old downtown church that was all quiet contemplative chanting. I quickly looked it up on my phone and realized I had just enough time to get there. I threw on some flats, washed my face with cold water, and ran my hands through my hair. I looked terrible, but I remembered this service was supposed to be very dark with just candlelight. Perfect.

The church was older, stone like St. Philips, but very imposing with tall Gothic archways and a rounded set of front doors. I followed an older couple through them, and we entered a vestibule that was almost completely dark except for one pillar candle on a small table by the sanctuary entrance. I could see by the way the people entering that we were to enter in silence, as no one greeted each other in the familiar way of a typical Sunday morning. People's faces were solemn, like they were going to a funeral. They filed into the cavernous, cool sanctuary walking quietly, like a procession of monks, taking seats in the pews, spreading themselves throughout the large, dark space. I followed and chose a pew by myself. Tapers placed in iron holders hanging from the large crossbeams flickered overhead. Votives lined the sills of tall, dark, stained-glass windows twinkling red, gold, and white. Candlelight was the only light present in the dim, empty space, creating a feeling of calm peacefulness, something I was craving.

Relaxing into my seat, I closed my eyes, sighing with relief, as a prayer of gratitude filled me. When I opened my eyes, I looked up at the one half-lit stained- glass window at the front of the sanctuary where reds, blues, and purples were illumined a bit by some kind of soft lighting behind it. Around the large hall, there were maybe 30 people there, all facing forward or leaned over in prayer, all still and waiting.

Then out of the absolute silence from the back of the sanctuary came one high soprano voice singing notes of an ancient Latin prayer, lifting up higher and higher as though calling God into this place. Or maybe it was calling us into God's place. While I didn't understand much of the Latin, I realized I didn't need to. The message was about praise, about awe, about holiness. I closed my eyes and sank into the presence of pure beauty. Other female voices joined in, weaving above and below one another into waves of harmony, and then tapering off into blessed silence. There would be a few moments of silence when I felt as though an angel had finished singing but was still there. Floating around me, breathing light into me. Then another voice would slice into the emptiness with blissful sound. Male voices joined the choir, deepening the range of wavering notes. A crescendo, high notes, low notes, all calling to God, all washing over me with peace, with comfort, with a feeling of unconditional love.

This bath of healing bliss went on for an indeterminate time. My bruised and hurting soul felt washed, and what scripture might call "made new." I knew that I would be whole again. I knew that God could heal and offer healing, because while I was certainly battered, I was not without hope. Not without light. Not without whatever it was that had brought me into the church. The light of the love from God is what made me feel whole. A wholeness of Spirit was back with me, even as I grappled with the failings of the people around me. Spirit calmed me and reminded me about my own humanness and that of others around me. Even though I still felt the painful hurt of disappointment and judgment.

Somehow, I got through Sunday by focusing on delivering my sermon, smiling at people, and engaging, even with my mind only halfway there. The other half kept bouncing back to Edwardo's revelation. I hoped that I was fooling people well enough, mechanically raising my voice to emphasize a point and noticing when their heads would nod in recognition of that point. But during coffee hour, Irene came by and put her hand on my shoulder, leaned in and said, "Rev. Sarah, are you feeling okay?" I answered vaguely about having some stomach issues that were nothing and I was sure would go away, and she seemed to accept that. I still wanted to call Marilyn but couldn't quite do it. I knew she would be devastated, and I knew she would want to reach out to him. I wasn't ready for that. I decided to hold off telling anyone. Part of me felt ashamed that I had gotten myself in so deep and now was treading water as fast as I could. But pushing it down felt worse.

I spent the next day at work staring out the window thinking about what to say to Edwardo. I knew I had to talk to him and give him some idea of what I was thinking but I wasn't sure. One minute I was thinking of jumping in my car, speeding over there, and greeting him with a huge sloppy kiss and telling him that of course I forgave him because I loved him. But living with someone who could hide something so big seemed like a huge red flag. So, the next minute, I'd think of sending him some flowers and writing a note that said, "My love for you has died. Sorry for your loss." Or something equally as dramatic and hurtful. So, I did nothing.

As soon as I got home that afternoon, I finally got up the courage and called Marilyn. She answered after a couple of rings but told me she had just finished a committee meeting and needed some time to take down some notes before she could talk. I asked her if she could come by, I'd make her a salad for dinner. She must have heard the urgency in my voice because she asked what was going on. I demurred and told her I'd explain when she came over. She agreed and said she'd be there in a couple of hours.

Once home I pulled out the makings for a salad and grabbed some leftover chicken breasts. I was slicing veggies when my phone buzzed. It was Edwardo. I hesitated. I wasn't ready to talk yet. My finger paused over the green button, but I just couldn't do it. I let it ring out, then sat down heavily on the couch, feeling like two opposing forces were pulling at me. One said "Call him back! He loves you!" The other said, "He doesn't deserve an answer yet. Let him wait it out. He lied to you." And then other voices clamored, "You better not lose him! He's the best thing you've ever had." And, "I cannot possibly be with someone who lies like that! What else would he lie about?"

My phone buzzed again, notifying me of a voicemail. I couldn't stand not listening to it. I gingerly pushed the button to listen to the voicemail taking care that I wasn't calling him back.

"Sarah, I just need to talk. Uh...please call me back. That's it. Just please give me a chance to explain." In his voice, I could hear his anguish, his seriousness. He hadn't meant to hurt me. But he had. He hadn't been completely honest with me, putting off telling me the hard facts. Making my decision for me. I couldn't let that go. Not yet.

I went back to cutting up cucumbers giving each piece an extra whack with the knife as my anger began to grow again. The front door buzzer sounded and I went over to push it to let Marilyn in.

I opened the apartment door, greeting Marilyn as she pulled herself up the stairs by the railings, huffing loudly and carrying a wine bottle wrapped in a brown bag.

"I picked up some wine just in case. This sounded like a two or three glass emergency. Was I right?" she asked with anxious eyes.

"Well, it's more like a fifth of bourbon emergency, but this will do. For now." I took the wine bottle from her hand and got out the bottle opener.

"What, tell me now. I can't stand to wait. You know me, I'm not patient."

"Okay," I said, taking a deep breath. "Cliffs Notes version. Edwardo told me yesterday that he's married."

Marilyn's jaw dropped and she put up her hands. "What? No! That's not possible!"

"Yep. He's been in a sort of arranged marriage with a family friend from Mexico. And he didn't tell me because they're separated and he hadn't decided yet whether I was worth the heartburn of letting me know that he was still married!"

Marilyn took the glass from me and gulped a large swallow. "God damn! I can't believe it! He seems so sincere and upright! I trusted him! Oh no! *I* introduced you to him! Shit! What have I done?"

I took a sip and motioned to the couch where we both sat down. "Marilyn, this isn't your fault. At all! I totally trusted him, too." I paused, pinching the bridge of my nose. "He says he's been separated for four years, and they just haven't gotten around to divorcing because his parents kept hoping that they could work it out. But that neither he nor his wife felt that the marriage was what they wanted. They felt forced into it by their parents when they were young."

"Jesus, you never would have thought he would be in an arranged marriage with his background! Whoa! Oh, my God, I don't know what to say, Sarah. What does he say about why he waited to tell you? And what does he want now?"

I felt this huge sense of anger, frustration, and sadness rising in my chest. It felt like the knot that had been sitting in my belly since yesterday now was moving up to my throat.

"I just don't know," I managed to mumble before the storm broke, and I couldn't stop the tears. Marilyn reached out and I fell into her arms and sobbed. All the hurt and anger just poured out as she rocked me in her arms, holding me tightly.

After a couple of minutes of this catharsis, the heaving stopped, and I was able to control it and leaned back on the sofa. Marilyn reached into her purse and handed me tissues. The consummate priest, always ready with tissues. She patted my arm as I wiped the snot and melting makeup off my face.

"I'm sorry. I just needed that."

"Of course, you did. I can't believe you didn't call me yesterday. How did you get through the morning?"

"Oh, you know. It's easier to focus on other people's problems than your own."

"Yeah, that's true. But this is huge. What are you going to do?"

I sighed and blew my nose. "I don't know. I really don't know. I mean, I still think I'm in love with the man. But..." I couldn't find any words for the disappointment and the hurt. More tears leaked out. I wiped at my face with the wadded-up tissues. "But maybe

I can't understand his culture, maybe a marriage like this is more common. And he had to be sure about me before he could finally divorce. He wrote an email to his parents just last week telling them about me and that he was going to finally divorce. And, well..."

"Yes?"

"In that email he says that he's in love with me and wants to marry me."

"Whoa! Marry you when he hadn't even told you his marital status? That's a little backward!" Marilyn shook her head in frustration.

"Yeah, can you imagine? But...well, maybe this really is a cultural thing? I don't know. I don't know whether to talk to him to understand it better. Or just break it off and realize it won't work if we have this much difficulty understanding each other."

Marilyn shook her head and took another sip. "I wish I could tell you. You're going to have to figure that out yourself. But I do hope you'll give him a little leeway. Maybe just pray to understand him?" She sounded hopeful.

"Marilyn, I can see you really hope I'll talk to him. It's all over your face. And there's a part of me that wants to go that direction, too. But it seems like a huge hill to climb to let him in again. To trust him enough to give him another chance. And if I let him talk me into this, wouldn't I just be letting myself into more hurt?"

Marilyn nodded and rubbed my shoulder. "I know. There just doesn't seem to be any good answer. Yet. But you will figure this out. I know you, and you know yourself. You will figure out what is best for you and this relationship. I have every faith in you. One thing I know about you, Sarah, is that you don't accept things that aren't right on face value. You dig deeper. You'll figure this out."

Chapter Twenty-Five

SARAH

The next day, I went to work moving by rote, not at all sure what I was doing considering my emotional state. I was working distractedly in my office when Mary buzzed me on the intercom. It felt so antiquated somehow to have Mary screen my calls for me instead of answering my line directly. It reminded me of Dad's secretary answering when I'd call for him. But it really was a help. There were times when I was not quite ready to give someone an answer about some parish matter and Mary was very skilled at the oblique excuse about my being "unavailable" or "in a meeting." I picked up, hitting save on the latest version of my monthly newsletter article which was limping along.

"Sarah, it's Jeffrey. Do you want to speak to him?"

Did I want to speak to him after hearing from Terry how he had been manipulating her? Yeah, I did. Or maybe I shouldn't. But yes, I had to.

"Sure, I'll get it." I pressed the lit button.

"Hello, Jeffrey. What can I do for you?" I managed to squeak out between my clenched teeth.

"Good morning, Sarah. How are you today?"

"I'm fine, Jeff. What can I help you with today?"

"Oh. Okay. Um, I was just thinking about the Christian Education position and wondering if you wanted to go ahead and set up some interviews. You know, we want the committee to interview Terry. We need to fill this position soon and we wouldn't want her to find something else, would we?"

I stopped, not quite believing that he was pushing on as usual when the Vestry had clearly voted to put together a job description and recruit more candidates before moving forward. And not to mention the fact that he was having an affair with her. The gall. I twisted myself around in my seat so I could look outside, as I seethed.

"Jeff. You remember what the Vestry voted, right?"

"What? Oh, you mean, the niceties of all that personnel stuff? You know, I've been thinking about it. I called Frank, and we agree that while that stuff is nice to have, it's just not necessary when you need to move fast. We need to get this taken care of right away for our kids. Right?"

"Our kids. Need us to take care of this right away?"

"Yes. They do."

I just couldn't keep down the reaction that was firing up all my senses. How could he pretend he was doing this for the kids instead of keeping Terry quiet? The nerve. I could barely keep the cold anger that was pushing up from overtaking my voice.

"Jeff, I think you and I need to sit down and talk. Today." My voice was tight and firm.

There was a definite pause on the line. Jeff didn't answer. Then he cleared his throat.

"Um. Why? What do we need to talk about?"

"I think you know."

Pause. "Um, I don't know. About what the board voted? Let me explain. I mean, the Senior Warden and the Junior Warden have executive privilege to make decisions that need to be expedited. You may not know this, but Frank told me about a few times in the past when this was necessary."

"No, Jeff. Not about that. About Terry."

Another pause. "Terry? Uh, okay. I guess I can come in. This afternoon? Maybe 5:30?"

"Yes. I'll see you then." I nearly slammed down the phone as I tried to contain myself.

I spent the rest of the long afternoon trying to get my emotions under control. I told Mary I needed some time to clear my head and was going to take a walk down to the post office. I grabbed a sweater and took the stack of letters sitting on Mary's desk. Mary looked surprised and looked like she was going to protest, but then she nodded, getting that it wasn't about the mailing.

I headed toward the post office but took the long suburban back streets with tall oaks lining the shady sidewalks. It was slightly chilly but sunny, a little breeze blowing my hair back now and then. I gathered the bundle of letters close against my chest and shoved my other hand in the deep pocket of my navy jacket. It was after 3:00 and school was out. Two kids were coming toward me, boys around ten. One had a scooter and was pushing it with one foot while the other ran beside him shouting encouragement. I stepped to one side to let them pass, smiling at their carefree enthusiasm. I wished I could feel that kind of joy these days.

I thought of myself at that age with Pam. We loved jumping rope with another girl on our block. We would chant the jump-rope ditties we had been taught but would soon tire of those. We began making up our own using our names as the anchors of the song. Silly things. When my mother heard them, she encouraged us to write them down. We laughed at her. No one wanted to remember those silly made-up songs. But now I did. I remembered the feeling of being completely silly and no one would care. We felt some kind of freedom, I guessed. Freedom to just be who we were. To make up stuff and not care what people thought. All that passed when puberty hit.

When I first noticed my breasts becoming rounder and having some definition, I was eleven. My mother noticed, too. She suggested a trip to the mall to find a "trainer's bra." I wondered what the hell I was being trained for. To become a woman? But after I came home with the little white bra with a tiny pink bow adorning the middle band, I felt proud like I had a secret with my mother. Pam wasn't a part of that secret. Not yet. I noticed when I ran my breasts bounced. At school, I was glad we stopped having co-ed gym in the sixth grade. That was the year my period started. My mother had warned me and I had started carrying a little pink pad wrapped up in my purse. When I noticed that my stomach felt funny and I asked to go to the rest room, I saw the bit of bright blood in my underpants. It was so strange. I wasn't bleeding because I was hurt; it was supposed to be normal. I fished out the pad unwrapping it and fastening it to my underpants. I worried all day that it would somehow give me away and I ducked into the girls' room between each class, checking to make sure the blood hadn't leaked.

That was the start, I thought now. Of being cautious around others. Of not letting some people know your business. My mother had suggested that I could tell my best friend, Kathy, but that it wasn't a good idea to talk about it openly. She said that the girls who hadn't gotten their periods might feel left out. Left out? I thought no one would want to be part of this club. But I was wrong. I soon heard the girls around me whispering and giggling about when they had gotten their periods. And I noticed other girls shrinking away from those conversations. In fact, I began to see a difference between those "mature" girls and the ones whose chests were still flat beneath their thin blouses, no telltale straps underneath. The boys noticed, too, I realized. They would grab the back of the blouses, pulling the bra straps of some of the more obviously well-developed girls, who would blush and tell them to stop, but also laugh. I wondered if Jeffrey had ever been one of those boys. The ones who would do anything to embarrass the girls, teasing them about everything. Especially about those horrendously private things like getting your period. And there I went again. Judging others. But I also realized my anger was justified. He was hurting others, and I wasn't going to allow it.

When I got back to the office, I felt ready. I was ready to take him on.

I was finishing up the first draft of my newsletter article when Jeff poked his head around the door. I motioned him in, greeting him tersely. He sat down, seeming a bit nervous as I stood and went to the door and closed it. I sat down behind my desk, instead of in the chair next to his, wanting to emphasize my authority, or at least my role as priest. I start to speak, trying to keep anger out of my tone.

"I've asked you—"

Jeffrey cut me off abruptly. "So, Sarah, I am interested in what you wanted to discuss. As I said, I don't think this hiring decision is yours to make. I think this is best left to the Vestry, especially since the decision has been put off for so long."

I eyed him directly for a moment. I took a breath, measuring out my words, aware that I was moving us both into new territory.

"Jeffrey, you cannot push through a hiring decision in favor of a woman with whom you are having an affair." I watched as Jeff's eyes widened in shock that I would stand up to him. His face was pink, especially his ears. He shook his head, seeming to want to shake all this off. He had clearly underestimated me. I took another breath and plunged in.

"Before you say anything, I want you to know that this is no longer just a private matter. It is affecting your ability to perform your duties as Senior Warden. You are obviously trying to manipulate the Vestry to make a hiring decision based on your personal preference putting undue pressure on the person involved. This could be seen as sexual harassment or as a quid pro quo. You get her the job, and she keeps quiet. You are placing the church in legal jeopardy by these actions. Therefore, I am asking you to resign as Senior Warden and to leave the Vestry. I can't force you to resign but I'm suggesting it strongly as it will only complicate matters if I need to go to the bishop to get him to take action."

Jeff's cheeks were shiny as his breathing became considerably exaggerated. He looked down at the floor as he seemed to consider his options. He stuttered as he began to respond.

"Now, Sarah." A big breath. "I think you have misinterpreted the situation gravely. I mean, my own personal relationships are my own business, not the church's. I chose to share that situation with you hoping you would understand how it came about. But you should know that my personal relationship with Terry has ended. I certainly hope you would keep my personal business confidential. But, as for the hiring decision, that is just not related to this. I mean, I can't imagine how you came up with this…this…accusation that I'm using my personal agenda to drive this. I mean, you have been after me ever since I suggested that maybe you didn't have the experience to…"

I watched him shake with his struggle to refute me. I wondered if I was enjoying this too much.

"Jeffrey. Stop now. Just stop. I don't want you to get yourself into deeper water. I just want you to go home, consider what I've said and write a letter explaining to the congregation that you must resign due to family concerns, or whatever excuse you want to give. I'll expect the letter in my email tomorrow morning with a copy to the Vestry."

"But, now let's talk about this more. You can't do this." Jeff stood up with his arms raised up.

"Yes, I can do this. I've actually consulted a lawyer, and they have confirmed that this is the right action. I want you to leave now." I was a little shaky since he seemed so upset and I felt a little frightened. Of what I didn't know. I was lying about the lawyer which I didn't usually allow myself but in this case, I felt it was warranted. I also needed to get the bishop involved but I didn't want to have to force Jeffrey's resignation through the bishop unless I had to.

Jeffrey seemed to lose momentum when I said "lawyer". He went to the door, turned as though he was going to speak, then lowered his head and opened the door. He started to walk out. I raised a hand, "And Jeffrey, I want you to consider Elaine and how your actions have affected her. And how the actions you are proposing will reflect on the church." Jeff started to protest, but simply emitted an exasperated huff, and stormed out.

I slumped into my chair. I felt totally deflated, like the breath had been knocked out of me. Then I got up and went quickly to the door and closed it. My heart was beating like a frightened animal. What was I afraid of? I knew I was in the right here, but Jeffrey held power in the congregation. I needed back-up. I picked up the phone. I needed to call the bishop. But I needed to let Irene know right away what was up.

I called Irene right away, explaining the situation with Jeffrey briefly, not specifically naming the affair but alluding to his "manipulating the Vestry to get the hiring decision that he wanted". Irene didn't waste any time in letting me know that she had already figured out about the affair, and was bursting with righteous indignation about Jeff's bold attempt to get Terry hired behind the Vestry's back.

"Sarah, you have absolutely done the right thing, whether you had a lawyer's advice or not, you've done the right moral thing! I just can't believe the nerve of that guy!" she gushed with exasperation.

"But, Irene, what will the rest of the Vestry say? I can't reveal the affair to them. They will just get this letter of resignation from Jeffrey and with a few phone calls, he could lead them to believe that I've pushed him out with no reason."

"Don't worry about that. I will call some of the other Vestry members to tell them that you have saved the church from an unsavory situation or even a possible lawsuit with Jeffrey and while you cannot reveal the nature of the situation, that you have every reason to ask for his resignation. After I speak with them, they will not question your decision."

I breathed a sigh of relief. I really wasn't sure that I was going to get away with this without being accused of sharing a confidence. "But you won't mention the affair?"

Irene laughed. "I don't think I'll need to. While Jeffrey has the support of the other men on the board because they admire his male chutzpa, the women have all noticed his flirtations over the years. They know enough to fill in the rest. Oh, but you need to call Frank, soon."

I sighed. "Yes, I know. I really don't know how he's going to take this."

"Just tell him you've asked for Jeffrey's resignation and ask to meet with him. Tell him it's a matter of utmost confidentiality but that you'd rely on his discretion. He'll be so pleased to be taken into your confidence that I think you could tell him the situation confidentially."

"Really? You think I should tell him?"

"You can tell him without saying the words. You could just say something about Jeffrey 'using his position to influence a hiring decision' in favor of a candidate with whom he had an 'unusually close relationship' and leaving you out of the hiring process. Something like that?"

"That's really telling him."

"Not in so many words. You're just pointing out the immorality of Jeff's position. As soon as he gets a whiff of a scandal, he will be with you."

"All right. I'll call him," I said. "But Irene?"

"Yeah?"

"I didn't go into ministry to be busting men's balls."

Irene laughed. "Yeah, but you have to ask yourself, 'What would Jesus do?'"

When I put in a call to Bishop Springer, I was told that he was away for a few days and would get back to me. I asked his assistant to please let him know that it was an urgent matter that I needed to discuss if he could get back to me as soon as possible.

I ended up meeting with Frank the next morning before the Ladies Guild met in the sanctuary. His face clouded when I explained the general situation, emphasizing the role that the Rector in charge should have in the hiring process. He asked about why I thought Jeffrey was pushing Terry's candidacy, not getting the implication. I demurred saying that I wasn't sure but I thought it was an "inappropriate" role for the Senior Warden to be playing with someone who seemed to be close to him. Frank agreed but said he didn't understand why I had asked for Jeffrey's resignation. I didn't want to be accused of breaking confidentiality, so I suggested that he ask Jeffrey why I had insisted. He agreed to support my decision but said he would also speak to Jeffrey.

After Frank left my office, I sat at my desk, looking out the window, giving myself some time to just rest. I knew we weren't out of the woods yet. Frank still needed to check in with Jeffrey, and I didn't know how that would go.

In the back of my mind, I also realized that this crisis had allowed me a distraction from making a decision about Edwardo. But that only brought back to me the realization that I had somehow, in the midst of all this, with some inkling of understanding, begun to accept that Edwardo's way of dealing with a difficult situation was based on his not wanting to hurt anyone. He ended up hurting me anyway, but not with any malevolence. He truly wanted to do the right thing. So, unlike Jeffrey who had wanted the best only for himself and ended up hurting everyone including himself. There was no comparison. I could not hold onto my feeling of betrayal for Edwardo when I could see the clear difference between a good man and a man only out for himself.

After sitting and breathing in some relief, the intercom buzzed surprising me. Mary wouldn't have interrupted unless it was important. "Yes?"

"I'm sorry to bother you, but Terry is on the phone and she sounds very distraught. I thought you'd want to talk with her."

"Of course. I'll get it." I took a second, giving myself a mental readjustment, getting ready to go back into pastoral mode.

"Terry, what's going on?"

Terry breathed noisily into the phone, obviously having been crying. "Rev. Sarah. I'm so sorry to bother you."

"No, it's fine. Did Jeffrey call you?"

Terry sighed and began sobbing in earnest. "Yes!" She continued crying as I told her to take her time. After a few seconds, she began again, "Yes, he called me and told me that since I had told you about our relationship that he was being kicked out of the church and he never wanted to see me again! It was all my fault, he said!"

I waited as Terry's breath came and went with new surges of emotion. I waited until Terry's sobs died down. "Terry?"

A moment passed while Terry blew her nose and caught her breath. "Yes?"

"This is not your fault. You shared with me because you sensed that the affair was a mistake, right?"

Terry thought a moment. "Well, yeah, I guess so."

"So, you probably knew that it wasn't going to end well. Didn't you?"

There was quiet while Terry thought that over. She cleared her throat. "I guess so. I wanted to believe that he would leave Elaine. He told me he would. I hate that here I am, the stupid manipulated woman. An old story that everyone..." Her voice shook as she started crying again but quietly.

"Terry. This is not your fault. Jeffrey deceived you, he deceived Elaine, and he was getting ready to deceive the whole board by pushing through your getting hired. He is a bully. And he is good at deception. Everyone thought he was a fine, upstanding man who should be respected and followed. But everyone was deceived, not just you."

Terry's crying stopped as she pondered this. "So, are you kicking him out of the church?"

I huffed. "No, Terry. I've asked for his resignation from the Vestry which I imagine he'll give. But we don't have immorality courts anymore." I just wished we did.

"Oh. Well, I hope he gets what he deserves!"

"Oh, believe me. I think he will."

"Does everyone know about the affair now?" Terry asked, the news starting to dawn on her.

I hesitated. I didn't want to lead Terry astray. "Terry, I have not revealed the affair explicitly. But I have to warn you that some people will put two and two together and guess."

Terry moaned quietly into the phone. "Oh, fuck! I'm going to be blamed for this. I just know it. That's what married women do. They blame the woman!"

"Now, let's not jump to conclusions. I think some people understand who Jeffrey really is and will understand that you were being used."

"Yeah. Why didn't I see that? The stupid, blind woman who bought his bullshit!" Terry was emitting little grunting sounds.

"Terry. Now, listen. Take some deep breaths. Breathe."

After taking some deep breaths, Terry's breathing eventually slowed down. "Okay, I'm all right. I'm sorry to bother you with all this, Rev. Sarah. Really, you shouldn't have to put up with all this."

"It's okay, Terry. I'll be thinking about you and sending you prayers. You remember that you are not to blame for this. And we'll talk more tomorrow."

Terry agreed quietly and hung up. She sounded absolutely done in.

I put down the phone, and tried to calm myself. I ran my hands down my arms, feeling the soft feel of my sweater. I slowed my breath and listened to my heartbeat. It was beating fast, trying to escape this conflict where I felt trapped. Here I was, only four months into my first ministry. How would I ever last?

I tried to reach for a place where I could feel ready to pray. I reached out for my image of the God I believed in. A force of loving, forgiving energy ready to hold me. But I couldn't even imagine it right now. All I could see was my own less than perfect self, judging Jeffrey. And in addition, not forgiving Edwardo.

It felt like a huge stone was sitting in my heart. My own pain and disappointment in myself. But also, anger. Anger at what this ministry brought me. Not the uplifting, inspiring leadership that I had imagined for myself. But instead, tawdry, secretive and manipulative behavior on everyone's part including my own.

It wasn't what I had wanted when I envisioned myself as a priest, a pastor. I thought I'd be helping people to find their own way to a spiritual path. Instead, I was helping people become judge and jury over others. Being my own judge over Edwardo as well as Jeffrey. This wasn't ministry. This wasn't what I had hoped for. Instead, here I was lost and confused and not helping anyone, including myself.

I was fooling myself if I thought I knew where God was in all of this. I had carried the faith that God was always with me since the time of Pam's death. I had built my whole idea of ministry on this confidence. That somehow even when I felt alone and lost, I thought God was with me. But right now, in the brokenness of the actions of Jeffrey and the dishonesty of Edwardo, I couldn't see what God wanted me to do. I felt very alone.

Chapter Twenty-Six

IRENE

I called Rowena Swift right away. I remembered when she had questioned the Nominating Committee's decision to nominate Jeffrey to the Vestry. "Too new," she said sniffing her judgment. "And too stuck in his God-given male authority. Huh, I don't think he even lets his wife have her own checking account!" I had agreed but we couldn't find anyone else who take the Senior Warden position. People who've been around the church long enough know that it's a full- time job without much recompense, except perceived power. Which Jeffrey was certainly attracted to. The reason why he'd take it. We had both voted no, but he got in because there wasn't another candidate. So, now when I told Rowen that our Senior Warden was up to his neck in 'conflicting interests' and possible unethical behavior, she laughed.

"What'd I tell you? Thinks he can get away with his flirting and flashing around his male prerogative? Don't worry, I've been on to him from the start!"

Then I called Phyllis Trimble, whose family had been in the congregation for generations. She was a harder sell on why she should vote to uphold the priests' decision to ask for Jeffrey's resignation.

She wanted to know more. She tended to trust the male authority in the room. I wasn't going to risk sharing a confidence which could backfire on Sarah. I just said that Jeffrey was recommending an expediated hiring decision without the priest's involvement when he had "ulterior motives." She said she thought it wasn't right not to involve Rev. Sarah in a hiring decision, but she wasn't sure it was right to ask for a resignation for that reason. Then I said, "What if there might be a lawsuit involved against the church for sexual harassment?"

"Oh!" she said. "That's a different matter. You should have said. Of course, I'd vote against the Senior Warden if there's any impropriety involved." I said there might be.

"Well, in that case, you've got my vote. We must protect the church's reputation."

Then I thought about the other two members of the Vestry beside Frank. One man had been playing golf with Jeffrey from the time they met on the Vestry. I decided to skip that one. The other was a woman who had only been around for four or so years. She was a little naive about church life, wanting to believe that everyone at church was there for the good of God and humankind.   When I called her, I just said that an upcoming vote was being held that would take away Rev. Sarah's authority to make contractual decisions about hiring. I remembered that she had been a small business owner and might identify with Sarah's need to have control over the necessary decisions to run a church. I was right. She agreed right away.

I called Sarah back and relayed my results. She was very grateful for my support. She was still a little shaken by Jeffrey's tactics. I reminded her that Jesus also had to fight against the structure of the Jewish priests, and it wasn't easy fighting immorality. She sighed and said, "Yeah, but we are all sinners, you know."

I said, "Some more than others."

Chapter Twenty-Seven

SARAH

I came home early that afternoon, changing into my comfiest yoga pants and sweatshirt, I swung the refrigerator door open, scanning for some wine. The only bottle was the one I had opened for Marilyn, some days ago. It seemed like a lifetime ago when I was just worried about Edwardo and now my job was imploding on me as well.

I poured myself a larger than usual amount, first sniffing the bottle to see if it was still okay. I wasn't usually much of a drinker, but this situation called for something. I had called Marilyn before I drove home, and she had promised to come over as soon as she could get out of a meeting that was scheduled for 5:30. She also promised to bring takeout and some "spirits", holy or otherwise.

I settled myself on the couch and picked up the remote for the stereo. What kind of music would speak to me now. I thought of one of the Indigo Girls songs that I used to love. I spoke the name into the remote, then sipped the wine, listening as the music spoke to me. They sang about taking life less seriously. Wrapping fear around yourself like a blanket. Yeah, that's where I was.

I remembered my therapist telling me that when I felt something, I should let my body express it. I felt my body wanting to move to push out the heaviness I felt. I stood swaying with the pulse. The pace rose as the notes followed along, then lifting, began a beat that become more regular, catching me up in the rhythm. Side to side, into the room, moving into a circular dance, my arms echoing the beat of the song as they sung it out. As I moved in circles, I felt myself just letting it all go. Throwing off my anger and my guilt, pushing it away like frightened birds. Finally, as the song ended, I collapsed onto the couch, catching my breath in short bursts. My heaving chest began to slow down as everything came to rest. My body and my mind came to rest as well somehow. Everything left me. I was emptied. Lying down, I buried my head in the cushions.

After a few minutes, my cell went off. It was sitting on the kitchen counter, and I would have to get up to see who it was. I let it ring. Then eventually, I fell asleep having exhausted myself with it all.

When I awoke, the sky outside had darkened into dusk. I remembered my phone and went to pick it up. It had been Irene. I dialed her back.

"Sarah. I'm so glad you called back. Have you seen it yet?"

"Seen what?"

"Oh, you haven't seen it. Open up your email and call me back."

"What? What is it?"

"Um, just open and read it and call me back."

"Okay." I ended the call and pulled up my email on my phone. There were several normal church business emails that I skipped over and then I saw it. An email from Jeffrey. It was titled, "Emergency meeting of the vestry. Wednesday night, 7:00". Wednesday was tomorrow. I opened the email which was addressed to all the Vestry members including me. It started with this sentence from Jeffrey,

Emergency Vestry meeting called Wednesday evening to discuss a recommended hiring of a Christian Education Director. The Emergency Session of the Vestry will be in Executive Session and therefore Rev. Piper is asked not to attend until she is notified by the Vestry.

I dropped my phone and sank back into the couch. Then I picked it back up and dialed Irene.

"Rev. Sarah. Don't worry," she said immediately after she picked up, "he can't get away with this."

I shook my head. "I don't know. But I have to get a hold of Bishop Springer right away. Which I should have done sooner."

"Yes, you need to do that. I should have seen this coming, but I didn't think he had this much gall. I'm so sorry."

"Thanks, Irene. I'll call you back after I speak to the bishop. But that may not be until tomorrow."

"Okay. But you should know that I have already talked to three other vestry members and they see right through him. They had already wondered if there was something fishy going on. They're on your side,"

"Yeah, I thought Frank was, too. But obviously, Jeffrey is very persuasive."

"Yes, we should not have underestimated Jeff. What about Terry? Do you think he got to her and has hoodwinked her?"

I sighed. I didn't want to deal with this. "I guess. Terry was very worried that all the church members would know about the affair and that she would be blamed. I wonder if he convinced her that they can just deny the whole thing."

Just then, I heard my bell. Marilyn must be arriving with dinner.

"Irene, I need to go. I will call you back tomorrow morning. I'm going to try to reach the bishop tonight. And, Irene, thanks for your support. I could not go through this without it. Thank you."

I heard Irene breathe a huge sigh of disappointment. "Sarah, I so wish this hadn't happened on your watch. I had convinced myself that with your guidance, we could overcome Jeffrey's tendencies. But obviously, that was wishful thinking. Okay, I'll talk to you tomorrow!"

I said my good-byes and went to answer the door. I saw Marilyn's grim face as she swung it open.

She hugged me awkwardly with one arm, the other holding a bag of takeout.

"Oh, God, Sarah! I'm so sorry you have stirred up the gods of patriarchy so quickly!" she said, moving into my apartment.

"Well, I guess I deserve it in threatening the beast," I responded, taking the bag and moving to the counter, unpacking the boxes of Thai food, and moving to the cupboard for plates. "Oh, and you haven't heard the latest."

Marilyn made a face, "Now what?"

"Jeffrey has called an Executive Session with the Vestry without me to discuss hiring the woman he's having an affair with."

"Oh, my God! Hot damn!! He really is the devil incarnate! This is unbelievable. Have you called Bishop Springer yet?"

I sighed and shook my head. "I've put in a call to him saying it's urgent. But I don't know him very well. Just had my initial interview with him. I hate that my first call to him is to tell him how I've truly messed up. What's he like? How's he going to respond to this?"

Marilyn took off her coat. Looking pensive, she moved to the kitchen. "First, spirits to calm the spirit," she said, pulling out the bottle of wine she had brought and opening the drawer looking for a bottle opener. "So, Bishop Springer is an interesting case. He came from New York. He's fairly new at his job, maybe 3 or 4 years. But when I've talked to him about social justice issues, he's been extremely supportive. Oh, and I just remembered. A friend of mine in Pittsburgh has gotten to know him. She says he's very supportive of women in ministry."

I looked hopeful. "Okay, that sounds good. I'll call his assistant back and tell her I need to talk to him tonight."

"Yeah, that's a good idea, and Sarah?"

"Yeah?"

"Don't forget that Mary Magdalene was one of the first to challenge the patriarchy."

I smiled. "Yeah. Okay." I went back into my bedroom with my wine glass and looked up the bishop's number. It rang and rang and I finally left a message on his assistant's phone. I relayed to him that the Senior Warden was involved in an affair with a congregant and that he was challenging me to a duel over the control of the Vestry. I asked that the bishop call me back tonight if possible.

Coming back into the kitchen and living area, Marilyn had already gotten out plates and was helping herself to the Thai food she had brought. She looked up at me.

"So, left a message?"

"Yeah. He didn't answer. But you know, I think I made a big mistake."

Marilyn frowned. "You're second guessing yourself? Having doubts about ball-busting the biggest sleezeball in your congregation?"

I shook my head. "No, I have no doubts about the need to put a stop to his power trip. But I just didn't go about this right."

"Because you didn't call the bishop first?"

"Well, yes, that. But also, because I didn't bring Jeffrey in with Terry and get it all out in the open first. Get Terry to admit the affair in front of me with Jeffrey in the room. Get it all on the record. I was so damn angry I didn't even think! I just reacted. Oh, and I lied, too."

"Wait, what did you lie about?" Marilyn asked skeptically. She had taken her plate into the living area and was beginning to eat.

"I told Jeffrey that I had consulted a lawyer and that there might be grounds for a sexual harassment suit."

Marilyn shook her head between bites. "You might have lied that you called a lawyer. But it's true. There certainly are grounds for a suit if he told her that she could get a job if she would just lie about the affair."

I thought about that. "Yeah, so maybe I should call a lawyer now..."

"Yeah, now you're talking. Hey, I've got just the person. A woman lawyer in my congregation who works for a corporation doing their labor relations stuff. I'll call her right now"

I was loading my plate with food and stopped. "No, let's slow down for a minute. I've already overreacted enough. If we call a lawyer, we may be setting up the church for liability problems."

Marilyn put down her plate. "Hmm. I know. I'll call her and not give any particulars. Just 'calling for a friend' kind of thing. Get her initial thoughts on this matter from an impartial viewpoint? What do you think?"

I came over to the couch and put my plate down, thinking it over.

Marilyn got out her phone and was scrolling down her contacts. "It wouldn't hurt anything just to get an idea about it. And it will fulfill your statement that you had called a lawyer. Right?"

I sighed, then nodded. "Okay. But just give a general idea of what happened. No specifics. Nothing about what kind of job or anything that would allow her to tie it to us."

Marilyn found the number and clicked. I could hear it ringing.

The lawyer answered and Marilyn filled her in with the general outline of the situation. I could see Marilyn listening as the woman talked. Marilyn thanked her and got off the phone smiling. She relayed to me that the woman said that she couldn't give specific legal advice to anyone since her corporation didn't allow her to do so. But she said she'd be happy to give Marilyn some general idea of what the legal issues were. She said that the organization was certainly liable to a sexual harassment suit if in fact, the job for the woman was implicitly tied to sexual favors.

"See, there you go. You just called a lawyer like you said you did."

My phone rang and looking down, I saw that it was the bishop.

"Gotta take this. It's Bishop Springer." Marilyn nodded for me to go ahead. I answered, taking the phone into the bedroom.

I felt uncomfortable filling in the bishop on all the events that had happened, realizing that I should have been reporting the animosity between myself and the Senior Warden from the beginning. Bishop Springer was mostly quiet but asked certain questions about what I had revealed to whom and when in the series of events. He was obviously concerned about confidentiality. After I finished, I asked, "So, I guess I'm in really deep and I know I should have called you sooner. I just didn't expect this to blow up like this."

The bishop sighed. "No, I know. We never expect the worst from people. But sometimes, that's what we get." He was quiet a moment, seeming to mull it all over.

"Sarah, I'm sorry that you are experiencing this right in your first year of ministry. It's really discouraging, I'm sure. I guess you've now realized how hard this job is. A lot harder than they told you in seminary, right?"

I felt like an idiot. Of course, it's a lot harder than I expected. I thought I could handle it. In fact, I still thought I could handle it if the bishop and the Vestry would back me up. But they didn't really know me yet. Why would they back me up?

"Yeah, it's hard, but I expected it to be hard. What I didn't expect is to find this level of hypocrisy and corruption in the Vestry. I mean, how do these people get chosen to lead their congregations?"

"Yes. I know. It's hard to understand. But as you know, we're all just human beings. Hoping to get some love. And, well, that's what this man is probably looking for. To be loved. For some, that looks like taking power and control over others. You just got in the way of that."

"Yeah, I sure did."

"When we become interrupters of corrupt power, we're doing God's work, Sarah. I know you've made some mistakes. Maybe you should have taken a step back and slowed it down. But you're doing what God called you to do. Don't you think?"

I felt a huge feeling of relief sliding into my chest. In fact, that's what I was hoping he would say. He saw that I was doing what I knew to be true. I was calling out misplaced power and dishonesty. I was doing it because that's what I knew was right. I didn't want to be in a position where I had the power to stop corruption, and I didn't do it. I felt the relief of being heard, of being validated. I let it wash over me for a minute.

"And now, what do you think you need to do?"

I thought about what needed to happen next. "I guess I will go to the Vestry meeting and confront him."

"Well, yes. You should. But you shouldn't go alone. I'm going to send you our Diocesan Liaison for Congregational Life, Jack Ritter. He will listen to you. Then he'll go to the meeting with you to hear how it goes."

I felt my heart leap. "He will? He'll go with me?"

"Yes, indeed. You won't face this alone."

Oh, my God, I wasn't going to burn out in this first ministry. I was going to be okay.

"Oh, thanks so much. But the meeting is tomorrow night? Can he get here by then?"

"Well, I think so. And Sarah, there is much here to learn. Jack will help you figure that out. I'll help you figure this out. There's a lot of careful steps involved before we change the systems of power that are so enmeshed in our congregations, you know? I will have Rev. Ritter call you first thing in the morning. And yes, let's get together and review all this in a few weeks. Okay?"

I agreed and hung up with gratitude washing over me. He was in my court. They would have my back. The congregation would survive this. I went out into the living room and opened my arms wide to Marilyn. Marilyn raised her eyebrows.

"Good?" She came over to me holding out her arms.

I nodded and leaned into a hug with Marilyn wrapping her arms around me. I felt the relief of being held both literally and figuratively.

"Oh, my, God! Thank you for being here! I'm so lucky to have you."

"You are loved, lady! And not just by God."

That night as I lay on my sofa, thinking over the long day, watching the sky darken with the bleak shape of a winter night, I picked up my thumbed- through New Testament, looking in Matthew. Yeah, there it was.

Blessed are those who are persecuted for righteousness' sake.
- *Matthew 5:10*

But I also thought of Jeffrey. What kind of place was he in that he would resort to such desperate tactics? What could I do to pull him back to a place of grace? Was there anything I could do?

Then I thought of that age old Matthew 7:7 passage: *"Ask, and it will be given to you, search, and you will find, knock and the door will be opened."* But of course, Jeffrey would need to knock.

Chapter Twenty-Eight

JEFFREY

When I talked with Frank Trumbore, I knew that I had to convey some urgency of why we had to move against Sarah. I sensed as soon as he answered that he had some real hesitancy going up against her. We had begun having coffee regularly a few months ago and I had built somewhat of a good relationship with him. Enough to have some common goals in mind.

One, we were both from working class families and had both risen above that into the middle class and were proud of that. We knew that value of working hard and being able to pick out a lot of bullshit like when those from the liberal elite started talking about "common objectives" and "transparency." Terms like that had been invented by people with too much education and too much time on their hands.

So, when I mentioned to Frank that while Sarah was a good person and wanted to do a good job that she really hadn't been in the trenches long enough to know what the common working person experienced, he had begun listening and kind of acknowledged he might be sympathetic.

But then he hesitated saying, "Jeffrey, I hear what you're saying and all. But she is our priest, and she says that she has the responsibility to hire staff. And she also says that there's a standard process to do that. Shouldn't we give her the benefit of the doubt?"

I talked about how she had been in school more than she had been working. That she was young and idealistic and just didn't have the experience of knowing how difficult it is for the young parents in our church who had to volunteer to run that Sunday School after putting in a whole week of work. I leaned heavily on his background as a business manager about how sometimes what is required for a job is the knowledge in the field not the piece of paper that had a degree printed on it, which is what Sarah had been expecting for the new hire. I pointed out that St. Philips had never had a college educated Christian Ed Director and didn't need one now. Besides which, we couldn't really afford it.

He sighed and admitted that she had called him in to talk about the necessity of following "proper procedure" for the hiring process. He said he thought she was trying to do an end run around the Vestry but that he had tried to give her a chance since she was so new. But that now that I had put things into perspective, he could see that Rev. Sarah wasn't really ready to take on this urgent task for getting someone hired as Christian Ed Director. Frank said he just didn't want her to feel unsupported when she was so new and trying so hard. I suggested that he talk to her after our meeting and explain why it was so urgent to have to vote against her. But then to mention that he would certainly support and help her bring the new Christian Education Director onboard. He grunted his acceptance of that idea, reluctantly.

I knew this was going to be tricky especially with Irene on the Vestry, but I could see that now that Sarah had decided that I was a terrible person that she wasn't going to give me a chance. I was sure she was going to go to the Vestry and oust me. I just had to give them a reason to see that she was out to get me. If I could show them her lack of experience and her need to control this hiring decision, then I could show them that she was going to try to imply that I lacked some basic morality or something. I had to get them on my side before she had a chance to do this. I didn't think she would uncover the affair. I had called Terry this morning and after much sweet-talking her got her to agree to backtrack about there being an actual affair and say that we had just gotten a little "too close". She was reluctant to go against Sarah but wanted to cover up the affair, if possible.

I figured that once they hired Terry, the Vestry would be happy and could convince Sarah that this was for the best. Because it really was for the best. For everyone.

CHAPTER TWENTY-NINE

SARAH

When I entered the conference room with Jack Ritter, the Congregational Liaison that Bishop Springer had sent, the Vestry were sitting in stony silence. I guessed they had been warned by Irene that we were on our way in. Most looked confused and wary. Jeffrey glared at us, teeth clenched, face tight. Irene held her head high in a somewhat defiant stance, nodding to me. I motioned to Jack to take the chair next to me, and I sat at the top of the table next to Jeffrey, where I usually sat at Vestry meetings. Then I nodded to Jeffrey to go ahead.

Jeffrey stood and looked down at the paper where he had apparently written an agenda. He looked up and cleared his throat, his face a bit cloudy, unsure what to do with us there to thwart his plans.

"The Vestry Executive Session is now called to order. I was just informed that Rev. Sarah and someone from the diocese would be attending. I didn't know this until five minutes ago. I strongly object since this is an Executive Session where we were to discuss confidential personnel matters. But apparently the diocese doesn't allow for that," Jeffrey said, motioning to me and Jack. "Perhaps,

Rev. Piper, you can tell us why you're here when you were not invited and who you brought with you."

My heart was beating loudly with both trepidation but also indignation. How did he think he had the right to treat me like this?

I glanced at Frank who looked caught out, and took a deep breath. "Good evening. I understand that the Senior Warden's intention was to meet with the Vestry to move ahead with a personnel matter that would exclude me from the decision of hiring a Christian Education Director. Let me introduce our visitor from the diocese, Rev. Jack Ritter, Assistant to the Bishop and Liason of Congregational Life. I spoke to the Bishop yesterday and conveyed to him what the intention of the Senior Warden was: to move ahead with a hiring decision and to exclude me. He recommended that I attend this meeting and sent along Rev. Ritter to accompany me. Jack can advise us on how the diocese would typically act on these matters. Rev. Ritter, can you tell the Vestry why you have taken this unusual step of coming to a parish Vestry meeting uninvited?"

Jack nodded and stood as Jeffrey clenched his jaw and sat down. Jack looked around the room, seeming to take in the tenor of the anxiousness. His manner was calm and even, quieting some of my own anxiety.

"Good evening, everyone. I am sure you're all a little concerned about why I am attending your meeting when normally the diocese does not intervene in vestry matters. But occasionally, when priests or vestry boards ask for our help, we will step in. I am here to represent Bishop Springer and the diocese. He was concerned when he heard that an ordained Rector, Rev. Piper, was being excluded from the Vestry of St. Philips' meeting where a hiring decision was being made. Now, there are cases when priests are not head of staff in congregations. Sometimes there are consulting priests who do not have full ministerial authority. But that is not the case here. Rev.

Piper is your called Rector with the full authority of the diocese to act as Head of Staff in all hiring decisions. That is in your contract with her. So, I'm here to ensure that she is a part of that process. Of course, vestries are consulted on hiring decisions and can recommend one strongly. But the ultimate decision belongs to the Rector when they are hired as head of staff. Perhaps you weren't aware of this?" Jack asks Jeffrey pointedly.

Jeffrey stood again, drawing himself up to his full height next to the tall, distinguished-looking Jack, who had no qualms facing off with him. It seemed a little like a male pissing contest to me, but I trusted that Jack had the experience of handling bullies.

Jeffrey scowled and puffed out, "So, you're here to overrule a decision that a vestry might make on their own?"

Jack took a beat before looking squarely at Jeffrey. "Mr. Trainor, I am not here to overrule anything. I'm simply here to point out the role and responsibilities of the Rector that has been called to this congregation by the diocese of Pennsylvania. In our polity, vestries have certain roles and responsibilities including confirming the appointment of a call to a priest. Your vestry called the Rev. Piper as Rector *and* as head of staff. Therefore, it becomes her responsibility to make hiring decisions for this church, acting in collaboration, of course, with the Vestry. Certainly, you could find a way to consult and collaborate together on this hiring decision?"

Jeffrey shook his head. He was utterly out of ideas and probably not familiar with Episcopal governance policy. I guess he thought that the Vestry was in charge. He focused his attention on Frank, telegraphing his need for help.

"Frank, could you help here?" Jeffrey motioned to him and sat down looking frustrated.

Frank's eyes were like a deer in the headlights. He was certainly out of his league.

"Um. I don't know, Jeffrey. It seems we've made a gross error here. I'm afraid that the diocese has come to point out our mistake, and I certainly can't, well, I can't refute it. I'm sorry, Rev. Piper, if we have stumbled here. Really, we want to work with you. I think Jeffrey was just trying to get a hiring decision made quickly since it seems urgent that we have someone in place. And the proposed candidate certainly seems appropriate from what I can see. I thought we were really trying to just, I don't know... expedite things." He stumbled through his words, looking down to hide his embarrassment.

Jack, who had sat down during Frank's bumbling, raised a hand.

"May I?" Jeffrey nodded to him scowling. "Could we ask Rev. Piper to share her plan for the hiring process?" Jack asked, glancing at me.

I looked at Jeffrey raising my eyebrows for permission to speak. He looked away like he wanted nothing to do with this. I stood, realizing that there was power to be expressed in the standing position.

"I understand that the Senior and Junior Wardens are anxious to move ahead with a hiring decision. They have expressed what they see as an urgency in the matter. However, the Christian Education Committee has now reviewed and passed on a job description for the Christian Education Director. We have placed a small announcement in the diocesan newsletter for this month. We are moving as fast as we can to identify appropriate candidates both inside the church and within the diocese. So, the next—"

Jeffrey put his hand up to stop me. "But how long will this process take?"

I looked at Irene who had been helping the Chrisian Ed Committee with this task, and nodded at her to urge her chime in.

Irene spoke confidently. "I believe that we should have a candidate ready to go in 6-8 weeks. We want to make sure we have qualified candidates, and people who will fit in well with our community."

Jeffrey shook his head again, as if the answer wasn't good enough. "So, we'll have to ask our parents to keep managing this program by themselves for another two months when we have a perfectly good candidate ready to take on the job. She fits into this community very well because she is a part of this community." He looked at me and then at Jack with a smug air.

I opened my mouth to speak but paused as I considered how to express the absolute injustice of what Jeffrey was doing. "I want to ask the Vestry to trust me in this process." I looked around at the faces, most of whom were avoiding eye contact. Irene looked defiant and satisfied that finally Jeffrey was being shown up.

Frank raised his hand in a conciliatory way. "Rev. Piper, it's not that we don't trust you. We are very glad to have you here as our new priest. But you've only been here a few months and don't know us very well. You may not know what our needs are. You may not even know this candidate well. But we do." He was offering a peace branch, but a broken one. I noticed his condescending tone. I quickly followed up before he could dig himself in deeper.

"The candidate that Jeffrey refers to has some experience in our Sunday School as a teacher, but she does not fit the qualifications that were outlined by the committee which include a college degree and some experience in Christian education. I don't doubt she is a nice person and we all like her, but I don't think she is the appropriate candidate. In fact," I said, taking a break to weigh my nerve. Could I do this? Or should I? Looking over at Jack and seeing his nod, I realized that I had to.

"I believe that this candidate is being railroaded through this process because she has a very close, personal relationship with our Senior Warden."

Jeffrey's eyes shot up and he immediately stood with his hands balled at his sides, his mouth working in a kind of a huff as spittle formed in the corner of his mouth. "I...that accusation...is absolutely...well, preposterous, and slanderous at that!" He jabbed a pointed finger toward me. "I demand you retract that statement." Expressions of surprise on the faces around the room turned to Jeffrey. Frank's eyebrows raised as his expression changed from surprise to shock as he looked accusingly at Jeffrey. Jeffrey went still.

I sat and shook my head in response. "I won't retract it, Jeffrey," I said quietly.   Just then, Irene raised her hand as if to quiet the arguments that might follow.

"I know this is a shocking accusation. Rev. Piper doesn't make it lightly. She has been working behind the scenes to try to forestall the need to even come to the Vestry with this. But Jeffrey made that impossible by calling this emergency meeting and trying to exclude her. I think we need to realize that most of us have not been privy to why Jeffrey has been pushing so hard for this hire to happen. We must listen to Rev. Sarah and trust her now!"

Jeffrey breathed unevenly, his voice raising as he stammered. "Jesus Christ! This is the thanks I get for volunteering to help this church move forward! I can't believe you would stoop this low! I will not stand for this. I resign my position. I'm done here!" He pushed back his chair and stamped out.

The air went out of the room. Absolute silence descended as people looked down uncomfortably. I finally cleared my throat and somehow managed to keep it together long enough to apologize to the board for not foreseeing the seriousness of Jeffrey's demands beforehand. Irene moved that the Vestry vote to allow the Christian

Ed committee to work with me to present an approved candidate to the Vestry. There was a unanimous affirmative vote with each person holding up their hands high, their faces somber.

I thanked them for having confidence in me. Jack quietly asked me if I would lead the Vestry in prayer. I looked at him with desperate eyes, and he added, "Since you are the leader of this church and together you must find a way to forgive each other and yourselves." When I still hesitated, he said, "Rev. Sarah, I know whatever you want, is probably what we all want. And maybe what God wants."

I sighed and tried to measure my breathing. What I wanted was just to get out of there and never come back. But what did these people need and want right now? What did I think I had left to give them in this moment? Nothing but grief. Grief and pain at the mess that humans make of our lives. All of us made messes and expected God to clean it up. *Oh, okay, maybe there's a prayer in that,* I thought.

I began by asking that we hold each other's hands. Frank and Irene looked doubtful but wanting, I guess, to support me reached for each other's hands, and everyone then grabbed a hand and bowed their heads. I'm sure they wanted out of there as much as I did.

"Dearest God, we come to you with our deepest sorrow. We know that you love us despite the messes we make in our lives. Despite the way we hurt one another again and again. Despite the way we make promises we don't keep. Despite all of this, you still offer us another chance—to be loved. We don't know why. But here we are, asking again, to be forgiven. We want to learn to love each other better. We want to learn how to be worthy of your love. And each other's love." I took a deep breath, and continued, "God of love, give us the wisdom to know that we are loved, and that you will keep loving us. Give us the grace to find the strength to offer each other trust, forgiveness, and imperfect love. Because that's all we have. Imperfect love. But we offer it again to you and to each other. In the name of that love, Amen."

I looked up and Irene smiled at me showing her appreciation. Jack gave a nod of confirmation. Despite the mess we were in, we could still depend on prayer. I thanked Jack for being with us.

Everyone slowly got up and began to make their exits. Irene gave me a side hug, then left with a couple of the other members. Frank came to me, his eyes troubled. He cleared his throat and began a stumbled apology.

"Sarah, I didn't have your back, and I'm sorry. I was momentarily dazzled by Jeffrey's quick talk and magic tricks, I guess. I hope...well, I hope you'll forgive me." I put my hand on his shoulder, assuring him that I totally understood how hard it was to turn Jeffrey down. I asked him if he would take on the Senior Warden position at least for the rest of the year, if the Vestry approved it, which I was sure they would. He agreed noting that he was so sorry to have let me down but would do his best to support me from now on. He left, nodding to Jack, but his shoulders seemed to carry the heavy burden of moving forward.

Jack accompanied me up to my office and sat down across from me as I sank heavily into a chair. He gave me a smile of resignation.

"You survived this well, Sarah. You didn't deserve having this kind of turmoil in your first year. But you got through it. You're okay, I think. Don't you?"

I could feel the heaviness of guilt starting to bear down on me. "I don't know, Jack. I don't think I could make it through another one like that! Whew!"

He smiled his agreement. "Yeah, I don't blame you. But you've proven your strength and they've seen that. You are their priest now."

I felt a huge welling of disagreement swell up. "What? Why in God's name would they want me as their priest when I let this all happen?"

Jack shook his head. "No, you didn't let this happen. This happened to you. All of you. Life happened. Sarah, you were there to hold them together and let them find a way to move forward. You still held to your promise to help them find God even in the midst of brokenness. You did that, even if you don't realize it now. You'll see a difference in how they react to you. You've proven yourself."

I laughed ruefully. "I just barely got through. I judged Jeffrey. I was angry with him. And I really hated him for a time. What kind of example is that? I didn't act like someone who held fast to God's hand. I could barely feel God in this. Where was God in this? I don't know!" I asked, showing my frustration. Feeling defeated, I sighed, my hands falling into my lap. "I really don't know anything."

"Sarah, right now, you are feeling the grief of disappointment. You must feel like this job is too hard. And that you don't want to do it anymore? Are you feeling that?"

I agreed with a slight nod and a grimace.

Jack leaned forward, his tone sympathetic. "This is just your first test. I don't mean that God is testing you. I don't believe God does that. But humans test us to see if they can trust us. Congregations especially. They saw how you stood up to Jeffrey. You didn't let him manipulate anything. You held him to account, and you held the Vestry to answer to their call, which is to hold the leaders of this church to act with God's love. You asked, no, you demanded that they support integrity! And they did. You need not feel that this was a failure. This was a success."

I shook my head. "Come on—a success?"

"Yes, believe it or not. And you ask where is God in this? You carried God into this. You carried his love into demanding justice and accountability. That's where God was. Right there with you."

Eventually Jack could see I wasn't up to his pep talk. He got up to leave, telling me he would call me later in the week. I thanked him with the little bit of energy I had left.

Then I just sat in my office and stared out at the dark sky with the sliver of a moon just beginning to shine through the bare branches. I had nothing left to give. I thought of Jeffrey, returning to an empty hotel room. Who would be there to encourage him? And after all this, did he deserve anyone's encouragement? I sure couldn't do it.

Suddenly I thought of Pam, and the day we learned of her illness. Maybe because it was also a day when I felt God was missing. I had been doing homework when my mom, dad, and Pam had returned from the doctor's office. Pam came upstairs and went into her room and shut the door. She never did that, so I knew things weren't right. My mom came up and also went into Pam's room. There was some quiet talking, then Mom came out, paused in the hallway, and came into my room. She looked at me and sighed, then shut the door behind her. I looked up. "What is it? Did the tests come back?"

She came around to my desk and sat on my bed before explaining the diagnosis and the treatment that would soon follow. I felt my fear rise especially seeing my mom's face so serious. That's when I knew our lives were about to change.

How did we get through that time? We didn't really connect with anything spiritual. My folks didn't talk about religion. They talked about getting through with hope and optimism. That we would get through this because we would get the best doctors, and we would try everything. They did try everything, medically. But nothing spiritually. I don't remember any kind of spiritual connection until after Pam died. My mom had asked Rev. Doug to say a prayer when he came to the house right after he heard that Pam had died in the hospital that day, despite the trying everything. He had prayed, but I saw how nervous that made Dad, who looked at the floor, fidgeting with his hands in front of him, not sure how it was done when you weren't sitting in a pew. My mom had cried through the prayer, holding onto my side. And I had just held onto her desperately. Thinking all the while, if God was around, why hadn't he done something to help us, to help Pam? I didn't get it.

But then sitting with Rev. Doug in his office for many visits afterward, he would ask if we could end with a prayer. It somehow felt right to me. He mentioned all the things we had talked about, like how sad I was, and how much Pam had been a part of my life that was missing now. He made a prayer sound like a summary of what was already in the room. My sadness and my hope for my parents to get through this. He made it sound like sadness was a holy thing, a thing that God cared about but couldn't make go away. But that God somehow was with us in all of this. That stuck with me, along with the love and care. Even in the overwhelming grief, it stuck. I began to get what God might be to me. The comfort of someone listening. The hope that somehow, we'd get through this.

I knew that in our brokenness we had to show people that we still had love to offer each other. We still could forgive each other. And try again to make it right. God was in all of that. In fact, that *was* God.

I tried to imagine how I could still reach Jeffrey, and thought again of what I had learned from the wisdom of the Gnostic gospels. I had begun to learn from the Gnostic gospels that God was found everywhere, even within people who were lost and broken. Even when people didn't accept Jesus as their savoir. Even from people who might persecute you. Even Jeffrey had God within him. But how could I help him see that? There was no way he'd accept that kind of theology from me now.

His disciples said to him, "When will the kingdom come?" Jesus said, "It will not come by waiting for it. It will not be a matter of saying 'here it is' or 'there it is.' Rather, the kingdom of the father is spread out upon the earth, and men do not see it.

    • *Gospel of Thomas*

People do not see it. The kingdom is within each of us, but we don't see it. I wondered what our world would be like if we did recognize God in all people.

***

"So, Jeffrey Trainor was kicked out of the church because he wanted to hire Terry as the Sunday School Director?"

———

"Um...I was just calling to find out if you're okay. I heard that the Sr. Warden tried to get you fired?"

———

"Rev. Sarah, I was a little concerned when I heard that Jeffrey and Elaine Trainor have left the church? Why? What were they mad about?"

———

I finally gave up trying to answer the flurry of phone calls with all the rumors that were piling up. I began crafting a statement for the newsletter that said that the Senior Warden decided to resign from the Vestry due to some "irreconcilable differences" in approaches to the hiring process.

Everyone heard something different, and I certainly wasn't going to tell them the bleak truth: that they had appointed a Senior Warden who wanted to manipulate people to get what he wanted. Mostly all they knew was that Jeffrey had tried to get the Vestry to hire Terry, and the Vestry had turned him down on the advice of the bishop who had sent a representative to back me up. But most were just curious about why the Senior Warden had resigned his position with a diocesan representative there to intervene. Most had no clue that there was anything untoward going on with Terry, except for the members of the Vestry who understood the need to be discreet.

After fielding these phone calls for two days, I was very ready for a break. Friday afternoon, I headed home, picking up some groceries on the way. When I got home, I sunk down in my cozy chair, exhausted, realizing I really needed to meditate to find some peace.

Closing my eyes, I took a deep breath, reaching for that calm place inside of me. I searched for the quietness within that sometimes helped bring the voices of discord to a halt. I breathed in and breathed out, moving the calm air in and out. Letting my breath quiet my chaotic heart, I began to feel a stillness of what I thought of as mindfulness. I could find peace within when I really searched for it. But even as I breathed, I felt the intermittent stabs of doubting myself. I leaned into it. Allowed it. Then I allowed myself to let it go for now.

Peace and stillness were still possible even when things were upside-down. I stayed there for a time, I don't know how long. Long enough to feel like I could find myself again. I was still hurting, I knew. And I was still missing Edwardo.

How could I have put off calling him so long? It had been ten days since our dreadful last meeting, where I basically threw him out. But now I really missed him. I so wanted to talk this over with him. I needed his calm presence. He would tell me I was okay.

Marilyn was always supportive. But she was also reactive and would want to go to bat, to go beat someone up for me. She would often get me more stirred up instead of calming me down. Jack Ritter, the diocesan guy, had been so helpful in helping me to see where my strengths were and where I could do better. But he was business-like, and I was just another problem he had to solve. I needed someone who both loved me and could be non-reactive. That was what I had come to rely on with Edwardo.

I needed to decide once and for all where we stood; whether I was ready to accept everything he had told me as truth. I missed him dreadfully, but his lack of transparency still smarted. Ultimately, I think he did what he thought he had to in order to get to know me. He was right that I wouldn't even have gone out with him if he had told me upfront that he was married. He took a huge risk getting involved without telling me this significant fact. But he was also falling in love as I was, and didn't want to risk the whole thing being put on hold which is exactly what happened when I found out. He deserved a chance to tell me what he had been thinking. I deserved a good explanation. Maybe he even deserved some forgiveness.

I looked at my phone. He had called many times and texted a few times in the couple of days after our meeting. But the last text had said: [I need to let you process. I will leave you alone and give you time to figure this out. But, please, please call me when you're ready to talk.] That had been a week ago. It was time. I was ready, or thought I might be.

I sat quietly looking at my phone, getting up my nerve. Oh, please, let him understand how hard this is for me. Please, God, let me listen and hear him and find out if I can forgive. Open my heart for this. Please.

Taking a breath, I text him, [Edwardo, I'm ready to talk. If you are.]

Nothing came back. He was probably with a client. I sat watching my phone. Nothing. Five minutes. No dots. I slipped my phone in my pocket with my hand clasped around it and slumped down in the chair, my heart beating fast. I tried to get back to a quietness. No deal. My mind was a chattering mess of questions. What would he say? How would I respond? Was I crazy to try again?

Moving and settling over on the couch, I felt the phone buzzing. I took out my phone and peeked – a text from him!

[I am ready whenever and wherever you want to talk. I've been anxiously waiting to hear. Just tell me where to meet you.]

I stopped to think. If he came to my apartment, I'd feel like I wouldn't have a lot of options for getting him to leave if I decide I'm not ready. But in a public place, I'll feel strange crying, which I will do, inevitably. I wanted him at my apartment. I wanted him near me where it was just the two of us.

My hands shook as I texted him back: [Come to my apartment. Saturday evening? 8:00?]

Dots. Then it came back. [Nothing could keep me away. I can't wait to see you.] Then a string of hearts.

I sighed. My heart let down. I still loved him. But I knew I had to protect myself if he wasn't trustworthy.

Saturday morning my nerves were at full speed. Up one moment "I'm going to see him today!" Anxiety overtaking the next "Why did I agree to see him?" I washed my hair, dried it quickly with my diffuser and tried to decide what to wear. Casual. Just jeans. Don't want to look like I'm trying too hard. Which of course, I was.

After a quick lunch, I decided to try out a city park next to the University I had never been to before. It was late afternoon by the time I got there. The light through the trees filtered through weakly, allowing a chill to claim the end of day. I pulled my jacket around me and shivered, reconsidering whether this was where I needed to be. Despite the slight breeze and waning light, being in nature was always a place I could bring my circling doubt and rising anxiety.

Zipping my jacket closed and pulling on some gloves from my pocket, I closed the car door, noticing the other few cars in the parking lot, one a green slightly battered hatchback with an old Obama sticker still clinging to the bumper. I headed down the trail, a feeling of much needed freedom opening within me.

Yesterday, when I had agreed to Edwardo coming over, there was a palpable sense of relief when he responded to my text with a series of hearts. But despite my longing to be with him, I also needed to consider what I was going to say to him. I couldn't just give in and say it's all right and let's just forget it. I mean, part of me wanted to move on and forget it. But I knew that if this was going to last, I had to be more confident that Edwardo was who he seemed to be, a sincere and trustworthy man, who had a serious lapse of judgment. I so wanted to believe that, especially when he looked at me with those eyes. Those eyes! I couldn't help but believe that he had the sincerest intentions toward me. But how many women had fallen into eyes like that and been lost like children in a wilderness?

Pushing my hands into my pockets, I looked up into the trees where the dark branches were lined with a bit of snow. A little brown ice clung to the edges of the path with dried leaves crumbling around it.

I moved down the trail, seeing the shimmering of the pond surface ahead, with a small gazebo next to it. I craved some quiet time to think this all over, so decided to stop there. As I got closer to the gazebo with its simple brown benches on three sides, I thought I saw something move behind a post. Oh, shoot, there was someone there. I'd have to keep moving unless I wanted to sit on the bench a few yards closer to the water. It seemed far enough away from the gazebo that I could still be alone. I skirted the path that led to the gazebo and crossed the grass to move around it. I glanced back to see if there was someone there and saw a figure hunched against the post, holding a shawl around them—an older woman with white hair pulled back, pensively looking at the lake. I smiled as I passed and held up a hand in greeting. But then as I looked away, I thought something seemed familiar about her face. I looked back a second time just as she glanced at me, and I knew. It was Gloria! The woman I had known in seminary who had first introduced me to the Gnostic gospels.

I turned right around, smiling, as I looked at her more closely. Yes, it was her. What in the world was she doing here? I moved closer.

"Gloria?" I ventured.

She tilted her head and looked at me, puzzled. "Yes. I'm Gloria," she responded hesitantly, clearly not recognizing me. "Do I know you?"

I smiled widely as I came to stand in front of her. "It's Sarah, from seminary!" I hoped she remembered me, because I certainly remembered her and our amazing conversations, before she disappeared sometime in my second year.

She narrowed her eyes and looked at me again. "Sarah? Is that you? Really? What are you doing here?" She looked startled, but got up, holding out her arms to me. "Come here! Give me a hug."

I stepped into her arms, and it was like getting a hug from a mother I didn't know I had. I felt engulfed in love and acceptance. I hugged her back, swaying with the gift of finding her again.

"Gloria, I didn't know where you went. Or how to contact you. I tried to email you," I said, trailing off.

Gloria pulled back to see my face, then motioned toward the bench for me to sit. "Oh, honey, I just had to get away fast. I'm sorry. I just shut everything down," she said shaking her head. "It was a bad time."

"What happened?"

"I don't want to burden you. It's family stuff. A bunch of shit hit the fan all at once! And I just had to drop everything I was doing and come here. That's why I didn't even tell anyone where I was going. I didn't know if I could go back, but I didn't think I could. Turns out I was right; I needed to be here."

"Oh, Gloria, I'm sorry to hear that. But you can tell me, if you want. What happened?"

Gloria shook her head. "It's bad. My son. He...well, he went to prison. And I had to rush back here to take care of my grandson. I'm afraid it's not a good situation," she said, looking at me sadly.

I blanched. I couldn't begin to imagine. "That's terrible!"

She nodded, rocking her head back and forth. "Yes. It is. It's very hard."

I didn't know what to say next but wanted to allow her to keep unburdening herself. "So, can you share what he did? Or would you rather not?"

Gloria stopped moving for a moment, and squeezed her eyes shut like she couldn't bear to remember it. Finally, she said, "He robbed a store with a gun. Luckily, he didn't hurt anyone, but he threatened someone with that gun. Oh, I just couldn't believe it at first."

"But is it true?"

Gloria looked at me. "Honey, yes. It is."

"Oh, my. That must be so hard for you."

"Well, yeah. It was at first. But now, I'm just.... raising my grandson. Best I can. Hoping the Lord will help me. And of course, some of those gospels. You know. The ones I showed you."

"Oh, yes. I can't tell you how helpful those gospels have been to me. Really. I have to thank you for introducing them to me."

"Well, now, Sarah, what are you doing here in Philadelphia? I thought you were a Boston girl."

"I was. But I'm pastoring my first church here. I just got ordained last year. And got called here in the fall. I've been here only a few months. But it's going...well, not so great, I guess. It's hard. It's not what I thought it was going to be like."

Gloria patted my hand. "I'm sure it is. It's hard to pastor to people. But they're lucky to have you, Sarah. You've got an open heart. And an open mind. I loved the way you kept asking all those questions in those religion classes. Just like me. Not going to just accept it all. That's right. I liked that."

"But I'm finding that seminary didn't really prepare me for the real challenges." I sighed thinking about all the events of the past weeks.

Gloria snorted out a laugh. "Hmph. Yeah, I can imagine. What kind of challenges?"

I smiled and shook my head. "I can't even begin to describe all the messes I've found in my church and in my life."

Gloria laughed. "Yeah, life. It's a mess! But you know what? The Lord doesn't judge us for that. The Lord, heaven help us, he's not about judging. So, I've learned that I've got to stop judging. You know?"

Surprised by this response, I stopped and considered. "I mean, I know that God is all forgiving. But how do we humans keep on forgiving? When people just keep hurting us? It's like, we humans can never learn. We just keep on hurting each other. I'm finding it very hard to forgive these people."

Gloria stopped and gave me a look. "You? With your big heart? You can't forgive a little mess? Why, honey?"

I felt a little ashamed. Why, indeed? "I don't know. I mean, people hurting other people. And not being honest? I guess that's what bothers me the most about people. People who just aren't honest and don't think ahead how their lying is going to hurt someone. I mean, Gloria, how do you forgive your son for what he did?"

She sighed and scrunched her nose like something smelled. "Phew! It's not easy, I know. Yeah, it's not easy. But you know what? My son had a hard life. His Daddy left us when he was just a little thing. And then I can't say I was the best mother back then. You know? I tried. But I was pretty lost. I was drinking and I even lost it at one time and my son had to go live with his uncle. So, I can't blame him. I can't even blame his dad. When it comes down to it, I can't even blame myself. But I did. I blamed myself for years."

I looked at her face, noticing how her expressions seemed to shut down for a minute. She closed her eyes and put her head back, and in the silence, I wondered if she was praying.

When she finally looked at me again, her eyes were filling. "Sarah, I finally heard from the Lord. You know, I'm not one to go about witnessing about Jesus and stuff. I'm just not that into that being saved stuff. But I finally got to the point where I was either going to get off the planet, just say good-bye to life because I couldn't deal with my own stuff, or I was going to find a way to move forward. The Lord gave me that way. Yeah, He did! He came to me and told me that He forgave me, and I needed to forgive myself. That was the only way forward. I had to forgive myself. And once I saw that I was still okay with the Lord despite all the crap I had given Him to put up with, then, I realized that the love that passes all understanding—you know all that stuff that we hear in churches, but we don't really believe—it finally got through. I forgave myself. I knew that I was still loved. Yes. I was." It felt like she was telling me something that I had been looking for. Something I needed. I began trying to connect it all together.

"So, when you forgave yourself, did you forgive everyone else?"

"Of course. Had to. If I was going to get all this forgiveness and love, then certainly others deserved it. Right?" I pondered that for a moment. It seemed so simple for her, but I knew it wasn't simple for me.

"I guess. I just don't know how. I mean, I get that we all get forgiveness, and God offers it to us. But I guess the problem is how do I forgive myself?"

Gloria nodded as I finally spoke the words out loud. "Uh-huh," she murmured, and then motioned for me to continue. "Why can't you?"

I really didn't want to admit it. But the thing I'd been holding back, the fact that I didn't forgive myself for actions long ago seemed to be at the heart of it all. "I don't know. I guess for all the things I could have done for my sister when she was dying but didn't. I just wasn't there for her the way I should have been." The tears started coming, and Gloria grabbed my hand and held it.

"Oh, honey. You've been holding onto that a long time. Way too long. Right?" I nodded as the tears streamed down my face. "Sarah, it's time to let that go. It's time to forgive yourself. I mean... well, your sister has probably forgiven you, don't you think?"

The idea of my sister's soul looking down on me and forgiving me had been plaguing me. I didn't know if I could buy that. But knowing my sister, and believing that some part of us lived on, then that was the obvious conclusion.

I nodded while wiping away tears. Talking with Gloria felt like coming home. She was someone who could hold my grief and just be with me.

"Thank you. Yes, it's been trying to come out, all that feeling, I just haven't let it."

Gloria squeezed my hand and let it go.

We talked some more about our lives, the ins and outs, the daily parts that got us through. And then she said she had to go. We exchanged numbers and agreed to get together again soon. Finding Gloria after all this time felt like a gift. A divine gift.

That night, after nervously choking down a sandwich for dinner, I tried to listen to music to calm myself before Edwardo was due to come over. I tried my favorite Phish songs, tried the Beatles, even tried Adele with her powerful emotion. But I was too nervous myself to find solace in any of it. I did feel hopeful, though. I felt a lot of different things all coming at me at once. Anger that Edwardo couldn't have told me sooner. Joy that he really did love me. Sadness that our time of admitting our love to each other was tainted by his cover-up. Anticipation at being back in relationship with someone who got me. Someone who understood the passion for helping others. All these feelings just mixed-up and not making much sense to me.

Offer him wine? No, that was like it was a social occasion when it wasn't. I kept checking my mirror, rearranging my hair, trying different expressions as though I could control how I might look to him.

Finally, I turned off the music at ten minutes before 8:00 and sat staring out the window, saying a quick prayer. Five minutes later the bell rang, and I jumped. *Here we go*, I thought, holding a hand over my startled heart. I didn't feel ready, but it was now or never.

I buzzed him in and waited by the open door. When I saw his face coming around the stairway, my heart was beating like a drum. When he saw me, his face lit up. As he came close to the door, I reached out and touched his arm, waving for him to come in, unable to say anything. He stood awkwardly after following me in, but once I closed the door, he began talking in a rush, his words tumbling out.

"Sarah, I can't tell you how hard the last ten days have been." He shook his head in frustration, searching for the words. "I wanted to just show up at your door so many times and sit there until you were ready to talk."

"I know," I said quietly, and motioned for him to sit down. I sat on the couch across from him. I noticed how his body leaned toward me, wanting so badly to touch me. But I knew that if I allowed that, the words we needed to say to each other would be lost. "Well, I'm very glad you didn't do that. I wasn't ready to talk."

He nodded sadly. "I understood that. But I thought maybe, if you just saw me, that maybe... well, anyway, here I am." He looked down and addressed the floor. "Sarah, I have never been more remorseful for my actions. I keep beating myself up for not being more upfront with you."

I could see how much he was struggling. But I just nodded and waited for him to go on, my hands knotted in front of me. He finally gazed at me with those deep, earnest eyes. He took a deep breath and started again. "Sarah, I care about you deeply. I'm in love with you." He waited to see if I would respond, but when I didn't, he continued.

"I keep trying to figure out why I didn't just tell you my situation sooner. I should have told you when I first called you. I should have told Marilyn before that. But there's something about my feeling of guilt in having agreed to a marriage that was never going to work in the first place. My guilt was so great for first thinking I was lying to

Luisa, then later, after it became clear that she felt the way I did, I felt guilty for having not told my parents sooner. Both our parents made the assumption that we were going to marry because we had been good friends. And our two families were so happy together. The assumption just continued without us even questioning it. None of us really examined it too closely until we were married and then we started trying to live with it."

"We both began to admit that we loved each other, but the passion wasn't there. We couldn't see a future together. And then, Luisa and I felt we couldn't just tell our parents we'd made such a big mistake. So, we decided to stay together for a year." He looked down at his hands and rubbed them together. "After a year, we talked and both felt it wasn't going to get any better. But we still didn't know how to tell our parents. So, I decided that I needed to come here to work. But really, it was just to escape from the situation. That's what it truly was—an escape." Edwardo paused, considering his words.

"Sarah, I have been here four years. It didn't seem necessary to get the divorce when we hadn't really been honest with our parents yet. Now I've told my parents, and Luisa has told hers. We are ready for the divorce. Even my parents have seemed to accept it. I was so relieved when they finally got it. My dad even apologized for putting us under that pressure. I've already seen a lawyer and he's preparing the paperwork. It should be ready in a couple of weeks." He looked over at me hopefully, but I still didn't respond. Edwardo could see he hadn't really gotten to the heart of it for me, and he nodded slightly before taking a breath and starting again.

"I'm so sorry for not being honest with you. It was something that I opened my mouth to say a million times, but then I'd think, 'But then I'll lose her.' And I wouldn't say it. My heart so wanted to tell you, but my mind kept thinking it was not the right time. At first, since I hadn't brought it up before we started dating, I thought,

I'll just wait to see if this is something. Why bring it up if we don't really end up wanting to be together? It's almost like I was making an assumption that bringing it up would be saying that we were getting serious and you needed to know. But of course, you needed to know. From the beginning. I can see that now. I can see that I was just putting off something uncomfortable. I'm so sorry. I hope you can forgive me." Edwardo looked at me with this heart-splitting entreaty on his face. Like I held his life in my hands.

I didn't know what to say. I loved this man. But what if hiding the truth was his character? What if he continued to hide things?

"Edwardo, I can see how hard this is for you," I began hesitantly. "But it's really hard for me to understand why you would keep this from me. I understand that your parents had put pressure on you for this marriage. But after all this time, it would seem as though if you were ready to start dating someone, you would be ready to get a divorce. Or at least tell the person you wanted to date what the story was." I looked at him and saw his deep pain. But I was in so much turmoil, I couldn't just let him in because he was sorry. I needed to understand who he really was. I felt my judgment of him rising up. What was so hard about telling his parents? There had to be more to this story.

"Can you help me understand why it was so hard to tell your parents?"

Edwardo's face sank, and I knew he could feel my harsh judgment of him. But he nodded again, attempting to get the words out.

"Why. It's so hard to describe why. My mother wanted this marriage to work because the families were so close, and it would have meant having her grandchildren close. She really loves Luisa like a daughter and wanted her to be her daughter-in-law. In Mexico, we're Catholic and no one is supposed to get a divorce. I mean, it's really not allowed by the church. The people my parents knew who were divorced always got an annulment and tried to make that work in the church. But everyone would know. And then there was my dad who was hoping for the two families to merge businesses. But that was never going to work. There was a big part of me that wanted my dad to see me as a success. But I knew that I couldn't stay there and try to meet his expectations of taking over his business. I had no interest. So, moving here was again, an escape. God, that makes me sound like such a...loser!"

"But Edwardo, didn't it take guts to move here? Why was coming here less hard than just telling them that the marriage wasn't going to work?"

He shook his head. "I don't know. I guess at first, because I told them it was a chance for me to get a good job doing something I cared about and then bring back my experience to Mexico and help people there. They thought it was a plan for the future of my family, I guess. But after so much time here, I'm sure they saw through that."

He shook his head and rose from his chair to sit next to me on the couch, taking my hands gently between his. Taking a deep breath, his face softened as he said, "Sarah, I began to love you when you first told me about how hard it was when you lost your sister. And then, how much you wanted to help other people so they wouldn't suffer. I could see what kind of heart you carry. The kind of heart that is soft and open to the world. I fell in love with you that first night we went out."

I could feel tears began to sting my eyes, and one tear escaped, falling softly down my cheek. Edwardo reached out to wipe it away.

"But if I told you then, which is what I should have done, what would you have done?" he asked.

I took my hands back gently, clasping them together. "Well, I probably would have said, stop, go get a divorce! I would have stopped what we were doing and told you to go away. Sometimes I wish you had." I felt some anger, but mostly I felt sad. I thought for a moment about why it bothered me so much.

Edwardo voice softened, and he looked pained. "Yes, that's what I was afraid of and why I just couldn't do it. I was falling in love, and I didn't want it to stop. It was selfish of me."

I got up and went to the kitchen counter, grabbing a napkin, wiping my face. I tried to figure out why I was finding it hard to just forgive him. He saw my hesitation and took a step toward me.

"Sarah, what are you worried about now? If we love each other, then can we not move ahead? Knowing that we will both make mistakes, I hope we can learn to share with each other and forgive each other."

I could feel his sincerity, but I also felt my cautiousness rise like a guardrail. "But that's just it, Edwardo! How do I know that you'll share difficult things with me? How do I know that you won't continue to hide what you're afraid of me knowing? I'm worried that this is a tendency you have. Especially since you were so afraid of telling even your parents about the end of your marriage." I went back over to the couch and sat down in an exhausted huff. "I just don't know," I said shaking my head in frustration.

When I finally looked at him, I took in the defeated look on his face. He was beginning to give up. I could see his breathing slow, his face moving into anguish. This man totally loved me. That was clear by the look in his eyes. I sighed, picking up his hand. Hope glimmered briefly on his face at this.

"Edwardo, I do love you." I said, knowing that I had to tell him. He took my other hand as I continued. "But I don't know how to move forward. I think we need to slow it down. Just...see what happens if we commit to being completely honest with each other. About everything. I mean, our fears about this not working out.

And our hopes that it might. Just take a step back from everything and be more intentional about how we are with one another." My tone was serious and deliberate, but his face relaxed in relief. He nodded and caressed my hand.

"Yes, of course. I get it. You aren't ready to fully commit to me. Ay, caramba! How can you be? I completely understand. I'm so relieved that you'll give me another chance. Ay Dios Mio! Gracias." He relaxed, his whole body coming down off the high anxiety of his fear. Then he leaned forward to kiss me. I let him, and the absolute release of that kiss told me more than any words. Our bodies knew and were stronger than the fear that was still hiding inside my heart.

But there was still fear; the fear of losing someone that I loved. Since losing my sister, fear of loss was just a part of me. I knew that every time I loved someone, I would fear losing them. But I couldn't let that stop me anymore, because loss is a part of love. I was beginning to learn that.

I also knew the feeling of not being forgiven. Gloria had helped me see that I was still carrying that stone of guilt. It was time to put it down and focus on forgiving others.

CHAPTER THIRTY

IRENE

DECEMBER, 2016

I fielded calls all weekend trying to quell the wild rumors that were circulating about Jeffrey and Rev. Sarah. The callers weren't sure why they were upset because they really didn't have a clue what had happened in the Vestry meeting. They only knew that something had happened, and they weren't getting the full picture. The gossip vacillated between Jeffrey trying to get Sarah fired, to Sarah getting the diocese to kick Jeffrey out of the church. That Sunday, more people shanghaied me at the end of my pew, while I tried to give them answers that were vague but true. Jeffrey Trainor was not kicked out, I insisted, he resigned from the Vestry. Rev. Sarah was only doing what she needed to do to protect the church. Some accepted that, but I'm sure some went on to call others on the Vestry who might have different versions.

I finally shook myself loose at coffee hour from all the speculation and went over to speak to Justine and Abigail. They, of course, seemed blissfully ignorant of anything concerning the drama that was swirling around them, which I surmised only because they didn't ask me any questions about it, and I certainly didn't bring it up.

Abigail was wearing a beautiful emerald-green sweater with a short black skirt. I complimented her on the sweater which was perfect for the upcoming holidays since it was already December. The parish hall was decked out with the traditional holiday decorations although they seemed cheap and a bit overly glittery to me, like we were trying very hard to be jolly but weren't fooling anyone. I knew Mary had spent some time over the weekend pulling the tired plastic garlands from the storage closet and draping them around.

I was not someone who enjoyed the holidays since I had spent many alone after my mother died. During the holiday season, seeing all the stores ablaze with white lights, evergreens, and brightly colored ornaments always put me in a diminished state. But the decorations at church, being pathetic, just seemed sad to me. I mentioned that to Justine and Abigail while asking them what they were doing for the holidays. Justine looked at Abigail as was her habit before she spoke.

"Well, we're not sure yet. I've invited my parents to come here but they've never visited us. They have kept me at a distance since I made it clear that I was living with Abigail. But my mother has been calling me lately. So, we're hoping that they'll come, but you never know. We'll probably have a quiet holiday as usual. Just have a nice dinner together. I like to cook, and Abigail makes a beautiful chocolate Yule log. What about you, Irene, will you be visiting with family?"

"I'm also really not one to play up the holidays. They have always seemed to me to be an excuse for toy companies to push their latest Barbie dreamhouse or toy machine gun on unsuspecting parents who are trying to make their kids happy. "

Justine looked momentarily surprised at my response, then asked, "Will you be with family over the holidays?"

I felt embarrassed. I usually tried to avoid this question. But with this couple, I had to be honest. "Uh, no. Since my mother died a few years ago, I haven't had any family that I wanted to be with. But I'll probably spend the day getting caught up with my Christmas cards which I never get out on time."

Abigail nudged Justine in the ribs and Justine quickly asked, "Irene, would you like to spend Christmas with us? I mean, it's not fancy, and if my parents come, it may be tense, but we'd love to have you." Abigail smiled and nodded before saying, "Yes, Irene, we would."

I can't tell you how much I had been hoping for this without really knowing it. I didn't want to be overeager, but I was excited. "Yes, I'd love that." I said, smiling with genuine gratitude. We agreed that I would bring my spinach casserole with nutmeg and cream cheese, my mother's recipe, and the fresh cranberry sauce that I loved to make. I thanked them again profusely. They were such a sweet couple, and I was so glad that they were sticking with St. Philips especially now that Jeffrey was gone. I looked forward to what could change. I didn't want to get their hopes up so soon, but I wanted to begin to put a plan in place.

But mostly, I was pleased that they saw me as someone they wanted to know better, despite the differences in our ages. I had gone to Shelley's home last Christmas and her family was always so welcoming, but I felt out of place. A lesbian aunt, hanging around without anywhere else to go. It felt awkward. As much as Shelley loved me, she couldn't quite bridge that gap with her grown kids who were very friendly and me who had not been a part of their lives growing up. I would try to figure out some generic gifts to bring them, but it just made it uncomfortable when they hadn't thought to get something for me. Justine and Abigail seemed to genuinely want me there and I was looking forward to being with them.

Seeing Rev. Sarah come into the parish hall, I made a beeline for her. So many people had been coming up to me and asking what the hell was going on with Jeffrey and the Vestry and I didn't know what to say. Rev. Sarah needed to announce his resignation and do it soon. I was getting weary of dealing with more of his shenanigans and I didn't want Sarah to somehow end up taking the blame for this. That man deserved what he was going to get, plenty of blame!

After making arrangements with Rev. Sarah to meet her in her office, I went and sat in the sanctuary for a few minutes. I often came here and sat, just to get my head on straight. I was feeling this anger about Jeffrey rising up in me. Sitting there, I began to realize that this anger felt familiar. It felt like the anger I had toward my dad. He had been absent most of my childhood, just too busy with his work to notice me much. And then when I was in high school, he left us. My mother told me it was just that they weren't compatible anymore, but I soon learned that he was living with another woman. I had stopped seeing him regularly after that, but never really had a real relationship. He died when I was in college. It had just felt so unfair. Like this was. Another man treating others with disrespect and disregard. My anger was palpable even today.

I tried praying, asking God to help me. But something nagged at me when I prayed about this, something unresolved. Did my dad leave because he sensed that I was gay? He seemed so disappointed when I never went to the dances. He'd ask me if I had a friend that I might want to invite to come over to dinner, meaning did I have boyfriend, and I'd roll my eyes and shake my head. He'd sigh deeply and mutter, "What's the use!" When I finally came out to my mom, I asked her not to tell Dad and she exclaimed, "Oh, heavens, I wouldn't think of it!" She told me later that it was a good thing that he'd died before he found out, because it would have killed him. Could I forgive him? I've never figured that one out.

I left for Rev. Sarah's office my heart still heavy.

CHAPTER THIRTY-ONE

SARAH

The next morning, my spirits were definitely lifted from my time with Edwardo. After our difficult discussion, we had gone out to dinner at our favorite small Italian trattoria down the street. I kept it light-hearted but also filled him in on all the drama that had gone on during the interim. He was horrified but was grateful that the diocese had been there to back me up. He smiled and reached over to touch my hand when I told him how relieved I was to have this episode somewhat resolved. I had been worried that I would lose my job and him both in the same week!

He had squeezed my hand and said softly, "Sarah, you won't lose me unless you decide that I'm not the right person for you. I do hope you know that." I had nodded gently and changed the subject since I knew I wasn't ready to make that decision. But I got the message. Edwardo was here to stay. I just needed to know if that's what I wanted.

We ended the evening in front of my apartment building. He sensed that I wouldn't invite him up to stay when I paused and turned to him before going in. I reached for his hand, but he pulled me against his chest, wrapping his arms around me, hugging me tightly before leaning down for a kiss. This kiss was a sweet one, one that promised more but wasn't an urgent push. I appreciated that he was responding to my request to slow down a little so I could see how my heart felt. He didn't let go, but looked at me and said softly, "Sarah, I love you with all my heart. But you set the pace, and I will follow." I smiled in agreement and let go, telling him I would call the next day. He squeezed my arm lightly in response, then walked away slowly, hands shoved in his pockets. I let myself into the building, slightly regretting my decision to slow things down, but I knew it was the right decision. I just had to honor the wisdom that had urged me to watch my heart and give it time.

Walking into the parish hall after service on Sunday, I saw Irene coming toward me briskly; her face was all business.

"Hey Irene, did you need something from me?"

"Yeah, if you have time, I'd like to go to your office," she said looking around to see if anyone else was pursuing me.

"Well, sure, but since I told people I wasn't free, let's not be obvious. Why don't I take a few minutes to greet people and then meet you there in ten?" She nodded and went toward the door.

I went right over to a young couple who were heading up the Christmas donation drive and checked in with them about how that was going, then saw Justine and Abigail about to leave. I raised my hand to stop them and went over and greeted them. Justine seemed very glad to see me.

"We've just invited Irene to come for Christmas dinner. Then we realized that since this is your first Christmas in Philadelphia that you might be without family. Do you have family you'll be joining for Christmas? Or could we invite you to come as well?"

I was surprised and pleased to hear their offer. I had told my parents that I couldn't come there until the day after Christmas since we had services on Christmas Day and I didn't feel like travelling that day. I wasn't sure what Edwardo would want to do, or even if he'd be in town. But maybe he wouldn't mind joining me.

"That is so sweet of you to offer. I haven't confirmed my plans yet, so I'd love to think about it and get back to you. Could I let you know by the end of the week? And could I bring a date with me?"

Abigail beamed and answered, "We would be so honored to have you join us and of course, your date would be very welcome. Yeah, just let us know!"

I told them I'd call them by Friday, and we said our good-byes.

I said hello to a couple of other congregants and then excused myself to hurry back to my office. Mary was pulling on her coat while talking with Irene. She saw me and turned as she fastened her buttons.

"Rev. Sarah, I've started a list of people who want to talk to you about the 'situation,' and I put it on your desk. A few of them seemed very anxious to do so, but I told them that you were busy this week and would get back to them as soon as you could."

"Thanks, Mary. You go on home. Why don't you take tomorrow off since you were here today?"

Mary looked surprised, "Oh, well, sure. I'd love that." She took her purse and bag and turned to leave. "Then I'll see you Tuesday?"

"Yes, see you then." As Mary left, I motioned Irene into my office and we went in, closing the door. Irene sat on the far chair near the window and I took the chair opposite.

"So, what's going on now? Have you been hearing lots of gossip about how I wrangled Jeffrey out of the Vestry?"

Irene sighed, sitting back. "Well, lots of different scenarios with varying conjectures. I think we need to clarify for people," she said seriously.

"I agree, and as I said, I plan on writing a newsletter article soon. But you know, I want to give Jeffrey one more chance."

Irene curled up her lip, frowning. "I don't know why. I think he's had plenty of chances."

I paused, taking my time. Then I decided to confess my revelation in the park the other day.

"The truth is, I've been judging Jeffrey and another man in my life very harshly. I couldn't see that they had acted in any way except very selfishly. I didn't want to give them the benefit of the doubt. All this was weighing on me so heavily that I just felt like I was carrying around a rock. My heart was so heavy. Then after just pouring this out in prayer one day, I realized that I was also not blameless. There are plenty of things I've done wrong. Now, and at other times in my life. And if I deserved to be forgiven, then they did, too."

Irene looked confused. "If you're saying—"

"Well, just wait. Let me finish."

"Okay."

"When I realized that I had been guilty of a few untoward actions in my life, I realized that I've never forgiven myself for some of them. Some of the things I've been carrying around like bad baggage. That guilt has made me judge myself and others without considering why we all screw up sometimes. You know, we all do."

Irene cocked her head to the side, as if to ask if she could finally interject, so I nodded. "Sure. We all screw up," she said. "We all need forgiveness. And God forgives us, I get that. Of course, we also need to forgive each other. That makes sense. But if we are accountable to each other, then there needs to be boundaries that people can't cross. Jeffrey crossed a number of boundaries. He may deserve forgiveness, but he doesn't deserve to be given any more chances."

I thought for a minute. "I get what you're saying. And I'm not suggesting that he remain on the Vestry. I'm suggesting that we invite him back into the church, so he has the chance to make amends for what he's done."

Irene raised her eyebrows at this. "Oh? How would he do that?"

"Well, that's something he would need to figure out. But if he was willing, I'd be willing to help him figure it out."

Irene sighed. "Ugh, I don't know, Rev. Sarah. I suppose I don't really forgive him. It's not about the affair. That's human. We all make mistakes. But I don't forgive him for leading Terry on and trying to get his way on the Vestry. And, of course, for getting the Vestry to prevent gay marriage. Sorry. I don't forgive him for that."

"I get it. That's pretty unforgiveable. All of it is. But would you want Jeffrey to walk away from this church feeling that he is unforgiven?"

Irene sighed in frustration. "I don't know, Sarah. I really don't," she replied.

"It's really hard. But I'm at least going to call Jeffrey and invite him to talk and ask him if he wants to start over. Make amends. He may very well say no. I mean, I'm not sure he'll even talk to me. We'll see."

Irene sighed, her exasperation with my approach apparent. I thanked her as she left.

I sat down and decided I better take some time to pray before I made the call. After spending a few minutes in silent prayer, I looked up and saw my New Testament on my desk and opened it to the passage I knew I'd find in Matthew 18.

Jesus told this story: "*If a shepherd has a hundred sheep, and one of them has gone astray, does he not leave the ninety-nine on the mountains and go in search of the one that went astray? And if he finds it, truly I tell you, he rejoices over it more than over the ninety-nine that never went astray.*"

If I could be forgiven, so could he. It was time to go find the one sheep who had gone astray.

***

The next morning, looking around my apartment at the mess that had accumulated over the past two weeks, I decided to start putting things in order by taking my clothes down to the laundromat. I stuffed the dirty laundry in a sack, avoiding the smell of ripeness, and grabbed some quarters from my bureau. The sun was shining and even though the temperature was brisk, I looked up at a beautiful blue-sky day. A bit weary from a night of worrying about Jeffrey, then Edwardo, those thoughts hung over my head, threatening my mood, despite the cheerful sky.

Deciding to enjoy the weather and walk the two blocks to the laundromat, I set out with the bag slung over my shoulder. Lots of people were out, some busy and pushing themselves forward into the exigencies of the day, some with worried expressions on their faces, some just bored looking. I flashed back to the expression on Jeffrey's face when he barreled out of the Vestry meeting. I had a strong urge to reach out to him. I knew he was hurting, and I felt some degree of responsibility for that. While I dreaded talking with him, I knew I wouldn't stop thinking about him like that proverbial lost sheep until I did something about it. At least tried.

After dealing with the laundry and having 30 minutes to kill, I decided to walk down the block to the little pocket park. Being a school day, there weren't any children at the park and I settled on a park bench near the swing-sets.

Preparing myself to make the necessary outreach to Jeffrey, I spent a few minutes just sitting quietly, trying to find as much calmness as I could. I was as ready as I ever would be. Although, in truth,

I wasn't ever going to be ready for this. I picked up my phone and texted Jeffrey.

[I would like to talk to you. Would you be open to meeting with me?]

No answer. I wait. Two minutes. Three. Then I see a text come back.

[What do we have to talk about? You clearly don't want me in that church.]

I thought for a minute, then answered back.

[No, that isn't correct. I do want you to come back to the church. We'd just need to talk about what that would look like.]

[So, you want to get me down on my knees asking for forgiveness, is that it?]

[Do you want to find a way back into this church? Do you want forgiveness?]

No answer. I waited and prayed. His reply came a few minutes later.

[I don't know. I know I've done wrong to Elaine. I want her forgiveness. But I don't think I've done anything wrong to the church.]

[Would you be open to talk about this? I'm not here to judge, just to help you decide how you want to move forward with your life.]

Another minute.

[Well, I might be open to talking. But not at the church.]

[Good. Meet at a restaurant? Tomorrow morning?]

It took a few more minutes and I thought I'd lost him, but then it came back.

[Okay. 8:30 at the Country Diner.]

I could barely believe that he agreed. *Now what would I say when we met?*

I spent the evening Googling "How to make amends in community," but there wasn't much help out there. Even looking at my diocesan handbook on healthy communities and re-building broken trust didn't yield much. Nothing seemed to fit this particular situation.

The next morning, I made sure that I arrived at the diner first, securing a table in a secluded corner. I ordered a tea and waited nervously. Jeffrey arrived a few minutes late and looked around scanning the restaurant. Spotting me, he walked slowly toward the back of the diner, his expression the picture of a "gallows face." He seemed puzzled when I offered my hand but shook it hesitantly and sat down.

"I'm really glad you agreed to see me today," I told him.

Jeffrey still looked wary and sighed. "Well, Rev. Sarah, I certainly didn't want you to think I blamed this all on you."

Yeah, sure, I thought. It sure felt that way.

The waitress came by and he ordered black coffee and toast. I told her I didn't need any breakfast. I didn't think I could eat anything with him there; my stomach was queasy enough as it was.

"I certainly hope you don't blame me. I've always been open to talking over this situation with you."

"Yeah, until you decided to put a stop to my trying to hire Terry."

"I told you that it wasn't appropriate to hire someone you were personally involved with."

"You also told the Vestry about that involvement! I asked you not to share that."

"Jeffrey, I did not share your personal information. I simply shared that you were not in a position to be objective since you had developed a close relationship. I also shared that the hiring process decided on by the Vestry was not being followed."

Jeffrey gave me a stone-cold look. He cleared his throat. "Rev. Sarah, I don't know what good it's going to do to re-hash this whole thing."

"I agree. I was hoping we could move on to how we could find a way for you to feel comfortable coming back to St. Philips."

His food was delivered then and Jeffrey got busy buttering his toast. He looked at me while taking his first bite, like he wished I would go away.

"Are you interested in coming back to the church?" I asked him.

Jeffrey took a sip of coffee, taking his time. "Well, because of everything that happened, Elaine kicked me out of the house. And my kids aren't talking to me. So, why would anyone want me back at church?" he asked defiantly.

I sighed. "Jeffrey, I don't think you can blame all of those problems on what happened in that meeting."

He sniffed and wiped his mouth. "No, not all of it. Some of it happened because you shared things with Elaine, so she knew what was going on."

I sighed heavily at that. *This may have been a mistake. We weren't getting anywhere.*

"You know very well that Elaine came to me and had already guessed what was going on with Terry. She was the one who confirmed it to me. I did not share anything that I had learned."

My tone was stern, and I felt like I was the principal calling in a naughty boy to receive his punishment. Jeffrey snorted in derision and looked away. Irene had been right—he wasn't taking responsibility for any of this. I had been very naïve, again.

I tried one more time. "Jeffrey, there's two ways this can go. You can stay angry and out of relationship with all of us at St. Philips. That is certainly your prerogative. But I hope you'll opt for the alternative, and that's you putting things right to make some things better. Because if you don't, you will lose your family, your friends, and your church."

Jeffrey took a sip of coffee his coffee and slowly took another bite of toast. He looked deflated, the righteous anger seemed to have evaporated, along with the arrogance. He seemed sad and no longer sure of himself.

"Sarah, I don't want to lose my family. I love my family. I love Elaine. And this thing with Terry, it was a huge mistake. I thought I loved her. But that was just my...boredom and unhappiness with my life. I mean, it's not Elaine's fault that I was not getting what I wanted in my marriage. It was my fault. I know that now. But..." He seemed to be at a loss for words. "I don't quite know how to ask for her forgiveness. I mean, I'm just not good at that."

I felt a little disgusted by his late-coming remorsefulness. But I also couldn't help but feel sorry for him—he looked so sad.

"No one is good at asking for forgiveness," I told him. "Believe me, I'm certainly not good at it." I sighed, summoning what compassion I still had for this man. "But nevertheless, when we hurt others, we need to ask for their forgiveness. You may not get it, even if you ask. But you can't move forward without asking. You know that, right?"

Jeffrey sat with his head down for a minute "I guess you're right," he said quietly. "But if I ask for forgiveness and people don't forgive me, then what do I do? I'd have made myself look ridiculous!"

I couldn't hide my impatience that response. I couldn't help it. But I tried to not raise my voice. "Jeffrey, is that all you care about? How you look to other people? Don't you care about how you hurt other people? Healing what you broke?"

He put a finger over his mouth for a minute, thinking. "Yes, I do care. I realize that it doesn't look like it. But I haven't been sleeping. I keep thinking about my kids and how I've let them down. And

Elaine, she didn't deserve this. She is such a good mother to those boys."

"So, why don't you start there? Go ask Elaine for your forgiveness. Explain to the kids that you made a mistake. A big one. See if you can start to put things back together in your family."

He nodded, his eyes down, lips tight.

"And Jeffrey, when you're ready, I'd be happy to talk more about the rest of it. Apologizing to Terry and to the church. When you're ready."

He shook his head. "I don't know if I can do that." He finished off his coffee and got up.

I extended my hand, and he hesitated before finally shaking it. After taking some bills out of his wallet and leaving them under his plate, he gave me a curt nod and left.

CHAPTER THIRTY-TWO

JEFFREY

Jesus H. Christ, she had some nerve! I mean, I get it that she thinks I need to apologize to Elaine. But for God's sake! Apologize to Terry? Terry's the one who led me on! She kept on saying things like, "Oh, Jeffrey, we have so much in common. I would just like to get to know you better." And more stuff about how she wonders if Elaine really "got me". She's the one who kept putting ideas in my head about the problems that I might be having in my marriage. Mistakenly, I had shared that sometimes marriage was really hard. And boom! After that, she just ran with it.

I mean, it's true. Our marriage has been stale. All we ever talked about was the kids. Whether Alan should try out for basketball. Whether Paul was spending too much time on his phone and should we take it away when his grades went down? But that's just the way marriage is. You put all your energy into the kids and pretty soon, your marriage is shot to hell! I don't blame Elaine for that. I'm just as guilty of turning away from her and toward someone with whom I didn't have to discuss all those mundane things.

But I want to change all that. I want my marriage back. I'm ready to work on it. I just have to convince Elaine.

I drove by our house. The van was in the driveway, so I knew she was home. It was Saturday so the boys might be home. I didn't want to text her because I'm sure she'd just tell me she's not ready. But if she saw me, maybe she would see the regret on my face. I got out of the car, hesitating, checking the windows before slowly walking to the front door. The boys had left their basketball in the driveway again. I paused, thinking I couldn't just use my key and go in because Elaine didn't want me there. Feeling like an idiot, I rang the door to my own house instead and hoped the boys wouldn't answer so I wouldn't have to face them.

The door swung open, Elaine's face seeing me and immediately shutting down like a window blind. I scrambled for the right words, but she held up her hand like a traffic cop.

"No," she half whispered, glancing over her shoulder. "I don't want you here."

"Elaine," I started, but she held up her hand again, and stepped outside the door shutting it behind her.

"Jeffrey," she said firmly, "I am not ready to forgive you. I don't know if I ever will. But I don't want you here now."

Frustrated, I tried to soften my response, and reached out my hand to touch hers, desperate to find some sort of lost connection. "I just want to talk. I want to apologize. I owe you so much. I screwed up bigtime. Can we just sit and talk? Maybe you're not ready now. But maybe in a few days? Please."

She pursed her lips, and her hands pulled away from mine. She glanced around the neighborhood to see if anyone was watching, but the street was quiet. When she looked back at me, her face was completely shut down, void of any expression. That got me sweating a little.

"I don't know when I'll be ready. I'll let you know. But I do want you to see the kids. I want you to try to explain what you've done. I sure don't know what to say." Her tone was punishing.

"Okay. I do want to see them. But wait, what have you told them?"

Elaine sighed, glancing back at the door. "I just told them that right now, we're having a little time out from each other. That it doesn't mean we're getting a divorce, but sometimes married people just need a break from each other." She frowned in disgust. "And boy, is that an understatement!"

I felt a bit encouraged by her characterization. It sounded like maybe this was not too serious. I nodded in agreement.

"Good. Can you ask them if they want to come out for pizza with me? Like now? Or maybe I could pick them up tonight?"

Elaine considered. "Not now. Paul's got homework and Alan is still sleeping. Tonight would be better. I'll text you what time—if they want to come. Which I can't control." She scowled.

I nodded. This was as good as it will get, I guess. "Okay. Tell them I'll take them for pizza and bowling if they want." Elaine nodded, then turned, grabbing the door handle.

"Wait, Elaine. I just want you to know that I know I made a huge mistake. But I want us to start over. Please give me another chance." I hated begging, but I truly wanted this more than anything.

Elaine didn't respond at first, possibly considering what I said. But then she just shook her head, and said tersely, "You should've figured that out a long time ago." She disappeared into the house, shutting the door behind her without looking back. I waited for a minute, hoping maybe she'd change her mind. Then when the closed door of my own house stared back at me disparagingly, I turned towards my car, hoping the neighbors hadn't seen any of it.

CHAPTER THIRTY-THREE

IRENE

I've never been the most feminine woman, but not masculine either. But I wondered what I had been thinking when I bought this lilac blouse with a self- tie, as I filled plastic bags with clothes from the back of my closet to take to Goodwill, late on a Saturday afternoon. I mean, I've never felt comfortable with the masculine way some lesbians dressed. I know I've inherited some of my mother's very antiquated views of dress. Clearly, there were times I let her influence me too much.

Taking a break in the soft comfy chair in my study, I grabbed my laptop from the side table, opening up my email. Rev. Sarah sent me a draft of her newsletter article describing the Senior Warden's resignation due to "irreconcilable differences with the Vestry and the priest around a hiring process". Hiring process, my foot. It was an unethical end-run around the priest to hire his bit on the side to appease her. But the article sounded professional and not inflammatory. I sent her back my approval and added a note.

[Rev. Sarah, you didn't deserve this mess happening in your first year. Let's hope that from now on the church gives you their gratitude and support. I certainly do. Thank you for hanging in there.]

I also asked Sarah if we could sit down with Frank, now the Senior Warden, so we could make a plan for major objectives for the Vestry to accomplish during the rest of the year. She knew that in addition to getting a Christian Education Director hired, we needed to start planning the approval process for gay marriage in the church. She wrote back that afternoon agreeing that we should plan a meeting with Frank. So, I suggested that I'd reach out to him.

Justine had called that week and confirmed the time for their Christmas dinner, and I found myself excited about it. I mean, this young couple were so sweet, and they deserved to have their wedding in a church where a community was ready to support them. They told me they were dreaming about adopting a child from China as soon as they could get approved. They had already started the paperwork with an agency that coordinated international adoptions, but it was complicated. Their marriage would help the process.

One day at the homeless shelter, I spied a big white box stacked under some plastic bags of clothes. I pulled it out and opened it. Inside was a white wedding dress in a dry-cleaning bag made of a polished linen, simple cap sleeves, and a scoop neck. It was in perfect condition. I immediately thought of Abigail in this dress. I closed the box and put it to one side. At the end of the day, I asked the director if she would mind if I directed it toward someone who might be able to use it. She smiled and said, "Please do, Irene! And blessings to them!" I stowed in the back of my car. Even if Abigail couldn't use it. Someone could.

CHAPTER THIRTY-FOUR

SARAH

Over the next month, the Vestry prepared to meet the new challenges of hiring a Christian Education Director, electing a new member to the Vestry, and responding to Irene's request to consider a new vote on marriage equality. There were a few old-timers who got their feathers all ruffled by this idea, but the majority of the congregation seemed very ready to move into the 21st century.

Irene spoke to the Vestry in a meeting where several congregants showed up, some to put a stop to the movement, and some who offered their support.

"You all know me," Irene told the group that day. "You all know that I have been loved and cherished in this congregation. I have been supported and encouraged as I struggled in my career and my life. And yet, I cannot understand how you can care about me, but not be ready to validate my life and who I am. I have not asked this congregation to bless a union for me. I have not had that blessing in my life. But we now have a couple in our congregation who is ready and asking if we would bless them in their union, as a fully accepted and supported couple in love. I am ready for this congregation to move ahead. But if this congregation is not ready, then, I may not be able to stay. I can no longer wait for this congregation to offer everyone what you offer each other."

Seeing Irene put herself on the line like that with the congregation where she has spent most of her adult life, I was moved to act. I felt something push me to stand up. I had to take my chances with her. I had to be ready, because the time had come.

"I am still new here. And I'm still working to develop your trust. But I have come to develop a great admiration and trust in Irene. She has given her life to this congregation, as many of you have over the years. So many of you have been faithful in keeping this church steady. But times have changed. Our faith has grown clearer in its understanding of God speaking to us with new words. It's become clearer that our faith should not be stymied by tradition. Tradition is filled with customs designed to maintain power and exclude marginalized people. Jesus taught us that we must love everyone, regardless of their place in society. In John 4, Jesus says, "Beloveds, let us love one another, for love comes from God. Everyone who loves has been born of God and knows God."

I looked around the room, many faces nodding and smiling. A few seemed unmoved. And two older members who had urged me not to vote on this now, looked down at the floor.

The Vestry voted to allow same-sex marriage in our sanctuary and to bless these marriages with whole-hearted acceptance. The two older members left the meeting abruptly, obviously upset. I would make sure I reached out to them later. But the rest of the Vestry and some on-lookers there to witness the vote, clapped and beamed with joy, looking toward Irene. She turned to me with the most grateful smile, taking my hands and said, "Thank you, Sarah."

***

Over the next few weeks, Edwardo and I found ourselves shifting back into a cozy, intimate, relaxed place, often seeing each other a few times a week, staying the night at each other's apartments. He wasn't pushing and I wasn't anxiously looking for cracks in the relationship. He shared openly about how things were with his parents as they had begun their acceptance of his divorce and their questions about me. He teased me about how they wanted to know more about my background and they were curious about me asking questions like: "Why does she want to be a priest?" Their experience with Catholic priests being one of distant, judgmental men who know nothing about family life. Edwardo teased that they probably thought I was not free to marry.

One evening after dinner, Edwardo was relaxing on the couch, looking over my selection of CDs while I finished up the dishes. He always jumped right in with the cooking, being very handy with chopping vegetables, or even showing his expertise with using a wok. He would often banish me to the couch after dinner to clean up when I was too tired. But tonight, I had assigned him to find some music for us to enjoy as we sipped another glass of wine.

After the first strains of the upbeat Miles Davis trombone wended its way into the room, I broached the subject of Christmas.

"So, I was wondering…. I mean, I've been thinking that maybe we should drive up to Boston over Christmas break to visit my parents." I had been thinking this over for a while and I was ready for him to meet them.

Edwardo's face lit up. "Really?" he asked with surprise. "You mean, you're not worried it wouldn't be moving too fast?"

"Well, we don't have to think going together to see my parents is some kind of commitment, do we?"

Edwardo shook his head. "Well, no. But wait…do your parents know about my former marriage?"

"They know that I'm very involved with you and ready to intro-duce you to them."

"Meaning they don't know," he said, with a concerned tone.

I frowned. "Edwardo, they don't need to know everything."

"Right...so, why don't they need to know?"

"Because they wouldn't understand. You know their generation! They're pretty old-fashioned." I stared at him with impatience.

"I see. So, I must be completely honest with you, but selectively honest with your parents?" he said with a raised eyebrow.

I rolled my eyes, sighing. "They're my parents, for God's sake! They don't need to know everything the first time you meet them."

"In that case, you know I'd love to meet your parents. I thought you'd never ask me, but I'm so happy that you want me to." Moving closer to me on the couch, he put his arms around me, pulling me to him. There wasn't any more discussion that night.

When I called my parents to tell them of our holiday plans, they were thrilled. I warned them not to jump to conclusions about our relationship. "No hints about getting married!" I insisted. My mother assured me that they would try not to make assumptions, but her voice sounded indecently pleased.

When I asked Justine and Abigail if I could bring a guest to their Christmas day celebration, they said they would be thrilled that we would join them for their holiday dinner. I checked with Edwardo about the plan. He thought it was a great idea. Since the invitation to come to Boston with me for Christmas break, we seemed to be relaxing into the joyful freedom of trusting that we wanted to be together and we would move forward with that goal.

CHAPTER THIRTY-FIVE

IRENE

When Justine called me the week before Christmas, I picked up eager to finalize the plans for Christmas dinner at their house. But as soon as she greeted me, I could hear in her strained tone that something was up.

"Justine, what is it? You don't sound great."

She emitted a slight groan. "Yeah. You're right. Things aren't great."

"What's going on?"

"Well, you know that we asked my parents to come for dinner next week," she sighed. "They aren't coming. But that's not all."

"Oh, dear, what else?"

Justine sighed again. "They told me that they don't want Abigail to be a part of my life, if we're going to be together in 'that way'. They basically said that they loved me, but they couldn't accept my lifestyle as it was against God."

My heart sank. I could imagine how this affront stung. I had felt it, but not with my mother, thank God! "Justine, I'm so sorry. I know this must hurt."

"Yeah, it does. I mean, I've known they weren't happy about Abigail. But they have met her and were at least polite about it. They've never invited us over again, but my mom would ask about her a bit. I had thought maybe they were softening. But apparently my dad suggested they go see their priest, and that was when they were told not to encourage my sin by accepting it."

She was silent for a moment. I just let it sit. Then I thought about what I did when I was hurt by others who rejected my life choices. Somehow, I found my way back to the church. Where I almost always found peace.

"Justine, I... well, I wondered what do you feel like you need right now? Is there a place you go or something you do when you're hurting?"

Justine made a quiet noise of frustration. "Well, that's just it. I mean, I do pray. I do find comfort in prayer. But when it's the church leading the mob against us, I just don't feel like God is on our side."

Hearing a priest who would break up a family like this made me so angry. I thought about how lucky I had been with a church who always backed me up.

"That's just a travesty. Telling you that God doesn't accept you! Of course, the love that God offers is not conditional! I just can't believe people who create this small God who is mean-spirited and prejudiced. It's not right!"

Justine's voice was not angry. It was sad and listless. "I know. It's not. But that's the world we live in. What can we do?"

"I don't know either. But I do know that our church and our priest offer something different. We offer everyone love and acceptance. Without judgment. Without conditions. So, would you like to talk to Rev. Sarah about it?"

Justine said she thought she would. And she agreed to call Rev. Sarah the next day and go see her with Abigail.

I checked in with Sarah and warned her about the situation. She was also furious with Justine's priest and how the Bible was used as a hammer against people.   She said she would expect Justine's call.

Later that week, Justine called me back. She said that she and Abigail had gone to see Rev. Sarah and had spent a long time talking about their families. She had given them time to express their anger and to envision a new future. A future in which they were loved and accepted by the people around them. Together, they talked about how to build that future. And it would start with joining the church and getting married in the church. Rev. Sarah had told them how the vote had gone to approve gay marriage and assured them that they could build a warm place for their family at St. Philips. Justine was thrilled and told me that we would hear more about it at Christmas dinner.

Christmas dinner at Justine's and Abigail's was more than I could have hoped for. I arrived a little early bringing my casserole carrier and the cranberry sauce in a festive glass container with a red ribbon. Justine and Abigail lived in a newer townhouse not far from the church. The front door was welcoming with a wreath decorated with pine cones and a bright plaid bow. Abigail welcomed me in with a little hug. She took me into the kitchen where Justine was basting a turkey.

"Merry Christmas, Irene!" she said, washing her hands at the sink and coming over to relieve me of the heavy casserole. We chatted about the meal before the doorbell chimed again with Rev. Sarah and her date arriving. Abigail went to greet them, and brought them into the kitchen where Justine had poured us some wine. Sarah's cheeks were rosy from the cold and her smile infectious as she introduced me to her boyfriend, Edwardo. She had told me very little about him other than he was from Mexico City but had been living in the U.S. for years. He seemed very warm, but stayed close to Sarah, a little shy in this new group.

After the introductions, Justine herded us into the living room, with Abigail following with glasses of wine. Their home was modern with clean, modern furniture, all blond wood and beige fabrics. Brightening the room were accents of scarlet and navy blue. In a corner of the room, next to the fireplace was a real fir tree in a bucket, decorated with small white lights.

Abigail disappeared back into the kitchen, and came back out carrying a bowl of chips and dip. Justine raised her glass, motioning us all to a toast. We grabbed our wine glasses and held them up, looking to her for the words.

"Here's to the spirit of the season which I think of as celebrating togetherness, all sorts of togetherness, whether it's family, or friends, or new friends, it's all about being with one another. Merry Christmas!" Justine raised her glass and we all followed, chiming in with "Merry Christmas!" or "Here, here!"

I added a hearty "And a happy new year!" which was truly how I felt. A good new year with these people who were becoming more important to me every day. Having Rev. Sarah there with her new boyfriend, Edwardo was such a delight. He seemed like a wonderful calming presence in her life. Justine and Abigail were good hostesses and made Edwardo feel welcome.

Justine called us into the dining room, which was beautifully set with a red tablecloth, white tapers, and a festive arrangement of glass Christmas trees. Justine asked Rev. Sarah to say a blessing which she did with a quiet grace. We started passing the plates to Abigail who had carved the turkey. The conversation started with sharing about our varying family traditions around the holidays, the Christmas Eve caroling, the gift giving, all those little things that somehow made Christmas unique for each family. But when Sarah turned to Abigail and asked if she'd like to share, Abigail got kind of flustered and blinked a few times, looking around the room.

"Um, well, I don't know. I guess, well, we had kind of quiet holidays. I mean, we'd get gifts, but they weren't exciting or anything. You know, it was considered more of a religious holiday than anything else."

Justine put down her fork, taking over from her. "Well, Abigail and I have had to invent our own holiday traditions since our families pretty much decided that we weren't welcome anymore. It got too hard after we went to Abigail's the year we met, and her father asked us to leave when I was introduced as her girlfriend. We haven't seen them since."

Everything got quiet then. My face was warm and my stomach felt queasy. It had been so many years since I had had to confront blatant prejudice. But these sweet women still had to face it in their own families. I focused on Abigail who had gone silent. "Abigail, I am so sorry that you've been treated that way in your own family. You deserve better."

Abigail nodded. "Well, thank you, Irene," she replied quietly, with a half-smile.

I continued, "Sometimes we have to make our own families. I've had to do that since my mother died. And here, tonight, by your inviting me and Rev. Sarah over, you're also doing that. You're creating a place for us to celebrate together. I think that's close to having something like family. At least, I hope you'll think of us that way."

Rev. Sarah nodded vigorously. "You're right, Irene. We need to create ways to celebrate what we do have."

When the meal was over, and we all moved back into the living room, Abigail got up and motioned Justine to follow her. She turned to us with a somewhat secretive smile. "This has gotten way too serious. It's Christmas and as we just said, it's time to celebrate. Are you all willing to experiment with something a little different, and hopefully, way more fun?" She gave a questioning glance to the group, and everyone nodded.

Abigail disappeared into the study at the end of the living room with Justine following, holding up a finger for us to wait. Sarah looked at me, eyebrows raised, wondering what they had up their sleeves. After a few minutes of hearing them whispering in low voices, Justine emerged wearing a red Santa jacket with the white trim, a furry white beard, and a Santa hat. She was carrying a large, fully stuffed bag.

"Ho, ho, ho!" she chortled. "Merry Christmas!" We all laughed at her antics.

"Ladies and Gentleman," she began in a deep voice, "we come together tonight to celebrate Christmas and it couldn't be Christmas without Santa! And of course, presents!" She held up the bag. "However, before you all receive your treats, you must show your true Christmas spirit! Right? We can't be jolly without some merriment. And what could be jollier than a Christmas pageant? A pageant where everyone participates!" She motioned around the room, gesturing to us all, a wide smile on her face. We looked at each other dubiously.

Rev. Sarah, laughed and voiced what we were all thinking, "Uh-oh! Does that mean, we have to wear costumes and play parts?"

Justine nodded vigorously. "Yes, indeed! Are you game?" she asked looking around. We nodded without much enthusiasm.

"Good! I introduce to you the director of the pageant, Miss Abigail, Spirit of Christmas Present!" She made a flourishing motion to the door, where Abigail stepped in, dressed in a pink, floor- length nightgown with some kind of tulle cape around her shoulders. She carried a sparkly wand and waved it a few times in the air.

"Welcome to our Christmas pageant! And now, Santa will give you all costumes and I will tell you your parts. Justine? I mean, Santa?"

Justine put her heavy bag down and started pulling things out of it. As she did, Abigail explained our parts. "First of all, this pageant is called, 'A Christmas Carol: Adapted to Modern Life'. Each of you will be given a costume and a role to play. Then, and this is the fun part, you will ad lib your role from what you might remember about the play, adding in what you think might occur given our current times," Abigail grinned, winking at all of us. I looked at Edwardo thinking that this might be a lot to expect of someone so new to the group. But he shrugged good-naturedly and got up with the rest of us to go along with the program.

What followed was creative mayhem with everyone doing their part to recreate something vaguely related to the Dickens piece but felt more like Saturday Night Live. Sarah played a priggish "Ms. Scrooge" with hilarious overtones of a society matron who belonged to the Junior League and patronized everyone with a "let them eat cake" attitude. I was assigned the part of Spirit of Christmas Past which I had to cogitate on for a minute. But soon enough, I invented a scene from Ms. Scrooge's past when she had a date with Donald Trump and was so disgusted with his attitude toward the less fortunate that she decides to start a homeless shelter. Sarah couldn't stop giggling as she responded to the assigned storyline. Edwardo revealed a whole other side when he, assigned to be Tiny Tim, imitated the falsetto voice of the strange 1970's singer with the same name bringing us all into paroxysm of laughter. "Tiptoe through the Two-Lips" will forever be burned in my mind now with Edwardo in a blond wig dancing with his imaginary ukelele.

Recovering from the absolute hilarity, we took off our costumes and were rewarded by Abigail with small wrapped gifts of Christmas candy. I noticed Justine glancing over at Rev. Sarah, and she nodded back.

Justine reached out and took Abigail's hand. She moved closer to her and pulled a small square box from her pocket. Abigail's face lit up.

Justine looked into her eyes, and said, "Abigail, you changed my life when you became my best friend. I cannot imagine my life without you. Will you marry me?"

Abigail just nodded, her eyes bright with tears. Taking the ring out of the box, Justine placed it on Abigail's finger. Abigail beamed with joy as she leaned over to kiss Justine while we all clapped and hooted.

Rev. Sarah came over, giving them both quick hugs, then added, "I hope you'll both do me the honor of allowing me to marry you in St. Philip's sanctuary!" We all clapped at that announcement, grateful for this moment to finally be here.

After so many years at St. Philips of carrying the torch for lesbians, now I hoped that the church was ready to accept these wonderful, young women for who they were. Maybe things were changing.

But it was more than just the attitudes of the congregants changing, it was also something inside of me. I had wanted family for so long, but had resigned myself to never having it. But now, I had begun to feel this tiny seed growing in me. The seed of me being some kind of mother- like figure. Justine and Abigail needed family and I needed family. We could create something like family together. To be needed and taken in and accepted as a part of someone's family, that was life-changing! I found myself praying that I could offer Justine and Abigail something that they needed, something that we could all trust.

CHAPTER THIRTY-SIX

SARAH

DECEMBER, 2016, BOSTON

The day after Christmas, Edwardo and I took turns driving my Honda Civic up the New Jersey Turnpike on our way to my parent's house in Boston. I loved sitting next to him while he was driving in relaxed togetherness. As the miles rolled by, the closeness of being in the car with him for such an extended time was an invitation for opening up.

He asked me about my parents and whether we were close. It was a hard question to answer.

"Close?" I asked. "Hmm. That's a tough one. I mean, I check in with them every couple of weeks. I tell them about my job. And I tell them about you. They know some about my questions of faith, but not a lot since I don't want them to worry about my future. I mean, you know how you want your parents to know about you, but you don't want them to worry or ask too many questions you can't answer?"

Edwardo shrugged, "I guess. Yes, obviously, I didn't share a lot with my parents which is why I got in such trouble. I should have shared more."

"Yeah, but that's what you were doing, protecting them from worrying and protecting yourself from having to answer the hard questions. I get it. That's what we all do, I think."

Edwardo nodded. "Yeah, but it seems to me like you're in closer contact with your parents."

I considered this for a minute. "Yes, but I don't share everything. So, don't assume that I'm closer. We all have things we keep from our parents." I laughed. "It's human nature to assume that your parents won't accept everything about you, don't you think?"

Edwardo grinned. "I guess."

When we arrived at my parents' house in Back Bay, Edwardo looked up at the stately brick townhouse, then gave me a nervous look. I tried to gauge what it was about but then decided not to focus on it. I had told him in the car that my parents would love him because of who he was, and he didn't have to be something different. I hoped that was really true. I also knew that my parents had always wanted me to be financially stable. They always hoped I'd marry someone who would carry the financial burden. With Edwardo's social work career, that wasn't going to happen. We both had decided to move away from the kind of lives our parents had given us, hoping instead to find more meaning in our careers.

Mom must have been watching for us, because the door opened just as we started climbing the steps. My mother beamed in delight as we came in.

"Sarah," she said, pulling me in for a brief hug. "And this must be Edwardo." She reached out for Edwardo's hand, enclosing it with both of hers. "We're so glad to finally meet you. We've heard so much about you!" Edwardo looked surprised and gratified by her warm welcome. He responded with something about how he was glad to have been invited.

My dad came running down the stairs gathering me into a hug as well. "Oh, so glad you're here!" he said. Then he also extended his hand to Edwardo, "Welcome, Edwardo!"

Edwardo shook it firmly. Smiling at me, Dad seemed very pleased we were there. It felt strange since so much of my time with my parents over the past years had felt muted. The warmth of their welcome was comforting.

My mother took our coats and asked my dad to take our suitcases to the guest room. She turned to me and winked. Apparently, my parents had reached an age where acceptance of one's daughter's partner didn't require marriage to share a bedroom.

My mother's usual understated display of white poinsettias placed next to the fireplace, white lights on the tree, and porcelain angels nestled in evergreen boughs on the mantel created an elegant holiday feel. A fire crackled pleasantly, and there were a few professionally wrapped presents under the tree in solid red or white, accented with silver, nothing garish. My mother was all about making things seem effortless as if these things just appeared on their own.

Taking Edwardo's hand, I led him on a tour through the kitchen and dining room, then showed him the small, cozy study where Dad did most of his work and where the two of them spent each evening reading the paper or watching television together, some PBS historical drama or political analysis.

On one wall were pictures of our extended family: There was my favorite Aunt Peggy, who lived in Florida, and who we had always visited during spring break. Several were of me and Pam when we were young. In one we were just toddlers sitting in front of the Christmas tree each holding a doll that must have been that year's gift. Another when we had both gone to overnight camp when we were about 10 and 12 standing in front of a school bus with tennis rackets and heavy duffel bags hanging from our shoulders. Pam was grinning wildly—she had been so excited about going to overnight camp for the first time.

There were few pictures after that since Pam died two years later.

As Edwardo glanced over the cast of characters that made up my family, I wondered what he was thinking. I tried to guess how he must be trying to draw some new knowledge of me by this sketch of my life through my family portraits.

"What do you think?" I asked him.

He looked pleased. "Your family looks a lot like mine in some ways."

"Yeah? How so?"

"Well, lots of activities together, always having fun, lots of laughter. Lots of extended family? People who love each other?" he asked hesitantly, as if he wasn't sure whether I could see that.

I looked back at the wall of pictures. He was right. When you didn't dwell on the tragedy and the sadness that followed the gaping hole of losing my sister, the pictures looked like a happy family. I had expected him to see how much the pictures showed Pam's absence. But instead, he saw the presence of a loving family. I guess it wasn't obvious, but there weren't a lot of pictures with smiling faces after her death. There was the picture of me at my college graduation, white cap and gown, standing stiffly between my parents. Another of a holiday with my Aunt Peggy who had started joining us at Christmas to try to bridge the tremendous emptiness we felt. To me, the wall showed a family who had lost its heart. Seeing the family from an outsider's viewpoint made me reconsider that perhaps I wasn't giving us enough credit. I felt myself considering perhaps a new view of my family.

Dad had returned from upstairs after I finished showing Edwardo the rec room downstairs and the small patio where we sat outside in the summers. My mom suggested that he get us some drinks and he disappeared into the kitchen, coming back with a glass for each of us.

My mom settled in her usual armchair and offered Edwardo a seat next to her. "Edwardo, tell us about your family. What's Christmas like in your home?"

I winced at the inquisition, but Edwardo didn't seem to mind.

"Our family is part of a larger extended family, especially when it comes to holidays."

My mother showed interest, cocking her head to ask for more, and Edwardo went on.

"My mother's sisters' families all come to our house for Christmas. There's lots of kids running around. Lots of noise, lots of food, and of course, lots of fun." He looked proud explaining this scene as Dad settled in his usual armchair.

My mother looked thoughtful. "So, do you have siblings?"

"No, I have no brothers or sisters. But, you know, I have many cousins. And family friends who are like family."

"So, have you been home for Christmas since you moved to the States?"

Edwardo looked embarrassed. "Well, I've been home a few times since moving here. I went for my mother's birthday one year. It was really important to her. But only once for Christmas."

"I'm sorry you haven't been able to go home more. But we're so happy to have you here this year, aren't we, dear?" Mom said, glancing at my father.

Dad nodded in agreement. "Edwardo, we'd love to show you Boston. Have you ever been here before?"

Edwardo admitted that he had not, and Dad seeming pleased about that, started to lay plans for a Boston whirlwind the next day. He smiled at me, eager to show Edwardo this city that he loved.

"Shall we start with Beacon Hill, Faneuil Hall, and the Public Garden?"

"Sure, Dad. That sounds good." I knew there was at least one place my parents would avoid: the cemetery where Pam was buried. They didn't ever visit as far as I knew. We never brought it up. Sometimes, it felt like Pam had never even existed. However, underneath this charade was the larger truth of her stark absence.

But somehow, with Edwardo here, the atmosphere that had been almost claustrophobic with my parents, so focused on Pam's absence for so long, now felt more relaxed. Like maybe he could fill this hole. I wondered, scrutinizing my parent's beaming faces, if the idea of my marrying and having a family of my own someday beckoned to them like the promise of life without this aching loss. Was it possible that they also carried the guilt that had been my burden? Or did I still carry the extra load alone; the one of not being fully present for Pam when she was sick, but also not being enough for my parents after she was gone? I felt like I was never enough for them. Was it possible that I could be now?

There was a certain arrogance in loving Boston as though the founding history of our country is imbued throughout all of this city and somehow makes those who live here heroes of the same ilk as John Hancock. We expected Edwardo to find our favorite nostalgic spots as flavorful as we did. Our favorite place for clam chowder, Durgin Park, where waitresses, with their natural brashness a part of the ambiance of this prior century sea-faring pub, would pick up an expensive camera sitting beside a tourist and start snapping pictures without asking. Edwardo laughed at the rude familiarity of the waitstaff. Afterwards, we walked through Quincy Marketplace window shopping at expensive boutiques and then made a quick stop at Faneuil Hall where my father waxed on endlessly about the Sons of Liberty. Edwardo turned out to be surprisingly informed about our revolution especially about Benjamin Franklin, with his well- known quips about living life. "He who lies down with dogs shall rise up with fleas!" my father intoned, and Edwardo joined in.

The second evening after dinner seemed a bit strained since my parents had done their best to buy presents for Edwardo but didn't really know his preferences. But he was touched by the way they had tried to include him in our present exchange, even buying him a warm scarf for the frosty Boston winters. Edwardo had reciprocated, even going so far as to pick out books for my parents based on what I had told them they liked. Mom was thrilled and impressed by the novel he gave her by Isabel Allende. He gave Dad a book on the Civil War which he had already read but said he'd be happy to pass on to a friend who was hoping to read it.

At the so-called 'Christmas dinner' the night after we arrived, my parents asked me to say the blessing which had been expected of me ever since I entered seminary. I always included a remembrance of Pam and "others who are gone from us". This year, I included a mention of Edwardo's family as well. I peeked at him through my clasped hands, noting his smile at being a part of family time. The empty chair at the table which had been staring at us since Pam's death was now filled with Edwardo's presence. It was not hard to imagine him becoming a new part of our family as he shared stories of his family and asked questions about ours. He was even able to broach the subject of Pam, asking if she had loved Christmas as much I did. That characterization of me surprised me, but then I realized my excited preparation for sharing my family's Christmas traditions must have seemed to him like a nostalgic love of the holiday.

My mom had seemed unusually upbeat throughout the three days of endless cooking, setting the table with the white linen tablecloth complete with the holly and berry centerpiece, and initiating conversations with Edwardo about his plans. I had to keep a cautious ear out for every conversation that started with, "Now, Edwardo, tell us about what you envision about…" I kept feeling like these fishing expeditions were designed to push him or perhaps me into speculation about when we were going to get married and start a family. Luckily, they never quite used that language but certainly skirted around it enough.

Edwardo took it all very well and side-stepped the conversation by mentioning that he was busy making plans for a city foodbank, and it took up most of his focus. My parents seemed satisfied by his answers, although I could hear their unasked questions lurking behind it all.

My mom did corner me one day when Edwardo and Dad had gone out to pick up some more wine. She looked a little coy, then asked that typical mother question, "So, Sarah, I know you told me not to read too much into your bringing Edwardo home at Christmas. But really, sweetheart, you both seem very taken with each other. Is it moving in a serious direction?"

My disdainful expression didn't discourage her in the least. "Really, Mom?"

"Well, I know you're not making future plans or anything, but are you in love? You can tell your poor mother that anyway?"

I pursed my lips, but the tender part of me couldn't help but breaking into a wide grin. "Okay, yes! We are pretty much head over heels, as you would say." My mom's face reflected a joyful light that I had not seen for years. I reached out to her and gave her a full-on hug. It felt good to bring her this bit of happiness. I hoped this would only be the beginning. Something inside told me, maybe this was going to last. But I was afraid to even say that.

We packed up to drive home a few days later. Having someone else to share all the logistical details of loading the car and extracting ourselves from the somewhat oppressive cheerfulness of my parents was a relief.

As we were preparing to depart, my parents christened Edwardo "a good sport" for putting up with endless stories about my youth. Driving away together, it felt like we were somehow different as a couple. It felt like a new chapter in our relationship. I felt something akin to being relaxed and peaceful. Dare I even say "happy"?

Chapter Thirty-Seven

JEFFREY

December, 2016, Philadelphia

Christmas was the most miserable one I've ever had. I guess I knew that was going to happen, and I know I brought it on myself, but I didn't realize how bad it was until I tried to invent a lame holiday time with my kids. Elaine arranged for me to pick them up Christmas Eve for an afternoon of bowling and pizza. She said Emily was looking forward to seeing me but she couldn't speak for the boys. Before she got off the phone, I took a chance.

"Elaine, wait. I want to sit down with you sometime before Christmas. Anytime would do. Can we do that?"

Silence for a beat. Then she answered, "Jeffrey, I'm still working on how I feel about all of this. So, I'm not ready to talk about it, yet. So, you'll have to wait. I'll let you know."

"Okay. I will. But can you just tell me...whether there's a chance for us? I mean, can I hope for that?"

"You can hope for whatever you want, but I can't promise anything. I'm sorry." She mumbled a good-bye and hung up.

I sat for a long time after that just starting out the window in my sterile Embassy Suite hotel room with the king- sized bed, for just one person. My empty refrigerator, the shiny polyester curtains, and bland blond furniture, all set up for a temporary stay. No Christmas decorations, no presents, and no one here that cared about me. Would they ever again?

I had spent a few afternoons taking Emily and Paul out for shopping trips to pick up gifts for their mother and siblings. Paul was quiet but engaged when we spent the afternoon in a bookstore thinking about what Elaine would like. He was thoughtful and eventually picked out a romance novel that he thought she would like. But then he turned to me while we were waiting in the check-out line, his worried face a little hesitant.

"But Dad, um, aren't you going to spend Christmas with us?" he asked.

I knew that Elaine had told them that I'd be with them on Christmas Eve but that she would be taking them to a friend's house for Christmas dinner. I wasn't invited. I explained the plan for the holiday. His face seemed to close down until we finished paying and went to the car. After I started the car and was ready to take off, he asked me to wait. I turned the car off, expecting the questions that I was sure were swirling around his mind.

"Dad, Mom told me that you guys are having... like a fight?" he asked uncomfortably.

"Well, not exactly a fight. Just having a difficulty. But that doesn't mean that we're getting a divorce or anything, buddy. I mean, sometimes grown-ups just need time to figure things out."

He looked confused. "So, do *you* need time to figure things out? Or does Mom?"

"Well, we both do. I mean, we still love each other. But we have to figure out what that means. Like sometimes when you've been married a long time, you kind of forget how to love each other. I guess, well, I kind of forgot how to love your mom the best way. So, I screwed up."

Paul nodded thoughtfully. "So, when Mom forgives you, will you come home?"

"I sure hope so. But I can't push your mom until she's ready. So, will you help Mom in the next few days? Just be really good and help around the house?"

Paul nodded vigorously. "Yeah."

He was the sweetest boy. He wanted for everyone to get along and for things to get back to normal. He would forgive me someday when I was able to explain it all to him. Assuming that Elaine would forgive me and we'd get back together. I guess that was a big assumption on my part.

But with Alan, being older and more aware that something fishy was going on, it was like a cold curtain of judgment had fallen between us. When I called to ask if I could take him out Christmas shopping, after some stern talk from Elaine to get him on the phone, his steely, low voice informed me that he could do his own shopping and he didn't need my help. When I suggested that we just grab a burger together, he said a terse, "No, thanks," and handed the phone back to his mother. It was a door slammed shut in my face. I barely kept it together, getting off the phone as quick as I could.

But when I took Emily out, she relished the individual attention, smoothing down the Sunday dress that she had insisted on wearing, and rattling on about her new best friend, Ally, and how they were building houses for their dolls out of cardboard boxes. She asked me if I would help her figure out if they could get a light inside the dollhouse they had made. After we picked out a purple, flowered silk scarf for Elaine, we had gone to the hardware store and bought a small battery-operated lamp that might fit inside her newly-made dollhouse. She had been clingy and wanted to hold my hand the whole time. In the front hall where Elaine was waiting after I brought her home, Emily asked me if I would stay in her whiny, tired voice. I looked up at Elaine's tense face and she shook her head, biting her lips firmly together. I bent down and explained to Emily that I had some work I had to get done and would come and see her in a few days. She grabbed my arm and began screaming "But, Daddy, we need you home. I want you home!" Elaine picked her up, and motioned for me to leave. I hugged Emily as best as I could around Elaine, and got out quickly. But I felt like such a bum that whole day. Just sat around my stupid hotel room, watching golf and kicking myself.

Then on Christmas Eve, I picked up all three kids, Alan dragging his feet and not meeting my eyes. Paul was okay, carrying a book on his hip to read in the car, sitting in the front seat but saying little. Emily, sitting primly in her car seat in the back, asked me if we could listen to Christmas songs. I scrolled around until I found a station with easy-to-sing carols. She launched right into Rudolph with childish gusto, hitting her nose each time they mentioned his shiny one. I tried the best I could to keep up, thinking desperately about how to involve the boys. She smiled, encouraging me, despite my feeble attempts. Alan just plugged in his earphones and paid no attention. Paul had his nose in a book as usual.

At the bowling alley, Emily and Paul really got into it, picking out their balls right away. I helped Emilly find a light-weight ball that was purple, her new favorite color.   Paul, after writing our names on the scoresheet, sat down to put on the soft bowling shoes. When Emily got up, holding her ball with both hands and positioning herself in front of the lane, Paul got up behind her giving her helpful, brotherly advice.

Alan mumbled that he wasn't into it and sat listening to Spotify on his phone. I sat next to him and tried to make light conversation.

It wasn't going well when he turned to me with eyes flaring and spitted out, "Dad, I don't need your feeble attempt to make everything all right! It's not all right! Okay? Just leave me alone." Then he got up and stomped up the stairs, walking angrily into the arcade.

Paul noticed Alan's tone and watched him disappear. Emily was busy watching her ball meander down the gully. I got up, whispered to Paul to take care of Emily and followed Alan. I saw him veer off toward the cafe and went after him. He was sitting at a table, scrolling on his phone, his face, stony and closed.

When I sat down across from him, he turned away, intent on his phone. My chest felt squeezed and heavy. How could this child of mine hate me so much? I deserved it, but it felt so hard to accept. Alan had always looked up to me before this. He had asked my advice; he had always wanted to know more about my own high school years. But now, it was like I was the enemy. And in fact, he was right. I was the enemy. I had harmed Elaine. And somehow, he knew that.

"Alan, I know you're angry at me. And you have every right to be," I said softly, leaning over to him. At this, he turned his head toward me.

"Damn right. I know what you did."

"How do you know?"

"I heard you talking to Mom in the kitchen. She said you were seeing this other woman. I know what that means. I'm not stupid, Dad!"

My chest got tighter as I tried to take a breath. "Yeah, I know that," I said softly. "And I have to find a way to make it up to your mother. I've apologized and I've asked her to forgive me."

"Has she forgiven you?" he asked, challenging me.

I sighed. "No, she hasn't."

"So, good for her. I don't forgive you, either." He got up, held up his phone and said, "I'm calling Mom to pick me up." He stalked off toward the front door.

Later, when I dropped off Emily and Paul, I asked Elaine if we could talk. She sent the kids up to watch a movie they had been wanting and motioned for me to follow her into the living room. It felt awkward sitting across from each other in this formal room where we had only entertained guests and hardly ever sat together. She kept glancing up to make sure the kids had disappeared into the boys' room where they had their television, then turned to me. I noticed that she had put on make-up and styled her hair. I wondered if it was for me, or just since it was Christmas Eve.

"Elaine," I began, my heart beating fast, "I miss you so much." I looked her in the eyes, hoping she could see my sincerity. She glanced down, unwilling to look at me. I continued. "There is no way for me to excuse what I did. I know that it was my mistake. I know that. But I hope you'll let us start over. Get some counselling. Do whatever you think we need to do to get us right again." I tried to reach out to touch her hands, but she moved away slightly.

"I know you want to fix this, Jeffrey. I'm just not ready to move ahead to solutions," she said, exhaling nervously. "I'm still hurting. A lot. And you need to let me figure this out on my schedule. I'm not ready to forgive you." She stood up. "Thanks for taking the kids out. I'm sure they were glad to see you," she said stiffly. "Except for Alan, of course."

She motioned for me to go. I stood and moved to the door, feeling like a complete failure. I could barely see, my eyes starting to tear up. I hurriedly said good-bye and got out the door.

And there it was. I wasn't forgiven. I didn't deserve it. If Elaine couldn't find it in her heart to forgive me, and I had to live without her, I didn't think I could forgive myself either. What would my life be without her?

Chapter Thirty-Eight

SARAH

On the road back to Philadelphia, December 30th

As we were passing by New York City with its heavy traffic, Edwardo was driving. It reminded me of times when my family would be caught in traffic on 95 driving down to Florida to visit my aunt at Easter.

"So, have I told you about the Easter hunt my aunt did one year for us once we were too grown up for Easter eggs?"

Edwardo looked amused. "I didn't know you could outgrow Easter eggs." He loved the American traditions around the holidays that were different from his family traditions.

"Well, you never outgrow the candy, but you do get too old to be racing around the yard looking for colored eggs. But Aunt Peggy, she knew that we enjoyed the whole hunting thing, so one year she hid pipe tobacco for my father, wine coolers for my mother, and CDs for Pam and me. She called it the 'Lent is Over!' Easter hunt since my father would often give up pipe smoking for Lent. We died laughing at finding pipe tobacco inside the refrigerator and a wine cooler stuck up inside a hat one evening long after the hunt was over."

Edwardo grinned, and I loved that he seemed to get a kick out of the family memories I shared.

"But you know, Edwardo, this Christmas was the happiest one we've had in many years," I said thoughtfully. Was I reading too much into Edwardo's presence? Or was it just the holiday lightening my feelings about my parents?

He smiled and reached out to squeeze my shoulder. "I also had a really good time," he said wistfully. "You know I've had some pretty lonely holidays in recent years. So, I'm very grateful to have been included in your family holiday. And...glad to be so welcomed by your family."

He took my hand and held onto it for a while as we drove. I could feel my hope for this relationship soar. I think Edwardo felt it, too.

Watching Edwardo navigate the highway through a light snow-fall, I was enjoying sitting back and letting him drive. I was just about to drift off into a hazy nap when I felt the phone in my pocket vibrate. I was very surprised to see that it was Elaine Trainor. I thought about letting it go to voicemail, but since I had been wondering how she was doing, I decided to answer.

"Elaine, Merry Christmas! So glad to hear from you."

Elaine's voice, tight and anxious, was hard to hear as though she was holding her hand in front of her mouth and didn't want others to hear. "Rev. Sarah. I am so sorry to call you. But...oh, God, how to tell you this? It's Jeffrey. He's in the hospital."

"Oh, no! What's going on?"

"Well, he...he tried to commit suicide," she said her voice muted.

"Oh, my God, Elaine. I am so sorry. Jesus...how is he?" She didn't answer right away, but I heard her breathing heavily. My heart was pounding as I tried to calm her, "It's okay. Just take your time."

After a few more gasps, she managed to answer with a raspy voice. "He...he's in critical condition. He shot himself but he missed and managed to just destroy his ear."

"What you must be going through. I'm *so* sorry." I couldn't even think straight to know what I should be saying.

"I feel so responsible," she said on the verge of tears. "I mean, I should have told him before that I've forgiven him. I really have but I just hadn't told him yet. I should have!"

"Elaine, you cannot blame yourself. You are not responsible for Jeffry's actions. No one is responsible but him. We can love him, but we cannot change his actions." I could hear Elaine's snuffling.

"Where are you now?" I asked.

Her voice got a bit louder like she had held up the phone closer to her mouth. "I'm in the hallway outside the waiting room. He's in surgery now."

"Okay, who's with you?"

Elaine hesitated. "Well, Jeffrey's mom is on her way from DC. And my neighbor is with the kids. I'm alone for now."

"Okay. I'm on my way back to Philly. We're probably..." I looked at Edwardo, and he held up one finger. "We're still one hour out. But I'm going to call someone to be with you. Can you think of anyone from the church you'd like?"

"I don't know. I guess Sally Rutgers, maybe. She's a good friend. But...I don't know if I want anyone to know about this yet. Jeffrey hates people to know his business, you know. I don't..."

Of course. Jeffrey probably wouldn't want anyone to know about this. But she needed support.

"I think you need some support right now. So, I'm going to call Mary, our administrator, to come sit with you. She is very discrete and won't share this with anyone. Okay?"

Elaine grunted in agreement.

"I'll be there as soon as I can, but call me if you need anything. I'm praying for him right now. And I'll be praying for you both all the way."

I got off the phone and filled Edwardo in. He flinched when I described what Jeffrey had done. I knew that he had experienced the suicide of a client. He knew what it was like. Holding the well-being of someone as part of your responsibility and then having them do the unthinkable was devastating. Quickly, I called Mary and asked if she could get to the hospital to be with Elaine and she agreed.

Under the shock and sadness, I felt the guilt crawling up my spine like a vine. Wrapping around and creeping up until I began to feel like I couldn't breathe. My breaths were coming hard and fast. The sobs pushed through and wouldn't stop, pulling me down into the shame. I had helped to cause this poor man's suffering. I had not helped him enough. How could I call myself a pastor when I wasn't there when he most needed me?

Edwardo put his hand on my shoulder rubbing it. He took my hand. "Sarah." I could barely register what he was saying through the tears. "Breathe slowly." I tried but started huffing instead.

Edwardo removed his hand and checked the rearview mirror. He pulled the car over to the shoulder and turned the car off, then enfolded me in his arms, rubbing my back gently.

"This is not your fault."

How did he know that's what I was thinking? But how could he say that?

I looked up and pulled away. "Yes. Yes, part of it is!"

He took my arm and held it. "That's what your over- functional, very compassionate heart thinks. But Sarah, mija, you did nothing to cause this."

I turned away, my heart racing. "You don't know how I acted in that meeting. I mean, I pretty much hung him out to dry! I did!"

Edwardo sighed. "I know you want to take responsibility. That's what compassionate people do. But you can't. All of his actions were his to make. His decisions. His actions. Not yours. You simply asked him to take responsibility for his actions."

My tears had slowed. I began considering his words. "I know what you're saying. But I could have done more to reach out to him."

"Sarah, didn't you reach out to him?"

"Well, I tried."

"And that's all you could do. You did what you could. This was his decision. None of this is your responsibility."

I sighed deeply. I knew that Edwardo had probably gone through something like this. And I knew what I would tell him if our roles were reversed.

"I know. I just feel so...terrible." I slumped down, raking my hands through my hair.

We sat silently for a minute. I took his hand. "I think I need to pray. Could we, just for a minute?"

Edwardo nodded. I stammered out a prayer for Jeffrey and Elaine and their kids. Oh, please God, stay with those kids. Then I squeezed his hand and suggested we get back on the road so we could get there as soon as we could. Edwardo started the car and checking the traffic, pulled back onto the road.

After dodging all the holiday traffic in the city, we got to the hospital where I jumped out of the car in the drop off area, and hurried up to the family waiting room. Seeing Elaine sitting there huddled in a corner, her face white as stone, I immediately went over and held her in a warm hug. She seemed glad to see me but was too shutdown to be able to talk. I relieved Mary who offered to go across the street and grab us a bite to eat before she left.

Elaine kept nervously checking the status board every few minutes, and then looking down at her phone. After a bit, Mary brought us back turkey bagel sandwiches and some chocolate chip cookies. Elaine thanked her for being there until I had arrived. Mary just patted her hand and slipped out. Having not eaten all day, I immediately devoured my sandwich, while Elaine just picked around the edges of hers.

A little while later, we saw on the board that Jeffrey was being moved to the ICU. Elaine was called to the desk and told she could go in to meet the doctor. She looked desperate and grabbed my hand and squeezed it before she followed the nurse into the recovery area.

I quietly said a prayer that Jeffrey could heal and find some peace and Elaine could find her forgiveness. I pushed down the feeling of guilt that was still nagging a corner of my mind, telling myself that I had done what I could. As I was sitting there staring into space, I noticed the families around me whom I hadn't really focused on before. Sitting across from me was an older woman, knitting a blue fuzzy thing. She looked up when she saw me noticing her. I smiled and indicated her knitting. "Looks cozy. Is it going to be a scarf?"

She nodded and sighed. "Yes. Someday, if I ever finish it. You know I start things like this, but I rarely finish them."

"Who's it for?" I asked.

"It's for my husband who's in surgery right now."

"I see. It's hard to wait, isn't it?"

She looked up like she wasn't sure. "Yes, it is. They're removing a tumor from his lung. I hope that's what they're doing. They weren't sure but that's what they're trying to do. They may need to remove part of the lung or the whole lung. I don't know." She sighed and shook her head.

I realized that maybe she didn't want to talk about it. "I'm sorry. I didn't mean to pry."

She looked up. "Oh, no. It's fine. We're very hopeful. I'm hoping that when I finish this scarf, he will be well and ready to wear it." She smiled and resumed her knitting.

Hope. It was a thing we all held gently in our fingers, like sand. Sometimes, it would begin to drip out slowly, bit by bit. Sometimes we'd throw it away in anger. Sometimes, we'd use it to build a whole sandcastle. I wasn't sure at that moment what kind of hope I held for Jeffrey. But I knew it was there.

Elaine came back, looking exhausted. When she saw me, she half-smiled. "The doctor said that he's out of the woods. Still not sure how the ear will recover. But it went well." Her voice showed her relief. "He's awake, but very groggy. He is very sorry he put me through this on top of everything else. But mainly, I just told him how much I love him and that we'd figure this out." She squeezed my hand, her face drained of the tension.

I squeezed back and sighed with relief. "Elaine, you are remarkable."

She shook her head. "No. I just love my husband enough that I can forgive. It hurts. But I now know that he was struggling as much as I was. I had been depressed about my mother's death for so long and I couldn't see outside of my own sadness. I wasn't much of a wife."

I couldn't believe Elaine was trying to excuse Jeffrey's actions by taking responsibility for the marriage.

"Elaine, you couldn't help being depressed."

"I know. I mean, I don't think what he did was right. He hurt all of us very deeply. But I can see how much he wants his family back. I can see how my rejection might have pushed him to try to take his life. I will always feel bad about it. But as you said, I know it was not my fault."

I nodded in agreement. "I'm glad you're starting to understand that. I know it's hard. I've also been feeling my own part in this. I hope you will forgive me for not seeing how much the action of the Vestry hurt him. You know, I tried to reach out to Jeffrey—"

"I know you did, Rev. Sarah. When I told him you were here waiting with me, he said he felt badly by the way he acted toward you. I wonder if you would mind visiting with him while he's in here?"

"Really?"

"Yes, I think he wants to make everything right again. He scared himself to death by all of this. And he wants his life back."

"Oh, wow. That just makes me so relieved." I felt a rush of hope filling my heart.

Elaine smiled. "I think you showed him you cared. He just wasn't ready to hear it since he was feeling so guilty. Maybe now he can hear whatever you were suggesting."

I nodded. Elaine started packing up her tote bag. "I'm going to go home and see the boys and tell them about their father. I called them once right after surgery, but I know they want to know more."

She promised she would let me know when Jeffrey was ready to have visitors. I held her hand and told her I would be sending them both my prayers. She reached over and hugged me.

Later that week, I got a text from Elaine that Jeffrey was ready for me to visit. I called her immediately to see how he was and told her I'd visit that afternoon.

While I was a bit anxious about seeing Jeffrey, since our previous encounters had been fraught, but I was also eager to see if there was a different side of this man, a better side. He had certainly been through a lot and maybe, just maybe, he had learned something.

Chapter Thirty-Nine

JEFFREY

December 30, 2016- January 4, 2017

Waking up in the hospital after surgery and seeing Elaine there, standing by my bed, her face filled with fear, I felt such gratitude that she was there with me after all I've put her through. She reached for my hand when I opened my eyes and saw her.

"Jeffrey. Oh my God, what a scare that was!" Elaine wiped away a tear with her other hand.

Clearing my throat, I took her hand and tried to find my voice although my throat was scratchy. "Elaine. I'm really sorry. I just... I just didn't want to live if you didn't love me anymore." My voice faltered as I told her that truth.

Elaine leaned over and kissed my cheek. "I'm sorry I led you to think I didn't still love you. Of course, I love you. I would be devastated to live without you. Please, don't ever do that again." She looked devastated.

Hearing her tone and her words was a great relief. "No, I won't. I promise."

She talked about the kids and how much they missed me and sent their love. All of this was healing. But my nagging guilt made me think I didn't deserve it. I told her so and she assured me that we would work it all out. I didn't expect this after all I put her through. Thank God!

When Rev. Sarah called to arrange a visit, I felt so ashamed about how I had treated her and everyone at church that I didn't really want to face it. Part of me wanted to just do a quick, polite expression of apologizing. Get it over with. But after almost losing my life, I knew I needed forgiveness more than anything. How could I show my face at that church unless I had truly apologized! I knew that since my family had found something at that church, I needed to make it right. So, I decided that I would ask for Rev. Sarah's advice after all. I knew I needed to turn it all around. I had a lot of work to do. I told her I would like to see her.

She came in smiling, and moving closer to my bed, asked how I was doing, like it was a regular pastoral visit. I was so taken aback by her demeanor that I was at a loss of what to say for a moment. Then I swallowed my pride.

"Rev. Sarah, I have a whole load of stuff I need to get off my chest."

She looked intrigued. "What would you like to tell me, Jeffrey?"

I didn't really know how to ask for forgiveness, even though I knew that's what I needed to do.

"Well, I have to admit that I was wrong about a lot of things. I acted selfishly and I hurt a lot of people. I know you asked me once if I wanted to—what did you call it? 'Make amends'?"

Rev. Sarah nodded. "Yes, that's what I suggested."

"Yeah. I didn't think I needed to ask for forgiveness from Terry since she had also acted wrongly. But I've thought about it. And it wasn't her that was cheating; it was me. I promised her things I shouldn't have. I led her to believe I'd leave Elaine—I see that was wrong now. I need to ask her to forgive me."

Sarah encouraged me to continue. It began to feel like I was unloading a lot of crap that had been weighing me down. "I admit that I tried to get the Vestry to hire Terry when it was just my own arrogance thinking I could control things. I mean, really, how could I have been so full of shit? Excuse my language," I added hastily.

Sarah smiled. "I'm so glad to hear you're seeing things differently now. I can't tell you how happy that makes me."

"Oh, and I want to apologize to you. I treated you badly."

She shook her head. "I appreciate that. It hasn't been that easy trying to get through to you."

"No, I know it hasn't. When I get out of here, I want to come back to church. Maybe not right away. I need some time to heal with my family. That's the most important thing. I'm the luckiest man in the world that Elaine has forgiven me and the kids are okay. I mean, Alan is still kind of cold to me. But Elaine says he'll come around. So, after I have time with them to get things straightened out, I'm going to come back to church. And I'm going to give my apology to the Vestry."

"I'm happy that you have seen this all differently. And glad you want to come back to church."

"Well, I mean, if they'll have me. I know people will probably ignore me at first. I get that. I have to prove that I'm really a different person. I want to treat people right. I want to be respectful of others, which I know I haven't been. I know this all sounds a little hypocritical right now, like I want to be forgiven so I'm just saying all this. But I can't tell you what I went through."

"It must have been hell. Whatever you went through must have led you to believe that your life wasn't worthwhile any longer."

"You can't even imagine."

"No, I can't. But it must have been horrible."

"When I came to after the gun when off and I fainted, I just felt this amazing feeling when I realized that I was still alive. I was just so grateful. I couldn't believe it! And really, I can tell you this, I think God saved me for some reason. I mean, I don't deserve it. But I survived! So, I really feel this kind of, I know this will sound strange but this holy kind of thing?"

Sarah acknowledge that with a nod.

"So, I definitely want to come back to St. Philip's. But not to be a big man on the Vestry or anything like that. I blew that. Just to be able to go to church with Elaine and the kids and maybe eventually have friends there again. That's all I want. Oh, and one more thing... Elaine has arranged for us to see a therapist together, and also for me to see someone alone. I don't know how that works, but I know I can use all the help I can get!"

She looked pleased and put her hand on mine briefly. "The people at church are going to be glad to see this change in you. And maybe they will be stand-offish at first. But once they see how good you are with your family and how you want to be a part of things, they will accept you. I'm pretty sure of it."

Before she left, she asked me if I'd like to pray with her. That felt weird, but I said, okay. She asked God to be with me as I figured out how to be in 'right relationship' with the people in my life. And all I could think was, yeah! That's what I need. I was so grateful to have my family back that I felt like anything was possible. Maybe even I could change.

Chapter Forty

SARAH

February, 2017

Since Christmas, I was watching my interactions with Edwardo with curiosity, viewing our growing relationship like we were in a movie. He had been sharing more of himself with me, and I was finding myself not wanting to analyze everything but to instead enjoy the ride.

I knew in the back of my mind that my cautiousness was settling into trust. Once in a while, I'd open my mouth to ask a question about his former marriage and then I'd just decide that I didn't want to stir the waters. But as we finished the breakfast dishes one morning at my place, him washing, me drying, I thought about his marriage and what it might have been like. While I no longer questioned his motivations for keeping his marriage a secret, I still had an underlying curiosity about how Edwardo had shown up in a marriage where he wasn't comfortable.

I finished drying the last bowls and placed them in the cupboard while Edwardo dried his hands on the dishtowel. He threw it to me as I turned, catching it in mid-air and smiling. I thought of what we looked like—a happily married couple.

"Edwardo, sometimes I find myself trying to imagine what your marriage to Luisa was like," I blurted out.

Edwardo's brow creased in concern. "What do you mean?" he asked.

"Well, um…did you enjoy being together? Or was it tense? Or did you have nothing to talk about? I just have a hard time imagining what didn't work in that relationship."

Edwardo paused, holding up a finger to ask me to wait as he considered. This was one of the things I loved about him: He knew my question was more than casual and wanted to give a considered response.

"Well, it was like being with a good friend at first, we were just having fun. But then, as we started talking about having a family, planning for long-term things, we realized we weren't ready. We stopped talking about those plans. We ignored it for a time, but I knew if it was on my mind, it was probably on hers. It was Luisa who first admitted she couldn't see staying together long-term. At first, I was so relieved since I agreed. But then it was sad and stressful—we didn't want to keep the façade up. That's when I started planning to leave the country. We both thought it was a good idea for us to separate for a time." Edwardo sighed and moved over to the couch, and I sat with him, taking his hand.

"Edwardo, I don't judge you for having had made a mistake in marrying her. Clearly, you both thought you were doing the right thing. I'm just…"

He interrupted me. "Yes, of course. You just want to understand. That makes sense. What else do you want to know?"

I squeezed his hand and released it while I thought. "I guess I don't understand how you knew it wasn't working. What wasn't working? Was it your interests? Your temperaments?"

Edwardo shrugged. "You know how you feel about a friend you like to go to the movies with, but when it comes to sharing how you feel about something serious, you just don't feel comfortable? That's what it was like."

I thought about the last guy I had been living with in D.C. He was fun and great to have around. Until I wanted to talk about something that was bothering me, then I called a girlfriend.

"Yeah, that makes sense," I told him. "I can see falling into that kind of relationship with someone who is fun and amusing. Been there."

Edwardo suddenly grew serious, moving closer. "Sarah, there just isn't a good way to describe the difference between a friendship and a relationship with someone with whom you'd like to spend the rest of your life. I feel like we can share anything with each other. I tell you about what my family is like, how difficult my job is and how important it is to me, and I can tell you how I feel when I'm very sad or extremely happy. I am very happy when I'm with you, Sarah. All the time." He gazed at me intently, waiting for a response.

"I'm so glad you feel that way," I said touching his cheek softly, "because I feel that way too." I could feel a "but" coming on, so I held my breath for a minute to see if it would push its way through. It didn't come. I was beginning to see my way through to trust him, completely.

"I wasn't sure if I could trust you after you withheld your marriage from me. But ever since, you've been so open. So willing to share. I know I can't keep pushing you away, and I don't want to." I reached for him, holding him tightly as he pulled me closer, stroking my head.

He pulled back and took my hands in his. "Sarah, will you consider marrying me? I'm ready. I'm fully committed. But I've been afraid to ask you. Are you ready?"

While I hadn't expected him to bring it up now, everything within me was hoping for it. I nodded. "Yes, I think I am. I mean, yes!" He pulled me into a long kiss, and I fell into it, holding nothing back. It was different; *we* were different, like we both were fully there. There was nothing left to hide, nothing to hold back. Nothing left to forgive. I felt the release within me of being ready to move into a future with this man I so loved.

I also felt myself letting go of a long held tension of not being able to forgive myself for not being enough. Not being enough for Pam when she needed me. Not being enough for my parents when they had lost Pam. But especially not being enough for myself. Now I was. The knowledge of being enough. Knowing that God loved me, I loved myself, and that I was ultimately loveable. That was true gnosis. And with that knowledge came the freedom to love fully.

CHAPTER FORTY-ONE

IRENE

MAY, 2017

The morning of the long-awaited day opened with a beautiful May scene of bursting forsythia and daffodils surrounding the church. As I passed the front garden, I noticed even some tulips were in bloom, nodding their heads in approval of the day. Entering the front door of the sanctuary, I carried the white tablecloth for the altar, drycleaned and crisp, which I lay carefully over the back pew as I made my way up the aisle. The flower arrangements had already arrived and had been placed on either side of the chancel. I saw the box of flowers ready to decorate the pews that had been left by the florists for me to fasten to the side pews. There was also a box with the bridal bouquets sitting on top of the altar. I peeked inside. Two beautiful sprays of white roses with pink ribbons were curled up snugly next to each other. Perfect.

Yes, I thought. Two bridal bouquets! Finally, we were breaking that homophobic barrier to gay marriage that had been resting here in its traditional garb for more than a century. St. Philips in his colorful robes depicted in the main stained-glass window at the front of the sanctuary seemed to kick up his heels in a little gay dance. It was finally here. Freedom for so many of us!

There was another small box laid next to the bouquet box, and I wondered what it was for. I pulled open the cover so I could make sure it ended up where it should be. Inside was a pink rose corsage with white ribbons. There wasn't a mother of the bride to be found in this wedding, I thought sadly. Who was this for? I saw a small gift card attached and peeked at it.

[For Irene, the "mother of the brides," in spirit. Thank you so much for your love and encouragement! Please sit in the front row as our family. Love, Justine and Abigail]

My eyes filled as I felt my heart spilling over. How I had been lucky enough to find myself, a lesbian spinster, as the chosen family for two amazing women? Truly God was in this place. Miracles do happen!

I grabbed the box of floral sprays and began fastening them to the pews. I heard someone enter the sanctuary as I was fastening the last small arrangement to a side pew. I turned as Mary came down the aisle holding a white bag. She beamed as she took in the sight of the decorated church.

"Oh, my, Irene! You have done wonders here! Really!"

I smiled and shook my head. "No, not me, Mary. Abigial designed this whole thing with the florist. They deserve the credit." I stood back and took in the whole scene, pulling my phone out to take a picture and send it to the brides before they came in.

"Let me show you something, Mary," I said as I walked to the front and grabbed the small box with the corsage. Opening the box, I showed her the card. I couldn't hide my joy and smiled as Mary read it and broke into the widest grin.

"Irene, you deserve this! You have done so much both for those girls and this church! You made the congregation finally come to their senses about marriage and who deserves to have it sanctified. I know Rev. Sarah is so grateful to you for bringing this whole thing forward. It's about time!" Mary gave me a tight hug.

As we broke apart, the door to the sanctuary opened and Rev. Sarah walked in, smiling. "Oh, my God! This couldn't be more beautiful! Thanks, Irene, for getting everything ready. The altar cloth is here?"

I pointed to the back pew. "Yep, all ready. I was just going to ask Mary to help me lay it."

"Good. And Mary, when you finish that, the brides are down-stairs in the brides' room getting dressed. Don't you love it? The "brides" are here. Both of them. Oh, Irene. What an auspicious day!" She moved toward me, pulled me into a hug, then reached over to include Mary. It was a day for hugging. And I loved it.

"Let's get this party started!" Sarah said and moved up the aisle to the sacristy. Mary and I carried the white tablecloth up to the front and started moving the candlesticks away from the altar. The altar cloth with its crisp whiteness completed the picture of this sacred space.

When the time came, the sanctuary was filled with members from St. Philips and some of the brides' friends. There were several lesbian couples present, and there was a great, palpable energy I'd never felt in St. Philip's before. Both beautiful brides wore long, white, simple gowns, one of them the one I'd found for Abigail. The ceremony was brief but included a part that Justine and Abigail had requested. They had asked for a question to be added to the ritual for the congregation to bless their union. We felt confident after the overwhelming support for the Vestry's proposal to sanctify marriage equality that almost everyone was finally ready for this.

Sarah held up her hands motioning to the congregation as she asked, "As a gathered religious community, we ask on this sacred occasion for the congregation to give their blessing to this couple. Will you do all in your power to support and uphold this marriage?" I looked around at all the beaming faces witnessing this historic wedding. In a rush of voices, we responded as one, "We will!" There was a spontaneous clapping, and suddenly everyone was on their feet, yelling affirmation and whistling their joy. Justine and Abigail turned to face us, nodding their thanks, Abigail teary-eyed. Long awaited joy is sometimes the best kind.

After the vows that Justine repeated loudly and Abigail shared softly, Sarah proclaimed them "partners joined in marriage." They kissed, then looked up as the applause and excitement swelled up again. They both smiled at me then, happily holding hands and their wedding bouquets. It felt very much like I had a place in their lives, almost like the mother of the bride(s). They marched down the aisle as the organist pounded out Joy to Man's (or in this case, Woman's) Desiring.

A new day was being born, not without its pains, but I was hopeful for the future, both theirs and St. Philip's.

Chapter Forty-Two

SARAH

Since we announced our engagement to the congregation, I'd started inviting Edwardo to attend some church events so that he might begin to understand what it might be like to be the priest's spouse. I'd assured Edwardo that he had no formal role to play; it was just an invitation if he wanted to observe what it was like to be in a congregation like this one.

But seeing him sitting in the back pew, hearing me preach about the Bible and how to relate these ancient scriptures to one's daily life, I had begun to feel more aware of my authenticity as a pastor. Having shared my theological questions with Edwardo, I found myself wanting to be completely honest about my views when preaching.

When I speak about how Jesus is teaching us how to love one another, I try to make it sound simple. But I find myself admitting that it's not always that easy to understand when I consider the doctrine of the church. There are plenty of passages in the Bible that I struggle with. Writing my sermons, I pick apart each scripture passage, arguing with Paul, or imagining myself as a woman disciple sitting at Jesus' feet, asking questions as Mary Magdalene would have. I want the Bible to give me answers to the predicaments we humans find ourselves in every day. Like how do you raise teenagers with compassion and firmness? Or how do you work in a corporation and remain ethical? I ask these questions in a sermon to stimulate more questions. I often find people coming in to talk this over with me later in the week. I was beginning to feel that questioning the Bible together is part of my ministry.

When I officiated the wedding for Justine and Abigail at St. Philips, I was touched by how much it meant to Irene and to the congregation as a whole. They all cheered, and I saw that Irene clearly had tears in her eyes. What a victory for justice!

After the reception where Edwardo and I danced together for the first time, we went back to my apartment, I asked him what he thought of the wedding ceremony.

"What do you mean?" he asked.

"What do you think of the Episcopal ritual and the words? Are they comfortable for you? Do you want to use similar words for our ceremony?"

Edwardo smiled, drawing me into his arms. "You know, it doesn't matter to me what words are used, as long as they mean that we'll be together for the rest of our lives. That's all I care about."

"But what about your parents? Won't they be sad not to have a Catholic ceremony?"

He paused, thinking. "They may be a little disappointed. But they are so happy to be coming to see me happily married that I don't think they will care that much. And besides, you have invited that priest friend of yours to do a Catholic prayer and that was so considerate of you. Sarah, they will love you and that's all that matters." He pulled me in for a kiss before breaking away to look at me with a grin.

"Oh, and Sarah?"

"Hmm, yeah?" I replied, turning away to examine what was in the refrigerator for dinner.

"I got some good news today."

"Yeah, what?"

"Just a sec."

Edwardo pulled out his laptop from his bag. He opened it and started scrolling. Finding the right email, he waited until I turned to listen, then he read.

"We are pleased to inform you that the Lilly Corporation has approved your grant for $400,000 to support the development of an interfaith food bank and homeless services center in the downtown Philadelphia area."

"Oh, my, God! That is so great! Congratulations, Edwardo!" I exclaimed. "I'm so excited for you!"

He nodded, pleased. "So, this means I can quit my regular job and focus just on this."

"Of course! This food bank and homeless center is so important to our city. I'm just so glad this is what you're choosing to do."

"Yes, and I'm so glad that St. Philips has finally decided to be a partner."

I went back to the kitchen, smiling. "Well, after they met you, how could they not?"

It was amazing to me how everything was seeming to fall into place.

CHAPTER FORTY-THREE

JEFFREY

SPRING, 2017

My entry back into St. Philips was a little awkward. I wasn't sure what the congregation knew about what had happened. The Vestry members who did know were a bit cool to me, especially Irene. But Frank Trumbore had called me once I told Rev. Sarah I wanted to come back and invited me to coffee. He had been very sympathetic when I shared that I wasn't sure that I would be welcomed back at church. He told me that he once had an "indiscretion" in his marriage, and that he never thought his in-laws would forgive him but after some time passed, no one mentioned it. He assured me that we all make mistakes, and I shouldn't worry so much. I told him I really appreciated that, but that I would never forget my mistakes and would work hard to "make amends" as Rev. Sarah had suggested.

But I told Frank that I didn't know how to make my apologies in the church. He thought for a minute and then said he didn't think that was necessary but if I wanted to, I could send an email to the Vestry explaining that I would be returning to church and apologize for any pain or discomfort that my actions caused. He seemed to think that an apology would be very well received. After I sent the email with some trepidation, most of the members replied that I would be very welcome at church. I tried not to worry about those who didn't respond.

I had been told by Rev. Sarah that Terry wasn't comfortable coming to church anymore and had found a new church where she was happy. I also sent her an email apologizing but didn't hear back from her. In a way, I was happy she didn't respond. I didn't want her to think I was trying to start something up again. I just needed to take responsibility for my part.

After a few months of Elaine and I planning family outings together, trying to get back to some normalcy with the boys, we finally had a family discussion about attending St. Philips again. We asked each child what they thought. The boys were tentative at first, voicing reservations about why we needed to attend church. We explained why being in a religious community was important so that we could all learn how to be better human beings. I saw Alan roll his eyes at that. So, I owned it. I said that I had not showed them how to be the best person they could be, and I needed a community to help me with that. Then he listened and nodded his head. Emily was excited and asked if she could wear her new dress.

So, one Sunday, my whole family showed up and filed into the pew we had occupied for years. My boys were a bit nervous and kept glancing around to see who noticed us. Emily held my hand tightly, beaming next to me, patting my shoulder occasionally just to make sure I was still there. Elaine seemed a bit self-conscious to have us all sitting there together. She nodded to her many friends who smiled at us. Observing this, I considered that maybe I didn't really have "friends" at church, just people I'd worked with on committees. Elaine seemed to know all about the personal lives of people at church like who was divorced and who had grown children that might be estranged. I just knew what we had discussed in our meetings: things like the church budget or the auction we'd hold to raise money for the playground equipment. Would I be able to change that? I didn't know. But all in all, I began to feel like maybe I could be accepted at St. Philips despite my missteps.

In some ways, I'm like a new man, with a busted ear due to my stupid attempt on making everything go away. I still know that I'm not the best husband or the best father, but I know that I want to be better. Remembering how I fell into trouble, I remind myself that you need to appreciate what you have when you have it, because it may not always be there. I may not be the most sensitive guy, but I can see that the quiet contentment I have now with Elaine and my family is what was there all along, but I couldn't see it while being caught up in trying to be some version of a "big man." Being on the Vestry, trying to control the church policies, and using Terry to make me feel more desirable. All of that was superficial window dressing. Having my family back, that's what's important. God, why couldn't I see that instead of throwing my weight around and hurting people?

I'm not one to be very religious, but I have found myself praying a kind of thank-you prayer. Thank you, God, for giving me a second chance. For staying with Elaine and my family while I bungled the job you gave me. That of being a good husband and father. I can try again to be that with your help.

CHAPTER FORTY-FOUR

SARAH

SPRING, 2017

Edwardo and I set a date for the wedding for the middle of June when I'm freer from many of my church responsibilities. We planned a honeymoon in Mexico with his family for a week, then time alone exploring the country. I was excited for the wedding but also just as excited to have time to learn more about his family and where he grew up.

But as we started to plan our future, I was still trying to resolve *my* future. Did I want to stay at St. Philips? Did I want to stay in ministry? After Jeffrey's coming to terms with his relationship with the church, I felt a little bit of ease at where I found myself now in this first year of my ministry. I realized that I'd had a tsunami of congregational events which would set almost any pastor's head spinning. But I also realized that I had stepped into a place of growing questions about my role as priest. I found myself noting moments at church when I felt utterly myself and those were cherished times. But then other moments were touched with more doubt. The quandary of whether the role of ministry was enough *for me* was still an open one when I made an appointment to have a heart to heart with the bishop to discuss all the events and my fitness for ministry. My nerves that day were off the chart, expecting to be found wanting since the whole Jeffrey thing exploded so badly. Bishop Springer was very pastoral. I mean, what did I expect? He's a priest. After I reviewed the series of events, he asked me what I had learned.

After really pondering it for a moment, I said, "I learned that judging someone without really knowing what's going on will get me into trouble. But then again, allowing that person to continue to hurt others is just delaying the ultimate resolution. So, I guess I would spend more time with the person making them aware that they were moving in a direction that wasn't going to serve them, and I would be more direct with them about how their actions were going to backfire. And," I added with emphasis, "I'd get more help sooner. I'm so sorry I didn't call you as soon as I saw the problem develop."

The bishop acknowledged my apology, but then he asked me an even harder question: in my own faith, what was my guiding principle? What did I depend on? I had been anxious about this interview and what the bishop thought about my performance. But I was more concerned with my own faith and whether it was really lacking, and his question got to the point quickly. I knew that my dependence on the Gnostic gospels instead of the gospels of Matthew, Mark, Luke, and John was pretty heretical. It wasn't that I didn't believe in scripture, I just found so many questions with some of the statements about finding salvation only through Jesus.

I paused to consider whether I was going to be truthful with him. I knew I had to be. I couldn't fake it any longer. If I was going to devote the rest of my life to the commitment of ministry, it had to be real. It had to be honest.

"I have been wondering whether my faith is the kind of faith the diocese wants in its churches. I'm just not sure. What I am sure about is that I have faith in God and how God acts in my life and in my ministry. My faith in God is a faith in how powerful love is. When I decide how to act as a priest, or as a person, it has to be grounded in love. I have begun to realize that I haven't always acted in love, especially over the past year. There were times when I was acting in fear, not in love. I feared how the people in my life were hurting me and hurting others, and I feared what harm they were doing. I tried to stop them with fear, with punishment. That never helps. But what I really feared was that I had hurt people in the past and that I couldn't be forgiven. I didn't think I deserved forgiveness. But then, I had a kind of revelation, about God's love and forgiveness for me. All the forgiveness that I had been needing but not realizing I needed poured down over me like healing water. Once I felt that pure love, I knew I could forgive others. That God forgives us all. We all deserve that. Even when we hurt others."

The bishop looked strangely moved. "And what are you not sure about?" he asked quietly.

This was the hard part. But I knew I had to share it.

"I'm not sure whether the scripture, the approved canon of the Episcopal Church, holds these answers for me. Scripture points us to how God loves us. Loves us so much He sent Jesus to us. That's what I preach. But then I think that in order to be a priest in this church I need to understand the salvation given to us by the sacrifice of the cross. I need to fully embrace that God gave his only Son for our sins. So that we could be forgiven. That's where I'm stuck. I think God forgives us every day in all ways. So, I don't really understand why the sacrifice of Jesus is necessary for our being forgiven. When people ask me about this, I simply tell them if they believe in God's forgiveness, then why do we need to question how?

I just don't see that it's necessary to go through all the ins and outs of being sanctified by communion, the body and the blood thing, just to understand that God forgives us! Why do we really need it?"

After sharing all of that, I glanced at him anxiously. I felt so completely at the bishop's mercy. Whether I could really say I was a true Christian or not. I didn't want to fool anybody anymore. So, this was it.

Bishop Springer sighed and looked at me with deeply earnest eyes. Blue eyes the shade of the sweet Williams flower. I thought that he wanted so sincerely for me to be okay in this church, but he was going to have to let me down gently. I wasn't really Christian, enough, I was sure.

"Sarah," he said gently, "You have the most loving heart. You truly want to offer your parishioners the kind of leadership that they deserve. I understand that you aren't exactly following the approved canon of the church. I urge you to keep studying the concept of substitutionary atonement and study different theologians to see how many views there are about this knotty subject. I think you have a keen intellect and a sincere commitment in forming the most insightful theology around this." He took a deep breath before continuing.

"But what I see is that you apply theology to real life. When you do that, God is with you every step of the way. When we ask for forgiveness, we are also offering ourselves for God's transformation. For being transformed by the Spirit. That's what the sacrifice of Christ was about—the transformation that occurs when we accept forgiveness and take communion. Communion, as you know, is an outer sign of our inner spiritual grace given by God."

As I listened, I felt a deeper understanding. Certainly, I had been transformed when I realized God's forgiveness for me. I closed my eyes and nodded in agreement.

"As long as God is with you showing you His ways," Bishop Springer said, "these deeply mysterious ways where we find Him in every part of life, then you are a good priest. An effective priest. I have talked with your Senior Warden, Frank Trumbore, and he told me about how you reached out to the man who had gone astray and pulled him back in. Like a good shepherd would. He told me that he'd never seen a more committed priest than you. That you pulled the Vestry together after the difficult incident and showed them the way. You showed them a loving path to become open and accepting to all. I was moved by the Senior Warden's words. I can say that I don't think the difficulty you're having with accepting the definition given for salvation by the church is going to stop you from trying. I think you'll keep trying to understand and wrestle with theology in a way that makes your faith real. Your parishioners will thank you if you share your struggles with them. Because you know if you struggle with it, they do, too."

I couldn't believe his gentle words. I was okay in this church. I could stay. I could keep trying to pastor to these people even with my unorthodox theology. But now that I realized that I wasn't going to be kicked out of the church, something began gnawing at me, something that had been there for a while: Did I want to stay?

During the last few months, after the fiasco with Jeffrey had resolved and the Vestry put their trust in me, despite a couple of older members who called me to task for shaking things up, I had begun to feel more confident in my role. I loved meeting with parishioners, hearing about their lives, and I had learned to be more comfortable praying with them after we talked things over. But when someone came to me with questions about salvation, truly wanting to know how to resolve their own questions about Christianity, I realized I had done just what the bishop had suggested. I was honest about my own struggles and encouraged them to study and pray with me.

So, I began to move towards a knowing, a gnosis, that my role in life was as a learner about God and a companion to those who also wanted to learn. As a learner, though, I needed to be more committed to the role as priest, a companion and teacher with all those who wanted to also learn about God. Within me, I could feel a new commitment starting to grow stronger, that building this community of learners was a role where I could grow and be comfortable.

I decided that I needed a partner in this learning commitment. So, I asked Marilyn if we could meet at her church for a serious conversation. She was amused at first, but agreed as I knew she would. We met there on a late Wednesday afternoon, when her staff had left and the downtown church building was quiet. It felt a bit strange going into her office, like I was a parishioner needing pastoral care. She greeted me at her office door with one of her enveloping hugs, but then with a smile offered me a seat in her rather disheveled office. There were books stacked everywhere with church circulars sticking out of them as bookmarks.

"What kind of 'serious conversation' were you needing? Are you wanting a confessor?" she began in a light tone after moving her briefcase to sit across from me.

"Well, kind of," I said trying to find the right words. "You know that I talked with Bishop Springer a few weeks ago, right?"

Marilyn nodded and waited for my explanation.

"Well, he listened to my unorthodox theology about not quite accepting the whole salvation- atonement thing. But he wanted me to continue my quest to understand it better. In fact, he kind of challenged me to share my difficulties with others and continue to be open to a deeper understanding. And that's what I want to do."

Marilyn heard that my tone was serious. "I get that, Sarah. I do. So, how are you going to go about that?"

"I wanted to ask if you'd be my theology partner. If you'd be open to meeting once a week to look at certain scriptural passages and share our doubts and our beliefs. A kind of open discussion where everything is open to questioning. No holds barred." I could see Marilyn's eyes getting wider. "I know this is asking a lot. A lot of commitment and time. But also, a lot of honesty. And if you're not into that, that's okay. I can ask someone else."

Marilyn smiled. "You are asking a lot. But you're offering a whole lot more. You are offering me the gift of coming along on a significant spiritual journey. I couldn't be more honored."

Marilyn hesitated while searching for the right words. I was waiting for the "but". She surprised me.

"I accept. This is something I've been craving. Really, it's what we did in seminary, but we haven't had the guts to continue that open journey. I think once I was ordained, I felt I had to sort of toe the line. And you know how bad I am at that. So, this is just right up my alley. Thank you. I couldn't be more ready for this." She reached out her hand and I took it, squeezing it. I felt such relief. If I could do this with someone like Marilyn, then I knew I would be okay. Embarking on this journey in a way to truly examine my faith, instead of a pretense for the sake of the bishop's agenda, felt like a saving grace.

Marilyn sat back and looked at me with a quizzical glance. "So, Sarah, I'm remembering some of our long conversations during seminary about salvation and all that. But I'm also remembering your own personal struggle with forgiveness for yourself. Is that still one of your dark- night- of- the- soul issues?"

"You don't miss a beat, do you?" I said wryly. "You've been witness to all that crap I've been carrying around for so long. I haven't really been sharing a lot this year since we've both been so busy. But yes, that was part of my continual search, my own need for forgiveness. You remember what I shared about how I felt when my sister died? I felt like I hadn't been present enough. And then after she died, I wasn't very aware of my parent's grief being so tied up in my own. I know you heard me mention that."

Marilyn nodded, smiling sympathetically.

"What I haven't shared is how much that has changed over the past year. You know I felt this hot judgment toward Jeffrey and then again toward Edwardo. My anger and disappointment toward them were pretty overwhelming."

Marilyn sat up, holding up her hand. "Wait, but that was valid anger and disappointment! I mean, they screwed up! Big time! You know, Sarah, you don't have to be a saint. We all experience anger and disappointment,' she said, shaking her head, wanting to disagree further.

"I know, I know. But I couldn't let it go. I was stuck in it. The judgment. I wondered how God could possibly forgive those things. But God is supposed to forgive everything, right? So, I realized that if they could be forgiven, then..." I hesitated, wanting Marilyn's full attention. She stopped her disagreeing stance and listened.

"Then?"

"Then, I realized I was forgiven. God didn't expect me to be perfect any more than God expected them to be perfect. And there's one more thing I needed to be forgiven for that I haven't shared."

Marilyn looked puzzled. "Yes?'

"I promised Pam I'd be over to the hospital to visit that afternoon. The afternoon that she died. I promised her. And then I got a better offer. A guy from school asked me to go get a milkshake with him. So, I went out with him instead of going to the hospital."

Marilyn nodded her head sadly. It was hard to admit this. It still hurt.

"And I even resented her for being in the hospital, so I had to go visit her. I didn't want to visit her." My voice wavered but got louder. "I wished that she would hurry up and die! That's what I was thinking that day. I just couldn't do it anymore. I was so selfish that I wished she would just go away...." I took a deep breath, wiping away tears. "And she did."

Marily waited with her kind eyes. "Yeah.. and?"

"And I've finally realized that even Pam would have forgiven me! She loved me so much, so would have understood that I was just being a teen-ager."

All the miserable feelings about myself were shaking themselves loose. How I felt I could never be forgiven. And yet I was. I knew deep down somehow that I was forgiven not just by God, but also by Pam. I took a deep breath and sat back. Marilyn handed me a tissue, and I blew my nose. The relief of sharing all that was palpable. Marilyn heard this confession and did not judge me. I knew that I could now move on.

Marilyn and I made a plan for our weekly "Big Questions" meetings. We decided we'd invite another couple of colleagues who were also open to questioning. My learning partnership began to grow before my eyes and it felt like I was opening myself up. To new gnosis about myself and about God.

CHAPTER FORTY-FIVE

SARAH

JUNE, 2017, BOSTON

I had never dreamed of having a big fancy white wedding like my friends had always described. With a long train and veil, throwing the bouquet, the tiered wedding cake with the edible flowers, my father leading me down the aisle, and the joyful couple dashing out the church door toward a car festooned with the celebratory streamers and "Just Married" written in shaving cream on the back window. That was someone else's dream. My mother might have harbored some of those illusions. But now with my father retired, money was a bit tighter for them, and certainly for us. We just wanted a celebration that stated the obvious. That we loved each other, and we had family and friends who loved us and wished the best for us. Edwardo was a little concerned that bringing his parents all this way would be a disappointment if there wasn't a lot of fanfare. But when I described what I wanted for our wedding, he just smiled and said, "Sarah, that is so you. No one will be disappointed at being invited to witness that kind of wedding."

Edwardo's parents arrived days before the wedding at Logan Airport, and Edwardo and I were there to greet them. I'd had the chance to get to know them when we had flown down to Mexico City for a weekend two months ago. They were the warm and quiet people that Edwardo had described to me, but his mother, Esmerelda, immediately seemed to be so taken with me and the idea of our marriage, that I could see I had won her over the minute she hugged me and kissed my cheeks murmuring, "Querida, querida!" in my ear. I knew that meant "Dear one!" and was so touched that she would see me in that way as soon as we met. I guess once she got over the shock that Edwardo was not going to stay married to Luisa and hearing the sincerity of Edwardo's voice when he talked about me, she had become my best supporter. His father, Alfredo, was a bit more stand-offish, simply shaking my hand, welcoming me to Mexico. Edwardo had warned me that his father was the best example of "macho" in that he needed to stay in control and not show his feelings. But his welcoming smile was enough.

So, when they arrived for the wedding, I felt like we were old friends. They had brought me a Spanish comb and lace mantilla that was Edwardo's grandmother's that I had already agreed to wear to the wedding. I didn't know how it would look with the short off-white lace dress that I had picked out as my wedding attire, but I was more than glad to incorporate something from their family that would give Edwardo's family a sense of tradition. The non-traditional wedding was enough for them to deal with.

After picking them up at the airport, we had driven them straight to my parent's house on Commonwealth Avenue in Back Bay. Driving up to it with his parents, and seeing his mother Esmeralda's face, I realized that they were relieved that it seemed that my background of well-to-do Bostonians was similar to the background in which Edwardo had been raised. The neat, manicured postage stamp yard gracing the front with a white dogwood in full bloom was a welcoming sight.

We'd arranged for his parents to stay with my parents over their week-long stay for the wedding. I thought they could use this chance to get to know one another. We, on the other hand, were staying at an Airbnb down the street so we could have our own privacy and not have to worry about what bedroom we slept in. I was also very glad to be able to have some private moments to process all the family interactions that were due to happen.

We took Edwardo's parents over to my parent's house to get to know one another, and take a nap after their long flight. Later, we showed up with a pecan pie that we picked up from a favorite bakery in Back Bay. It felt so much like we were already married, coming in together, my mother greeting us, proud and pleased, taking the pie and hugging us briefly. She carried the pie to the kitchen, turning to call to the others that we had arrived. Both fathers came slowly down the stairs, dressed a bit formally, both with long sleeved button downs and ties. My mother returned to the living room, stylish as always in her slacks and lacy blouse, with a tray of cheese and crackers. Esmeralda was trim in a flowered dress, smoothing down her hair, seemingly fresh from a nap. She kissed my cheek and patted Edwardo's shoulder as she settled onto the loveseat next to Alfredo.

My father negotiated the drinks, going around to each person to get their order, even translating wine and beer into Spanish when he came to querying Alfredo's preference. He couldn't quite manage "bourbon" or "whiskey" since they were different things apparently than Alfredo was used to, but they finally settled on "tequila" which needed no translation.

Our parents were a bit formal with each other. Edwardo's father's English was not that great, so Edwardo's mother and Edwardo would take turns translating. The two different translators gave very different perspectives on what was being said. Although I still hadn't picked up much Spanish, I could tell by Edwardo's father's reaction what was being communicated. When his wife translated, he would get very serious and nod slightly. When Edwardo translated, he would break into a wide smile and respond enthusiastically.

The next day we took Esmeralda and Alfredo to the Public Garden where our wedding would take place. My mother, who was on the garden's board, had gotten permission for us to use it. She also gave a donation to the fund for the garden which helped. We only had the space for an hour and we had to pay a couple of Boston cops to inform the public what was happening and to keep people from interfering. But this setting, which had been my favorite place in the world growing up, was just idyllic for our wedding. Edwardo also loved the swan boats and the winding trails, and his parents seemed charmed. Those pre-wedding days were filled with delightful planning and conversations with our families about our respective histories, which made our time together a magical one.

The night before the wedding, instead of the traditional rehearsal which I had deemed "not necessary", we had a small dinner at my parents' with a few friends from out of town. Marilyn was going to officiate the ceremony, of course, and she and Bob had arrived in Boston that afternoon. I introduced them to both sets of parents and Marilyn was immediately taken aside by my mother and Esmerelda, who wanted to understand their part in the ceremony since we weren't having a rehearsal. I could see by their pleased chatter that Marilyn was assuring them about the plan, and charming them as she described the flow of the ceremony. Bob was bending the fathers' ears about the current political situation in Philadelphia. Edwardo stood to one side translating for his father and casting me amused glances as I filled wine and water glasses at the festive table.

When one of my uncles asked about Edwardo and where he worked, my father jumped right in,

"Edwardo will be running the center—it's called the 'City Center for Community Assistance' and he'll be the director." I noticed that he shared this with a proud kind of demeanor. Edwardo smiled and nodded. My father asked him to describe the work the center did, and Edwardo described the food bank, the tutoring, and the mentoring that staff and volunteers would be providing.

Marilyn heard the conversation and joined in, placing her hand on Edwardo's shoulder affectionately. "And this guy, he has done an amazing job of outreach to the faith communities. I mean, he's really good at twisting arms without their even noticing the pain. My church has signed up for staffing the tutoring center three days a week! I could never get volunteers to commit to something as significant as that! I can't even get them to sign up to make coffee."

Not being able to contain my own feeling of pride, I stepped over and added, "And St. Philips has also volunteered a large group of people to help with the food bank. But it was Edwardo's enthusiasm that convinced them."

Irene, who had arrived with Bob and Marilyn, came over, joining the discussion. "You can say that again. I've seen members of that church who haven't volunteered for anything for years jump right in! I have to hand it to you, Rev. Sarah. You're marrying someone who has single-handedly pushed St. Philips into social ministry without even a fight!"

I thanked her, then suggested we all move to the dining room where I could see my mother and Esmeraldo carrying platters of food. The dining room had been set with two long tables side by side with flower arrangements of blue and white hydrangeas and white tapers in my mother's silver candlesticks. We wanted the dinner to reflect my parent's traditional white tablecloth style, with both mothers' collaborative cooking and decorating.

While I was helping clear the dessert plates, I found myself in the kitchen with Esmeralda. Smiling warmly at me, she took my hand and asked if we could step out to the patio for a chat. I was a bit nervous, considering that our wedding was the next day and I hoped she wasn't going to bring up some deeply held belief in my converting to Catholicism so our children would be raised in the church. But she took my hand and patted my shoulder.

"Don't worry," she said. "Just a minute to have you to myself." We stepped through the back door without being seen and she faced me with a serious expression.

Uh-oh, I thought.

"Sarah, my dear Sarah," she said touching my cheek. "I want to apologize to you."

That was very puzzling. "Whatever for?"

"Edwardo told me about how he had not shared his marriage with you for a few months when you were getting to know each other. He told me how wrong that was and how devastated you were when you learned."

I started to shake my head, and she held up a finger. "No. Let me speak. You gave Edwardo another chance. Thank goodness for that! But I want to explain that it really is my fault that Edwardo felt he couldn't tell us about his failure in his marriage. We had been pushing him into this marriage from an early age due to our closeness to the family. And it seemed right to us, but we didn't know that those kids weren't really in love. They were just friends, Edwardo tells me. But he was so afraid of disappointing us, that he couldn't tell us." Esmeralda took a breath and gave me a wavery smile, as if she was on the verge of tears. "Sarah, I'm so grateful that you could see that Edwardo was not a lying fool. I mean he was lying and he was a fool for not telling you, but he doesn't lie in his life normally. So, please forgive me, for making this so much harder for

Edwardo and for you." She held her hands together in a prayer like gesture, like she truly wanted forgiveness.

I wrapped my arms around her in a tight hug, then took her hands. "Esmeralda, you have given me the most cherished gift of my life: your son. And while it wasn't easy at first, I think it was meant to be. God wants us to be together, I think."

She smiled, a tiny tear in the corner of her eye. "Yes, indeed, Sarah. I couldn't agree more."

The next day bloomed beautiful and bright with the kind of voluptuous spring air that just demands a celebration. This one was not going to disappoint.

As this wasn't a traditional wedding, I arrived by horse drawn carriage with Edwardo by my side instead of my father. I felt the tradition of a father "giving away" his daughter was fraught with patriarchal symbols. My father had been disappointed at first until we explained that all four parents would be involved in blessing the marriage.

Edwardo held my hand tightly as we arrived. All of our family and friends were decked out in their brightest summer finery and were gathered by the white chairs set up near the pond. As we were helped down from the carriage by the driver, and I glanced at Edwardo.

He was beaming. "Ready, querida?" he asked, taking my arm.

"I couldn't be more ready, my sweetheart. Let's get married!"

We moved slowly down the trail toward the pond. Standing just behind the chairs, waiting for us, were our parents, one couple on each side, smiling with pride. Marilyn stood at the front of the assembly and motioned for the guests to stand. My parents came to us first as planned, hugging us both, then presenting us with the first part of my bouquet, some flowers from my own mother's garden. I took them and kissed them both. Then Edwardo's parents came over and Esmeraldo handed me the next flower to add to my bouquet, a Spanish flower that had arrived the day before. Esmeraldo had carried these kind of flowers in her wedding bouquet.

Esmeraldo whispered to me, "You are the daughter we always dreamed of having," and kissed my cheek, then turned to Edwardo, hugging him tightly. Alfredo came to me and handed me another one of the Spanish flowers with a shy kiss on both my cheeks.

Our parents preceded us down the aisle and took their seats. The musicians, a flutist and violinist started playing and we started slowly down the aisle. As we went, we stopped at each row of guests where they each handed us flowers of their own, adding to my bouquet, which grew larger and more beautiful with each glorious addition. Edwardo helped me gather the flowers and incorporate them. Eventually, when one bouquet was full, and he gathered the flowers for another bouquet that he carried.

At the front, Marilyn took the bouquets from us and placed them in huge vases set on small tables on either side. Smiling, she explained the significance of having our bouquets created by all our family and friends to symbolize what they each brought to our marriage. She then explained the ofrenda, the altar table set with all the traditional elements added by each family to represent the tradition and history that preceded our marriage.

One of the elements on the ofrenda was the picture of Pam and I spitting watermelon at each other. Seeing it, I felt like she was there with us, watching with great joy, as Edwardo and I joined hands in front of Marilyn.

The ceremony was short. One of the readings that I had asked Marilyn to share was this one from the Gospel of Thomas, "Split a piece of wood, and I am there. Lift up the stone, and you will find me there." Marilyn explained that it meant that our marriage and our lives were not separate from God. That we would always find God everywhere in our lives. How could we not be happy if we found God every time we looked at each other, as we created a new life together?

Instead of traditional vows, we wrote our own. Edwardo went first, holding both my hands in his.

"I can't tell you what this marriage means to me," he began, "because there are no words to describe it. I never thought I'd find someone so attuned to who I was and what I saw as my goals in life. You have opened my eyes to what happiness means and shown me what it means to be in an honest, intimate relationship. I hope that we will always help each other keep our relationship fresh, and honest, and real. That is my deepest prayer."

Pushing down the threatening tears, I responded with my sincerest wish for a deepening partnership and honoring the special knowledge of seeing God in each other. When I finished, Marilyn told the gathered group that she didn't need to pronounce us married, because we had married our hearts to each other long ago and everyone was a witness to that sacred marriage. She suggested that we might want to share a kiss which we did. She offered a simple blessing on our long and happy marriage. The Catholic priest, who was a friend from Philadelphia, stepped forward and blessed our marriage in Spanish. Alfredo and Esmeraldo beamed at this.

As the music started up again, Marilyn handed us our bouquets and we began to distribute the flowers back to the guests as we walked back up the aisle, each person receiving a different flower than the one they had brought, symbolizing the community our marriage was bringing together.

We were careful to hold onto one Spanish flower from Edwardo's parents, and one of the blue hydrangeas from my mother's garden, which Edwardo tucked into my hands, taking from me the remaining blooms. As we approached the waiting carriage, we turned, and he hoisted the remaining flowers into the assembled crowd spraying them with petals as they cheered. I took his hand and holding up my skirt, stepped up into the wagon, waving to our parents and friends.

Edwardo turned to me as the horse and buggy made its way down Arlington Street with the late afternoon sun behind us, the vivid green of the Public Garden still in view. He took my hands, putting aside the flowers I was clutching.

"My dear Sarah. I don't know how to tell you how happy I am," he said, stroking my hand.

"And you don't need to," I said, pulling his lapels forward and meeting his kiss, both of us relaxing into this brief time with just each other.

As we settled back into the seats, we watched as the cherished, familiar sights of Boston surrounded us down Commonwealth Avenue to my parent's house. Inside my white satin slipper, I felt the scratchiness of the page I had folded up and placed inside as my "something old". It was a page from the Gospel of Thomas. I remembered quite clearly what it said,

Rather, the kingdom is inside of you, and it is outside of you. When you come to know yourselves, then you will become known, and you will realize that it is you who are the sons of the living father.

I felt known, both by myself, by God, and certainly by all those who loved me. How known can a person be? The feeling of being utterly known and utterly loved was nothing short of becoming whole.

ACKNOWLEDGMENTS

First of all, I am so grateful for my dear my husband, Bill, who puts up with my need to write and the time it takes away from him. Then, I have so many dear friends and family who have read these chapters over the years, giving me feedback and generally egging me on. I want to gratefully acknowledge:

My editor and midwife for the birth of this novel, Jenna Robinson, for her tireless effort and amazing vision in developmental feedback and line editing. I could not have finished this without her. My writers' group: Helene Negler, Bill Shields, Mattie Coll, and Cat Dino. Helen Foster who took time away from her own writing to provide feedback on the entire first version, giving me encouragement to go on. Rev. Jenny Montgomery, Episcopal priest, and my sister, Marcy Fisher who helped with terminology. Many friends including Renee Hill who have read excerpts and kindly given their feedback.